BROTHERS
IN ARMS

BROTHERS
IN ARMS

Hans Hellmut Kirst

TRANSLATED FROM THE GERMAN BY
J. Maxwell Brownjohn

HARPER & ROW, PUBLISHERS
NEW YORK AND EVANSTON

Author's Note

On the night of 20 April 1961, sixteen years after the last war to date, the body of a man was found in a West German town which we shall call Rheine-Bergen. Preliminary inquiries established that death had occurred the same evening, as a result of a bullet through the heart.

Further investigation disclosed that the same man had already been listed as dead sixteen years earlier—in 1945, during the final days of the war.

The material for this book was supplied by a man known as K. R., who compiled the full details of the case. He has described the cause of death as ' an overdose of esprit de corps '.

Here, then, is the strange story of the man who officially died twice and of the consequences —even stranger, perhaps—which stemmed from his double demise.

Contents

1. *Requiescat in Pace*

Just as Karl Schulz thought he saw the man who was dead, it started to rain again.

At the same moment a livid jet of flame raced round the neon tubes, which emitted an angry hiss. Karl Schulz stared unflinchingly into the face he thought he knew.

The face had the greyish pallor of parchment. Long, narrow and pinched, it floated behind the bus window with an air of unreality. There was an infinite melancholy in the large deep-set eyes.

The harsh glare of the neon light which Karl Schulz had been trying to repair danced over the gas station's two petrol pumps, sharply outlining the decrepit bus a few yards away.

Then the dead man's face behind the bus window was grotesquely distorted by the streaming rain. In the end it was obliterated by dirt and moisture as the warm exhalations of the occupants of the bus began to build up on the inside of the glass.

Schulz crouched on his ladder, scarcely moving even when the tube beside him flared up again, illuminating his surroundings with weird clarity—the expanse of concrete in front of the petrol pumps, the stolidly waiting figures of his two employees and the blurred shape of the bus, streaming with grime and rain.

For an instant or two darkness closed in again.

' There's a short somewhere,' one of the pump attendants said.

Schulz did not reply. He began to climb slowly down the ladder, his eyes still on the bus.

The driver of the bus, Bennicken junior, strolled from the direction of the lavatory, adjusting his fly:

' What's so interesting about my bus? ' he inquired. ' I don't have to pass an inspection every time I buy a few litres of petrol, do I? '

Schulz shook his head and took the slip of paper recording

quantity and price from one of his men. Then he retired to his office, still watching the bus out of the corner of his eye. Bennicken junior followed him, striding along with the bow-legged gait of a cowboy who has spent hours in the saddle. Bennicken junior modelled his manner on the screen idols he worshipped in his spare time.

Schulz said: 'Give your father my regards and ask him to 'phone me tonight if he gets a chance. I've got to speak to him. It's urgent.'

'Nothing to do with me, is it?' Young Bennicken's bubble of self-assurance burst abruptly. 'The old man gives me hell if anyone complains. He's a bastard when he's roused.'

'You ought to speak about him with more respect, you know.' Karl Schulz's tone was admonitory.

'It's all right for you to talk—he's not your father. All I know is, he'd make mincemeat of me if you told him I needed it. A nod from an old soldier means more to him than the word of God!'

'Don't worry,' Schulz said absently.

Bennicken junior heaved a sigh of relief. He could stand most things, but intensive parental control was not one of them. 'That's all right then. You're one of the best, Herr Schulz—everyone says so.'

'All right, all right,' Schulz said curtly. He disliked flattery, however well-merited. 'You can do me a favour, though, if you like.'

'Name it,' Bennicken junior replied promptly.

'There's a man sitting at the back of the bus—maybe you know him? He's on the right, next to the window.'

'I don't pay much attention to my passengers—the men, that is—as long as they pay up and don't make trouble.'

'You don't know who he is, then? You've never seen him before?'

'That long streak of misery at the back? Not that I know of.'

'Where did he get in?'

'Not a clue—Babenburg, probably.'

'Where's he bound for?'

'Rheine-Bergen—where else? There's only one stop to come after this, and that's the cattle market. That's where I unload this lot. I could hold a ticket check, if you like.'

'No, don't do that!' Schulz's voice took on a sudden note of urgency. 'I wouldn't want any unnecessary fuss. It might make him suspicious.'

'On the other hand, I could sound him out gently—if you're as interested as all that.'

'I'm not really interested.' Schulz did his best to look unconcerned. 'But if you could find out—casually, so to speak—where the man comes from, where he's going, what his name is, what sort of luggage he's got with him, whether he's travelling alone or not—you might let me know some time.'

'Leave it to me.' Bennicken junior was starring in a Western now. He slapped the imaginary holster on his thigh. 'I'll give him the once-over.'

'No fuss, though,' Schulz stressed. 'It's not really worth bothering about. I'm just curious, that's all.'

'Don't worry, Herr Schulz, I'll play it cool.'

'Is anything wrong?' Eva Schulz eyed her brother in-quiringly. 'You're home a good bit earlier than usual.'

Schulz mustered a smile. 'Any objections?'

'Of course not. It's a nice surprise.' She took his briefcase and helped him off with his overcoat. Karl was her big brother, the person who looked after her and protected her. She was more than grateful to him—she loved him dearly.

She hurried to the bathroom ahead of him and swept an armful of clothes off the line above the bath. Eva knew that Karl's first act on coming home in the evening was to have a wash—a ritual which he performed less for reasons of hygiene than for the benefit of their lodger, Marlene Sonnenberg.

Karl Schulz usually hummed or whistled a popular tune while he was getting ready to spend an evening at home in the flat. He was a man who took an uncomplicated view of life and believed in the essential goodness of people, especially when they were well-disposed towards him. This evening, however, the atmosphere of cosy domesticity failed to instil its usual sense of well-being. He washed his hands and face thoroughly but in silence.

'It's a plain impossibility,' he murmured. 'Dead men don't ride on buses.'

'What did you say?' asked Eva, who was watching him from the doorway.

'Nothing important, love. I was just thinking.'

Eva eyed Karl with covert concern as she handed him a towel. She was nearly twenty years younger than her brother, a belated afterthought on the part of her parents, who had died in an air raid at the end of the war.

'You're not yourself this evening,' she said cautiously. 'Did something happen at work?'

'It's hardly likely, is it?' Karl spoke with an assurance he didn't entirely feel. 'I lead a quiet sort of life—no surprises for me.'

He liked to preserve a light-hearted front. He set great store by his reputation for cheerful optimism and enjoyed being regarded as 'one of the boys'. In fact, he had been happy for as long as he could remember. There were only two days in his life which he recalled with distaste. One was the day he heard of his parents' death and the other—well, the other was the day that had come alive again in his memory when he saw the face at the bus window.

'Where's my box of old photos?' he asked. 'The ones from the war, I mean.'

'They're in a trunk in the attic. Shall I look them out for you now, or will tomorrow do?'

Karl did not reply. He seemed to be lost in his own thoughts. 'Tell me, Eva,' he asked at length, 'have I changed much in the last fifteen or sixteen years—outwardly, I mean?'

'Not a bit, as far as I can judge,' Eva assured him. 'To me, you look just the same as you always have.'

'So you reckon a man's face doesn't change all that much in fifteen years? For instance, if I met someone I'd served with in the war—we'd recognize each other straight away, wouldn't we?'

'It's quite possible.'

'Mistakes can always happen, though. After all, fifteen or sixteen years is a long time.'

'Of course, Karl.' Eva agreed, sensing that he needed reassurance.

'And then again, what about doubles? It's easy to mix people up when they belong to the same type.'

'You're telling me!' Eva said promptly. 'I can think of a lot of women like that, especially the ones who try to look like something out of a film magazine.'

Karl chuckled. 'Is that meant to be a dig at Marlene?'

Eva denied the charge, but Karl knew that she was thinking of their lodger. She obviously saw Marlene Sonnenberg as a *femme fatale* and a potential threat to the even tenor of their domestic life, whereas Karl regarded her as a welcome hobby and distraction.

That was no concern of his sister, however. At eighteen she was far too young to worry about such things. Her duty was to look up to her big brother, and Karl Schulz was sure that she did precisely that. He was her entire family, her mother and father combined—with the emphasis on father.

'You're my favourite girl,' he said tenderly. 'Nothing can alter that.'

'Of course not.'

Karl patted her affectionately on the arm. 'So don't go getting any silly ideas—it's bad for you at your age.'

'Don't worry about me—it's you who ought to watch your step.'

He eyed her cautiously. She wasn't exactly bursting with sex-appeal, but she dressed with admirable propriety and kept herself scrupulously neat and clean. She looked as virginal as untrodden snow—and she was, too, Schulz would have staked his life on that. He was firmly convinced that she never did anything without his prior consent and approval.

'What do you want?' inquired the maid. 'Not that it matters—we're not receiving visitors.'

'I'm not a visitor,' said Karl Schulz, who had planted himself four-square in the doorway. 'I've come on business. Kindly tell Herr Gisenius I'm here.'

The maidservant of the Gisenius household was a thin elderly creature with skin like the rind of a pickled gherkin and two narrow coin-slots of eyes which she screwed up even tighter as she scrutinized the newcomer. The stringy grey hair bristled on her pear-shaped head as though she had hurriedly clapped a horse-hair wig on it before answering the door.

'What name?' she asked suspiciously.

'Schulz, Karl Schulz. I run the gas station north of the town, on the Babenburg road. Herr Gisenius knows me.'

'Herr Gisenius knows everyone,' the maid observed.

So saying, she vanished, giving Schulz ample opportunity to examine his surroundings. It was his first visit to the house. Gisenius preferred to meet his friends, cronies and former comrades-in-arms elsewhere—usually at the *Hotel Drei Kronen* —and Schulz began to have a vague idea why. Despite the opulence of the establishment, the atmosphere was an oppressive blend of varnish and mildew, floor-polish and decay—simultaneously genteel and sickening.

Claus Gisenius, not noted for any great resemblance to his father, Conrad, Schulz's revered friend and fellow-veteran, emerged into the hall and walked across to Schulz. 'Well well,' he said with a provocative grin, 'a personal visit from Dad's war-time pal—hero of a thousand battles and champion of the fight for peace and freedom, 1939 version. To what do we owe the honour?'

'I wanted to speak to your father,' Schulz said tersely. 'Kindly tell him I'm here.'

Claus Gisenius was the sort of young man who got under Karl Schulz's skin. He was obviously devoid of the gratifying respect due to a member of an older generation tempered in the furnace of war. He belonged to those who had no faith in the ordeal by fire, the mission against the East, the preservation of Christendom and the sacred cause of Western civilization.

'My father isn't at home,' Claus announced. 'I can't say I'm heartbroken.'

Karl Schulz had some difficulty in maintaining his composure in the face of the boy's deliberate provocation. 'Can you tell me where I can reach him?' he asked irritably.

'How you get hold of him is your business, Herr Schulz. Surely you're not asking advice from an unblooded noncombatant like me?'

Schulz ground his teeth. 'All I meant was, do you know where your father is?'

'Sorry, Herr Schulz, I'm afraid I don't.'

'Doesn't anyone here know?'

'My mother may. Would you like to speak to her?'

'Yes, please.'

'The only trouble is,' Claus said amiably, 'my mother's not speaking to me at the moment. Her views on my father are a luxury I can't afford to indulge in.'

'Very regrettable, I'm sure,' Schulz grunted.

'As a staunch friend of many years' standing, Herr Schulz, what do you really know about my father? What do you think of him?'

'That's a most unsuitable question for you to ask,' Schulz said indignantly. 'I know your father pretty well—well enough to respect him, anyway. He's always been a good friend to me.'

Claus Gisenius was visibly unimpressed. 'You've squatted side by side on the latrine and shared the same mouldy straw, put a few Russians under the sod and bedded the odd girl together, and you think that entitles you to claim you know my father? You may know what his backside looks like, but he's got other attributes, and they're not necessarily any more edifying.'

Karl Schulz was speechless by this time. He glared at the grinning youth with contempt. Then, making an effort for his old friend's sake, he growled: 'That was meant to be a joke, I suppose?'

'Could be. If I've said anything to annoy you, forget it. You're welcome to assume that I didn't mean to rub you up the wrong way—especially as you've got such an attractive sister.'

Claus Gisenius walked over to the sliding doors that led into the drawing-room and threw them open with a gesture of invitation. 'Mother!' he called. 'A visitor for you!'

'Come closer, Herr Schulz, come closer!' urged Frau Gisenius. 'I won't bite. I'd like to sometimes, but I'm past it.'

Heavy red plush assaulted Schulz's eyes wherever he looked. A standard lamp with a dark red shade cast its rays on a sofa, table-cloth and arm-chair, all in the same muted tones. The colour-scheme extended to Frau Gisenius's dress, the puffy skin of her face and the contents of the glass at her elbow.

'You'll have a little one with me, won't you?' Frau Gisenius went on. 'You've never been a teetotaller, as far as I can recall—it was one of the things I liked about you. But perhaps the years have changed you, too.'

Schulz felt uncomfortable. He said with attempted jocularity: 'My friends tell me I can still put it away.'

'Then have one with me.'

'Thank you. I didn't mean to disturb you, though. I just wanted a little information.'

15

'Nothing disturbs me, Herr Schulz. Visitors are always welcome, especially as I don't have many these days. Sit down.'

Frau Gisenius's face preserved a mask-like rigidity as she spoke. Only her mouth moved. The voice that issued from it was commanding, but it belonged to someone with a slight speech impediment—someone who had drunk too much.

'Your presence here, Herr Schulz, seems to indicate that you're either brave or unsuspecting—which often amounts to the same thing.'

'I don't quite follow.'

'Drink up and things may become clearer. Your health, Herr Schulz.'

Karl Schulz saw a brimming glass in front of him, presumably placed there by the servant who had greeted him at the door. Reaching for it, he put the amber liquid to his lips and poured an appreciable quantity of it down his throat.

Watched attentively by Frau Gisenius, Schulz gagged violently and turned puce. It was not vermouth or sherry, as he had anticipated, but undiluted brandy. With streaming eyes he watched Frau Gisenius drain her glass at a single draught.

'Don't tell me you've lost your taste for the good things of life, Herr Schulz?' Frau Gisenius's tone was slightly mocking.

Schulz picked up his glass again and emptied it. It began to dawn on him that there were complications ahead, and his ingenuous nature was ill-equipped to deal with them.

'It's a long time since we last met, Herr Schulz.'

'Five or six years, I'd say.'

'Eight,' she said firmly. 'I've been ill for eight years now, gravely ill without any prospect of recovery. I began by feeling permanently sickened. The world—your world— nauseated me, so I started to drink. Now I soak it up like a sponge.'

Schulz poured the contents of a second glass down his throat in an attempt to banish his embarrassment, but it had no effect. On the contrary, the dryness in his throat increased. He felt hot and thirsty. Gratefully he watched the impassive maidservant refill his tumbler yet again.

'The petrol station's doing well, I trust?' Frau Gisenius inquired abruptly.

'I can't complain,' Schulz replied. This was a characteristic understatement. He had a regular job and a steady income, his employees liked him and he was popular with his friends. He could afford to feel pleased with himself.

'Well, well,' she said, studying her glass pensively, ' and they say virtue goes unrewarded.'

Schulz looked uneasy. ' Excuse me,' he said, ' but I really mustn't detain you. I was looking for your husband. I've something rather important to discuss with him.'

' Is that so? Your health, Herr Schulz.'

It was an unmistakable challenge as well as a token of respect, and Schulz up-ended his glass. When he put it down, the maid refilled it. She had exchanged the dead bottle for a full one and seemed to regard his intake of brandy with approval.

' Why do you think I'm letting you see me in this state, Herr Schulz? ' Frau Gisenius demanded, turning her puffy face to his. Schulz saw her fingers tremble violently. She enunciated her words with extreme care. ' I haven't received a visitor in years. Why do you think I saw you, of all people? '

' I've no idea.' Schulz looked genuinely perplexed.

The room began to dance and sway until he seemed about to be borne away on a whistling carousel of crimson light.

' Because I'm sure you're a good man,' Schulz heard Frau Gisenius say in a voice that seemed to reach him through layers of felt. ' Because from what I remember of you in the old days and all I've heard since, I feel you may be the only man who can help me and my husband.'

' I'll be glad to do anything I can,' Schulz heard himself saying, ' but I'm a pretty ordinary sort of chap. I sell petrol and enjoy my friends' company. That's about the extent of it.'

' On the contrary, you're one of the few people I know who could be trusted implicitly—' she stumbled over the word '—implicitly. You have a very rare characteristic: you're an unselfish man.'

' Oh, I wouldn't say that, Frau Gisenius,' Schulz protested. He was having trouble with his tongue now, and the merry-go-round had started to revolve with him on board. ' I'm only human, after all. I've got my faults—plenty of them.'

' But if someone was in need of your help, you'd give it, wouldn't you? '

17

'Certainly I'd help—as far as I could, that is.'

'Even if my husband was involved?'

'Especially if he was involved. I'm indebted to your husband. He's always been a good friend to me—always been there when I needed him. He's the sort of person you can rely on. I'd do all I could for him, believe me.'

'Ruin him, then.'

'What did you say?' Involuntarily, Schulz put a finger in his ear and started to excavate it. His body swayed gently as he reached for his glass. 'You'll laugh at this,' he said finally, 'but I thought you just asked me to ruin your husband.'

'I did. Ruin him, compromise him, force him to abandon the ghastly life he leads. It would be a kindness, like throwing cold water over a mad dog. I'm telling you this, Herr Schulz, because you're probably the only decent man my husband knows—and because I love him.'

'My dear lady,' said Schulz, rising to his feet with a groan. He staggered slightly and recovered himself with a supreme effort. 'My dear lady, I must ask your permission to leave.' His stomach heaved. He made a last attempt to look her in the eye, but she was hidden somewhere behind a curtain of red light.

'You'll find my husband at the *Drei Kronen!*' she called after him. The words rang in his ears like a command.

'Yes, ma'am!' he said, clinging to the doorpost for support. 'The *Drei Kronen!* Yes, ma'am, certainly ma'am!'

'Hey, taxi!' Karl Schulz called.

He stumbled to a halt at the edge of Bahnhofstrasse and stood there, swaying. He had to get somewhere urgently. He knew where, but the world was spinning round him so crazily that he needed a helping hand.

Schulz groped clumsily for the lamp-post beside him. He needed support even more urgently than transport, but his surroundings seemed to be made of cotton-wool, rubber and candy-floss.

'Stop!' he shouted. 'Over here! Taxi, blast you!'

The vehicle which he had mistaken for a taxi came to a halt. It was a prowl-car. Two policemen got out and approached him.

'To the *Drei Kronen*,' Schulz said dully, clinging to the car. 'The *Drei Kronen*, got it?'

He took no special notice of the policemen. He regarded every non-soldier in uniform as a sort of chauffeur.

He slumped exhaustedly into the back seat, subsided into a heap and almost at once began to snore.

The two policemen examined him curiously.

'What do we book this as?' asked the younger of the two. 'Jay-walking?'

'Maybe,' drawled the elder, a sergeant named Brahmvogel. 'It all depends.'

'Do you know him?'

'I shan't know who he is until he identifies himself,' said Brahmvogel. 'He doesn't look up to it at the moment.'

'Shall I see if he's carrying any form of identification?'

Brahmvogel raised a restraining hand. 'Let's get in first.' He installed himself in the passenger seat while his companion squeezed in behind the wheel.

The younger policeman maintained an attentive silence. Brahmvogel not only outranked him but was a man of infinitely greater experience. He was reputed to be a first-rate police officer—the sort who could pass on a useful tip or two.

'We'll take him to the *Drei Kronen* for a start,' said Brahmvogel. 'After that—well, we'll have to see.'

His companion nodded obediently, let in the clutch and pulled away from the kerb. In spite of his limited experience, he was already familiar with a few of the town's unwritten rules.

The situation was comparatively straightforward. Most of the communities round Rheine-Bergen, the local parliamentary constituency and the province as a whole were controlled by a certain political party. The municipality of Rheine-Bergen itself was under the ægis of another party whose adherents included not only the mayor but the chief of police. The results of this dichotomy were plain enough. In theory, the police were neutral, but local bias could never quite be eliminated in practice.

Thus, the town hall was the stronghold of one party, while the stronghold of the other and its unofficial headquarters was the *Hotel Drei Kronen*, Karl Schulz's current destination.

The police car screeched to a halt outside the hotel entrance. The two officers got out and bent amiably over their passenger's recumbent form.

19

'We're there,' Brahmvogel said, doing his best to shake Schulz into a state of semi-consciousness. 'It's time to get out—this is the *Drei Kronen*!'

Schulz struggled to his feet, aided by the two policemen. They seized him under the arms and half carried him up the imitation marble steps into the hotel.

After a moment's shocked immobility, the receptionist hurried round his desk to meet them. The few guests who happened to be in the foyer regarded the strange trio with a blend of interest and genteel distaste.

'For Heaven's sake, Sergeant,' hissed the receptionist, 'what's all this about?'

'One of your guests,' Brahmvogel replied. 'He was a bit the worse for wear, so he asked us to get him here.'

'There's been some mistake,' the receptionist said firmly. He took another look at Schulz and shuddered. 'This man isn't one of our guests.'

Brahmvogel was not surprised to hear this, but he took care not to show it. It wouldn't do the *Drei Kronen's* reputation any good, of course, but it might make a private joke which the mayor and police chief would appreciate hugely—though secretly—when they heard about it.

'Are you absolutely sure?' Brahmvogel demanded. His manner was sternly official.

'I don't know the man, I tell you!' the receptionist protested. He was new at his job and unfamiliar with the local set-up. Visions of losing his position reduced his capacity for rational thought. 'Please don't let's have any fuss. I really don't know who he is.'

'That doesn't necessarily mean he isn't a guest, does it?'

'Please, Sergeant!' The concierge cast a horrified glance at the now sizable crowd of guests who had gathered to stare and express their disapproval at the unseemly incident. 'Take this gentleman away, I beg you. I've never seen him before in my life!'

'Disgusting!' a loud voice chimed in.

The concierge turned paler. He knew enough to realize that disaster was not far off.

'It's all a mistake,' he said soothingly, 'an unfortunate mistake. There must be some explanation, ladies and gentlemen. Please be patient.'

'Taxi!' Schulz mumbled to himself. 'Taxi! Take me to the *Drei Kronen*—and step on it!'

The receptionist was bereft of speech and bright ideas.

'Outrageous!' the guests exclaimed in concert.

'A misunderstanding!' moaned the receptionist.

'Most regrettable,' observed Sergeant Brahmvogel, 'but you can hardly hold us responsible for the behaviour of one of your guests.'

It was a bell-hop who finally settled matters by alerting the hotel management. Gisela Wandel, the manager's secretary —slim, poised and energetic—hurried out and brought the impromptu comedy to an abrupt end.

'This gentleman,' she said, indicating the unstable but amiably grinning figure of Schulz, 'is a friend of Herr Hirsch, the manager.'

''Sright,' declared Schulz, emerging from his torpor for a few seconds. 'Lance-Corporal Hirsch—to the cookhouse, for spud-bashing, quick march!'

'Kindly see that Herr Schulz is conducted to Herr Hirsch's private suite,' Gisela Wandel told the bemused receptionist. 'You will be given further instructions later.'

She spoke with equal briskness to the two policemen. 'I'm extremely grateful to you and your colleague, Sergeant. It was very thoughtful of you to bring Herr Schulz here. Herr Hirsch will no doubt wish to express his gratitude and settle any outstanding points.'

'All I need now are Herr Schulz's personal particulars,' said Brahmvogel.

'Is that necessary?' Gisela Wandel glanced at Brahmvogel in surprise. 'His name is Schulz, and I'll be happy to supply you with his address. That's good enough, surely?'

Brahmvogel fought a half-hearted rearguard action. 'I'm the best judge of police requirements, Fräulein Wandel.'

'Surely you're not thinking of preferring a charge?'

'I'll just make a few notes to begin with. Whether any further action will be taken is another matter.'

Karl Schulz came to about an hour later. He opened his puffy eyes with an effort and saw three things: a plaster gnome, his own likeness hanging on the wall, and a girl undressing.

The sight of the gnome told Schulz where he was—in the private apartment of Martin Hirsch, formerly one of his lance-corporals and now manager of the *Drei Kronen*. Schulz remembered that the gnome stood on Hirsch's bedside table, from which it followed that he must be lying on Hirsch's bed.

As for the picture hanging on the wall beside him, it did not portray Schulz alone but was a much-enlarged photograph of which Schulz occupied the focal point. Grouped round him were six men in well-worn but spotless uniforms.

Gnome and photograph obtruded upon Schulz's attention because they were illuminated by a shaft of light which came through the half-open door leading to the next room—Martin Hirsch's sitting-room—where the girl was undressing.

Schulz tried to sit up. For a moment or two he felt as if he had woken up in the middle of a mountain of cotton-wool. Then he became conscious of a searing pain in his head, apparently caused by someone trying to cleave his skull with an axe. If the girl in the next room hadn't proved too great a distraction he would have groaned aloud.

She was a fine figure of a girl—even Schulz's bleary eyes could see that—a graceful little creature of about twenty, with well-rounded curves in all the right places. Having taken off her dress, she was now perched on the arm of a chair removing her stockings. She did this with deliberation, almost with reverence, like a child absorbed in some secret game. Then she draped the stockings across the small table beside her. Her brassière, a confection of black lace, was laid out on the seat of the arm-chair. By the time she had finished, all her garments were scattered round the room, lending it an air of bizarre disarray.

Schulz temporarily forgot his lamentable condition. He was being presented with a private spectacle, and, as a man and an old soldier, he was enjoying it hugely. Women were no mystery to him, and he could only congratulate Hirsch on his catch.

The girl next door stretched luxuriously and clasped her arms above her head. Schulz felt tempted to give vent to some vigorous and appreciative applause, but he realized that these delectable posturings were destined for other eyes, so he refrained from interrupting them.

Sitting there in the darkness, he could already hear his

friends' virile laughter as he related the story in the fullest detail. Martin Hirsch would make a splendid butt for some hearty masculine jokes at the next veterans' reunion.

The girl concluded her strip-tease act with a few callisthenics. She sauntered over to the bedroom door, pushed it open and switched on the light.

'Can I do something for you?' inquired Schulz, grinning companionably.

The girl promptly switched off the light, but she displayed neither shock nor surprise. Instead, there was a hint of curiosity in her voice when she spoke.

'What on earth are you doing here?'

'Just what I was going to ask you,' Schulz replied with a waggish chuckle which jarred his head horribly. 'You make a gorgeous silhouette, you know—beats any nude film I've ever seen. Don't let me interrupt the show.'

'Thanks, but I'm choosy.'

'I'm not just anyone, you know. I'm quite an expert on women, so they tell me.'

'Not on this one, you aren't,' the girl said coldly.

'Besides, I'm a friend of Martin Hirsch.'

'Maybe, but you're not my type.'

'Let's make sure,' Schulz said enthusiastically, endeavouring to get up.

'You try anything and I'll hit you over the head—preferably with that frightful ornament there.'

'Don't move—I'll get it for you!' Karl Schulz made another vain effort to rise and slumped back on the bed, helpless as a baby. His head pounded like a steam-hammer. 'Blast!' he groaned in bewilderment. 'What's the matter with me?'

At that moment Martin Hirsch appeared, a tall, slim, rangy-looking man in his late thirties.

He stood in the doorway and took in the situation at a single glance. His immediate reaction, which was to try to close the door behind him, was frustrated by the figure of a floor-waiter, who stood with popping eyes and a tray wobbling in his hands. A man in his job was equal to most delicate situations, but he had seldom been confronted by quite such a stark fact before, and never in the manager's private apartment.

Martin Hirsch seized the tray, shoved the waiter firmly

out of the room and shut the door behind him. This took him perhaps four seconds, but it was three seconds too long. The waiter had seen quite enough to stimulate his fertile imagination.

' Don't get any wrong ideas! ' Schulz said.

' What is there to misunderstand? ' Hirsch asked acidly. ' The situation seems clear enough.'

' No, honestly! ' Schulz's voice rang with sincerity. ' I've no idea how I got here or how the young lady got here. Would you mind introducing us? '

' Sure there isn't anything else I can do for you? ' inquired Hirsch.

The girl stood there like a statuette. Her eyes were fixed on Hirsch, but if she was waiting for him to look at her she waited in vain.

Hirsch threw her a blanket. ' Get dressed and get out! ' he snapped. He carried the tray into the bedroom, put it down beside Karl Schulz and said: ' Here's some coffee. Get some of that down you and we'll have a little talk.'

This was the signal for all hell to break loose inside Schulz's head again. The aroma of strong coffee only underlined his unenviable condition. His hangover assumed volcanic proportions.

He poured out some coffee with a trembling hand and sipped it, keeping his head as still as possible. Hirsch's voice, clear, cool and reproachful, rang out behind the now closed bedroom door, but Schulz had no time to spare for the discussion in the next room.

His eye fell on the idiotic gnome. It grinned at him in a malevolent way until, irritated, he switched his gaze to the photograph on the wall. At once the dense mists that still shrouded his memory rolled away and everything came flooding back—the face at the bus window, the face that could have belonged only to a dead man, the face that figured in the photograph on the wall beside the bed. It belonged to one of the seven men in the picture, the only one who had never come back. Or had he?

Mustering all his strength, Schulz heaved himself to his feet and tottered resolutely over to the photograph. Then, propping himself against the wall with one hand on either side of the frame, he bent forward and peered at the face he thought he had seen in the bus.

24

He was still in that position when Martin Hirsch came in.
' Fantastic,' he mumbled. ' It couldn't have been him.'

Martin Hirsch took a step towards him. ' Had a skinful,
eh? ' he asked, not unkindly.

' You can say that again,' answered Schulz.

' And the sight of our youthful faces did the rest. It's a
unique picture, isn't it? Shows us in a historic rôle—lambs
on the threshold of the slaughterhouse.'

' We did our bit. No one can say we didn't—least of all
one of us.'

' Fair enough,' Hirsch said placatingly. ' Maybe it's a
lamb's duty to get itself slaughtered. Let's not argue. I'd
far rather talk about the girl you saw just now.'

' So would I.' Schulz was not averse to discussing the
subject. ' She's a sight for sore eyes,' he said, trying to sound
jocular. ' I congratulate you.'

' I want you to forget you saw her here.'

' Why? She's a credit to you.'

' I'm sorry to disappoint you,' Hirsch insisted, ' but there's
absolutely nothing between me and that girl. I give you my
word.'

' Of course not.' Schulz giggled. ' A lady's man must
always be ready to commit perjury to protect a lady's honour
—and no one can say you aren't a lady's man.'

' For God's sake! ' Hirsch exclaimed indignantly. ' I'm
telling you the truth.'

' There's no need to be so modest.' Schulz's eyes twinkled
at his friend affectionately. ' All right, if it means so much to
you, I didn't see a thing—not a thing! '

' It's all very simple, really.' Martin Hirsch seemed
genuinely determined to clarify the situation. ' The girl's
an irresponsible little creature. Don't misunderstand me.
I'm not saying she's immoral or depraved. It's just that she's
what our grandmothers might have called a bit wayward.'

' That's the impression I got.' Schulz grinned again.

' Karl,' Hirsch said imploringly, ' I'm being serious, please
believe me. The girl says she's in love with me, but I can't
afford to encourage her for a number of very good reasons. Is
that good enough for you? '

' If you say so.'

' That's all right, then.' Hirsch breathed a sigh of relief.

25

'Let's talk about something else—that photo, if you like. Anyone would think you'd never seen it before, the way you were poring over it.'

Now it was Schulz's turn to sigh. 'I'm afraid that's just what I've got to talk to you about.' He paused for a moment. 'Do you know who I saw this evening, outside the gas station?'

The hotelier shrugged.

'Michael Meiners.'

Hirsch stared at Schulz incredulously. His eyes narrowed and a look of cool appraisal came into them. Then he burst out laughing. 'You really must have been stoned.'

'No, that was afterwards!' Schulz protested. 'I saw him before I'd touched a drop.'

'You were stoned,' Martin Hirsch said flatly. 'You've been seeing ghosts. The whole idea's crazy. Meiners is dead. You're just trying to take my mind off your behaviour earlier this evening.'

'No, I'm not,' Schulz protested, 'really I'm not. I'm sorry if I made trouble, but I had to talk to someone about it.'

'So you get blind drunk and stagger into my hotel with a police escort!'

'I was trying to find Gisenius. I had to tell him.'

'All right,' said Hirsch, suddenly compliant. 'We'd better have a word with Gisenius in any case. He's probably the only person who can straighten things out with the police. Come on, let's go and find him. He's here, attending one of his regular meetings. I know he hasn't got much sense of humour, but your ghost-story may give him a bit of a laugh.'

'I'm rather pressed for time.' Conrad Gisenius glanced at his watch. 'We're in the middle of a private session of the Party's social welfare committee. Some important decisions are being taken, so I can't stay long.'

'I'm sorry to have disturbed you,' Schulz said, 'but I think it's important.'

'If you think so, Schulz, it must be,' Gisenius placed his finger-tips carefully together. Given a dim light and the benefit of the doubt, he might have passed for an illustration from *Lives of the Saints*.

'Let's take a seat first,' he suggested. He made a gesture of invitation which signified that even here, in Martin Hirsch's private suite, he was entirely at home and in full command of the situation. ' We can chat better sitting down.'

Karl Schulz looked pale and his eyes were bloodshot, but he had plastered his hair down with some of Martin Hirsch's hair-lotion and combed it carefully. He had also borrowed one of the hotelier's elegant ties. His expression was chastened and pensive.

' Take your time,' Gisenius said with an air of natural superiority. ' Even if I am in a hurry, my friends always take priority. What's the problem? '

' It's like this,' Hirsch said firmly. ' Karl here is convinced that he saw Michael Meiners this evening.'

' Whom did you say? ' Gisenius asked, raising his head slightly. ' Michael Meiners? '

' Precisely.'

Gisenius exhibited no surprise. Not a muscle of his face moved, but his voice sounded slightly tense as he asked: ' Where and when? '

' Earlier on this evening, when the rain started. He was outside my gas station, on the bus from Babenburg.'

' And you got a really close look at him? '

' Well,' Schulz puffed like an engine climbing a gradient, ' yes, up to a point.'

Gisenius leant forward as though he had not been hearing well until then but was determined to catch every subsequent word of the account. ' What do you mean, " up to a point "? Do you mean you think you saw Meiners but you're not a hundred per cent certain? '

Schulz nodded obediently. ' More or less. It was dark already, and the lights weren't functioning properly. Also, I only saw him for a few seconds before the bus windows misted over. It was raining.'

Gisenius sat back again in an attitude of relief, a small, short-legged man who contrived to look above medium height when seated. He dressed quietly, in clothes of excellent quality. Gisenius was, in a sense, a man who obtruded by virtue of his very unobtrusiveness.

' My dear Schulz,' he said with deliberation. ' If I understand you correctly, you think you saw Meiners. You think so, mark you—but you can't say so for certain. Ergo: you couldn't swear to it. Am I right? '

27

'I suppose so.'

'Some people look alike,' Gisenius pursued. 'Everyone knows that—it probably happens more often than we think. There are also instances where ideas, thoughts and subconscious reflexes create the strangest illusions. The human brain is the plaything of a thousand fortuitous factors. Apart from that, my friends, don't forget how long ago it was. Fifteen or sixteen years leave their mark on a man's face!'

Karl Schulz's spirits soared like a thermometer in a heatwave. He was only too ready to believe what he wanted to hear. Glancing at Martin Hirsch in search of sympathy and encouragement, he saw him nod and smile, and cheerfully overlooked the fact that his smile contained a hint of friendly irony.

'The main thing,' Gisenius declared, 'is that Michael Meiners is dead. We all know that. There's no room for doubt, so we ought to forget the unfortunate circumstances surrounding his death as quickly and conclusively as possible. It would be far better for us all.'

'And far more convenient,' Hirsch cut in.

Gisenius turned his long, monkish countenance towards Hirsch. 'I prefer to let the dead rest in peace,' he said, 'especially in this case. Don't you agree, Schulz?'

Karl Schulz grabbed the life-line without hesitation. 'What you say sounds pretty convincing to me. You're right, I mean.'

Gisenius rose and took his leave with the formal courtesy peculiar to him. He gave them each a parting nod—a cordial smile for Schulz and an admonitory frown for Hirsch—and departed. The audience was at an end. Gisenius was clearly in a hurry. The social welfare committee was waiting, and it was preferable that important decisions should not be taken in his absence.

'I'm glad that man's on our side,' Martin Hirsch observed when the door had closed behind him. 'We couldn't afford to have him as an enemy.'

2. *Live and Let Live*

Willy Kerze looked at his housekeeper. 'You look as if you've had another bad night, Frau Brandstädter. I'm delighted—it makes you a glutton for work.'

'Breakfast is served, Herr Direktor,' said Frau Brandstädter. She stood staring mournfully into space like a hippopotamus in a drought.

Willy Kerze, chairman and managing director of the 'Stabilator' synthetic building materials factory at Uhlenhorst, just outside Rheine-Bergen, was an imposing-looking man of forty-seven, tall, bulky and endowed with a commanding voice. His manner was generally amiable, even when issuing orders, but if his edicts were not promptly obeyed he could emit a bellow which inspired universal trepidation—justifiably so, since Kerze's bark often heralded a bite.

This happened comparatively seldom, however, and virtually never at breakfast-time. Kerze claimed to relish the quiet country life, and to sit down in the breakfast-room, overlooking his spacious garden and the waters of Lake Uhlenhorst, was one of the most pleasurable features of his day.

Willy Kerze breakfasted alone every morning. It was not merely that he liked breakfasting alone. The Villa Kerze had no legitimate mistress, so he had no alternative. His first wife had left him in 1946 and he had thrown his second out of the house in 1958. One was unable to endure poverty and the other had proved unequal to the stresses and strains of newly-acquired wealth. Kerze mentally consigned them both to perdition, telling himself that he missed neither of them.

Both women had, however, left children. Karen, now nineteen, was a product of the first marriage—pampered, pretty, and hardly a model of maidenly virtue, despite her sojourn at a leading Swiss finishing school. The living monument to Kerze's second marital fiasco was his son Konstantin, a gentle, dreamy, pale-faced boy of eight. He had fortunately inherited little of his mother's character but owed even less to his father—if, indeed, Kerze was his father at all.

'Where's my daughter?' demanded Kerze.

'She's still asleep,' Frau Brandstädter said with disapproval. 'Would you like me to wake her?'

Kerze shook his head indulgently. 'That girl seems to be making quite a hobby of sleeping, but as long as she does it on her own I suppose we might as well let her. What's Konstantin up to?'

'He's already left for school.'

'Did you check his suit? Were his nails clean?'

'I made sure of that, sir. He's due to have his hair cut this week, too.'

'Good.' Kerze had a grasp of detail which he was systematically perfecting. He liked his factory employees to imagine that he counted each individual brick produced by Stabilator Ltd., and at home he fostered the idea that no one could lose a pin without his becoming aware of it. 'But make sure they cut his hair a bit shorter this time. He's not a girl.'

Willy Kerze thoughtfully set to work on his four-minute egg. If his marriages had been disastrous it was no fault of his. At least, he was not solely responsible for their failure. Things had conspired against him and his trust and generosity had been disgracefully abused.

The factory, which now claimed his undivided attention, was going from strength to strength. Turnover and productivity were increasing, and his 'Stabilator' building materials had won a reputation for quality throughout the Common Market. Stabilator Ltd. would, he promised himself, become a world-wide concern with subsidiaries in Latin America and the Near East. In 1946, with three labourers, he had started to produce primitive bricks in a shed beside the Uhlenhorster See, on the outskirts of the up-and-coming town of Rheine-Bergen. Now he owned an ultramodern, multi-bayed factory, two store depots with loading-ramps, an administrative block and a canteen. Over two thousand workers and executives jumped to obey his every command. He was someone at last!

'You've forgotten the pâté de foie gras, Brandstädter.'

Yes, he was someone, all right. He was one of the two or three dozen most influential people in Rheine-Bergen. His housekeeper occasionally treated him as though he was her employee, but she had been with him for more than fifteen years. Brandstädter was a formidable creature, but she was honest, frugal and clean. His house shone like a new pin, and that was worth a great deal.

Brandstädter unearthed the pâté from behind the coffee-pot and plunked it down in front of him. ' By the way, sir, Herr Gisenius rang. He's on his way over.'

' At this hour? ' Kerze exclaimed. He pushed his plate away impatiently. ' Doesn't he realize my time's worth money? '

Kerze retired to his private study, a small secluded room dominated by a massive desk. He put a call through to the office, told his secretary he would be late and asked for the plans of the forthcoming Rheine-Bergen Building Exhibition to be sent up to the house.

Kerze whiled away a few minutes by scrutinizing his bank statements, a pastime which had lately become a source of unadulterated pleasure. His personal finances left little to be desired these days and his resources were mounting in a way which could hardly fail to bring him recognition and esteem as well as commercial success—commodities for which he was prepared to pay an exorbitant price.

There was a discreet tap at the door. It was a sound which conveyed deference and respect, the sound which only an employee with a yearning for directorial approval could have made. ' Come in! ' Kerze called.

Saffranski, one of the Stabilator accountants and universally known as ' the Snake ', silently entered the room.

' The plans for the Building Exhibition, sir.'

Saffranski had a soft, sibilant voice which went well with his nick-name. His keen eyes darted swiftly round the room. His hands, as he proffered the file containing the plans, looked abnormally long and thin, and his yellowish-white fingers seemed to be articulated with knots rather than joints.

Kerze took the file and opened it. The first sheet was dominated by the word ' Stabilator ' in fat black lettering— Stabilator, the name of his most representative product, a form of synthetic slab available in six different colours and six standard sizes, light, rugged and durable. He turned the page to reveal an artist's impression of his stand at the Rheine-

Bergen Building Exhibition, a miniature house in bold colours, almost reminiscent of Paul Klee, with an imaginative design worthy—Kerze told himself—of Frank Lloyd Wright. This, however, was intended more as an eye-catcher, a decoy. Inside the stand itself, prospective customers would be confronted by décor of the more solid, reliable, conservative kind. It was a cosmopolitan shell with a cosy interior.

'I have taken the liberty, sir, of checking the estimated cost of our contribution to the Building Exhibition,' Saffranski said deferentially.

'I don't remember telling you to.' Kerze's tone was guarded.

'No, sir, I did it on my own responsibility, out of hours.' Saffranski retracted his head, tortoise-like, and almost closed his eyes. 'According to my calculations,' he continued, kneading his fingers, 'a number of savings could be made, especially in respect of the architect's fee for the design of the stand.'

'Prickler's not cheap, I know, but he's competent.'

'And ambitious, sir, we mustn't forget that. I rang Herr Prickler the other day—off the record, of course—and hinted that you weren't overjoyed with his design. I gave him to understand that you were considering a last-minute switch to a design submitted by someone else.'

'Not bad!' Kerze commented approvingly. 'How did he react?'

'Just as I thought he would, sir. Prickler's worried about his reputation. He said the fee was a secondary factor, and that his primary concern was prestige. I think we'll be able to save at least three thousand marks on him.'

'Very good, Saffranski.' Kerze beamed. 'Ten per cent for you, as a mark of appreciation. Keep up the good work and you won't regret it.'

Saffranski's long bony fingers cracked—a sign of deep satisfaction. Willy Kerze dismissed him benevolently, confident that Saffranski would produce further surprises in the future. He was not to be disappointed.

'My dear Willy!' Gisenius greeted his friend like someone returning from an Odyssey. 'It's wonderful to see you again!'

'You could have waited till midday. We'd have been bound to see each other at the opening of the Building Exhibition—or didn't you get an invitation?'

'I should have been very hurt if I hadn't, my dear chap!'

The two men exchanged a knowing smile. They were past masters in the art of wire-pulling, experienced jugglers with legal regulations, financial complexities and patriotic sentiments.

'Can I offer you something—brandy, coffee, a glass of milk, a little snack?'

Gisenius declined urbanely. 'You know me, Willy. I haven't the slightest hankering for the so-called pleasures of the flesh.'

Kerze chuckled. 'You don't know what you're missing!'

'My dear Willy,' Gisenius said pompously, 'I think I can claim in all modesty to lead an exemplary life. No one knows the personal difficulties I have to contend with better than you do.'

'And no one sympathizes more.'

Gisenius laid a friendly hand on Kerze's arm. 'In spite of all my difficulties, I can safely claim to have an irreproachable reputation, and I don't live in a glare of publicity like you, for instance.'

'I think I follow your meaning. You're wondering whether I keep my nose clean. Well, don't worry, nobody can prove I've ever done anything to be ashamed of—not that I ever have, of course.'

'Of course not.' Gisenius smiled. 'As your legal adviser, I'm confident that your business affairs are in order from the legal aspect. I know you're no bank-robber!'

'Founding a bank would be more in my line. It's less risky and more profitable.'

The lawyer spread his hands. 'On the other hand,' he observed with a thin smile, 'there are times when it's far less risky to steal a million than rob a widow of her mite—or a woman of her reputation. A private individual can do it innumerable times and get away with it, but one false step can ruin a man in the limelight.'

'Don't worry,' Kerze assured him. 'I'm done with women.'

'You mean it?'

' I give you my word.'

' Well, that's cleared the ground. Now let's get down to brass tacks. I'm prepared to use my influence on your behalf —that's to say, I'm ready to act as your guarantor—but what exactly do you want? What are your ambitions in life? Be quite frank, my dear chap.'

Kerze's reply came back pat. ' The Federal Order of Merit and a seat on the Industrial Council.'

' Both those things could be arranged—under certain circumstances.' The lawyer knit his brows in a way which disguised the fact that he was engaged in mental arithmetic.

' I'd also like the Party's support in my business activities.'

' That shouldn't present any difficulty. I think I can say that no policy decisions are taken in this part of the world without my prior approval.'

Kerze nodded. ' I have the fullest confidence in you, you know that.'

' The welfare and housing committee held a session at the *Drei Kronen* last night. We discussed your proposals until long past midnight.'

' What was the upshot? '

' The committee isn't fundamentally averse to meeting your special requirements. It realizes that the project would bring you—I mean, Stabilator Ltd.—considerable financial benefits—not, of course, that this would be against the public interest. On the other hand, it would be glad to receive some definite, unmistakable token of your genuine appreciation of the Party's aims. The committee will be making its final decision at midday today, just before the Building Exhibition opens.'

' How much? ' Kerze demanded bluntly. ' Will thirty thousand be enough? '

Gisenius smiled. ' You have a regrettable way of over-simplifying things, Willy. However welcome, a contribution of that sort can never influence any decision. It does not place the Party under any obligation—it merely symbolizes the donor's goodwill and strengthens us in our determination to reward him for his faith in us. Thirty thousand marks is a handsome sum, but in my opinion fifty thousand would carry even more weight.'

' Done! '

Kerze opened the cheque-book that lay ready to hand in front of him and filled in the agreed sum.

Gisenius took the cheque and tucked it away in his brief-case. There was no need to express his thanks. He had merely performed a kind and doubtless profitable service. If all went well, Kerze would be the principal beneficiary.

'One more thing before we change the subject, Willy. You've convinced me that you'll play the game in your private life, but can you say the same of your daughter? From all I've heard, Karen appears to err on the side of frivolity. I'll refrain from employing any stronger terms in this connection.'

Kerze felt stranded. 'Karen takes after her mother,' he said. 'There's not much I can do about that. Her behaviour seems to be hereditary.'

'Perhaps you took her away from finishing school too soon.'

'I had no choice, Conrad. They wouldn't keep her any longer.'

'There are other schools. She could go to Paris and learn how to cook, for instance, or study art in Rome—at least until the situation's clearer at this end. Some pretty important decisions will be taken here in the next few months, and any hitch could prove dangerous. One can't afford to indulge in Montmartre or St Tropez behaviour in Rheine-Bergen. If she insists on having her fling and you're incapable of con-trolling her, she'll have to disappear until further notice.'

'I've thought of a more worthwhile way of exploiting Karen's energies.' Kerze's fleshy face broke into a satisfied smile. 'I'll marry her off.'

'To whom, may I ask?'

'Bartosch, right-hand man of the provincial president, friend of ministers and confidant of diplomats. He's crazy about Karen.'

'That would be splendid,' Gisenius said, his face betraying interest for the first time. 'An admirable solution.'

'I was hoping you'd think so. It could bring all sorts of other advantages with it. Advantages for us both, of course,' he amplified.

'Have you found out what Karen thinks of your wedding plans?'

'Karen won't make any fuss,' Kerze said confidently.

' She may be an irresponsible little slut, but she's got a lot of common sense—she inherited that much from me. Don't worry, I'll talk her into it. It just needs a bit of psychology, that's all.'

' What about Bartosch? Are you sure he seriously intends to marry her? '

' Pretty sure. He's already dropped a few hints. Actually, I'll be almost sorry for him if the thing comes off. Karen's as unreliable as they come. Still, he's a man. He must know what he's letting himself in for.'

On this note the two men retired to the garden for a breath of fresh air. There they met young Konstantin, who was loitering near the carp-pool. He hurried over obediently at his father's call.

' Finished school already? ' asked Kerze.

' Yes, Father,' Konstantin said politely. ' They sent us home early.'

' Were you feeding the fish? '

' No, Father.' Konstantin looked apprehensive. The paternal edicts and prohibitions which ruled his existence were a source of almost physical pain to him. ' You forbade me to.'

' What about that bread floating in the water—did you throw it in? '

Konstantin failed to produce a reply.

' Konstantin,' Willy Kerze said sternly, ' bread isn't baked to be thrown away. You can eat as much as you like, but I won't have you filching it to feed dogs and fish with. Kindly remember that. And now shake hands with Herr Gisenius— providing your hands are clean. Say how do you do properly, the way you've been taught.'

Konstantin hastily pulled a handkerchief from his pocket. Having wiped his hand, he extended it to Gisenius with a bob of the head.

Gisenius addressed the boy with a touch of schoolmasterly geniality. ' I trust you're well. Don't let us disturb you.'

' Make yourself scarce now,' Kerze said, ' and find something useful to do. You can sweep the back path. I may drop by later and inspect it.'

Konstantin ran off with evident relief. He vanished behind the nearest hedge and stood there panting like a frightened leveret listening for sounds of pursuit. Willy Kerze's booming voice drifted across the lawn.

'The boy's too soft—got no guts—needs toughening up.'

Gisenius betrayed no form of emotion, favourable or otherwise, but Kerze felt called upon to justify himself. 'You must try to understand, Conrad,' he appealed. 'I may be strict with the lad, but I've got my reasons.'

Kerze did have his reasons, and Gisenius was aware of them. Rather than touch on a dangerous subject, he deemed it wiser to steer the conversation into other channels.

'I almost forgot, my dear Willy. I meant to tell you about a strange thing that happened to our friend Karl Schulz yesterday.'

Willy Kerze brightened slightly at the mention of Karl Schulz. 'Go on,' he said, intrigued, 'don't tell me anything strange ever happens to good old Karl. He's far too staid and strait-laced—except when he gets drunk, which isn't often.'

'That's precisely what I thought,' Gisenius agreed quickly. 'Even Martin Hirsch seemed to share the same opinion.'

Gisenius had scarcely uttered Hirsch's name when he realized that it had been a mistake. He had introduced it too early and at the worst possible juncture. Willy Kerze's abruptly darkening brow confirmed this assumption.

'I follow your train of thought,' Kerze said morosely. 'So you find my son reminiscent of Martin Hirsch, too. You're another one who takes for granted what I've suspected for years.'

'Allow me to correct you.' Gisenius fell back on the cool manner which always stood him in such good stead. 'You're making assertions for which no evidence exists whatsoever, except in your imagination.'

'But you've seen it for yourself!' Kerze protested. 'You've only got to look at Konstantin—he gets more like Hirsch every day.'

'Sheer imagination,' Gisenius insisted. 'You go on telling yourself that and waiting for someone to agree with you. Besides, I was talking about Karl Schulz, not Martin Hirsch.'

But Willy Kerze was not so easily placated. The more closely he had observed Konstantin in recent months, the more his suspicions had mounted and the greater the boy's likeness to Hirsch had seemed to become.

37

'Listen, my dear chap.' Gisenius prepared to deliver a discreet warning. 'Every successful man has enemies—it's the most natural thing in the world. But anyone who deliberately makes enemies for himself is not only being irresponsible—he's making a serious blunder.'

Kerze looked slightly abashed. 'I'm sorry, Conrad. Please forget what I said just now. Tell me about Karl Schulz.'

'He's seen a ghost.'

'Just as I thought—he must have been drunk. Schulz can't take much, we all know that. A few glasses on an empty stomach and he heels over like a ship in a storm. Do you remember that time in the war, when he held a long conversation with a cow? Tried to sell it on the idea of being slaughtered! Another time he thought he saw an angel in a burning bush holding an infantry training manual.'

'This time,' Gisenius said quietly, 'he thought he saw Michael Meiners.'

'The man's mad!' Willy Kerze spoke without hesitation. 'Completely off his rocker or dead drunk—one of the two.'

'That's more or less what I told him, though not in quite those terms.'

'He needs his head examined,' Kerze said confidently. 'No one could be deader than Meiners, and that's the way it should be. Don't you agree, Conrad?'

'It's the only possible view to take,' Gisenius declared. 'To think anything else would be courting disaster.'

'You're up late this morning,' Kerze told his daughter. 'Too late, if you ask me.'

Karen smiled at him indulgently. 'That's because I got home late.'

Kerze leant back in his chair. Disregarding a few minor setbacks, the day seemed to be shaping nicely. He had supervised last-minute preparations for the Building Exhibition, taught his son Konstantin a lesson, concluded a highly promising agreement with Gisenius and reinforced the bonds of friendship between them.

Now he was back in his study again, sitting opposite his daughter Karen, instrument of directoral policy. Another high-spot in a momentous day was in the offing. He reached for the telephone, which was connected to his factory exchange by direct line.

'Get me Councillor Bartosch,' he said. 'It's urgent and personal. I'll hang on until you get through.'

Willy Kerze watched his daughter as he spoke, and Karen stared warily back at him. She was sitting curled up in the big leather arm-chair with her legs tucked under her.

'Ah, Herr Bartosch,' Kerze said courteously, 'I hope I shall have an opportunity of welcoming you privately at my stand after the official opening of the Exhibition today. I should be delighted to see you, and so would my daughter.'

Kerze scrutinized Karen as he said this, but she betrayed no reaction.

Kerze concluded his conversation and replaced the receiver with a gratifying sense of achievement. 'I've been thinking about you, lately, my dear.'

'I think about myself sometimes,' Karen said. 'It's not a particularly edifying subject.'

'Now, now!' Kerze did his best to radiate magnanimity. 'Everyone does stupid things occasionally. The thing is to acknowledge one's failings and then eliminate them.'

'What am I supposed to do—go down on my knees and say sorry?'

'I've always given you a great deal of rope, Karen. Remember how you had to leave school here when the mistress found you in the lavatory with another girl—smoking, you said?

'We were studying comparative biology. Girls of that age generally do.'

'I'm aware of that. I'm not completely ignorant of the facts of life, but that's beside the point. I turned a blind eye, but it wasn't the last time. I send you to one of the best finishing schools in Switzerland, and what happens? You have to leave because you're found in a hotel during class—with a man.'

'At least it was a man—that was a step in the right direction.'

'Don't be frivolous, Karen. I don't bear malice and I'm not reproaching you or being petty—I'm merely pointing out a few facts and asking you to acknowledge them. But to proceed: you've been home for a bare three weeks now. I try to introduce you into polite society, and what happens?

The proprietor of some disreputable tourist hotel turns up at my office and presents me with an item of your underwear. I'll refrain from indulging in greater detail.'

'My panties,' Karen said calmly. 'I left them behind by mistake.'

Kerze resolutely refused to give vent to his justifiable wrath. 'Listen, Karen,' he said soothingly, 'I was young once myself. I did a lot of stupid things, but at least I took a bit of care. I didn't get caught all the time.'

'I'm unlucky from that point of view,' Karen said. 'Believe me, Father, nothing much has happened that you don't know about already.'

Kerze realized he would have to cut proceedings short if he wanted to make Rheine-Bergen in time for the opening of the Exhibition.

'If I understand you,' he said in conciliatory tones, 'you regret having landed yourself in these embarrassing situations.'

'I haven't enjoyed it particularly, if that's what you mean.'

'And you're aware that your escapades are harmful to my reputation as well?'

'If you say so, Father.'

'I'm on the threshold of great things, but your behaviour could wreck everything.'

'I'm sorry.'

'I don't want you to be sorry, Karen. I want you to rectify the situation.'

'How do you suggest I start?'

Kerze stood up. The crucial moment had come. His voice took on a note of solemnity.

'I can still see you as you used to be when you were a little girl, Karen. I used to pick you up in my arms and carry you up and down the room—we only had one in those days. And when your mother ran off with that American soldier— he was only a private and I'm not sure he didn't have a touch of the tar-brush—I even did my best to sing you to sleep. I remember sitting on your bed for a long time that first night, thinking hard. I swore to myself then that my little girl would have a bright future—no worries, no cares, no financial difficulties. Well, I made it, but I still need one thing to complete my happiness.'

'What's that?'

' Can't you think, Karen?—Why, to see you happily
married, of course.'

' Who to? '

' Anyone you like, providing he's honest, respected and
influential.'

Karen sat up slowly; her face wore a faint smile.

' You've guessed who I'm talking about, of course.'

' I'm afraid you'll have to tell me, Father. I wouldn't
dream of trying to guess your thoughts.'

' I'm referring to Bartosch, of course, Councillor Bartosch.'

It was like a dam bursting. Karen shook with laughter
until the tears streamed down her cheeks. Then her laughter
subsided. ' I'm afraid that's not on, Father,' she said gravely,
the corners of her mouth twitching with suppressed merriment.

' Why the devil not? '

' Do you mean you really don't know? Have I got to
spell it out for you? '

' I insist! '

' All right.' Karen's tone was devastatingly meek. ' If
you really want me to, I will. I'm afraid Councillor Bartosch
isn't equipped for marriage. He's what polite people call
a homosexual.'

Kerze stared at his daughter in consternation, the fruits of
victory turning to ashes in his mouth. He was speechless, but
not for long.

' What did you say? ' he demanded hoarsely.

' He's a homosexual, a queer, a pansy, a consenting adult.
Is that plain enough for you? '

' Get out of here! ' Kerze bellowed, clinging to the edge
of his desk. ' You've wounded me deeply enough already,
but this is the last straw.'

' It's all going according to plan,' Gisenius told Kerze in a
confidential whisper. ' Everything's shaping nicely.'

Kerze had arrived minutes late, thanks to his unproductive
and distasteful interview with Karen, so his schedule was not
operating with the requisite precision. The inaugural ceremony
had already begun.

This was embarrassing, but it also had the advantage of
absolving Kerze from the necessity of smiling mechanically
into a series of mechanically smiling faces during the lengthy

ritual of welcome. He wasn't in the mood for that sort of thing. Karen's insinuations had left him floundering in a mental morass which threatened to overwhelm him.

He hurriedly made for his reserved seat. The municipal symphony orchestra was already playing as he took his place. He bowed to his immediate neighbours with an earnest mien and then gazed into space.

Kerze had naturally been allotted a place in the front row. It was yet another token that he now belonged to the upper crust. Even an important and influential personality like his friend Gisenius was consigned to a seat in the second row, immediately behind him.

'You can congratulate yourself,' Gisenius whispered over his shoulder. 'Things are going splendidly.'

Gisenius was not a man to be distracted by ceremonial music. The orchestra was playing Beethoven so loudly that it effectively drowned any exchange of confidences. The fact that Gisenius was sitting in the second row did not reduce him to silence. Having addressed himself to his next-door neighbour, a provincial Member of Parliament, who listened attentively, he leant forward again and whispered in Kerze's ear: 'The committee has adopted all our suggestions—all of them, Willy!'

Kerze nodded without enthusiasm. He felt uncomfortable. He was preoccupied with homosexuality, fatherly love and his factory's potential. Vague but distressing thoughts flitted through his mind, lending him an air of profound concentration.

The ceremonial opening of the Building Exhibition was to take place in the central hall of the newly constructed pavilion on the Jacobsberg, an edifice of concrete, steel and glass, interspersed—needless to say—with slabs of synthetic material supplied at favourable prices by Stabilator Ltd.

Flags, concealing the rough walls, were designed to conjure up a festive impression. In the centre hung the Federal flag, bounded on either side by the flags of the province and municipality. Other flags of lesser symbolic significance but similar atmospheric effect were draped round the podium.

Beneath them sat rows of distinguished guests, feeling, almost to a man, like cocks of the roost. They were there! They sat to the right of the Minister, to the left of the Minister, behind the Minister—all representatives of some authoritative, influential, vitally important organization or other. Without them there could be no inaugural ceremonies of any kind. They were the navel of their own little world. They listened to Beethoven, they would shortly listen to the Minister, and in everything they heard themselves.

The official speeches began. The first man to take possession of the rostrum rejoiced in the title of ' Exhibition Director '. He welcomed the guests by reading out a carefully prepared list of names.

This gave Gisenius another opportunity to whisper to Kerze. ' All we need now is the approval of the provincial president, and we shouldn't have much trouble getting that, eh? ' He smiled thinly. ' Bartosch is our open sesame! '

Willy Kerze's head drooped in a gesture which Gisenius interpreted as agreement. The fact that Kerze felt as though he had a ton weight on his shoulders was not apparent.

As inconspicuously as possible, Kerze glanced along his own row to where, in the centre, sat the mayor and his public works adviser, the provincial Minister of Finance with his secretary, and the provincial president with his personal assistant, Councillor Bartosch—Johannes Bartosch, until barely two hours ago a prospective son-in-law but now a disastrous disappointment.

Kerze saw a dark-suited, slim, elegant man in early middle age. He noted the gleaming black, narrow, pointed shoes, the blue silk socks, the razor-sharp creases, the Morocco briefcase in the slender, well-manicured hands, the raw-silk tie of the same shade as the socks, and the well-chiselled, vigorous, athletic-looking face.

Kerze studied Bartosch with minute care. He searched doggedly for signs of soft, sloppy effeminacy, but in vain. Bartosch looked the acme of virility. Could Karen have been mistaken?

Meanwhile, the mayor had concluded his address, and his place was taken by the provincial president.

' This should be interesting,' Gisenius hissed. ' Our friend Bartosch wrote his speech.' He already referred to him as ' our ' Bartosch, Kerze noted.

The speech differed very little from that of the mayor, and the ensuing address by the provincial Minister of Finance would undoubtedly be much the same. The usual platitudes were paraded in orderly succession: justifiable pride in a unique feat of reconstruction . . . hard work plus vigour plus efficiency equals success . . . solemn obligation to posterity . . . and so on and so forth.

'Nevertheless,' intoned the provincial president, 'there is something which should not be forgotten, something which merits our heartfelt gratitude and appreciation. I refer, ladies and gentlemen, to the outstanding achievement of some of our industrialists, manufacturers and economic planners.' He paused to let this sink in. 'I am thinking above all of those whose unwearying efforts and inexhaustible reserves of ingenuity have, as it were, conjured new branches of industry out of thin air: those whose hard work and self-sacrifice have enabled them to develop hitherto uneconomic fields of activity and increase the productive capacity of our beloved country in such a fruitful and socially beneficial manner.'

Here applause rang out and the provincial president took advantage of this contrived pause to drink a little of the mineral water which stood ready to hand, giving Kerze a meaningful smile as he did so.

Kerze drew himself up with a mixture of pride and gratitude, and Gisenius, who had no need to whisper during these few moments of noisy appreciation, said contentedly: 'There, you see! We can rely on Bartosch, he's on our side.'

Kerze nodded, this time in wholehearted agreement. The prolonged applause had acted as a tranquillizer. The courteous presidential smile from the rostrum was as good as a medal, and Gisenius's remarks had given him renewed hope. Karen's story about Bartosch couldn't be true. It must be a misunderstanding or a piece of malicious gossip. If he, Kerze, was to have any sure prospect of realizing his grand design, he needed Bartosch. With this in mind, he caught the Councillor's eye and gave him a discreet nod.

'A complete success!' Gisenius whispered in high delight. 'There's absolutely no doubt about it.'

True to form, the Finance Minister's speech was equally complimentary, enthusiastic and elevating. To an audience unanimous in its belief that a Minister was no common mortal, his pedestrian phrases seemed to sparkle. Even those who yawned did so with reverence.

After that, to everyone's relief, the orchestra struck up

44

the national anthem. Willy Kerze, his horizon bright once more, joined in lustily.

The official tour which followed the inaugural ceremony gained further ovations for Kerze. The provincial Finance Minister evinced a personal interest in the Stabilator stand and shook Kerze's hand warmly. ' Permit me, Herr Direktor,' he said in tones loud enough to be heard by everyone in the vicinity, ' to express my appreciation. Without men like you we shouldn't be where we are today.'

Kerze received an equally cordial handshake from the Minister's secretary, the mayor, the provincial president and other dignitaries.

On the heels of the official party came personal friends and associates. The Minister and his entourage had departed, but ordinary visitors had not been admitted yet. The doors of the Building Exhibition would remain barred to the common herd until early afternoon. Until then the exhibitors would be alone with their personal friends and guests.

Kerze took up his post in an inner sanctum at the rear of the Stabilator stand which was reserved for private conferences. Out in front, at the information desk, the indefatigable Saffranski was already lying in wait for the first visitors, although he knew that none could be expected for another hour. His zeal rejoiced Kerze's heart.

' Keep up the good work, Saffranski,' Kerze exhorted him. ' You won't regret it, mark my words.'

Saffranski bowed low, a model of devotion and gratitude, and Kerze withdrew to supervise final preparations for the reception of his intimates: champagne for the connoisseur, brandy for the average consumer and schnapps for the hearty drinker. Cigars were also provided. Anyone who wanted to smoke cigarettes would have to bring his own.

The first to appear was Conrad Gisenius. He greeted Kerze with a triumphant smile and sank into the most comfortable arm-chair. ' Your cheque's in the right hands, Willy,' he said. ' Faith and generosity don't go unrewarded, you'll see.'

' Let's hope not.'

' It's a fact. I haven't been idle since we last met. I've been putting out feelers.'

' What about? '

'The Federal Order of Merit.'

'Did you have any luck?'

'It's in the bag.'

Kerze stood in silence for a moment, deeply stirred. One of his major objectives was in sight. He gripped Gisenius's hand in mute gratitude.

'What's more, the Minister would regard it as a privilege to invest you with the F.O.M. personally when the time comes. Bartosch helped to push the idea—he's really doing his best for us. I'm more and more convinced that he'll make a perfect addition to your family.'

Willy Kerze looked round carefully to satisfy himself that no one was listening. Then he leant forward. 'Between you and me, Conrad,' he murmured, 'I've heard he's queer.'

Gisenius raised his head as though snuffing the air. 'Who told you that?' he asked indignantly.

'Karen.'

'How does she know?'

'She just knows—so she says.'

'From first-hand experience—or did she just make it up to get out of marrying him? Personally, I'd lay odds on the latter. Surely you've got enough authority over your daughter to convince her you know what's best for her?'

'All the same, Conrad—what if the man really is a homosexual?'

'Oh, come now, Willy! Even if he were something of the sort, there's a cure for everything. Besides, it doesn't affect his influence—or his usefulness.'

Further discussion had to be deferred because at that moment the cheerful, sturdy figure of Karl Schulz appeared in the doorway. Almost bursting with amiability, he strode over to them and shook them both vigorously by the hand.

'A jolly impressive performance,' he told Gisenius. 'Your people certainly know how to lay these things on.' He turned to Kerze. 'Fabulous bit of work, this,' he said admiringly, indicating the stand. 'Congratulations, you certainly know your business.'

Both men were aware that the worthy, reliable Schulz was a person who wore his heart on his sleeve. He made a habit of speaking his mind, except that he sometimes had no mind of his own. On such occasions he deferred to others.

46

' Well now, you old ghost-monger! ' Kerze cried, slapping him on the back. ' What are you going to have? '

' I had enough yesterday evening to last me a lifetime,' Schulz said, glancing across at Gisenius.

' Actually, Schulz, I ought to be grateful to you,' Gisenius said quietly, without looking up. ' From what I've heard, you made appreciable inroads into my wife's stock of liquor. Anyone who does that benefits her health, if only temporarily.'

' Poor woman! ' Schulz exclaimed sympathetically. ' I can't tell you how sorry I am for her—and for you too, of course.'

' Don't mention it, Karl.' Gisenius's tone was even milder than before. ' Perhaps it was a good thing for a man of your discretion to be given an insight into what I have to contend with. It may help you to understand me better.'

' I always do my best,' Schulz said stoutly. ' I like people to be able to rely on me.'

' We do, Karl, we do.' Kerze glanced at Gisenius. ' But tell me about this ghost of yours. Did you really see one? '

' Did I! ' Schulz was now prepared to regard the whole affair as a big joke. ' It looked just like that poor sod Meiners —you know, all pale and big-eyed. Gave me quite a turn, I can tell you! '

' Let's drop the subject,' Gisenius urged. ' It won't get us anywhere.'

' But it's very funny, really,' Kerze insisted. ' How could Karl have seen someone who wasn't there? Our old company commander wouldn't be pleased with you, Karl. Remember what he used to say? You aren't paid to exercise your imagination. Keep a tight arse-hole and concentrate on your job, and you'll come through.'

' Those were the days! ' Schulz exclaimed, reaching for a glass.

The fourth fellow-veteran to arrive was Frammler, Christian name Ludwig. He lumbered across to Kerze with elephantine tread, his twenty-stone bulk swathed in a double-breasted suit of impeccable cut. The flower in his button-hole and snow-white handkerchief in his breast-pocket invested his normally solemn appearance with a festive note. Although his spherical countenance beamed, he still contrived to look as though he might express his heartfelt condolences at any moment. This

47

was part of Frammler's stock in trade as proprietor of a locally renowned establishment known as Frammler's Interment Institute—Burials and Cremations.

'My dear Kerze,' Frammler said unctuously, enveloping Kerze's hand in both of his, 'permit me to convey my heart-felt—my heartiest congratulations. Rest assured . . .'

'Rest where?' Kerze bantered. 'Not in my grave, I hope! I'm good for a few years yet.'

'Don't tempt providence!' The undertaker's tone was business-like. 'Death comes when we least expect it, and your way of life isn't of the healthiest—not that it's anything to do with me, of course. I ought to be glad, I suppose, but then my business sense isn't as highly developed as yours.'

'That's enough of the funeral oration,' Kerze said gaily. 'What'll you have?'

'Schnapps,' Frammler said, 'in a champagne glass. It holds more and looks better. I don't want to let you down.'

Frammler greeted Gisenius and Schulz with equal warmth, and they made him welcome—as a friend who could be relied upon in the hour of death.

Shortly afterwards Bennicken senior appeared. Officially known as a haulier, Bennicken was in reality what he had always been: a taxi-driver. He dressed accordingly in leather jerkin, neckerchief and peaked cap, all in faded shades of brown, green and blue. He seldom removed his huge, wrinkled, bulging leather gauntlets except to shake hands.

Bennicken elbowed his way towards the group at the back of the stand. He waited until the others extended their hands, then enclosed them briefly in a vice-like grip and bowed, growling a few incomprehensible words as he did so. This done, he accepted a glass of schnapps and retired to a position on the outskirts of the circle.

'Well, my dear Bennicken,' Gisenius said, 'and how's business?'

'Can't grumble.'

'We're almost at full strength,' Schulz announced, looking round. 'The only one missing is Hirsch.'

'As usual,' commented Willy Kerze. He reacted to Hirsch's name like a bull to a red rag. 'He obviously doesn't appreciate our company.'

'Oh, come,' Gisenius said placatingly. 'He's probably

been detained, that's all. The banquet for the guests of honour is being held at the *Drei Kronen.*'

'That's right,' Bennicken said. 'He asked me to send his apologies.'

'You see!' Gisenius said.

'All the same,' Kerze insisted, 'if Hirsch found it necessary to cry off he ought to have made his excuses to me personally. I'm the host this time.'

'Listen, lads,' called Schulz, prompted to restore general harmony by a glance from Gisenius, 'let's not make a big thing out of this. I know Hirsch isn't exactly a model of discipline, but he's one of us—one of the old mob. What I mean is, let's give him the benefit of the doubt. He's sent his apologies, so let's leave it at that.'

'All right.' Kerze spoke with comparative docility.

'That's that, then.' Schulz's honest countenance broke into a delighted smile as an idea came to him, an idea which —in his humble opinion—was perfectly calculated to inspire general hilarity. 'After all, it's not a tragedy, even if it isn't the banquet that's keeping him. Maybe it's a bit of fluff. They can't seem to resist him.'

'What, in the middle of the day!' Frammler's display of unbelief did not conceal his eagerness to spur Schulz on.

'You never know with Hirsch,' Schulz said, 'especially where women are concerned.'

'You're right,' said Bennicken.

'How do you know?' Frammler demanded, all ears.

'I drive a cab,' Bennicken said shortly. 'I get around.'

'But surely he doesn't . . . not in the middle of the day!' Frammler was immensely titillated by the subject of sex, which he looked upon as a form of spiritual counterpoise to his activities as an undertaker. To him, procreation and death were long-term partners: the more children, the more potential clients. 'Hirsch seems set on remaining a bachelor,' he said. 'That has its advantages, I suppose.'

'You're telling me!' Schulz replied eagerly. 'I could tell you a story that would send your blood-pressure up a few points.'

'Well, fire away!' Frammler's voice registered delight. 'Let's have it!'

'I don't know,' Schulz prevaricated. 'We're here to help Kerze celebrate.'

'He'd be happy to hear about it,' Frammler insisted, 'wouldn't you, Willy?'

'Why not?' Any slightly smutty story about Hirsch was all right by Kerze. The more aspersions were cast on the man's personal character, the more his own sense of well-being increased. 'Any objections, Conrad?'

'As far as I'm concerned,' Gisenius said indulgently, 'anyone can amuse himself any way he likes as long as he doesn't upset other people. I'm broad-minded.'

'Me too,' grunted Bennicken.

'All right,' Schulz said, confident that he was going to gladden his friends' hearts, 'but mind you keep it to yourselves.'

He leant back in his chair.

'Well,' he began, 'it was like this. I had a few too many yesterday evening—it doesn't matter why, but I had to put my head down somewhere and I ended up in Hirsch's bedroom. How I got there doesn't matter either, but I did. Anyway, there I lay . . .'

'By yourself?' inquired Frammler.

'There I lay,' Schulz repeated, 'by myself . . .'

'You said that already, Karl,' Kerze was growing impatient. 'What happened then?'

'I came to,' Schulz recounted, 'with the light shining through the doorway into the next room. Then I caught sight of the girl.' He paused.

'What's so special about that?' Frammler demanded. 'Women make up more than half the human race.'

'This one was taking her clothes off.'

'Ah!' said Bennicken.

The others maintained an expectant silence.

'She was quite a girl, too,' Schulz went on, '—like something out of a magazine but made of flesh and blood—and what flesh! The lamp shone straight on to her—like a searchlight. I could see everything, I tell you, everything.'

'Lay off the poetry,' Frammler said impatiently. 'Let's have some details.'

'I'm a gentleman,' Schulz said, relapsing into a nostalgic day-dream.

There were loud protests at this.

'I'll roast you over a slow fire if you don't finish the story off,' Frammler said.

Suddenly Schulz froze. 'That's her!' he cried with mingled delight and incredulity. 'The girl who did gymnastics in Hirsch's bedroom!'

They all rose, with the exception of Bennicken, who was already standing, and pressed their faces eagerly against the glass partition. An attractive girl was walking across the exhibition hall, making straight for the Stabilator stand.

The old comrades gave vent to a concerted 'Ah!' of expert appraisal and admiration.

'Christ Almighty!' Willy Kerze bellowed hoarsely. 'That's Karen—my daughter!'

'You mustn't take everything at its face value,' Gisenius urged. 'Even if she was the girl Schulz saw, there may be some perfectly reasonable explanation.'

As always, Gisenius was playing the part of guide, philosopher and friend. His was the voice of authority.

'Regrettable,' Frammler murmured, 'most regrettable.'

The cheerful clamour of male voices had been replaced by an oppressive silence. Kerze hurried out and persuaded his daughter to wait for him in the exhibition restaurant, while Karl Schulz did his best to produce a string of explanations and excuses. His sense of integrity would not, however, allow him to take refuge in white lies. He stuck to his story.

'Let's assume it was all a mistake,' Gisenius said.

'I'm sorry,' was Schulz's blunt comment before leaving, 'but these things happen.'

'Fundamentally,' Frammler said as he made his exit, 'I've always been more interested in the dead than the living. What did it amount to, after all? Just a little lapse.'

'Strange business,' grunted Bennicken. Then he, too, departed.

Kerze and Gisenius watched the departure of their comrades-in-arms with mixed feelings. Gisenius played the expert judge of human nature, while Kerze strove to live up to his reputation for imperturbability.

'All right,' Kerze said finally, 'so women are impressionable—especially at her age. But why in God's name did it have to be Hirsch of all people?'

'I'm sure the situation will clarify itself,' Gisenius told him suavely. 'But even if your worst fears are justified,

Willy, this affair could be turned to good advantage—if handled the right way.'

' I'll slaughter that man Hirsch! ' Kerze hissed with sudden fury.

Gisenius shook his head reprovingly. ' One has to make the best of things,' he said, ' and that means making the best use of them.' He glanced through the partition. ' I'd better leave you now. I can see Bartosch coming.'

' How shall I treat him? '

' Like a prospective son-in-law, of course. How else? '

Gisenius departed, Bartosch entered, and Kerze radiated cordiality.

' Welcome, Councillor! ' Kerze exclaimed, carefully gauging the quality of Bartosch's handshake and finding it satisfactorily firm. The white teeth bared by the beaming smile looked equally masculine. The man exuded a certain fragrance, true, but it was an astringent scent. Bartosch was a member of the *beau monde*, after all.

' This is a pleasure! ' Bartosch exclaimed.

Councillor Bartosch was accompanied by a gentleman of nondescript but prosperous appearance whom he introduced as the managing director of Europa Hotels.

' You're acquainted with our company, I imagine? ' said the managing director.

Kerze nodded. ' Of course.'

' I'm afraid I can't linger,' Bartosch said gracefully, before taking his leave, ' but I hope you two gentlemen will find you have business interests in common.'

The gentlemen recognized each other as equals and got down to business without delay.

The managing director of Europa Hotels was looking for suitable business partners. A number of new prestige hotels were to be built, and the participation of an influential and reputable manufacturer of building materials would be most desirable.

The managing director mentioned the capital reserves at his company's disposal and named some of the better-known properties already controlled by Europa Hotels. ' One of them,' he concluded, ' is the *Drei Kronen*.'

Kerze's interest was aroused, but he did not impair his business prospects by showing it. ' At least that's something for me to go on,' he said, stroking his chin.

'You're not opposed to the idea, then?' the managing director asked hopefully.

'Far from it.' Kerze equated the *Drei Kronen* with Hirsch, which meant that he regarded it as a rival concern whose unwelcome competition could be eliminated by a take-over bid. 'You understand, of course, that I should need the most detailed information before proceeding further.'

The managing director nodded. 'Naturally.'

'Would you be prepared to allow me to inspect the books of one of your establishments—the *Drei Kronen*, let's say?'

'We should indeed.' The managing director's tone was approving. Kerze, he felt, was a hard-headed, practical business man endowed with a praiseworthy sense of caution. There was nothing to suggest that personal motives were involved.

'I'll think it over,' Kerze said. 'But if I wanted to submit the running of one of your hotels—the *Drei Kronen*, for instance —to detailed examination, I should have to insist on one proviso: absolute secrecy. Even the present management mustn't know I'm interested.'

'I could arrange that without any difficulty,' the managing director replied. 'Let me know your requirements as soon as you can. I'll look forward to hearing from you in the near future.'

On that note the managing director of Europa Hotels withdrew. Willy Kerze, far-sighted business man and harassed father, stood there for a moment, lost in thought. Then he glanced towards the front of the stand.

Saffranski was talking eagerly to a visitor. Snake or not, Kerze thought, he was a useful young man—just the man for a job which demanded meticulous care, perspicacity, and discretion.

Saffranski left the information desk and stood in the doorway of Kerze's lair waiting humbly for permission to speak. Kerze granted it with a wave of the hand.

'May I take the liberty of offering a suggestion, sir?' Kerze nodded graciously. 'Have a word with the gentleman I've been talking to outside. It might be worth your while.'

'We'll see,' said Kerze. 'Show him in.'

Conducted to the door of the office by Saffranski, the man entered. He was short, plump and greasy-skinned, and his manner bordered on the obsequious. His ingratiating smile was evidently designed to inspire confidence but was not an unqualified success. He bowed, doubling up as though his waist-band concealed a hinge.

'What can I do for you?' Kerze inquired in guarded tones.

'Perhaps,' the visitor replied meekly, 'it will be I who can do something for you. Allow me to introduce myself—Lehmgruber's the name.'

'You can speak freely.' Kerze waved his visitor into a chair.

Lehmgruber obediently took a seat and cleared his throat. 'I have certain contacts.'

'Contacts are always useful,' Kerze conceded. 'What sort do you mean?'

'I'm on close terms with one or two members of the Polish government.'

'Now listen!' Kerze spoke sharply, as befitted one whose steadfast principles were being called in question. 'Let's get this straight. I'm utterly opposed to the establishment of any form of relations with the so-called Eastern bloc. It's a matter of principle with me, so you might as well save your breath.'

'Even if the contacts I refer to are purely commercial?' asked Lehmgruber. 'One gentleman of my acquaintance is the chairman of a Polish trade delegation.'

'That's quite another thing, of course,' Kerze parried, '—always provided there are no political strings attached. And there's something else I must make absolutely clear, Herr . . .'

'Lehmgruber's the name.'

'. . . Herr Lehmgruber. I never pay middle-men on a percentage basis. A lump sum in return for an introduction —yes, possibly, but a fixed commission—never!'

'The business which I could put your way might be worth a considerable sum.'

'There's no price-tag on my principles!' Kerze protested righteously. 'Anyway, what do you mean by considerable?'

Lehmgruber gave a polite smile. 'Perhaps we can discuss that later—in private. You can reach me at the *Drei Kronen*.'

Kerze dismissed his visitor without arranging another appointment. Experience had taught him that the best way to handle such individuals was to let them stew in their own juice for a while. Besides, renewed mention of the *Drei Kronen* had steered his thoughts in a certain direction again. He rang for Saffranski.

' Tell me, Saffranski,' he said. ' Do you know anything about hotels? '

' I'm an accountant, sir. I know my way round balance sheets and tax tables. My speciality is audit work.'

' Just the man I need,' Kerze said. ' Hold yourself in readiness for a special job—a confidential one. Report to me at the villa tomorrow morning and we'll take it from there. But there's one thing you might as well know now: I want a thorough job done—a thorough job, do you hear?—and if you abuse my trust it'll be for the first and last time.'

' We're going to have a straight talk, the two of us,' Willy Kerze told his daughter, who was waiting for him in the almost deserted exhibition restaurant. She stared back at him with defiance. As usual, her conscience was anything but clear.

Kerze summoned up a fatherly smile for the benefit of anyone who might be watching. Being a well-known local figure, he found it advisable to maintain an air of dignified composure in any situation.

Karen said: ' I suppose you want an explanation.'

' What possible explanation could there be? '

' If you knew the whole truth you mightn't be so hard on me.'

Beckoning a waiter, Kerze ordered tea for Karen and a bottle of mineral water for himself. A few visitors had started to drift in, so there was no harm in demonstrating the abstemious habits of the Kerze family.

' Your behaviour is scandalous,' he said, when the waiter had gone.

' If you're referring to my so-called affair with Martin Hirsch . . .'

' Don't mention that name in my presence! ' Kerze said sternly.

' What have you got against him? I thought he was a friend of yours.'

' He's no friend of mine,' Kerze snapped. ' We served together, that's all.'

'What if I told you I'm in love with him?'

Kerze said brutally, 'There's no question of that.'

'I thought you'd understand.'

'Then you've got another think coming. You can't go on leading your sort of life in Rheine-Bergen. The only solution as I see it is marriage.'

'To Bartosch, do you mean?'

'What have you got against the man, Karen?'

'I thought I'd made that clear.'

'You made a totally unfounded allegation. That's all it was—unless, of course, you mean me to believe that you're speaking from personal experience. Is that what I'm supposed to assume?'

'How do I know what you assume, Father?'

'My dear girl, all I want you to do is lead a normal, decent family life.'

'With Bartosch?'

'How many more times must I tell you, Karen? Think carefully for a moment. Bartosch is a fine figure of a man and he knows his way around. You might even be a Minister's wife in a few years' time. But apart from all that, aren't you attracted by the thought of a settled life, a handsome husband, children . . .?'

'By Bartosch?'

'Your sarcasm is out of place, Karen. Besides, an abnormal condition needn't necessarily be permanent. It's a form of disease—they can treat it these days.'

'Tell him to see a doctor, then.'

'The best medicine for that sort of trouble is love,—love, marriage, a permanent relationship with someone of the opposite sex.'

Kerze was in full spate now. He felt almost certain that he could convince Karen. 'Can't you see what a wonderful opportunity you're being offered?' he continued with fervour. 'If you're looking for a deeper meaning in life—this is it!'

'Not for me, it isn't,' Karen said stubbornly. 'I'm not a psychiatrist.'

'No, but you're my daughter,' Kerze retorted, 'and that's why you're going to give the whole thing further thought. I'm not trying to dragoon you into anything. The choice is up to you: either Bartosch, a banking account of your own

56

and a fat allowance, or back you go to finishing school with ten marks' pocket-money a week. You won't get a pfennig more either, not even when you're twenty-one, so make up your mind and be quick about it.'

Willy Kerze was used to being stared at. He almost invariably felt himself to be pursued by looks of admiration, goodwill and respect, or envy, incomprehension and indifference.

Kerze had a fleeting impression that someone in the crowd which now filled the hall outside was watching him closely. A brief moment's reflection sufficed for Kerze to dismiss the man as an inquisitive onlooker, and he immediately forgot about him.

Striding out of the exhibition restaurant into Hall A he again had a fleeting sensation of being watched by someone in the background, but before he could take a closer look he was buttonholed by the municipal Board of Works superintendent.

'A great success, particularly from your point of view.' Kerze detected a note of suppressed envy in the man's tone. He was not unduly surprised. The superintendent not only belonged to another faith but espoused a different party platform. What was more, he had not been one of the organizers of the exhibition.

'A great success for all of us,' Kerze said magnanimously, 'including you and your department. After all, we have the same things at heart.'

They smiled at each other a trifle thinly. The words that were customary on such occasions flowed effortlessly from their lips, and since this demanded no great degree of mental concentration both men were left free to pursue their own thoughts. The Board of Works superintendent gauged the flow of incoming visitors and was forced to admit that the exhibition—not his exhibition, unfortunately—showed every sign of being a success. Meanwhile, Kerze covertly scanned the hall for the man who had been staring at him so intently.

It was an instinctive reaction to begin with, unaccompanied by any great sense of compulsion. Kerze was merely pursuing a subconscious train of thought. His memory stirred, sluggishly at first, until it dawned on him that he must have seen the man before—somewhere, sometime, possibly long ago, under circumstances that now seemed strange and unreal.

Kerze screwed up his eyes and, still mouthing platitudes, made a systematic search of the figures that thronged the hall.

And then, over the heads of the surging crowd, through a sea of scaffolding, posters and bunting, he caught sight of the face he was looking for. It was a pale, chalky face, sharply contoured yet curiously flat. Its pallor may have derived from the harsh glare of the spotlight which illuminated a nearby stand, but to Kerze the light seemed to shine with pitiless brilliance into the man's mutely inquiring eyes.

In that moment Kerze knew, with piercing certainty, that the face belonged to Michael Meiners.

'Our slaughter-house project,' the Board of Works superintendent was saying, 'is slowly taking shape. We're determined to plan for the future . . .'

Far from listening to the superintendent's monologue, Kerze thrust him aside without a word of apology and plunged into the crowd, making for the man he thought was Meiners.

He forced his way through the press of human bodies, ploughing through a forest of arms, heads and shoulders, being shoved aside and shoving back, deaf to indignant protests. All his senses were focused on a single goal: the brightly-lit stand, and beside it the man whose name he hardly dared admit to himself.

When Kerze reached the spot, breathing heavily, there was nothing there except the stand itself, a steel edifice surmounted by a seal balancing a gigantic ball-bearing on its nose. The ball bore the legend: 'The builder you can trust —makes German steel a must.'

Now it was Kerze who stood in the beam of the spotlight, but he failed to find the man he was looking for—the man he had thought was dead and in whose death he, too, had played a part.

INTERIM REPORT NO. 1

STENOGRAPHIC RECORD OF A POLICE INTERVIEW

WITH CONRAD GISENIUS

conducted by Chief Inspector Sand
on 1 May 1961
in connection with the events of 20 April 1945

Having been informed of the subject of the interview and cautioned, Herr Gisenius made the following statement:

My name is Conrad Gisenius. I am fifty years old and a lawyer by profession.

I was a private soldier at the time in question, having been in a reserved occupation until fairly late in the war. I was aware of the hopelessness of the general situation—not that this deterred me from doing my duty like millions of others. I was posted to an infantry company, where I was assigned to a rifle section commanded by Sergeant Karl Schulz.

Sergeant Schulz had the reputation of being an able and efficient N.C.O. We had every reason to value his leadership. We had heard that he was an experienced section commander, and we respected him wholeheartedly. While it is only natural to adopt such an attitude toward any superior officer, I should like to stress the point.

As far as the events of the day in question are concerned, my recollection of precise details is naturally blurred. The incident took place sixteen years ago, after all, and even today I can hardly see it as particularly significant. On the contrary, it was a minor and not unusual occurrence in time of war.

I should like to emphasize that ordinary soldiers like myself and my friends were merely defending their homeland. They had nothing in common with the Nazis. We did our duty and nothing more. It would be absurd, in retrospect, to associate our readiness to defend our country with power-complexes or criminal machinations.

I say this because I consider it not only important but

relevant to the matter in hand. We old soldiers know what war is. As a result, we are determined opponents of it—not that this makes us traitors or pacifists. We realize that some sacrifices are unavoidable.

But to come to the actual sequence of events. On the evening preceding the day in question, our section was billeted on the edge of a small village—Steinwiesen, I think it was—in a small farm whose name I cannot recall. Our company was taking part in a general withdrawal, so we were only to be at the farm for one night.

Sergeant Schulz presented a billeting chit and we moved into the quarters assigned to us in an orderly manner. This was on the evening of 19 April. We checked and cleaned our equipment in the usual way, and then set about preparing an evening meal. Afterwards, we chatted a little with the owners of the farm and a few of the refugees who were billeted there temporarily. A sort of harmony reigned among us all, probably because we felt drawn together by a sense of common adversity.

It cannot be denied that we had something to drink that evening, but I must stress that the amount of liquor consumed was negligible—little more than a bottle per man, in my estimation. It should also be noted that the farm people and refugees drank with us. The drink presumably came from an abandoned supply dump—I cannot say for certain. I only know that Lance-Corporal Hirsch came in with a crate of bottles and dumped it down in front of us with some such words as : ' With the compliments of our beloved Führer, for us to drink his health in! '

Irrelevant as it may seem, this remark is worthy of comment because it sums up the special situation in which we found ourselves and helps to place subsequent events in clearer perspective. Lance-Corporal Hirsch's remark was purely ironical, of course. It typified his attitude, though not necessarily that of the others.

We were profoundly worried that evening, primarily for the Fatherland. This may sound dramatic, but for most of us this mood was the product of a bitter realization that the end was near. I venture to say that we were almost physically oppressed by an awareness of impending doom—with the possible exception of Lance-Corporal Hirsch, who behaved with his usual flippancy. The other exception may have been

Grenadier Michael Meiners, who was eighteen or twenty years old and thus too young to appreciate the full gravity of the situation.

The older, more serious-minded and experienced of us saw a little further beneath the surface. The enemy was deep in the heart of Germany. Our territory had been violated not only by the fair, friendly Americans but by savage, bestial Russians, most of them Asiatics. The latter were heading straight for us. We were thus confronted, if I may so describe it, by twin manifestations of bestiality: the birthday of Hitler, a misguided man and ultimately a sick one—remember what happened on the 20th of April?—and the onset of the Red hordes. That was why my fellow-soldiers drank, deeply but not to excess.

I cannot guarantee that everyone was sober, of course, but I saw nothing to justify a contrary assumption. I myself was feeling exhausted, so I turned in comparatively early, leaving my friends still drinking. As I have already stated, I cannot recall any details. My sole surviving recollection is that most of the section were drinking and chatting with the locals and refugees, and that Lance-Corporal Hirsch was lighthearted enough to make jokes. Meiners sat next to him. Hirsch shouted out something like: ' Drink up, fellows! Get enough liquor on your breath and the Russkis may turn tail and run! ' I can't remember his exact words, of course, but that was the gist of the remark. It was typical of Hirsch to shrug off disaster in such a flippant way.

I can't remember any further details, but I think I lay down in a corner somewhere and went to sleep. It was dawn when I woke, and I found it hard to rouse myself—not because of what I had drunk, which was negligible, but because of mental exhaustion. After all, the war-years had left their mark on me, too. In retrospect, all I know is that 20 April 1945 was a turbulent day for all of us.

The first thing that happened was that Sergeant Schulz came in and told us there was a dead body in the barn. Well, a dead body is nothing out of the ordinary in war-time— regrettable, but hardly remarkable. I then learnt that it belonged to a girl from a refugee family, but even that meant little. It was merely one tragic incident among the many which occurred as our heroic struggle was drawing to its close.

The Russians were advancing, foreign labourers from the East had deserted their employers, there were reports that so-called Resistance fighters had been sighted, and criminals from a local concentration camp were already on the run. There was more than one dead body to be seen on the two fronts in those days—and I am not being cynical, I assure you.

In the middle of all this commotion Lieutenant Kronshagen, our company commander, appeared. He ordered Sergeant Schulz to take the section and block the road into Steinwiesen from a position on the edge of Copse 307. Once again, I cannot recall any exact details. I only know that the section was divided up in accordance with combat requirements. I was assigned to a group—with Bennicken and Frammler, if I remember rightly—which had the job of collecting timber for a road-block. This we did.

While we were still constructing our wooden road-block, large numbers of Russian tanks rumbled up the road, heading straight for us. They opened fire with everything they had, and all hell broke loose. The main target of this brutal attack by immensely superior forces was our M.G. position on the edge of Copse 307.

Question:

Who was manning it?

Answer:

I can't remember exactly—Meiners, anyway.

Question:

Why do you remember Meiners but no one else?

Answer:

Because after the first burst of firing the word went round that Meiners had been fatally wounded. I don't recall who told me.

Question:

So according to you the section was split up into two parties, one manning the M.G. and the other, yourself included, building the road-block. Who was working on it besides you?

Answer:

I can't give an exact answer to that question. The situation was extremely confused. Besides, one could hardly say that the section had been split up—we were all within earshot of each other. Kerze was somewhere near me, but that's all I can remember.

Question:
What happened after firing broke out?
Answer:
We were outnumbered and forced to give ground—there was no alternative. We had not only lost Meiners, but our M.G. had been put out of action. The road-block was unfinished, and there was no prospect of completing it. Russian tanks —four or five of them, possibly more—were virtually on our doorstep. Even so, we waited until we received the order to withdraw.
Question:
Who gave the order?
Answer:
The only man with authority to do so: Sergeant Schulz.

I should like once again to summarize the essentials of the situation, if I may. Sergeant Schulz's section had been given a dangerous assignment but one which any combat unit might have been called upon to undertake. We were fully prepared to carry out that assignment, and we continued to do so until our original instructions had been superseded. Such are the facts.

We were only one small unit among many, and I am confident that the others conducted themselves in much the same way. This goes without saying, and my only regret is that circumstances compel me to make a point of it. In my view, we ought to be gradually habituating ourselves to the traditional idea that a soldier's reputation is not something to be impugned lightly. He does his duty, and any man who does his duty merits our deepest respect.

3. *One Good Turn . . .*

' My name's Saffranski,' said the man. ' What's yours? '

' My name's Konstantin Kerze.' The boy stared back at the tall, slightly stooped figure above him.

They were standing at the gates of the Villa Kerze. Saffranski had rung the bell, and Konstantin, who happened to be in the garden, had let him in.

' I'm one of your father's employees,' Saffranski explained. ' He's given me a special job to do, so I shall be working here in your father's study. I hope we'll become good friends.'

The tall figure extended a long, bony hand and stroked Konstantin's head. The boy shrank back. He was unaccustomed to caresses.

' We'll get on well together, you'll see,' Saffranski said softly. ' I like boys like you. They can twist me round their little finger.'

' My father isn't at home,' Konstantin said stiffly.

Saffranski watched the boy with a slow smile that exposed his teeth. They glistened wetly. An abnormal amount of saliva had collected in his mouth and he felt his palms start to sweat like those of a sick man. There was something appealing about the sight of Kerze junior's silky skin, long eyelashes and soft smooth hair.

But Saffranski was not given a chance to enjoy the entrancing spectacle for long. An imperious voice called ' Konstantin —come here at once! ', and he turned to see a sturdy female figure standing at the door of the villa. This, he knew, was Frau Brandstädter, the managing director's housekeeper.

Saffranski found her repulsive, but then he found almost all females repulsive. To him, they were torpid dairy cattle whose lot it was to be denied an insight into the nature of true beauty. A lust for power was written all over Frau Brandstädter's countenance, but Saffranski favoured her with a courteous smile.

The housekeeper concentrated her attention on Konstantin.

'What have you got in your trouser-pocket?' she demanded. The boy produced a crust of bread. He held it out, averting his eyes from her face.

' It's always the same story,' Brandstädter said reprovingly. ' You take bread from my kitchen and feed the fish with it, even though you know perfectly well it's against your father's orders.' She stood looking down at him with her arms akimbo. ' Well, I'm giving you a chance to say sorry.'

' I'm very sorry,' Konstantin said in a small, polite voice, glancing shyly at Saffranski. Saffranski gave him an encouraging smile from behind the housekeeper's back.

' I'll overlook it this time,' Brandstädter pursued, ' but don't do it again, do you hear? The path leading to the fish-pond needs weeding, so take a hoe and a rake and get busy. Make yourself useful—that's what your father's always telling you, isn't it? '

Konstantin hung his head. ' Yes, Frau Brandstädter.' He shot another quick glance at Saffranski and trotted off.

Brandstädter now turned her attention to Saffranski. Studying his face closely, she was gratified to see that it wore an expression of humble deference—a quality which she greatly appreciated in others.

' Allow me to introduce myself.' Saffranski bowed. ' My name is Saffranski.'

' I know, I was told you were coming,' Frau Brandstädter replied. ' The study's all ready for you.'

' I hope I'm not being a nuisance.'

Frau Brandstädter was seldom treated to such a display of courtesy. Normally, her bluff and blustering employer was the only man in the house, and Saffranski's gentle manner made a welcome contrast.

She led him through the garden and along the veranda to Kerze's study, where a file marked ' Europa Hotels Ltd.' was lying on the desk. Saffranski advanced on it as though drawn by a lodestone.

' I hope you'll like it here. This is a well-kept house.'

' It does you credit,' said Saffranski. ' One notices the feminine touch.'

Frau Brandstädter swallowed this compliment without

difficulty. After all, Saffranski was only voicing her own deeply felt convictions. ' Can I get you something to drink —a little snack, perhaps? '

' How kind,' Saffranski replied, bowing. ' I'm much obliged, but there's nothing I want. Unless . . . well, if it's not too much trouble, perhaps a cup of coffee and two slices of bread and butter—nothing more.'

As she left the room, Frau Brandstädter gave him a look which plainly conveyed her approval of his simple tastes.

Saffranski surveyed his place of work. He was surrounded by the trappings of wealth—strong-smelling leather, heavy velvet, gleaming wood and steel. The sight stirred something within him.

What also stirred him was the view from the window, the spacious, neatly kept garden. Konstantin Kerze was standing there day-dreaming, a vision of forlorn beauty mirrored in the still waters of the pool.

Saffranski felt disposed to enjoy his surroundings. An awareness of the perfection he had always yearned for surged through him. He had never felt so close to it before.

He endured the reappearance of Frau Brandstädter almost effortlessly. Even the smell emanating from her black dress failed to revolt him as he stared past her to where Konstantin still stood, framed by his carefully landscaped surroundings.

When Frau Brandstädter had departed, Saffranski waited for two or three minutes. Then he pressed the slices of bread and butter together, stowed them away in his coat pocket with a secret smile and left Kerze's study by the door leading to the terrace. His nose sniffed the spring air outside. The well-tended garden looked inviting, and a short stroll would help to stimulate his faculties. He sauntered, as though by chance, in Konstantin Kerze's direction.

The boy saw Saffranski coming, but the faint look of apprehension on his gentle, girlish face gave way to one of interest. He stood beside a young poplar whose slender branches overshadowed the pool.

' Are the fish hungry? ' Saffranski asked.

' Fish are always hungry.'

' In that case, we ought to feed them when we get a chance.'

' But we can't,' Konstantin looked at Saffranski with sudden hope. ' Can we? '

Saffranski put his hand in his pocket, withdrew the bread-and-butter sandwich and gave it to the boy. ' Here,' he said, ' try them with that.'

Konstantin took the bread without hesitation, crumbled it and threw the pieces into the pool.

' These fish eat like mad.' He stared avidly at the fishes as they churned the surface, relishing every moment with a child's delight in observation and discovery. ' Like mad!' he repeated.

Saffranski said softly: ' What you're doing is forbidden, isn't it? '

Konstantin started violently. ' Are you going to tell my father? ' His voice trembled with apprehension.

Saffranski put a hand on the boy's shoulder. ' We'll keep this to ourselves, Konstantin,' he said. ' Call it our little secret, if you like—no one else need know.'

' That's all right, then! ' The boy sighed with relief. He turned round to face Saffranski and gave him a look of trust and gratitude. He was beginning to like the tall thin young man.

' Do you know something? ' Saffranski said. ' We ought to stick together, the two of us. It's a good thing to have a friend.'

Konstantin nodded. ' Shall we feed the fish again to-morrow? '

' We'll do that,' Saffranski promised, ' that and other things.'

Frau Gisenius eyed her husband nervously. ' Why don't you reproach me—go on, why don't you? '

' I'm trying to read the paper,' Conrad Gisenius replied. His tone was informative rather than reproachful.

' Speak to me! ' she insisted. ' Swear at me if you like, but don't sit there saying nothing. It gets on my nerves.'

She was sitting in her wing-chair near the window. The cold light of April fell on her face, exploring it with unmerciful clarity. It was the face of a prematurely ageing woman, blotched and sagging, with the reddish eyes of an albino rabbit.

' Don't I deserve a word occasionally? '

' I haven't finished reading yet,' Gisenius said.

He looked covertly at her hands, which were trembling

with nerves and a craving for alcohol. Gisenius could assess her habits and reactions accurately. He knew, for instance, that her sense of desperation reached an unendurable pitch in the morning because she could not drink while he was still in the house. He refused to tolerate it.

Constance Gisenius closed her red-rimmed eyes in anguish. 'I know—it was a mistake,' she said with an effort. 'I'm sorry, I shouldn't have spoken to Herr Schulz.'

Gisenius lowered his newspaper. 'But you did, didn't you?'

'It'll never happen again,' she promised humbly. When she was not under the influence of alcohol she looked shrivelled up, dwarfish and ugly.

'I seem to have heard that before,' Gisenius said. 'No doubt I'll hear it again.'

The tremor in her hands grew more pronounced. She knew what this preamble was leading up to. She was forbidden to talk to outsiders, and any contravention of the rule resulted in punitive measures. Gisenius had been quite explicit about this, and he made a point of carrying out his threats at the first opportunity. There was no way she could evade what he considered to be a well-merited penalty.

'We're alone,' he said with agonizing deliberation. 'Claus is at court and I sent Martha off on an errand. She won't be back for another hour.'

'Conrad, please—I beg you!' Constance implored. 'You mustn't!'

'Get started,' he said without moving. 'Put all the bottles on the kitchen table.'

Her limbs began to twitch. She got to her feet and turned her blotchy red face to his with a look of entreaty which he rejected with bored indifference. Then she clawed her way to the window and flung it open.

Conrad Gisenius still made no move, but his eyes narrowed as he took in the scene: a dusty, neglected-looking room furnished in dark-red plush and lit by a tall window through which could be seen an expanse of pale-blue spring sky. Silhouetted against this, swaying gently, stood the human wreck that was his wife.

'I'll jump!' Constance shrilled.

'Go on, then, jump.'

' I'll make an end of myself,' she cried. ' If you don't stop tormenting me I'll throw myself out! '

Gisenius settled back in his chair. The alert glint in his eyes faded. ' Why all the fuss? ' he said harshly. ' You haven't the courage to jump. You're finished, washed up, sodden with drink. You're only capable of meanness and malice. How could you behave so badly, pestering an outsider with your cock-and-bull stories behind my back? Is that all the thanks I get for my patience and consideration? I'm ashamed of you.'

He rose and walked over to his wife. Without touching her, without even looking at her, he closed the window. Contempt glimmered in his eyes, but Constance Gisenius thought she saw something else, something horrifyingly akin to disappointment. She stumbled back to her arm-chair and slumped into it, exhausted.

Gisenius proceeded to inspect every hiding-place in the room. He worked methodically, without hesitation. One bottle came to light in the pocket of an overcoat hanging in a cupboard, two more were hidden behind some books, the fourth and fifth were camouflaged by a jardinière and the left-hand curtain.

Gisenius made for the kitchen without bothering to see if his wife was following; she tottered after him.

He deposited the bottles in the centre of the kitchen table, glancing at the sink as he did so. Then he turned an expressionless gaze on his wife, who was leaning weakly against the door-post.

Gisenius uncorked the first bottle. He carried it over to the sink and poured it away, making a loud splashing sound. ' You've poisoned your life,' he said. ' You might have had the right to do so if you'd been alone in the world, but you weren't alone. You had to poison my life as well.'

He emptied the second bottle. ' I know how it all began. I had my work, but you were lonely. I exploited every minute of my time, but you lived in a vacuum which you couldn't fill. While I was doing my best to enrich our lives, you showed a total inability to appreciate the value of my efforts.'

The contents of the third bottle cascaded into the sink. ' A woman's life ought to be dedicated to her family, and that means primarily to the man she belongs to. All your energies, all your womanly devotion and maternal unselfishness should have been centred on me and on what has become the focal point of my life—a resolute endeavour to make the Fatherland a better and happier place for people to live in.'

His hand reached unerringly for the fourth bottle. 'What happened? Did I drink, gamble, have affairs with other women? Was I malicious, ill-natured or self-centred? Oh no, all I did was pledge myself to the service of the community. My only fault has been a love of mankind.'

He picked up the fifth bottle with undiminished enthusiasm. 'All right, perhaps you weren't capable of keeping up with me. The least I might have expected was a little toleration, a modicum of self-control. Don't you realize what immense lengths I go to on your behalf—how many sacrifices I make for you? It's not merely because you come from a good family or because you happen to have a private income. It's because we're bound together by an indissoluble vow. My generosity and consideration are prompted by purely ethical motives.'

Constance Gisenius made a renewed effort to hold herself erect. It took all her strength and left none to spare for following the thread of his remarks—not that this was necessary. She knew every one of his arguments by heart, just as he knew hers. She was utterly at his mercy.

'May I go now?' she asked wretchedly.

'Not yet. I have something else to tell you. If your illness assumes dangerous proportions—dangerous to other people, that is—I shall have to consider taking certain precautionary measures. To be blunt, you may have to be put away. People who endanger my work have to suffer the consequences. Kindly bear that in mind.'

'There are two people waiting outside,' said Gisela Wandel.

Martin Hirsch frowned. 'I don't remember arranging any appointments.'

'Well,' replied Gisela, sounding a shade less matter-of-fact than usual, 'maybe I ought to have sent one of them straight up to your apartment, but I'm not too au fait with your private affairs.'

Martin Hirsch's expression of easy amiability faded. His face grew serious, losing none of its charm in the process. 'I'll lay ten to one it's Fräulein Kerze.'

' The same.'

Hirsch was blessed with a certain natural nonchalance. His composure had only been shaken once, but that was sixteen years ago.

' I think I'll deal with the other visitor first, Fräulein Wandel,' he said casually.

Gisela Wandel reacted with the precision of a computer. ' Your other caller is a Herr Lehmgruber, at present occupying Room No 73. His weekly account was due for settlement the day before yesterday—you'll find all the particulars in the red file. He failed to pay again today, so I did the usual thing and asked him to call at your office.'

' Send him in,' Hirsch said, ' and ask Fräulein Kerze to possess her soul in patience for a little while longer.'

Gisela Wandel nodded briefly and withdrew. Hirsch opened the red file and studied the contents. It was a record of the expenses incurred by the guest in No. 73 and covered accommodation, room service and restaurant chits. The total was DM 284.60, which made Herr Lehmgruber's patronage worth having—provided he paid.

Lehmgruber entered. He bowed twice, once at the door and a second time in front of Hirsch's desk, in a manner which sought to convey cordiality, courtesy and eagerness to please. His bland, vacuous features were moulded into a permanent smile and his voice had the glib persuasiveness of a born salesman.

'Lehmgruber's the name,' he announced, bowing once more. ' Exceedingly sorry if I've caused you any inconvenience.'

' I'm sorry too,' said Hirsch.

Lehmgruber sat down without waiting for an invitation. He started to speak, and Hirsch let him run on. He produced the time-honoured story of a remittance which was on the way but had unfortunately failed to arrive as yet. Hirsch listened with half an ear while he meditated in a slightly apprehensive way on the probable reasons for Karen Kerze's visit. He wondered what it was this time. Anyone would have thought he was a social worker, the way the female members of the Kerze family came to him with their problems.

Meanwhile, Lehmgruber had brought his recital to a close and was waiting vainly for some reaction on the manager's part. 'I hope you understand,' he concluded, cocking his head on one side.

'I'm afraid not,' Hirsch said bluntly. 'There's only one thing I understand, and that's hard cash.'

'You'll get it within two or three days,' Lehmgruber assured him eagerly.

'That'll be two or three days too late.'

'But surely we'd do better to wait than cause each other unnecessary trouble?'

Hirsch pricked up his ears. This was something new in his experience. If anyone could make trouble, he was the one, not Lehmgruber. That being so, what did 'each other' mean? 'That's an interesting statement, Herr Lehmgruber. You must explain it in more detail.'

'Herr Hirsch,' Lehmgruber said, deferential as ever, 'I know enough about your line of business to realize that you require cash or some form of security from me. I can't produce either at this moment. On the other hand, I do have something else—something which may be worth a great deal of money. To be quite frank, I am in possession of certain confidential information about matters of—how shall I put it? —far-reaching political importance.'

'Oh, come now, Herr Lehmgruber, what's that got to do with me? I'm a hotel manager, not a politician.'

'Exactly. You run a hotel which is used as an unofficial headquarters by the local branch of a large and influential political party. I happen to be acquainted with certain facts about several of its leading members, and that, to put it mildly, is worth money in the bank. You may not wish to comment on this or commit yourself, but you could do one thing for me.'

'What's that?'

'Put me in touch with someone in the party who has genuine influence.'

Hirsch found the suggestion unusual but not undiverting. It might give a new twist to the almost mechanical routine of a hotelier's life. What was more, it might give him a chance to be of service to an influential friend—to wit, Gisenius. Grateful friends were always welcome, if only as a bulwark against Willy Kerze's hostility.

'What happens if you find I've sent you to the wrong man?' Hirsch inquired.

'He won't be the wrong man,' Lehmgruber said simply. 'He's bound to be interested, and I shall convert my information into money.'

'All right, Herr Lehmgruber.' Hirsch prepared to enjoy the game. 'I'll give you another two days to settle your account. In the meantime, keep this evening free. I'll see if I can get you an introduction to Herr Gisenius.'

Lehmgruber's smile broadened. 'I'm greatly obliged. You won't regret it, I assure you.'

'You're right. If anyone regrets anything round here, Herr Lehmgruber, it won't be me.'

Lehmgruber retired, and Karen Kerze stormed impatiently in.

'You've got to help me,' she began without preamble. 'Something awful's happened. Come on, let's go to your flat where we won't be disturbed.'

'No,' Hirsch replied with unexpected vigour, 'not unless you want something even worse to happen. And while we're about it, Karen, I see no reason why I should help you, particularly if your father's involved. In any case, I've no time to spare now. I'm needed in the dining-room.'

'All right, I'll have lunch there,' Karen said stubbornly. 'Afterwards we can talk, and if you're wise you'll listen. I'll wait, but don't keep me waiting too long.'

'I'm conducting a sort of ethnological survey,' the boy said. 'I'm interested in finding out where the warriors of yore are pitching their tents these days.'

'If you mean my brother, he's not here.'

'But you're here, Eva. That's good enough for me.'

Eva Schulz peered through the half-open door of her brother's flat with genuine astonishment. The boy on the landing had short, smoothly brushed hair of an indeterminate colour. Beneath it was a pair of pale-grey eyes, shrewd and observant, and between them an aquiline nose which dominated his mouth and chin.

'Don't slam the door,' he went on. 'I'd only put my foot in it, and my shoes are pretty tough. These modern doors aren't up to much, you know. You'd probably wrench the hinges off if you tried to force it.'

73

'Very interesting,' Eva said scathingly, 'but I'd sooner you told me who you are and what you want.'

'You mean to say you don't know who I am, Eva?'

'I've been spared that pleasure so far.'

'It only goes to show how unobtrusive I am. Modesty in person—that's me. You've got to admit that's a point in my favour.'

The boy moved closer, but Eva stood her ground, radiating poise, self-assurance and common sense.

'I stand beside you in the tram, I breathe down your neck while you look in shop windows—I even sit behind you in the cinema for hours on end, and you don't notice me! Ah, Eva, what have I done to deserve this?'

The boy struck an elaborate pose, bowing his head and clasping his brow like an allegory of despair. Whoever he was, he clearly enjoyed playing the buffoon.

Eva Schulz found the spectacle diverting, but she also realized that his play-acting had presented her with a chance of getting rid of him. Quick as lightning, she slammed the door in his face.

'Well I'll be . . .' The boy grinned appreciatively at the speed of her reaction. 'Do you always treat visitors like that?'

'Go away!' Eva shouted through the closed door.

'Give me a chance!' he shouted back. 'I'm only trying to repay a social call. My name's Claus Gisenius, if that means anything to you.'

Eva knew the name well. She donned an expression of youthful dignity and opened the door again.

'Good morning,' she said formally, every inch the mistress of her brother's house. 'I'm sorry I spoke to you like that just now, but you should have told me who you were in the first place.'

He nodded and came closer. Claus Gisenius was no lover of outmoded convention.

'Disappointing, this,' he said, indicating the neat but conventional décor of the passage behind her. 'I expected the walls to be plastered with war-time souvenirs—guns, steel helmets, pieces of shrapnel. Haven't you got a mess-tin or a canteen somewhere? I could do with a drink.'

'I must say, you've an odd way of putting things.'

74

'I'm merely displaying my expert knowledge, Eva, trying to adapt myself to the old soldier's mentality. We've got to convince our veterans that there's a rising generation which revels in the language of heroes.'

'You might as well save your breath—I don't understand a word you're saying. And if you're hoping to impress my brother, I told you already—he's not at home.'

'Can't I wait for him?'

'You can wait if you like, but not inside the flat.'

'Ah!' Claus moved closer. 'So visits from young men aren't encouraged.'

'You're no young man of mine.'

'Don't say that!' Claus exclaimed. He clasped his chest and staggered as if hit by a bullet. 'You've cut me to the quick,' he moaned theatrically, 'to the quick, I tell you!'

Eva Schulz laughed aloud. At this stage, Claus Gisenius struck her as no more than an amusing boy—slightly deranged, it was true, but in the nicest possible way. He appealed to her much as a playful puppy would have done.

'Come inside,' she said, yielding to a sudden impulse. 'I've got some things to do in the kitchen. You can help me if you like.'

'I'm deeply wounded,' Claus said. 'Not to put too fine a point on it, you've shattered my ego. I'll never be able to look another woman in the face—not unless you call me Claus, that is. It might give me new heart.'

'All right, Claus.'

They made their way to the kitchen. Claus inspected the tidy shelves and whistled. 'Very neat! Are all those pots and pans just there for show, or do you actually use them?'

Eva smiled modestly. 'I've got to get lunch ready now,' she said. 'My brother will be home in an hour.'

'That gives us an hour to get to know each other. Why spoil it by working? Just give your brother a tin of bully-beef and half a loaf of army bread. That's quite good enough for an old soldier.'

Eva smiled. 'You're quite funny sometimes.'

Claus agreed without hesitation. 'I know I am. It comes from living in such a funny world, I suppose.'

'What do you do all day, Claus—I mean, when you're not keeping other people from their work?'

'My life is dedicated to the cause of justice!' he intoned dramatically. 'To be more prosaic, I'm studying law.'

'Funny, I thought you might be part of a circus act.'

'It's the same thing,' he said promptly. 'Circus artists are considerably more honest and hard-working, but otherwise they're just like lawyers: they help to create an illusion.'

Eva was busy washing a lettuce, but she glanced up from her work as he spoke. Claus had spread his legs and was gazing at her with his elbows propped on the kitchen-table. He looked at ease, but a cool, analytical glint had come into his eyes.

'You see, Eva,' he went on, 'in my job I acquire some deep insights into human nature. I come into contact with honest crooks, lecherous schoolmasters, murderers who wouldn't hurt a fly, pimps who go to church every Sunday, respectable blackmailers—all of them worthy members of Greater German society.'

'There are other kinds.'

'Of course. For instance, there are people who pass for honest citizens because they're too old and apathetic to stick their fingers in the till, or people who are clever enough not to get caught, or people who get on very nicely with the laws of the moment, either because they made and moulded them or because they're adaptable.'

'Which category do I and my brother belong to?'

Claus Gisenius grinned. 'That's just what I want to find out.'

'You'll have a hard job.'

'Not if you help me, Eva. You'll be working in a noble cause, I assure you. It always worries me when I can't pigeon-hole people. I was curious about you the first time I saw you, but when I met your brother the day before yesterday—well, that settled it. Your brother's an unusual sort of person. He gives such an impression of decency and honesty.'

'That's just what he is,' Eva said stoutly, '—decent and honest.'

'In that case,' Claus drawled, 'the man's a challenge to his environment—and so are you, for that matter. Tell me, are you going steady with anyone?'

'You'd better ask my brother about that, Claus. But I warn you, his arm's as strong as his character.'

'Is it, now!' Claus looked delighted. 'That fits my picture of him to a T. I'm getting more and more curious, Eva. It's fascinating!'

'You've been long enough, haven't you?' Karen Kerze said petulantly. 'I'm not used to being kept waiting like this. Can you spare me some of your precious time now?'

'A minute or two, that's all,' Hirsch replied tersely.

'In that case I'll come straight to the point. It's not very pleasant sitting here, though. Couldn't we go up to your flat?'

Hirsch shook his head.

'But everyone's staring at us. You ought to select your staff more carefully. That waiter over there has been leering at me like a randy old goat.'

Hirsch did not comment on this. Then: 'Why did you want to speak to me? What can I do for you?'

'A great deal.'

'That sounds like a great deal too much.'

'Aren't you in love with me, then?' Karen complained in a low voice. No one in the room could have heard, Hirsch felt sure. He was well acquainted with the acoustic properties of his hotel.

'Come now, Karen,' he said, faintly amused. 'When did I ever give you that impression?'

Karen looked astonished. 'What about four days ago, when we were sitting in the Blue Bamboo?'

'That was four days ago. We met there by chance, and all I did was tell one of your boy-friends to get lost because I didn't like the look of him. I then took the liberty of telling you that you were an extremely attractive girl—which is true. I wanted to wean you away from the road-house set, but not so that I could get you into bed.'

'But you kissed me!'

Hirsch took a cautious look round. Karen's uninhibited temperament had its dangers, but no one was paying any attention except Paul, the waiter, who was still eyeing Karen with suppressed lust, as he had been, on and off, for the past two hours.

'Listen, Karen,' Hirsch said in a low, persuasive under-tone. 'Please don't exaggerate. We'd both had a couple of drinks and I was enjoying your company. Of course I kissed you, but it was more of a fatherly sort of kiss.'

' Is that so? Father's never tried anything like that with me, I can tell you.'

' Your father's attitude to life is quite different from mine. I may be an irresponsible idiot compared to him, Karen, but I'm not a cad.'

' I know you're not,' Karen said with passionate intensity. ' That's why I don't care if you are twenty years older and a friend of my father's. I know all the conventional objections by heart, but they don't alter the fact that I could love you if you wanted me to.'

' Quite frankly, Karen, I don't.'

' Are you in love with someone else—your secretary, for instance? '

' Steady on! ' Hirsch took another cautious look round. ' Don't you see, Karen? You can't coerce someone into loving you—certainly not by doing a strip-tease act, anyway.'

' I need someone I can love, Martin,' she insisted. ' I'm desperate.'

Hirsch leant forward. ' Look, my girl,' he said with as much of an avuncular manner as he could muster, ' we all need people we can love, but they don't grow on trees. You don't find them on every street corner, and you certainly don't find them by jumping into bed at the drop of a hat. You've got to be patient and shop around.'

' I haven't got time for that,' Karen said impatiently. ' I've been told I've got to get married as soon as possible.'

' To whom? '

' Father's trying to palm me off on that jumped up pansy Bartosch—Bartosch of all people! '

Martin Hirsch leant back in his chair without comment. His sardonic expression softened, and his hands, which were still resting on the table, clenched slightly.

' You see, that's reduced even you to silence, hasn't it! ' Karen cried triumphantly.

There was a long pause. Then, speaking without a trace of irony for the first time, Hirsch said slowly: ' I'm afraid that's something you'll have to work out by yourself. I can't help you.'

' So that's it! ' she exclaimed furiously. ' You're scared of my father like all the rest.'

' Rubbish! ' Hirsch's manner grew more relaxed and his eyes started to sparkle again. ' It's just that I'm not particularly keen to make trouble for your old man. I've already blotted my copy-book with him once.'

' I know all about it, Martin. That's mainly why I came to see you. You were generous enough to help my stepmother —she told me the whole story. That's another reason why I love you.'

' The fact that I helped your stepmother very nearly put paid to a friendship of long standing, Karen. Why should I be foolish enough to finish it off completely? '

' What if you haven't any choice? '

' Is that a threat? '

' You're forcing my hand, Martin.'

Gisela Wandel appeared, looking cool and business-like. Hirsch hailed the distraction with relief.

' Herr Bennicken is outside in the foyer.'

' Does he want to speak to me? ' Hirsch asked hopefully.

' No, he said it would be good enough if I gave you a message: Herr Kerze is inviting the members of his old unit to a reunion here in the hotel at eight o'clock this evening. Your presence would be greatly appreciated.'

' Tell Herr Bennicken I'll be there, and make sure the Oak Room is free.'

' Certainly, Herr Hirsch.'

Gisela Wandel withdrew, leaving Hirsch impressed, as usual, by her air of self-assurance. He never failed to marvel at the timely nature of her interventions.

' Now, Karen,' he said firmly, ' you're going to be sensible. Stop trying to bully me. I'll have a hard time as it is, explaining to your father why you were doing the dance of the seven veils in my flat.'

' What if I told him you asked me to ? '

' I'd simply say you were a complete flop—not even worth taking to bed. I hope you've got too much womanly pride to force me into making such a disclosure.'

Karen glared at Hirsch with mounting rage as he calmly produced a cigarette and lit it. She found his display of indifference infuriating. Convulsively, she looked round for a suitable target for her wrath. She soon found what she wanted.

'Hey, you!' she called peremptorily across the dining-room. 'Come here!'

The few remaining guests raised their eyebrows at this disturbance with irritation. Hirsch tried to intervene, but Karen's chosen victim was already approaching.

Paul bowed deeply. 'Yes, madam?' he inquired.

'Kindly keep your eyes to yourself. It's indecent, the way you've been leering at me!'

'It's all right, Paul,' Hirsch said, controlling himself with difficulty. 'You can go.'

Paul departed stiffly and in silence, visibly mortified.

'Disgusting brute!' Karen said in a loud voice.

'And you're a hysterical little bitch,' Hirsch growled at her. 'Honestly, Karen, I don't know which is worse, your bad temper or your lack of common sense. Paul is the last person you should have antagonized—he knows too much about you.'

'About me?'

'Certainly. He was the waiter who saw you doing gymnastics in my room.'

'So what!' Karen said fiercely. 'He's not the only man who's seen me like that.' A calculating smile came over her face as she added, with an abrupt change of mood: 'Anyway, who knows? It may be a good thing. Witnesses can be useful sometimes, can't they?'

'Listen a minute, all of you!' Schulz called amiably. He repeated his request in a slightly louder voice, but without success.

'Silence!' roared Schulz.

Conversation ceased abruptly. When Schulz really turned up the volume he seldom failed to produce the desired effect. Discipline still ran in his friends' veins, a fact on which they all prided themselves to a greater or lesser degree.

'Kerze has the floor,' Schulz announced.

'Before he gets under way,' Hirsch interposed, 'I have a purely administrative query: has everyone got enough to drink?'

There was a chorus of assent. With his usual foresight,

Hirsch had laid on adequate supplies. The bottles were carefully marshalled in neat groups: Kronen ale for Schulz, Rheine-Bergen lager for Kerze, Munich Löwenbräu and Danish schnapps for Bennicken, ice-cold Steinhäger and kirsch for Frammler. Gisenius favoured a velvety Moselle, and for his personal delectation Hirsch had selected a sparkling Anjou rosé.

'This kirsch is only fifty per cent strength,' said Frammler. 'I prefer the fifty-five per cent stuff.'

As usual in such circumstances Schulz felt entirely in command of the situation. 'Then go on drinking until you've made up the extra five per cent.'

'Fair enough.' Frammler shrugged. 'Orders is orders. I was only a lance-corporal, after all.'

'Right, friends!' Schulz called, seizing the initiative once more. 'Perhaps we can get started. Let's have you, Kerze.'

Kerze cleared his throat importantly. 'Well, I asked for the floor, and now I've got it, I don't know where to begin.'

'What about beginning at the beginning?' suggested Frammler.

'You won't like what I've got to tell you,' Kerze went on. 'It's awkward, but I'm afraid you'll have to know sooner or later.'

'Carry on,' Schulz said squaring his shoulders confidently. 'We can take it.'

'All right, then.' Kerze gathered himself for another attempt. 'Perhaps it would be best if I brought you into this, my dear Schulz. You remember what happened to you the day before yesterday?'

'Nothing special happened,' Schulz said. 'I had a few too many and started seeing things, that's all.'

'Naughty things,' Frammler said with relish.

'Cut it out!' Hirsch snapped. 'That item isn't on the agenda, and it won't be, either, if I've got anything to do with it. Any objections? What about you, Kerze?'

Kerze's eyes flashed menacingly and he made a movement in Hirsch's direction, but Gisenius laid a restraining hand on his arm.

'My dear Willy,' Gisenius said, 'you know I always try not to take sides, at least where the ex-members of No. 2

Section are concerned, but in this case I feel that Hirsch is right. Some things are better forgotten.'

'Why?' Frammler demanded, grinning.

'Because it's bad form to mention them,' Gisenius said simply.

'Gisenius is right,' growled Bennicken.

'You misunderstand me,' Kerze said. 'I had no intention of discussing any such thing. But while we're on the subject, gentlemen: if anyone tries to spread obscene slanders about my daughter, I'll sue him for defamation of character.'

'And I'll break his neck,' added Hirsch.

'Let's get down to business,' Gisenius urged. 'Come on, Willy, you're in the chair.'

Kerze collected himself with an obvious effort. 'All right, it's like this. The day before yesterday, Schulz, you specifically stated that you had seen a face known to you and all of us.'

'Oh, no!' Schulz replied promptly. 'It was all a big mistake—no doubt about it—a clear case of hallucination. What's the point of bringing that up again?'

'I'd like to know what we're talking about in the first place,' Frammler said. 'There are no secrets in our mob, are there? All right, then, what's it all about?'

'Schulz made a mistake,' Gisenius said suavely. 'It's not worth discussing. Let's forget it, Willy.'

'Forget what?' Frammler insisted. 'Who did Schulz think he saw? What's all this about hallucinations? Come on, let's have it!'

Willy Kerze said firmly: 'What it amounts to is this: Schulz told us the day before yesterday that he had seen Michael Meiners.'

Frammler looked dumbfounded. 'Who did you say?'

'Michael Meiners.'

'That's crazy,' Frammler said with finality. 'He's dead.'

'Dead as a doornail,' Bennicken chimed in.

'Cheers!' Hirsch said, raising his glass. 'Let's drink to his memory.'

No one followed Hirsch's suggestion. Willy Kerze said deliberately: 'I'm satisfied that there's been no mistake. Schulz did see Michael Meiners.'

'No,' Schulz protested. 'No, I'll admit I don't often

make a mistake, but I did in this case. Why not drop the subject? As far as I'm concerned, it's closed.'

'It's not closed for you or any of us,' Kerze said significantly. 'Get this straight, gentlemen—I saw Michael Meiners too. I saw him as plainly as I see you, standing under a spotlight only a few yards away. It was Meiners all right, I promise you!'

'Let's not leap to conclusions.' As was customary in awkward situations, Conrad Gisenius had assumed command. 'We must think this over calmly and carefully.'

Martin Hirsch rang down to the hotel kitchen for two jugs of black coffee as an aid to clear thinking and opened another bottle of rosé for himself. The 'ghost story', as he privately christened Schulz's and Kerze's revelations, did not impress him unduly. He had long ago realized that the world was a place where few things were impossible.

'I saw him, and that's all there is to it,' Kerze said stolidly.

Karl Schulz's first reaction was to feel gratified that his powers of observation had been vindicated. 'I was pretty certain I'd seen him myself,' he announced. 'Maybe I did the right thing when I put young Bennicken on his trail.'

'What's that?' demanded Gisenius, pricking up his ears.

'Bennicken junior—he was driving the bus. I told him to keep an eye on the man sitting at the back.'

Gisenius wasted no time in following up this clue. 'Bennicken,' he said, 'where's your son now?'

'Driving the cab,' said Bennicken.

Martin Hirsch acted with characteristic speed. He picked up the house 'phone and asked to be put through to the desk. 'Call Bennicken's,' he ordered. 'Tell young Bennicken to get here at once—I repeat, at once. When he arrives, send him up straight away.'

'You're all crazy,' Frammler said complacently, 'absolutely crazy.'

'You're not qualified to judge.' Kerze sounded indignant that anyone should treat his first-hand evidence with such scant respect.

'It's ridiculous, I tell you.' Frammler looked to Gisenius for support, but the lawyer was pursuing his own line of thought.

'You say you saw him, Willy,' Gisenius said. 'You didn't speak to him, did you?'

'Ghosts don't often give tongue,' commented Hirsch. 'Anyway, what would you have expected him to say: Grenadier Meiners reporting from the grave for a chat about old times?'

'Hirsch,' Gisenius said sternly, 'I don't think you quite appreciate the gravity of the situation.'

'I can't say I do.' Hirsch drained his glass. 'I'm not particularly keen on ghost-stories.'

'What do you mean by that?' Gisenius asked swiftly. 'You're not going to leave us in the lurch if our suspicions turn out to be correct, are you?'

'If you run out on us, Hirsch,' Kerze said accusingly, 'all I can say is, it's only what I'd have expected.'

'Oh, come,' Hirsch drawled, 'where's your team spirit?' He grinned wickedly. 'All the same, the thought of you in a convict's uniform isn't without its charms.'

'Gentlemen, gentlemen!' Gisenius exhorted. 'The last thing we can afford at this juncture is a split in the ranks.'

'It's fantastic,' muttered Frammler, taking a swig of his under-strength kirsch. 'I've never heard anything so ludicrous in my life.'

Two things occurred in quick succession to terminate the argument: coffee arrived and was dispensed by Hirsch, and Bennicken junior appeared, clad in a shabby blue serge chauffeur's uniform which he had presumably inherited from his father.

The youth ambled in nonchalantly in his best cowboy fashion, but as soon as he saw that one of the six men watching him was his father he adopted a stance which might charitably have been described as attention.

'Something to drink, lad?' asked Hirsch.

'Not when he's on duty,' interposed Bennicken senior.

'What about a cup of coffee?'

Bennicken senior was implacable. 'Bad for the nerves.'

'My dear young friend,' Gisenius said, bearing down on the youth with an ingratiating smile. 'Do you remember Herr Schulz asking you to do something for him the night before last?'

Bennicken junior nodded.

'If my information is correct,' Gisenius continued, 'he asked you to keep an eye on one of your passengers.'

'I did, too,' Bennicken junior spoke with pride. 'Gave him a proper once-over.'

'With what result?'

'There wasn't anything special about him. He was about forty, maybe thirty-five. Stared into space the whole time. He had big eyes—sort of cow-like, they were. There were scars on his face as though he'd been in a fight somewhere, but his voice sounded soft, like a parson's. Thin and narrow-shouldered, he was, and a bit bow-legged.'

'It sounds like him,' Kerze said.

'It sounds like a few thousand other people as well,' Hirsch commented.

'He had a bag with him,' Bennicken junior added.

'Any identification?' Gisenius demanded briskly. 'What about a label or a name—or a monogram?'

'Yes, it did have something like that on it. Two letters— M's, they were—you couldn't miss them.'

The ensuing silence was broken by Karl Schulz. 'Michael Meiners,' he murmured with something akin to awe. 'And they tried to tell me I was wrong!'

'Come off it,' said Hirsch, 'M.M. could stand for any number of things—Matheus Müller the champagne firm, for instance. Maybe he's one of their travellers.' He turned to Bennicken junior. 'Do you know where he came from or where he was heading for?'

'I couldn't say.' Bennicken junior stood there stolidly, savouring his unaccustomed sense of self-importance. 'At the end of the line he just picked up his bag and vanished. Haven't a clue where he went.'

'It's quite simple,' Hirsch said. 'He disappeared into thin air. Ghosts always do.'

Gisenius ignored the remark. 'Good,' he told Bennicken junior. 'That will be all, thank you. You can go.'

'There's three marks fifty on the clock.'

'Charge it to petty cash,' decreed Bennicken senior. 'Dismiss!'

The youth departed promptly, leaving the six men a prey to conflicting emotions.

'Gentlemen,' said Gisenius, 'let's recapitulate for a moment.

85

Kerze and Schulz saw a man who is, or was, familiar to all of us. However acute their powers of observation, one of them might possibly have been mistaken, but I consider it almost inconceivable that both should have fallen into the same error. I am forced to conclude that all is not as it should be, and this fills me—and presumably all of us—with a measure of concern. Only Frammler and Hirsch seem to find the matter in any way amusing. Would you mind telling me why, Hirsch? '

' Yes, let's share the joke,' Kerze said acidly.

' The answer's quite simple,' Hirsch replied, '—so simple that you may take offence at it, but I can't help that. As I see it, there are a few unalterable facts of life. One of them is procreation, which leads to birth, and another is death—the final solution, if you like.'

' Procreation! ' growled Kerze. ' You've got a one-track mind.'

' Very well, let's talk about death,' Hirsch said. ' It comes to everyone, but it only comes once.'

' That's just what I've been trying to say all this time,' complained Frammler.

' Exactly,' Hirsch said. ' We ought to have consulted our celebrated expert on death in the first place.'

' Except that in this case Frammler knows as little as we do, if not less,' Schulz put in.

' You're wrong,' Frammler said confidently. ' I know considerably more about dead bodies than the bulk of ordinary mortals. I saw Meiners's body, and it was deader than most, believe you me.'

' What do you mean? ' Gisenius asked in a flat voice.

' I conducted a sort of post mortem,' Frammler said, relishing the others' attention, '—about two weeks later, when all the fuss had died down. I went back to the spot—taking great care, you understand—and had a good look round. I've always been thorough—it's an important asset in my job. Thoroughness, accuracy and precision: that's my motto. No one jumps off the embalming-table while I'm around! '

' Get to the point, man! You went back to the edge of the wood? '

' I did,' Frammler continued, ' and everything was just as

it had been a fortnight before—apart from the stench, that is. Smells don't affect me, though. That's another trick of the trade. We all acquire it sooner or later, and with me it was sooner. I had a strong stomach even as a child.'

'All right, all right,' Gisenius said impatiently. 'You got to the edge of the wood. What did you see?'

'What I expected to see—the hole in the sand, the path, the fir-branches over the slit-trench.'

'They were pine-branches,' Schulz interposed.

'Have it your own way,' Frammler said with a touch of annoyance. 'I'm not a botanist. I happen to specialize in another field, and I know more about it than most. Anyway, I took a look round. The area looked pretty churned up— I'd hardly have recognized it. And then I saw what I was looking for. He was lying all crumpled up with his arms and legs smashed and his chest caved in. His head looked like a bowl of porridge—dried porridge. I told you, I've never seen anyone deader than he was.'

'Any questions?' asked Hirsch.

The old comrades—impressed, thoughtful or merely relieved—remained silent.

Only Frammler raised his hand. 'Yes, I've got one. Why are you keeping us so short of liquor, Martin? I call it downright unfriendly of you.'

4. *Social Life and its Consequences*

'I'm an artist,' Quahnke declared. 'I have my pride.'

Martin Hirsch looked amused. 'I hope that's not all you have.'

He was sitting in the office of the *Café de Paris*, facing Wilhelm Quahnke, self-styled artistic director of that establishment. Quahnke was a majestic man in his late fifties, de Gaulle-bellied, Adenauer-nosed, slightly unkempt and a little dirty, but indisputably majestic.

The *Café de Paris* came within the domain of the *Hotel Drei Kronen* both from the point of view of administration and location, since it occupied the basement of one wing of the hotel. It was a relatively innocuous dive which local burgers patronized on the rare occasions when they felt sinfully inclined.

'Herr Hirsch, I should like to draw your attention to Fräulein Marlene Sonnenberg.'

'Aren't you happy with her? Her singing doesn't seem to have deteriorated in the three weeks since you engaged her —or improved, for that matter.'

'I know,' Quahnke conceded. 'Her artistic ability, in so far as one can use the phrase in connection with her, remains unaltered, but her personal behaviour has left much to be desired recently.'

'The personal behaviour of your so-called artistes is your business, Quahnke.'

Quahnke flung himself into the role of Talleyrand soliciting Napoleon's sympathy, his portentous manner indicating clearly that this was a matter of the highest moment.

Hirsch sat back to enjoy the spectacle, pretending to study the office décor with an expression of faint ennui.

'The fact of the matter is this,' said Quahnke. 'When I engaged Fräulein Sonnenberg she still possessed the humility which I consider to be so absolutely essential in any artiste.

Unfortunately, this is no longer so, and for reasons which seem only too plain. You may remember, Herr Hirsch, that I advised Fräulein Sonnenberg to accept the offer of private accommodation which you were kind enough to recommend.'

Hirsch feigned incomprehension. 'What do you mean? Herr Schulz mentioned to me that he had a furnished room to let in his flat, and I passed the information on to you. What's so extraordinary about that?'

'Nothing—nothing, of course.' Quahnke wrung his hands. 'Except that it may have been a mistake on my part to send Fräulein Sonnenberg to Herr Schulz.'

'You could always have sent someone else—one of the band, for instance."

'I know, but I thought I'd be doing Herr Schulz a favour. After all, he's a friend of yours.'

'Quahnke!' Hirsch said sternly, the corners of his mouth twitching, 'I hope you're not suggesting that I indirectly told you to act as Fräulein Sonnenberg's pimp.'

Quahnke threw up both hands in horror. Without meaning to, he had ventured on to thin ice. To impute improper and underhand behaviour to a man in Hirsch's position could cost a man like Quahnke his post.

'Herr Direktor,' he said hastily, 'if a blunder has been made it goes without saying that I alone am responsible. But I'm at my wits' end. For some time now—especially in the last two days—this creature, this Fräulein Sonnenberg— well, she's been treating me like an inferior being!'

Hirsch could well imagine the cause of Quahnke's torment, and he found it grotesque. Marlene Sonnenberg had obviously been trying to exploit her connection with Schulz. Hirsch wondered what her object was. Who was she trying to provoke—just Quahnke or Hirsch himself?

'Now look, Quahnke,' he said in a matter-of-fact tone, 'what employees of this establishment choose to do with their private lives is no concern of ours. If they fall down on the job because they're careless, incompetent or lazy, they must be dismissed—sooner rather than later. In this particular case, as long as the Sonnenberg women is punctual, sober and hard-working, she stays. If not, she goes out on her ear. Got it?'

Saffranski was huddled over a pile of papers when his managing director entered the room. Leaping to his feet and bowing in one continuous movement, he stationed himself deferentially on one side of the desk, near the safe.

'Well, Saffranski, how's the job coming along?'

'Quite well, sir. I venture to say I've already formed a good general picture of the business. Hotel bookkeeping follows the usual pattern. It's only the items entered that seem a little unfamiliar at first, but the same goes for any specialized field. Its peculiarities can always be mastered in time.'

'Very good, Saffranski.' Kerze gave a benevolent nod. 'Prucker, the chief accountant of Europa Hotels, will give you all the records for the financial year '57–'58. I want you to bring them back here and go through them with a tooth-comb.'

'With a tooth-comb—certainly, sir.'

'I'm not so much interested in working out any schemes for increased profitability—there'll be time enough for that later. Your first job is to spot any mistakes or inaccuracies. You never know, you might even come across something fishy. Do you follow me, Saffranski?'

'Perfectly, sir.'

'That's all right then.' Kerze treated Saffranski to another nod of appreciation. 'Incidentally, I hope you're making yourself at home here.'

'Yes, thank you, sir.'

'My housekeeper tells me you've taken my son Konstantin under your wing. I appreciate that, Saffranski. It won't hurt the boy to be given a few hints on how to fill his time. He needs to be kept occupied. He day-dreams too much for my taste. I'd sooner see him wielding a spade occasionally.'

'I understand, sir.'

'Carry on, then. I shall show my appreciation in due course, don't worry. I'm not a mean man, and I've always acted on the principle that everything has its just reward—everything, Saffranski.'

'Don't be alarmed, I'm quite harmless today,' Karl Schulz said genially. 'I'll do my best to behave, I promise you.'

Gisela Wandel got up from her desk with her usual air of

formality and reserve, giving him a brief but penetrating glance as she did so.

Schulz smiled at her disarmingly. ' I must apologize for the other night.'

' There's really no need, Herr Schulz.'

' Oh yes, there is,' Schulz insisted. ' I must have behaved like a wild animal, and I'm sure I gave you a lot of trouble. I can't tell you how sorry I am.'

' Please think no more about it, Herr Schulz. If you want to see Herr Hirsch, I should go straight in.'

' Unannounced? '

' I'm sure he won't mind.' Gisela Wandel gave him another brief smile and sat down again.

Schulz walked into Hirsch's office to find him lolling back in his chair with his feet on the desk. He was puffing at a cigarette and contemplating the blue haze of smoke above his head with rapt attention. He squinted briefly at the door but did not move.

Schulz grinned. ' Sorry to disturb you in the middle of your work, but I was hoping you'd do me a favour.'

' What are friends for? ' Hirsch waved his visitor vaguely towards a chair. ' As far as my work's concerned, all I can say is: happy is he who has never managed a hotel. Even so, I don't indulge in the luxury of despair. What can I do for you? '

' I'm taking the afternoon off.'

' No need to be embarrassed, Karl. Taking an afternoon off isn't so reprehensible—it's what it develops into that matters. What are you after, anyway—a gala dinner in the Silver Room, a tour of the wine cellars, our best bridal suite? Your wish is my command.'

' Well, if you really insist . . .'

' I do, my dear fellow, I do! '

' All right, I'd like to pay a visit to the *Café de Paris*, if it's no trouble.'

' Our sink of iniquity doesn't open till this evening, Karl, but I'll willingly arrange a special booking for you in the so-called directorial box.'

' I realize nothing goes on down there in the afternoons officially, but what about rehearsals? '

' What about them? ' Hirsch asked, amused because he

knew what Schulz was driving at. He had nothing against Schulz's affair with Marlene Sonnenberg as long as it didn't go too far. Marlene was all right for a bit of slap and tickle but not for a serious relationship.

'I'd like to see one, Martin,' Schulz pursued doggedly.

'That won't be too easy, my boy. It's not usually allowed. They're frightfully sensitive, these artistes. When they're performing in public they love people gawping at them—but when they're rehearsing they scream like banshees if anyone so much as tries to give them a pat on the arm.'

'Well, that's that, I suppose.' Schulz looked crestfallen.

Martin Hirsch swung his legs to the floor and got up, feeling a twinge of remorse at his friend's obvious disappointment. Schulz was the one person he disliked hurting.

'There is one possibility,' he said. 'Outside observers aren't welcome at rehearsals, however great their personal interest, but nobody objects to the presence of the management. I'll pay the dive a visit in my official capacity and you can come with me.'

'Can I really, Martin?'

'Don't bother to thank me, old fellow—I'm doing it for my own sake as well as yours. Quahnke tells me he's discovered a splendid new specimen of femininity, so why shouldn't I take a look at her? Who knows, she may be worth it!'

'More soul!' Quahnke trumpeted into the spotlight. 'Lots more soul! You've got to feel it oozing out of your finger-tips, darling.'

The object of his adjurations was standing on the minuscule stage—twelve feet by nine—of the *Café de Paris*, endeavouring to shed the first of her seven veils with the maximum of allure. She was not succeeding to any marked degree, hence Quahnke's cry from the heart.

Quahnke turned and plunged into the semi-darkness of the auditorium, which was empty save for Martin Hirsch and, behind him, the awestruck and expectant figure of Karl Schulz. 'She'll make it,' Quahnke promised fervently. 'She's on the point of losing those stupid inhibitions of hers —I can feel it in my bones.'

'I hope your bones know their business,' Martin Hirsch said. He eyed the wares displayed on the podium with total indifference. A young girl stood pin-pointed by the beam of a spotlight, trembling slightly with cold, nerves and a desire to make good—a replica of thousands of other girls in thousands of other third- and fourth-rate night-clubs.

Quahnke turned and fluttered towards the brightly-lit stage again, a moth drawn to a flame. 'Your hips are too stiff!' he called. 'You're not putting enough expression into your backside, darling. You won't get anywhere like that.'

Karl Schulz at last made out the figure of Marlene Sonnenberg and raised a hand in greeting. She was sitting in front of the band on the right of the stage, just outside the circle of light.

Marlene also raised a hand in greeting and followed it up by blowing a kiss in the direction of the two onlookers. 'This is a real treat!' Schulz told Hirsch in a grateful whisper.

'If you go for that sort of thing,' Hirsch retorted. 'Personally, all I can see when I look at women like these is price-tags and directions for use.'

Meanwhile, the figure on the stage was striving to shed her second veil as erotically as possible, still without any notable success. Salome might be a hackneyed role, but it provided a good basis for a strip-tease act—and every woman had her own individual approach to that, Hirsch reflected ruefully.

In fact, the girl on the stage was far from being a woman, however desperately she tried to appear such. Hirsch was not slow to spot this. 'You,' he called, 'come over here.'

'Hurry up!' Quahnke said in admonitory tones, adding in a whisper: 'Now, Brigitte, show him what you can do!'

Instead of showing what she could do, Brigitte chose to show what she had—which was incomparably more. Flanked by Quahnke, she stationed herself in front of Hirsch and fluttered her eye-lashes strenuously.

Hirsch thought it time to dispel a few illusions. He eyed the veil-clad body dispassionately and said: 'How old?'

'Eighteen,' the girl replied eagerly.

'Too young.' Hirsch's voice was curt.

'With respect, sir,' Quahnke cut in, 'she's legally old enough to be employed in an establishment of this sort. I plan to make her a star attraction.'

Hirsch was aware that the qualifications demanded of a star attraction in the *Café de Paris* were not high, and he also sensed that Brigitte had her share of drive and ambition. She did not interest him in the least as an individual, but as a business man he had no objection to engaging her.

'Off you go, darling!' Quahnke exhorted. 'Take it from the beginning again, and put a bit more soul into it this time.'

'Do you fancy her?' Hirsch murmured over his shoulder.

Schulz demurred vigorously. 'I'm not a cradle-snatcher. Girls of her age ought to be in cookery school or learning about baby care. If I were her father or brother she wouldn't be able to frisk about like that—her bottom would be black and blue.'

Hirsch turned to Schulz and said, without a trace of reproach: 'I gather you told our friends about the girl in my apartment.'

'I know I did,' Schulz said. 'I'm sorry, but how was I to know she was Kerze's daughter? I hadn't seen her since she was in pinafores.'

'It's all right, I'm not blaming you,' Hirsch replied. 'All I would ask is that you don't let it go any further.'

'Rely on me,' Schulz assured him staunchly. 'What do you think I am, anyway? I don't hawk things like that all over town. It was just a joke among friends.'

'I'm not worried about the others, Karl, but I'd be obliged if you wouldn't tell anyone else about it—Fräulein Sonnenberg, for instance, or your sister Eva.'

'Of course not,' Schulz said. 'I understand. You'd find it embarrassing if Marlene spread it around here, but you needn't worry about her, nor about Eva. Eva's far too young for that sort of thing.'

'You know, Karl,' Hirsch said after a moment's hesitation, 'it's quite amazing, the way you cosset that sister of yours.'

'It's only natural. I've had to be a second father to her.'

'You've done a good job, too. There aren't many girls like Eva around these days. They're all spoilt to hell.'

Schulz smiled fondly. 'Believe me, every time I come home in the evening and find her waiting for me, neat and tidy and unspoilt, it gladdens my heart. And I'll tell you another thing: if anyone comes along and tries to get his hands on her—and he's not good enough for her—I'll break every bone in his body, so help me!'

Martin Hirsch glanced away as though urgently in need

of distraction. On the spotlit stage the fourth veil was just drifting to the floor, but the sight only irritated him. He was glad when a genuine distraction presented itself. One of the waiters came up with a telephone on a long lead and announced that his office wanted him.

Hirsch took the receiver and heard Gisela Wandel's voice telling him that Herr Gisenius was with her and wanted to speak to him in person.

'Tell Herr Gisenius I can't get away, but I'd be delighted if he'd join me here.'

'I'll pass your suggestion on straight away,' she replied promptly.

Hirsch turned to Schulz. 'Did you hear? We're going to have a visitor.'

'I can hardly wait,' Schulz chuckled. 'It ought to be a sight worth seeing—a model citizen like Gisenius in this den of vice. I bet he won't come.'

'He'll come all right. Gisenius would travel to hell and back if he thought it was worth it. While I'm talking to him, perhaps you'd look after the performers for me.'

Schulz grinned. 'Thanks, Martin. You're one in a million.'

'Just you go on thinking that. I may take advantage of it one day.' Hirsch swivelled in his chair. 'Ah, here comes his grey eminence in person!'

Gisenius stood in the doorway, escorted by a page-boy. He seemed to be dazzled by the spotlight, which might have been why he closed his eyes briefly. On the other hand, it might have had something to do with the veil-shedding Brigitte, who was standing motionless while her fifth veil—a scrap of flesh-pink chiffon—floated gracefully to the floor.

'That's it, darling!' Quahnke hissed from the wings. 'Just give it a bit more bosom—you shouldn't find it too hard.'

Gisenius passed a hand over his eyes, though whether to shield them from the light or shut out the sight of Brigitte was still not apparent. Some moments elapsed before he saw Hirsch, who waved to him, and Schulz, whom he had not expected. He approached their table with measured tread and shook hands.

'I was just going,' Schulz announced.

'Please don't go on my account,' Gisenius said, adding quickly: '—not, of course, that I want to detain you.'

Schulz grinned at him and got up. 'It's all right, I'm here as a student of the arts.'

Gisenius stared after him as he made for the stage. He saw Schulz greet a woman sitting beside the band and retire with her to more dimly-lit regions. Then he looked back at the stage. His eyes no longer seemed dazzled by the spotlight.

'Nice little piece, eh?' Hirsch said, watching him closely.

'A loathsome sight,' Gisenius declared with vehemence, but he continued to watch the stage, presumably to convince himself that his indignation was fully justified.

'A display of feminine pulchritude, my friend, that's all.'

'You hire her out as well, I suppose?' Gisenius's tone was heavily jocular.

'If you're really interested in our little Salome,' Hirsch said, 'I'll put a word in for you . . .'

'You're quite incorrigible, Hirsch. I came here to discuss something of the utmost importance. Can we go somewhere a little less public?'

They moved to the rear of the café. Hirsch sat down with his back to the stage and pulled up a chair for Gisenius opposite him, so that the stage—where Brigitte was just shedding her sixth veil—lay directly in the lawyer's field of vision.

Gisenius, however, seemed determined to ignore all distractions. He got down to business without further preamble. 'Hirsch,' he said, 'yesterday, when Frammler was telling his story, I was struck by something which made me think.'

'I think I know what it was,' Hirsch said slowly. 'Something to do with the difference between a fir-tree and a pine-tree—am I right?'

Gisenius gave an approving nod. 'Precisely. We appear to have been thinking along the same lines. If Frammler is a funeral expert he should know the difference. He must have seen a lot of wreaths in his time.'

'The only question,' Hirsch said, 'is whether he knew the difference then. We can't tell whether he's wrong or not until we know that.'

'But it doesn't preclude the possibility of a mistake, and that's what worries me.'

'There are a few more points in Frammler's story which

deserve closer study,' Hirsch said in a quiet, persuasive voice. 'For instance, he said he saw Meiners lying stone-dead in a hole in the sand, but the ground was marshy.'

'Incredible!' Gisenius stared past Hirsch at the stage, where the last veil had fallen to a crash of cymbals, but it was uncertain whether he saw it. 'Incredible, to think he may still be alive!'

'It's a possibility.' Hirsch derived secret satisfaction from seeing Gisenius a prey to dark thoughts. 'I noticed a couple more points, too. Frammler doesn't seem to have paid much attention to his surroundings when he was searching for Meiners's body. Everything looked churned up, he said. He found a body which he thought he recognized as Meiners's, but it was completely mutilated. The head was like a bowl of porridge—that's what he said. I ask you, Gisenius—how can a man identify anyone on the strength of something that looks like a bowl of porridge?'

At that moment the band came to life with every available instrument functioning at full blast. Trumpets, trombone and saxophones, accompanied by a crash of drums, blared out the opening bars of 'Sing, brother, sing!'

'This is disastrous,' Gisenius said.

Hirsch chuckled provocatively. 'I find the whole thing rather amusing. We're doing precisely what we accused poor Schulz of: indulging in a ghost-hunt.'

'I can't see anything to laugh at.'

'I can. Think it over for a moment, soberly and logically. Either Meiners is dead or he isn't. If he's dead, which seems pretty certain, the situation remains unchanged. If he isn't, so what? I don't suppose it would matter at this late stage.'

'You forget the special circumstances,' Gisenius said coolly.

'What circumstances?' Hirsch demanded. 'I don't know of any.'

'Do you mean to say you've forgotten what led up to his death?'

'What did? Nothing that's made me lose a night's sleep in the past sixteen years, anyway.'

'Hirsch,' Gisenius said significantly, leaning forward, 'have you really forgotten, or is it just that you don't want to remember?'

'You mean to say there's something I don't know?'
Hirsch demanded, raising his eyebrows.

Gisenius sank back in his chair, almost as though his
strength had failed him. 'Are you for us, Hirsch, or
against us?'

Hirsch disregarded the latent menace in the lawyer's
tone. 'I can only tell you this, Gisenius. I'm quite convinced
that Meiners is dead. I'd stake my life he is.'

'I may take you up on that,' Gisenius said thoughtfully,
'—if no better alternative presents itself.'

'Councillor Bartosch, Herr Direktor.'

Willy Kerze's secretary was a middle-aged mouse-grey
spinster with a razor-sharp mind. An outside observer might
have supposed that any woman who looked as insignificant
and held down such a job must possess special qualifications,
and he would have been right. Expert knowledge was valued
more highly at Stabilator Ltd. than an expert use of make-up,
and shirking was discouraged. Those who aspired to breathe
the same air as Kerze had to work hard for the privilege.

'Please ask the Councillor if he'd mind waiting a minute
or two.' Kerze glanced at the man in the visitor's chair.
'Tell him I shan't be long.'

'Certainly, Herr Direktor.'

Kerze surveyed his office with satisfaction. It conformed
perfectly to what was regarded within the Stabilator organization as the ethos of the firm: simplicity, durability and
solidity. The décor of the managing director's office was of
oak and steel, linen and leather, arrow-straight lines and neat
rectangular planes.

'Let's stop beating about the bush, Herr Lehmgruber.
As you've gathered, I've got a senior government official
waiting outside. I can't keep him hanging around for hours,
so tell me what you propose, preferably in words of one
syllable.'

'Well,' Lehmgruber said tentatively, 'I can supply you
with information of two kinds: first, particulars of the quota-
tions submitted by all the German firms which have tendered
so far, together with the relevant estimates and costing details;
and, secondly, the price limit imposed by the Polish government on its purchasing commission.'

Willy Kerze folded his large fleshy hands in an attitude of prayer, but his mind was intent on worldly matters. Possession of the information offered by Lehmgruber would mean that an enormous volume of business was virtually in his pocket. 'But what guarantee would I have that the information is genuine?'

'My personal integrity, sir. It's a principle of mine to give value for money.'

Kerze couldn't be bothered to dwell on the relative integrity of an obvious rogue. Bartosch was waiting outside and, besides, it didn't matter a row of pins whether or not Lehmgruber was an honest man. His information might very well be useful.

'Now listen, my friend,' Kerze said bluntly, determined not to be bamboozled like a mere novice, 'I wasn't born yesterday. I think it's about time we got down to brass tacks. Here's my proposition: you pass over your information, and if I land the contract I'll pay you commission—a percentage of the gross value, let's say.'

'Might I suggest a small advance? Just a few hundred marks—five hundred, perhaps?'

'What security can you offer, Lehmgruber?' Kerze felt entirely in command of the situation. He gained the impression that, for whatever reason, Lehmgruber would accept all his conditions. 'Everything has its price, you know. I don't even give away my factory waste for nothing. Let's call it two hundred.'

'Three hundred would be more acceptable.'

Kerze's pen sped swiftly over a cheque, which he tore out and pushed across the desk to Lehmgruber. It was for two hundred marks. 'Take it or leave it.'

Lehmgruber picked it up, ran his eye over it, folded it and tucked it away in his pocket before taking his leave.

To Kerze, Lehmgruber represented only one of many trial balloons, and two hundred marks hardly amounted to more than a pourboire dispensed by a traveller on the road to success. He had risked far greater sums in the past, but equally trivial amounts had occasionally brought very gratifying returns. Lehmgruber was merely one item in a long list. Another item, though of appreciably greater importance, was Bartosch.

Kerze opened the door to the outer office. 'Come in, come in, my dear Bartosch. I'm sorry to have kept you waiting, but perhaps we can have some time to ourselves at last. Please sit down. To what do I owe the pleasure?'

'I had a long talk with the Minister about an hour ago.'

'That sounds interesting.'

'In the course of our conversation the Minister passed on a piece of news—in the strictest confidence, of course. He told me that your recommendation for the Federal Order of Merit, First Class, has already reached the Villa Hammerschmidt. Since the Federal President normally endorses all such recommendations without question, the award is as good as yours.'

'I'm delighted,' Kerze said, 'really delighted.' It meant that one of his pipe-dreams had become reality. The honour that was to be bestowed on him represented one of the milestones in a career that richly merited acknowledgement and recognition—and it was Bartosch who had brought him the news!

'There's more to come,' Bartosch pursued in confidential tones. 'The Minister has expressed his willingness to invest you with the order personally. A special ceremony might be arranged.'

'I'm deeply indebted to you, my dear Councillor. I only wish there were some way of repaying you.'

'Perhaps there is, Herr Kerze.'

'Then tell me—you can speak freely.'

'In that case, since you insist . . . May I ask what your reaction would be if I asked you for your daughter's hand in marriage?'

The question came as no surprise. Only yesterday, Kerze had been dreading it; today he felt that the obstacles to the attainment of his dearest ambitions had melted away. Karen needed a husband, his friend Gisenius had stressed the value of useful connections, and he himself was quite willing to accelerate the fulfilment of his plans. In short, Bartosch was an insurance policy. He was also—praise be to God!—a man. Kerze made a solemn resolution never to doubt that again.

'I'm not averse to the idea.'

Bartosch looked worried. 'But you have reservations?'

'Of a purely parental nature,' Kerze assured him swiftly. 'Your proposal comes as no surprise to me, of course. I've got a pair of eyes in my head, and you've already dropped a few hints on the subject. Apart from that, I've already prepared my daughter for such a contingency.'

' Am I right in inferring that your daughter wouldn't be averse to the idea either? '

' I'm her father,' Kerze said simply, ' and I'm a tradition-alist. That doesn't mean I'm a slave-driver in my own home, but it does mean that nothing happens there without my say-so.'

' I'm sure it doesn't.'

Willy Kerze's eyes focused themselves on some distant horizon. ' I wouldn't be giving away any secrets, my dear Bartosch, if I told you that Karen has inherited quite a few of my own personal characteristics. She's not easily led, and she doesn't sell herself short.'

' No one appreciates that more than I do.'

Kerze studied Bartosch as if he were a vital clause in a contract and came to the same conclusion as before: the man's appearance was impressive. More than that, the man had connections and knew how to cultivate them. Ergo, he was a desirable son-in-law.

' Done! ' Kerze said decisively. ' You have my blessing—my blessing, mark you, not my official or quasi-legal approval. Don't worry, though, I'm sure everything will work out to our mutual satisfaction.'

Hirsch strode into his office to find Gisela Wandel waiting for him. She looked stern.

' All right, light of my life—fire away and don't spare my feelings. Let's hear what unpleasant surprises you've got in store.'

' A complaint from Room 217. Frau von Plönitz misses Paul's personal touch and insists on her room service being dealt with by him.'

' Paul stays in the dining-room from now on,' Hirsch said firmly. ' If the lady doesn't like it she can take her custom elsewhere.'

' I already told her that, though not in those exact words. Herr Lehmgruber offered to pay a hundred marks on account. I accepted, but I told him it didn't make any difference to your conditions.'

'Excellently put, Fräulein Wandel—as usual. Any idea where Lehmgruber got the money from? No? It might be interesting to find out. All right, anything else?'

'Fräulein Kerze rang three times while you were out.'

'If she tries again you can put her through.'

'She said she'd ring back in about twenty minutes. Herr Kerze has also rung, only once so far.'

'Get him for me.'

Hirsch threw a swift glance at his secretary but couldn't detect any particular reaction. She was already in the process of dialling Stabilator Ltd. Her total impassivity was a good thing on the whole, but Hirsch would have welcomed a little more warmth, a little easy-going informality. Hotel management often entailed dealing with problems of a delicate nature, and just recently his personal problems had been obtruding as well.

'Your call, Herr Hirsch. I'll transfer it to your own line.'

Kerze's tone was unusually cordial, as though he were paving the way for a business deal of some importance.

'I've a feeling we ought to have a frank chat some time. What do you say?'

'All right, Willy, if that's the way you feel.'

'When could you spare the time? What about this evening? There are a few unpleasant points—misunderstandings, perhaps I should say—which ought to be cleared up as soon as possible. Don't you agree?'

'Nothing would please me better,' Hirsch said warily. 'You'll find me in the manager's box in the *Café de Paris* from nine o'clock onwards.'

A faint but clearly audible sound of throat-clearing came over the line. 'It's not that I have anything against the place, my dear Martin, but . . .'

'Why should you have, Willy? I remember a time when you were a regular customer.'

'That time is past,' Kerze said firmly. 'In any case, it doesn't strike me as the ideal place to discuss what I have in mind. Couldn't you come to my house?'

'Sorry,' Hirsch said. 'I've got business to attend to. Of course, we could always postpone our discussion.'

'No, no,' Kerze said hastily. 'You know me—I like to

settle things on the spot. I accept your suggestion, and many thanks for being so co-operative. I'll see you this evening, then.'

Martin Hirsch hung up gingerly, as if the receiver were made of spun glass. He didn't know the underlying purpose of the conversation, but one thing was certain: Kerze's overture had not been prompted by a feeling of new-born friendship. It was far more probable that he meant to pay off old scores, and Kerze would never attempt such a thing unless he had a card up his sleeve. Hirsch carefully reviewed his defences and found them not as impregnable as he could have wished.

Uneasily, he got up and walked to the window. Minutes passed in indecision before Hirsch abruptly came to life again. He strode across to his safe, opened it, and produced a thin file from the back of the lowest compartment.

Taking it to his desk he opened it and extracted a slip of paper hardly bigger than a postcard. It bore the date 6 January 1958, the words ' promissory note ' and the sum involved, 5000 marks. The signature, written in a large sprawling feminine hand, was not easy to decipher.

Martin Hirsch took out his lighter and spun the wheel. The wick flared up. He held the I.O.U. over the flame until it caught and smouldered. In a moment, all that remained was a piece of charred paper which he dropped into an ashtray and ground to fragments with the end of a pencil.

'Five thousand marks for a spark of decency.' Hirsch gave a suppressed laugh. ' I wonder whether that's the official rate—maybe Kerze can tell me sometime.'

'What a woman! ' Karl Schulz said admiringly. ' One in a million! '

His remark referred to Marlene Sonnenberg and was addressed to Martin Hirsch. Hirsch made no comment. He knew his friend would never be deterred by sarcastic remarks.

They were sitting in one of the enclosures lining the left-hand side of the *Café de Paris*, the so-called manager's box, a compartment with room for five or six people. It was slightly raised and commanded a fairly good view of the stage, the first few rows of tables and the dance-floor.

The *Café de Paris* was sparsely patronized at this hour.

Apart from Schulz and Hirsch, the only customers were a few odd couples, two assorted groups of young people, three family parties enjoying an evening out, and, somewhere in the gloom at the back, near the door leading to the lavatories, a man sitting by himself. The place would not begin to fill up until later, when the last cinema showing ended.

For the moment, customers were being treated to an alternation of dance-music and popular ballads. The resident band was doing its unremarkable best, but Marlene Sonnenberg—engaged, in the words of her contract, as a 'mood singer '—had the knack of distracting people's attention from the music in an agreeable and time-honoured way: she sang with her hips.

'A fabulous creature,' Schulz evidently yearned for his friend's confirmation. 'Don't you think so? '

Hirsch nodded obediently, but his eyes wandered to the entrance. The thought of Willy Kerze's arrival filled him with a certain uneasiness.

'Are you serious about her, Karl? ' Hirsch inquired cautiously.

'I always get serious about women,' Schulz said with a slightly shame-faced grin. 'It's one of my failings.'

Hirsch almost guffawed, but his affection for Schulz prevented him from shattering his little idyll. Prudently, he said: 'It's womanly qualities that matter, Karl. No man wants to spend the rest of his life in bed. What he really looks for is a potential wife and mother, and from that point of view you've got a splendid example on your doorstep—your sister, I mean.'

'You're right,' Schulz conceded readily. 'Eva's a girl anyone would be proud of. You don't find her sort every day.'

'You can say that again.'

'But you hardly know her.'

'I've often chatted to her—enjoyed every minute of it, too. She's a very responsive person.'

'What do you mean by that? ' Schulz demanded with sudden suspicion.

'I mean mentally responsive, receptive—intelligent, if you like.'

'You may be right.' Schulz's misgivings vanished as quickly as they had come. 'You know, Karl, I'm not much

of a reading man. Most books are above my head, but Eva
enjoys them. Sometimes I think she's too well-educated, but
I suppose reading is better than gadding around.'
    ' That'll come in due course.'
    ' Maybe, but not for a year or two yet. Eva's hardly more
than a child. I bet she still believes in the stork.'
    ' Don't make her more childish than she is.'
    ' All right—so she doesn't still believe in the stork.' It
evidently depressed Schulz to have to admit this. ' She may
know about that sort of thing, but she's got no desire to
experiment in that direction.'
    ' How do you know? '
    ' I just do—I'm absolutely positive. Anyway, why are
you so interested? '
    Martin Hirsch parried the question swiftly. ' I was hoping
you'd make a few comparisons, Karl—comparisons between
Eva and Marlene Sonnenberg.'
    ' But they're two completely different people.'
    ' That's precisely what I mean. Marlene may be perfect
for a roll in the hay, but she couldn't be more different from
your sister if she tried. Eva's the marrying kind.'

    ' My brother's not in,' Eva Schulz said.
    ' To be honest—which I always am,' Claus Gisenius
replied, ' the news doesn't break my heart.'
    ' You always come when my brother isn't at home.'
    ' I know. Anyone would think I did it on purpose.'
    Eva was standing in the corridor and Claus on the landing.
    ' Aren't you going to ask me in, Eva? '
    ' I'm afraid not,' she said firmly. ' I'm alone in the flat.'
    ' Ask me in and you won't be alone any longer.'
    ' It's out of the question, Claus, please try to understand.
I can't invite you in at this hour. You may think I'm old-
fashioned, but it's simply out.'
    ' Very well,' he said. ' Far be it from me to violate your
principles. But if I can't come in, why don't you come out?
Think it over. I'll wait. I've got plenty of time—for you.'
    Claus sat down on the stairs leading to the next floor and
smiled at her. The pale-green walls of the landing were
bathed in moonlight. It was a light evocative of delicious
summer nights to come.

Eva regarded Claus with a mixture of exasperation and amusement. ' You can't sit there like that. What will the neighbours think? '

' Neighbours who mind their neighbours' business have usually got dirty minds.'

' You're impossible, Claus! '

' Of course I am. Everyone says so, but I take it as a compliment. In any case, may I draw your attention to the fact that spring officially arrived on the twenty-first of March. That was nearly a month ago, and it looks as if spring has finally filtered through to Rheine-Bergen. It's an annual miracle, Eva. Don't you think we ought to make the most of it? '

' Maybe tomorrow or the day after. What about one afternoon next week? '

' This evening,' Claus said firmly. ' Look, I'm giving you a choice of three alternatives—I call that pretty generous of me. One: you invite me inside the flat. No? All right. Two: you come and sit on the stairs with me. No? Fair enough. I understand—the neighbours' ignorance is your bliss. That only leaves the third alternative, but it's probably the most acceptable of the lot: a stroll in the great out-of-doors, asphyxiated by passing cars, dazzled by neon lights, jostled by indifferent passers-by and pestered by early drunks and officious policemen.'

Eva smiled. ' I might manage that,' she said. ' I could get Karl some cigarettes from the machine on the corner at the same time.'

' Come on, then,' Claus exhorted her. ' Let's get moving. I wouldn't want your brother to go without his fags.'

' You can go and visit your girl-friend in her dressing-room, if you like.'

Schulz beamed. ' It's good to have a friend like you, Martin.'

' I hope you never change your mind,' Hirsch said with a wry smile.

Schulz trotted off just as Willy Kerze, whom Hirsch had seen out of the corner of his eye, approached the manager's box. He extended his hand at a distance of ten feet and advanced on Hirsch with an air of resolute goodwill.

' Our friend Schulz is hot on the trail again, I see.'

' Don't begrudge it him,' Hirsch said. ' We're only young once.'

Kerze laughed raucously. ' You know,' he said, ' it's a waste of time, really, all that business. Women aren't a man's life-work, after all. What are they—compared to a factory, say? '

' Everyone has his own idea of heaven on earth,' observed Hirsch. ' The main thing is to let everyone find it in his own way. Not many of us are privileged to be married to a factory.'

For the moment, comparative peace reigned in the *Café de Paris*, the audience was impatiently awaiting the late-night show, the artistic presentations, the juggling and acrobatic numbers and the strip-tease act.

The place was gratifyingly full. Dense clouds of tobacco-smoke dimmed the harsh glare of the lights and the patrons were beginning to fidget with pleasurable anticipation. The lone man sitting at the back, in the gloom between the lavatory doors, ordered a third double schnapps and a third beer chaser.

' Why did you come, Kerze? Surely you don't propose to sit here lecturing me on your philosophy of life all evening? '

' I was wondering if we could do a deal.'

' What have I got that you might want to buy? '

' A scrap of paper, but I'll offer you five thousand marks for it.'

' For that and what else? '

' Look, Martin,' Kerze said genially, laying his palms flat on the table, ' we've known each other for many years . . .'

' True. There isn't much we don't know about each other.'

' We've clashed from time to time, I know, and I also know that you claim to be entirely in the right.'

' I still do.'

' All right, I'm prepared to believe you.' Kerze's eyes narrowed slightly, but his voice rang with sincerity. ' I think it's time we buried the hatchet.'

' You mean we've been playing Red Indians all this time? '

Kerze summoned up a half-hearted smile. ' There's the business of my second wife, for instance. You say it was all above-board—an innocent friendship, nothing more. I can't bring myself to believe that, but I can't prove the reverse. That being so, some people might say you had right on your side. Very well, I'm prepared to accept that view, and to demonstrate my sincerity I'll pay you back the five thousand marks you gave her—the five thousand marks that enabled her to break up our marriage.'

'You're wrong,' Hirsch said. 'The break-up was a foregone conclusion. I only did what you ought to have done—made sure she didn't have to walk the streets.'

'Very well.' Kerze swallowed Hirsch's indigestible imputation without flinching. 'Let's assume you're right once again. All the more reason to call it quits. I'll give you back your five thousand marks—with interest, if you like.'

'What else?' demanded Hirsch. 'What do you want from me in return? You surely don't expect me to believe you're doing this out of the goodness of your heart?'

'Let's fortify ourselves first,' Kerze said with a wry smile. 'What about a toast to the things we hold most dear?'

'Let's drink to your factory, then—and to pretty girls. May they make good wives and better mothers.'

'Old soldiers are always blathering about esprit de corps and team spirit—but what does it really mean?' Claus Gisenius demanded. 'Do they really believe in it, or is it just a load of hot air?'

'They believe in it,' Eva Schulz said warmly. 'My brother does, anyway. I honestly think he'd lay down his life for his friends.'

Claus grinned. 'All things are possible. Maybe his friends'll give him a chance to prove it some time.'

'Your father's one of them,' Eva said reprovingly. 'Haven't you any respect for him?'

'Masses of it.' Claus rubbed his hands gleefully. 'I respect him for being a clever fraud. Believe me, the more I get to know him, the happier I am to be his son. At least it gives me an outside chance of evading his clutches.'

'I think I'd better go home now,' Eva said with perceptible coolness. 'You needn't bother to see me to the door.'

She made no move to retrace her steps. Anyone but Claus might have attributed her reaction to typical feminine incon-

108

sistency, but to Claus Eva was unlike other girls, and he took it for granted that there was a good and sufficient reason for everything she said and did.

Keeping their distance, they strolled down the station road to the main square as though the cracks between the paving-stones concealed a thousand natural hazards.

' You've no need to explain anything to me,' Eva said.

' But I want to! ' Claus cried fiercely. ' I want you to know everything there is to know about me. Do you know why I called my father a fraud? Because he is one. When I was young he played the part of a war-hero—though only when he was on leave, of course. He enjoyed my admiration, and I was young and stupid enough to give it to him. Later on the war-hero turned into an anti-militarist democrat and became a humble servant of the Allies, which rather surprised me. In the end, the humble servant turned into a partner, and the spirit of heroism raised its head once more. I became suspicious. I began to wonder what my father was—a weak-ling, an imbecile or a fraud. Eventually I gave him the benefit of the doubt and decided he was a fraud.'

' You know, Claus,' Eva said softly, ' you must be a very unhappy person.'

Claus stopped in his tracks as though someone had butted him in the chest. Looking at the radiant face of the girl beside him, he thought he detected something he had never seen before: utter sincerity. There was something else, too, something which he had always shied at until now: affec-tionate concern.

' Me—unhappy? ' he said. ' I've never thought about it.' He grinned. ' But if I were, I'd need someone to make me happy. That's logical, isn't it? '

' We're men of the world, you and I,' Willy Kerze said per-suasively. ' We know which side our bread's buttered.'

' Except that we occasionally like it buttered on both sides.'

Kerze dismissed the objection with a wave of the hand. ' We're realists—we look facts in the face. For instance, I accept the fact that my wife ran out on me. It's all that bastard Hirsch's fault—that's what I told myself at the time, but I've now reached the stage where I'm grateful to you for helping to get rid of her. As far as I'm concerned, the stupid bitch can do what she likes. It spares me a lot of unnecessary fuss and unpleasantness.'

' Carry on like that,' Hirsch said drily, ' and you'll end up by calling me the only honest man in Rheine-Bergen.'

'Appearances can be deceptive, my dear fellow.' Kerse made as if to give Hirsch an affectionate pat on the shoulder, but the hotelier sat back abruptly in his chair. ' For instance,' Kerze continued, undeterred, ' just because a girl undresses in your room it doesn't mean you asked her to.'

' True,' Hirsch said warily. ' Go on.'

' She could have been taking a bath, say.'

Hirsch gave a shameless grin. ' Extremely plausible, I must say! '

' It's just a question of filling in the background,' Kerze insisted. ' For example: a car might have driven through a puddle and splashed her dress, so she had to change or have it cleaned. Since she happened to be in the vicinity of a hotel managed by an old friend of her father's, she naturally turned to him for help. Well? '

' Did it rain that day? ' Hirsch inquired. ' I can't remember.'

Kerze restrained his irritation. ' It could just as easily have been something else—any story will do, as long as it provides her with a good excuse for undressing in your room.'

' What if I said the reason wasn't so innocuous? '

'It would be typical of you! ' Kerze snapped. ' I mean,' he amended, choking back his fury with an effort, ' if you wanted to hurt me, that would certainly be one way of doing it. But I ask you, whose reputation would suffer most? Not yours or mine, but Karen's. Do you want to expose the girl? Do you really want to ruin her good name, perhaps for ever? '

' Very well,' Hirsch said. ' I'll say that the whole thing was entirely harmless.'

' Splendid! ' cried Kerze. ' You can have that cheque for five thousand marks any time you like, provided you hand over the I.O.U.'

' You've no need to increase your overheads, Kerze—there isn't any I.O.U.'

' What the devil do you mean? ' Kerze felt like an angler who sees a record salmon vanish through a hole in his landing-net. 'I know perfectly well my wife signed some piece of paper or other.'

'That doesn't mean the piece of paper, as you choose to call her I.O.U., is still in existence.'

'You're not being straight with me!' Kerze, his opinion of others coloured by self-knowledge, distrusted the world in general and Hirsch in particular. 'What are you playing at?'

'Nothing,' Hirsch said with a provocative smile. 'I've given you my word—what more do you want?'

'And as far as Karen's concerned you'll tell the same story to anyone else who expresses an interest in the matter?'

'We can put an advert in the paper if it means so much to you.'

'You're incorrigible, Martin.' Kerze gave a smile in which relief battled with lingering suspicion. 'All the same, I'll accept your word—for Karen's sake.' He rubbed his hands contentedly. 'Well, that ought to kill the whole damned story stone dead.'

'Don't forget there were two other witnesses apart from me: our mutual friend Schulz and one of my waiters.'

'Your evidence is what counts. Schulz is no problem—appeal to his loyalty and he'll shut up like a clam. As for the waiter—well, you're his boss. It's up to you to decide what he saw or didn't see. You shouldn't find him too difficult to handle. If you incur any expenses, don't hesitate to debit them to me.'

'I want to be absolutely honest with you,' Claus said. 'I realize it may scare you off, but that's a risk I'll have to take. I don't want you to have any false illusions. For instance, I haven't got a bean.'

Eva laughed. 'Do you want me to pass the hat round for you?'

'I'm not joking. It's a bit hard when someone wants to buy a girl the earth and his finances won't even run to a drink in a third-rate café.'

'What a shame!' Eva said with gay unconcern. 'I've got frightfully expensive tastes, too.'

They crossed the market-place and entered the Kronenstrasse. The street had been named after Theodor Kronen, the nineteenth-century entrepreneur who had also founded the

Drei Kronen—' Drei ' because three members of the Kronen family had owned it conjointly; grandfather, father and son. One of them, the grandfather, had died in bed, the father fell for Kaiser and country, and the son was consigned to a concentration camp in the name of Führer and Volk and there thrashed to death. The hotel had since passed into the possession of Europa Hotels Limited, but not before a number of middlemen had lined their own pockets.

' I could run to an ice-cream or a couple of frankfurters,' Claus suggested.

' You save your money, Claus.'

' Save it? What for? I'm not a family man. It's pointless saving for the future until you know you've got one. You see,' he went on, ' my financial situation's rather complicated. My father gives me a fixed allowance. He might increase it considerably if I asked him. On the other hand, he might not. I've a shrewd suspicion he knows what I spend it on. I lend it all to my my mother, if you want to know.'

' What's the matter with that? I think it's a very nice thing to do.'

' You're a dear girl,' Claus said tenderly. ' In a way, I wish you'd stay just as sweet and innocent as you are now, but perhaps that would be dangerous in the long run.' He shook his head. ' No, I'd sooner not hide anything from you. My mother uses the money I give her to buy drink with. She drinks, you see—she's an alcoholic. Didn't you know? '

' No,' Eva said uncomfortably, ' I didn't.'

' Hasn't your brother ever mentioned it? '

' My brother treats me like a child,' Eva replied. ' He'd never discuss anything like that with me.'

' Very creditable of him, though I can't make out what people like your brother really think. Are they honestly trying to persuade us that the world's become a place worth dying for again? I'll tell you what their little world is—it's a cess-pit. Oh, sure, it's warm, weather-proof and well-lit, full of cosily complacent people and mass-produced comforts, but that doesn't stop it being a cess-pit.'

' Think about something else, Claus.' Eva laid her hand affectionately on his arm. ' Try to forget it, just for a few minutes.'

They left the main thoroughfare and turned the corner

into Parkstrasse. The crunchy gravel paths which skirted the geranium-beds, rose-bushes and clumps of lilac and laburnum were interspersed at mathematically predetermined intervals by benches which found favour during the day with dozing pensioners and children and at night with courting couples and drunks.

'This is a good time of year,' Claus said, taking Eva's arm. 'The benches are almost always empty in April.'

'How do you know, Claus?'

'Guess-work,' he replied with a grin. 'Most people don't feel it's summer until the calendar says so. The open-air courting season doesn't begin until mid-May. Actually, Eva, you're right—I have been here before, but not with anyone else. You needn't believe me if you don't want to. I come here to get some of the fresh air I can't get at home. Besides, I've a weakness for dance-music. Do you hear that?' He nodded in the direction of the *Café de Paris*. 'Those boys play pretty well when they don't overdo the saccharine. Come on, let's sit down. The air's better out here—cheaper, too. Just the job for paupers like us.'

'We ought to crack a bottle of something to celebrate,' Willy Kerze suggested, '—at my expense, of course.'

'This is my home territory,' Hirsch said. 'I buy the drinks here.'

'On the house, eh?' Kerze threw out the remark casually, but he soon realized that it had not been the height of tact. 'I'm only joking,' he added hastily, summoning up an innocent chuckle but simultaneously reflecting that it might pay to run a check on Hirsch's expense account. He wondered what the manager's outgoings on personal entertainment amounted to. It was a point worth bringing to Saffranski's notice.

'Any objection if I ask Schulz and his lady-friend to join us?' Hirsch inquired.

'The more the merrier!' Kerze's spirits rose. With Hirsch's assistance, Karen was going to recover the whiter-than-white reputation so essential to a public servant's future spouse.

Hirsch entrusted a hovering waiter with an invitation to Herr Schulz and Fräulein Sonnenberg to join the manager's table. While the man padded off he surveyed the establishment with a practised eye. It was almost full, as it generally was after eleven o'clock, and the patrons were in an advanced stage of aimless but cheerful loquacity. Sundry lone males, most of them regular customers, had secured seats near the stage in anticipation of the first leg-show of the evening. The solitary figure at the back, in the semi-darkness near the lavatory doors, appeared to be soaking up double schnapps and beer chasers like a sponge. His twin glasses were hardly ever empty.

'The place seems to be doing well,' Kerze commented approvingly.

Karl Schulz and Marlene Sonnenberg came over to the table. Schulz introduced Marlene with an air of proprietorial pride. She was a tall, full-bosomed creature who had a habit of tossing her head like a high-spirited filly, and her eyes sparkled. She was visibly flattered when Kerze kissed her hand.

'Delighted to meet you at long last!'

Marlene bridled. 'The pleasure's mutual.'

While she turned her attention to Hirsch, Schulz nudged Kerze in the ribs and winked with his customary lack of guile. 'Well, what do you think of her?' he asked in a confidential undertone.

'I congratulate you, my dear chap,' Kerze murmured, returning the wink. 'She's a bit of all right!'

'I like you, Eva,' Claus Gisenius said, adding, very softly: 'I don't think I've ever liked anyone so much.'

'Do you always say that when you're alone with a girl on a bench?'

'Always,' he said, resting his arm on the seat behind her. 'If you'd like me to, I'll say it every evening, every hour on the hour from now on.'

Eva did not reply. She felt his arm brush her back, so lightly as to be scarcely perceptible, and she glanced up at the street-lamp shining through a delicate tracery of spring foliage. Its light hardly reached the bench where they were sitting, and yet, when she turned her head to look at Claus, she seemed to see his face with overwhelming clarity. It looked sad, gentle, weary, a melancholy mask fused into the magical dusk of the April night.

Claus did not look at her, but he felt her eyes on his face.

He slid his arm over the back of the seat until it hung limp and forced himself to concentrate on the music drifting across from the *Café de Paris*. Three saxophones were moaning their way through ' Charmaine ' while the drummer plied his wire brushes with feeling. Applause rang out, hesitantly at first, like isolated rain-drops falling on a tin roof. Then, with a crash of drums, the band plunged into a heavily mock-oriental number.

' I can guess what they're up to now,' Claus said, '—waggling their hips and waving feathers, sweating like pigs and discarding their underclothes. Don't you wish you were in there? '

' No,' Eva said firmly.

' I'm sorry, Eva,' he said, leaning back, ' you're out of luck tonight. You've picked on someone who can't offer you anything—not even a bottle of wine in that crummy joint over there. A bottle of wine would cost at least ten marks, and that's about eight marks more than I've got. I've got nothing, I am nothing, and I'll go on being nothing for years to come. Would you like to go home now? '

' No, Claus.' Eva leant towards him slightly. ' I'm beginning to like it here.'

' I've got some pretty nasty characteristics,' he said doggedly, '—inherited them, probably. I don't believe in anything and I've never been capable of feeling deeply about anything, even temporarily. Apart from that, I'm lazy, greedy and deceitful. Your best bet would be to head for home as fast as you can.'

' It's getting quite chilly,' Eva said softly. ' You can put your arm round me if you like.'

Claus looked at her quizzically. ' Who taught you to be so forward? '

' You did,' Eva said, nestling against him.

' Clever little thing, that.' Kerze's comment, delivered in a loftily objective tone, was inspired by Brigitte and her dance of the seven veils. ' Has she had a lot of experience, or is it just an act? '

' It's instinct,' Marlene Sonnenberg said. ' They say it's the first time she's performed in public.'

' Shameless little piece,' observed Karl Schulz.

'What do you expect?' Hirsch demanded equably. 'She's just joined the oldest profession in the world—shows promise, too.'

Glowing rosily in the dim, atmospheric light, Brigitte displayed her not inconsiderable charms to their fullest effect. She felt a hundred eyes appraising her, and her knees trembled with apprehension. Then, spurred on by the determinedly exotic music, she began to use her body more confidently. With a frisson of excitement, she realized that critical appraisal was giving way to delighted admiration. Her movements grew more supple with every passing minute, looser, lither, more suggestive.

'Is she expensive?' Kerze inquired. 'I mean, how much do you pay her a week?'

Hirsch told him, and Kerze, ever the man of business, judged her to be cheap at the price. He privately conceded that Hirsch wasn't bad at his job, and the admission depressed him. He wondered if it would be hard to find a suitable replacement when the time came.

'Who's your second-in-command here, Hirsch?'

'My personal assistant, Fräulein Wandel.'

'Efficient?'

'Efficiency in person.'

Brigitte was about to delight a now enthusiastic audience by discarding her seventh veil, but Schulz continued to gaze at Marlene with steadfast satisfaction. Willy Kerze, too, took a closer look at her and seemed to like what he saw. His eyes narrowed as he scrutinized her ample décolletage. Meanwhile, Hirsch quietly assessed the evening's takings.

An elderly waiter passed their table carrying a tray on which stood a large beer and a double schnapps. Gustav, who had grown grey in the service of the *Drei Kronen* and could afford to indulge in such familiarities, gave Hirsch a smile as he went by.

Hirsch nodded affably. 'Business seems to be brisk tonight, Gustav.'

'I'm glad to see some gentlemen still know how to put it away, sir,' Gustav murmured in an admiring undertone. 'This is his ninth round—pays cash each time, and he isn't mean with his tips.'

Hirsch gave another friendly nod. The old war-horse

with his forty years of customer-contact deserved a decent tip occasionally. He watched Gustav's retreating figure as he threaded his way through the tables and made for the dimly-lit recess where the solitary man sat communing with himself between the lavatory doors.

The man had a hunched look about him, as though he might creep off into the darkness at any moment. He sat there almost without moving, but there was something alert and tense about him—something watchful.

For a moment, Martin Hirsch had the strange sensation that the man's eyes were looking in his direction. What was more, they seemed to be focused on him alone.

'You'll regret it,' Claus said, almost inaudibly. 'You should have been home hours ago. It would have been better for both of us—especially you.'

'What makes you think you know what's best for either of us?' Eva asked tenderly.

Claus had his arm round her shoulders now. They were frail, slender shoulders which felt soft and warm to the touch.

Eva leaned against him, conscious of nothing but the warmth emanating from their two bodies. She trembled a little as he laid his hand on her shoulder in a half-protective, half-possessive gesture. It did not linger there but travelled downwards, hesitantly and almost timidly. She shifted her body against him so that her breast slid into his palm, and she felt his mouth, hot and moist, against her cheek.

'I love you,' he said. 'I can hardly believe it, though,' he added helplessly.

Her own voice seemed to come from far away. 'I love you too. The only difference is, I know I do.'

'Excuse me,' Hirsch said, rising.

No one at the table appeared to notice him. Schulz was still gazing at Marlene and Marlene was swapping glances with Kerze. Music throbbed around them and the whole scene seemed to be shrouded in a thick alcoholic haze.

Hirsch found it an effort to walk. It was as if something were holding him back. A casual observer might have thought his destination the gentlemen's lavatory at the rear of the night-club.

Hirsch moved with almost machine-like tread towards the man who was sitting by himself at the small table in the dimly-lit background, a beer and a double schnapps in front of him. The large eyes which had seemed to be watching Hirsch, and Hirsch alone, now looked lifeless and blurred, like the surface of a muddy pool.

'Meiners,' Hirsch said heavily. 'It's Michael Meiners, isn't it?'

The man rose abruptly, jolting the table as he did so. His beer-glass fell over and deposited its contents on the white marble top, where it formed an obscene-looking puddle, reminiscent of urine. 'I'm sick of this place,' he said, swaying slightly. 'It makes me want to puke.'

'Meiners,' Hirsch said again, but the man spun on his heel and disappeared through the door marked 'Gentlemen'.

It was as though he had never been.

INTERIM REPORT NO. 2

STENOGRAPHIC RECORD OF A POLICE INTERVIEW

WITH WILHELM KERZE

conducted by Chief Inspector Sand
on 1 May 1961
in connection with the events of 20 April 1945

Having been informed of the subject of the interview and cautioned, Herr Kerze made the following statement:

My name is Wilhelm Kerze. I am forty-seven years old and an industrialist by profession.

Yes, I used to be a member of Sergeant Schulz's section, and I'm proud of it. We weren't an élite unit—far from it—but we weren't run-of-the-mill material either. Karl Schulz was a typical, reliable, professional N.C.O., Gisenius had brains, I had drive, Bennicken had as much muscle as the rest of us put together, Frammler handled all the dirty jobs, and Hirsch could have laid on caviare and champagne in the middle of a desert if he'd been asked to. All in all, we were a first-rate mob—everyone said so.

Question:

Haven't you omitted someone from your list?

Answer:

You mean Michael Meiners, I suppose. Well, he wasn't a proper member of the section, you know. A nice youngster, I wouldn't deny that, but never really one of the boys. He only spent a few weeks with us, and I can't say I got to know him very well.

The evening before this frightful business we landed up in some God-forsaken hole—Steinwiesen, I think it was called. We were billeted in a farm on the outskirts of the village. When we arrived we found a lot of people on the premises. Apart from the farmer's family there were a number of refugees. Two of them caught my eye at once, a mother and daughter. They were both attractive in their way—in fact it was hard to know which one to look at first. When Hirsch clapped eyes on them he let out a whoop—I remember it to this day. Hirsch behaved like that even in those days—he didn't need any Americans to teach him how. Not, of course, that I'm saying anything against Hirsch—or our American allies either, for that matter.

I'd like to make one thing quite clear before I go on: our morale was first-class, so don't let anyone tell you it wasn't. Time had welded us together, in a manner of speaking. Weeks and months spent together under the toughest conditions had left their mark on us. Although there were times when we couldn't stand the sight of each other we knew we had to rely on each other and we did so without hesitation—we had no alternative. That's what I call genuine team spirit.

There was an illustration of this on the evening in question. Hirsch, who was a marvel at that sort of thing, had laid on a crate of bottles, as well as several tins of beef in gravy and some sausage. Treats like this came our way oftener in the closing stages of the war than they had in the previous four or five years put together, because so many supply-dumps were being abandoned. Not, of course, that I'm trying to minimize Hirsch's services to the section. He performed miracles of organization for us on many occasions.

Anyway, this made it something of a gala evening. There's nothing very wonderful about a few bottles and some tinned meat, I know, but I mention it to illustrate what sort of situation we were in. It was less of a festive evening than a last despairing fling—not that our morale was low. I'd like to emphasize that. We didn't know the meaning of the word despair.

We politely invited the civilians to join our little banquet and they accepted with alacrity, especially as we were supplying the wherewithal. Incidentally, I think it was Hirsch who issued the invitation, but I could be wrong. I only know that he took a pretty lively interest in the refugee mother and daughter. He divided his time between them equally—to begin with, that is. Young Meiners was hot on the trail, too, but he concentrated more on the daughter. Today, after all that has happened since, I find it almost pathetic to look back on.

Be that as it may, the party was quite a gay affair in spite of the general situation and the proximity of the Russians. You might say that it united soldiers and civilians in a way which recalled those memorable years before the war. For a short while, an almost peace-time atmosphere reigned, and the night air rang with popular ballads and patriotic songs until the early hours. I've often wondered what a lurking enemy would have thought if he'd heard—not that there was anything exceptional about us. However black things look, we Germans always put a bold face on it.

The following day was April 20th 1945.

Question:

Did you stay up until the end of the party? If so, who stayed up with you? Who spent most time with the daughter of the refugee woman, Frau Boddanski?

Answer:

It's no use asking me. I'd had a strenuous day, and I hadn't held back when it came to drinking with the civilians and my fellow-soldiers. I was extremely tired, but I can't say exactly when I finally fell asleep. I only know that the party went with a swing while I was still awake, and nothing occurred to mar the atmosphere.

Next morning at about five o'clock all hell broke loose. Everyone was shouting, the civilians loudest of all, but Schulz's voice drowned the lot. He had a splendid word of command in those days. In fact, he was a splendid chap altogether. I can still hear him now, yelling: 'Rise and shine, you dozy lot!'

When we staggered to our feet Schulz told us that we weren't continuing our march as had been expected. Instead, we were to block the road from a position in the copse near our billet. 'You've got to hold it at all costs!' That's what our company-commander, Lieutenant Kronshagen, told us before he rushed off to join the rest of the company.

Question:

Did you personally hear the company-commander's order? Do you remember his exact words?

Answer:

After a lively little party like that—what do you think? I can take a lot, but I had a man-size hangover that morning and everything was pretty hazy. I'm not a tape-recorder, you know. I'm merely telling you what I definitely remember.

I'm trying to be strictly objective, but I naturally can't swear to every tiny detail.

To proceed: we assembled in the yard and fell in, all six of us—seven, including Schulz. All thoughts of the party the night before were banished. We stood there, checking our weapons and being briefed by Schulz. Then we got ready to march off.

All this time the refugee woman had been racing around like a mad thing, looking for her daughter. She said the girl hadn't been with her during the night—although this was hardly an uncommon experience for a mother at the end of the war. Who are we to judge? Who knows where a young girl's instincts will lead her? Let's call it human nature and leave it at that.

Anyway, the daughter was eventually found in the barn, dead. When we heard the news we were already on the way to Copse 307, which was in the neighbourhood of the farm. Schulz was very concerned about the poor girl's fate, I remember, but he decided that our assignment had to take priority over everything else.

Question:

Didn't it occur to anyone that the death of the refugee woman's daughter—her name, as I have already stated, was Boddanski—might have been occasioned by a member of your section?

Answer:

You surely don't expect me to believe that a member of my own unit was responsible for a thing like that? True, Hirsch made a play for both the women, and poor little Meiners obviously fancied the girl, but what does that add up to? The daughter was a desirable young thing, certainly, but we weren't the only men around. There were a couple of hundred more soldiers and dozens of civilians in the neighbourhood.

Let's stick to the facts. Our section occupied Copse 307. The M.G. was sited on the edge of the trees and a road-block was constructed at the same time. We worked like Trojans, I don't mind tell you, felling timber for the barricade and expecting to see the enemy bear down on us at any moment.

So we waited for the enemy, feeling more resigned than anything else. It wasn't the first time we'd faced death, which is worth bearing in mind. People living in this cosy little world of ours can't grasp a lot of the things which we took for granted when we were risking our lives every other day. That's why we oughtn't to be blamed if we're out of sympathy with the footling preoccupations of a younger generation which has precious little idea of what we endured for the sake of our families, our homes and our Fatherland. I've no hesitation in saying this, now that traditional values are beginning to be appreciated once more.

That morning the enemy attacked in such overwhelming numbers that, with the best will in the world, we were unable to cope. Not one of us failed in his duty—I'd like to make that absolutely clear—but we were seven men against several Russian tanks—at least three of them, with others in support—and behind them, at a conservative estimate, came a whole battalion of subhuman Asiatics.

We engaged them straight away. The odds against us must have been at least a thousand to one, but none of us spared a thought for that. I can still remember someone beside me—Gisenius, I think—saying: ' Christ Almighty, now we're for it! ' Just a terse, soldierly comment—that's all. Perhaps it wasn't Gisenius who said it—perhaps it was Frammler, or even me, but what's the difference? That was the prevailing mood, the mood of the fighting soldier—a mixture of dogged determination and grim humour.

I need hardly add that I'm not trying to paint our conduct in heroic colours—nothing could be further from my thoughts. We only did what millions of others would have done in a similar position—except that few men had to go through what we did. We met the Russians' display of naked force head-on, but the loss of our M.G. reduced our fire-power so greatly that we were forced to withdraw.

Question:
Who was manning the machine-gun apart from Meiners?

Answer:
I'm not sure—not me, anyway. I was actually inside the copse. After the first burst of firing, which put the M.G. out of action, I wanted to push forward to the edge of the wood, but the order to withdraw came through first.

Question:
Who gave the order to withdraw?

Answer:
I can't say for certain. I only know that Hirsch passed it on

to me—at least, I think he did. The situation was pretty confused, don't forget.

It was just one more demonstration of the fact that even the finest unit sometimes has to give ground in the face of barbarous numerical superiority. I'm satisfied that we halted the enemy's advance, if only for a matter of minutes, but that sort of thing takes a toll—a tragic but inevitable toll—of human life.

Any German who dares to reproach us for having made such a sacrifice is unworthy of the name.

5. The Hunt Begins

Conrad Gisenius was kneeling, as he did on so many mornings, in his second-row pew in the Church of the Holy Trinity. He liked to begin his day in this way because, apart from providing him with a source of strength and consolation, it afforded a praiseworthy example to others.

As the last notes of the organ died away, Gisenius rose to his feet. He knew that the church would be virtually empty by now save for a sprinkling of elderly ladies, the sight of whom he always found so touching—and instructive, too, since they exemplified the shabby gentility into which he personally intended never to descend in old age. He decided to give them a friendly nod as he passed.

On this particular morning, the elderly ladies were not alone in their devotions. In their midst sat a most unexpected figure, familiar enough to Gisenius but strangely out of context. It was Martin Hirsch, swathed in a modish grey overcoat of English cut.

' You here? ' Gisenius inquired in a surprised undertone.

' Any objections? '

' Knowing you as I do,' Gisenius said, ' I don't imagine you came to pray.'

' No,' Hirsch replied, ' I came to tell you something.'

' Something to do with Meiners,' Gisenius said, with the dispassionate assurance of a meteorologist forecasting rain.

' You don't seem very surprised.'

' I'm not,' Gisenius said. ' It's part of my job to be prepared for any eventuality. Well, let's hear the details.'

Hirsch described the incident of the previous night while Gisenius listened attentively. As he talked, they strolled back and forth between the main portal of the Holy Trinity and the edge of the square that separated the church from the road.

' Anything you're not clear on? ' Hirsch asked, when he had finished.

'A great deal,' Gisenius replied promptly. 'But first, there's one point which strikes me as strange. Those present apart from yourself included Karl Schulz and Willy Kerze, who also think they've seen Meiners. Was it purely coincidental?'

'It was me who saw him this time.'

'Only you—not the others?'

'Only me.'

'And the others didn't see him, even though they were in the same room? Seems a little strange, doesn't it?'

'The room's about forty yards long.' Hirsch felt vaguely irritated by Gisenius's pedantic tone. 'It's pretty dimly lit at the far end—saves electricity and suits the courting couples. That was where he was sitting.'

'What made you go over?'

'I was heading for the gents. I recognized him and called his name.'

'You actually addressed him as Meiners?'

'Michael Meiners.'

'What happened then, Hirsch? It's vitally important to remember what happened next. Did he recognize you? Did he address you by name? What was his reaction—try to remember his exact words.'

'He looked at me,' Hirsch said, striving for precision, 'and then he stood up and said something like " I feel sick ". He said something else—" It makes me want to puke ", I think it was. He looked like it, too. He'd had plenty to drink by that time—nine doubles and nine beer chasers spread over a period of two hours. Anyway, he got up, swaying slightly, and disappeared into the gents.'

'You followed him, of course.'

'No, I didn't.'

'You didn't?' Gisenius said slowly, cocking his head a little like a dog scenting distant game. 'Why not, Hirsch?'

'Well, for one thing, it's not my habit to escort people to the lavatory.'

'I thought you said you wanted to disappear yourself.'

'I suppose the urge must have deserted me. Besides, there's no rear exit from the gents—just a door into the garden, but that's usually kept locked until the summer.'

'So you waited until he reappeared?'

'No,' Hirsch said, manifestly annoyed by the lawyer's

cross-questioning. 'I rushed back to Schulz and Kerze and told them the news.'

'If I know them, they immediately congratulated each other on their remarkable powers of observation.'

'You're right,' Hirsch said, 'but they didn't waste too much time slapping each other on the back. It was Schulz who took the initiative. He made for the gents and charged through the door like a tank, with us behind him.'

'And?'

'It was empty.'

Gisenius felt a fleeting urge to sit down somewhere. A spasm of emotion flitted across his normally impassive features. 'Empty, you say? No Meiners?'

'No Meiners. No one at all. The door to the garden was open, but the garden was deserted.'

'How much had you had to drink?' Gisenius demanded.

'Steady on,' Hirsch protested. 'You can't brow-beat me the way you brow-beat Schulz, you know. I never drink much and I'm not subject to hallucinations. I merely saw a man who might have been Michael Meiners—might have been, mark you.' He shrugged. 'Those are the facts. If you want to proceed on that basis, go ahead.'

Gisenius concurred at once. He was not rigid in his views, nor had he ever been, and when circumstances warranted it he was capable of rapid changes of tack. 'If what you say is true,' he said, 'there's a man in this town whose physical appearance is such that he might be mistaken for Meiners. Whether or not he really is Meiners remains to be seen.'

'Exactly, though we could have arrived at the same conclusion four days ago if we'd taken Schulz's story seriously. Any steps we take now will be four days in arrears, which may be unfortunate, so there's no point in wasting any more time. Let's proceed methodically, on the assumption that the man looks like Meiners as he might be today.'

'The resemblance may be purely coincidental—in fact, that's the likeliest assumption of the lot. Everything we know points—or, rather, seems to point—to the fact that Meiners is dead. That being so, we have to concede the probable existence of someone who may be entirely harmless but bears a strong resemblance to Meiners.'

'We certainly can't dismiss the possibility,' Hirsch agreed.

'But there's a further possibility: His resemblance to Meiners may not be coincidental at all—it may be entirely natural. That wouldn't be quite so harmless, would it?'

'It might be dangerous in the extreme,' Gisenius said gloomily. 'The same thought struck me the first time I heard Schulz tell his story.' He paused. 'What if the man turns out to be Meiners's brother?'

'In that case,' Hirsch replied, 'the situation might become really tricky. We should have to assume that this hypothetical brother has an ulterior motive for turning up here. What's more, we'd have to find out whether Meiners really had a brother, whether he resembled him and whether their ages tally.'

'To sum up,' Gisenius said firmly, 'our only course is to trace the man who looks like Meiners.'

Hirsch nodded. 'And quickly at that.'

Gisenius lowered his voice as though communing with himself. 'There's one feature which strikes me as particularly suspicious.' He did not look at Hirsch as he spoke, but stared down, thoughtfully, at the flagstones beneath his feet. 'If this man isn't Michael Meiners but knows something of the circumstances surrounding Meiners's death, where could he have got his information from? If anyone has divulged anything, it could only be one of us.'

'It's eleven o'clock, sir,' announced the chief clerk.

Gisenius glanced at his watch. 'Ask Herr Dänkel to come in.'

'There's a Herr Lehmgruber to see you too, sir.'

'Tell him to come back tomorrow,' Gisenius ordained, feeling confident that, as so often in the past, time was on his side. Lehmgruber was obviously in a hurry, which was a very good reason for displaying tepid indifference. The waiting game almost always paid dividends in the end.

The door opened and Siegfried A. Dänkel—the A stood for Adolf, a rash aberration on the part of his over-patriotic parents—bounced into the room. He was a short, rosy-cheeked, rotund young man who strove to radiate an aura of brisk efficiency. His manner seemed to proclaim that those who engaged the services of Siegfried A. Dänkel were getting a bargain too good to be missed.

128

'I've got a job for you,' Gisenius began without further preamble, 'a job which demands the utmost discretion.'

'Just my line,' Dänkel declared promptly.

'This job,' Gisenius continued, 'demands not only the utmost discretion but a certain talent for detective-work.'

'I'll take it on.' Whatever the circumstances, Dänkel was never backward in coming forward.

'Personally?' Gisenius inquired. His voice carried an unmistakable note of misgiving.

'It all depends.'

Gisenius cleared his throat. 'The gist of the matter is that I want all the information I can get about a man who's been staying here in Rheine-Bergen for the past few days.'

'Sounds simple enough,' Dänkel observed confidently. 'May I have some details?'

'I'm not in a position to give you any. Details are what I want from you.'

'Of course, but I must have something to go on.'

'You're well-known in this town, Herr Dänkel—at least, it's well-known in certain quarters that you occasionally work for me. In view of that, I should prefer you not to conduct inquiries personally in this particular instance.'

Dänkel nodded intently. 'I follow you.'

'On the other hand, I'm sure you could get hold of someone who would have the important asset of being virtually unknown here.'

'I could indeed.'

'Who, in your opinion, would be the man for the job?'

'Tantau,' Dänkel said, in the tones of one imparting a revelation.

'Who's Tantau?'

'An old fox.' A note of professional admiration crept into Dänkel's voice. 'An ex-chief superintendent who used to run the Berlin homicide department. He retired some years ago and settled in the neighbourhood, but he's quite happy to earn a few hundred marks on the side occasionally—only if the case interests him, though—that's his one condition. If it does, he worries at it like a terrier. The old boy's a genius, take it from me.'

'Expensive too, I imagine.'

'Yes, but a genius. Do you remember the series of sabotage

acts at the electricity works in Babenburg? The police ran round in circles for weeks on end until the management called Tantau in. He solved the case inside forty-eight hours.'

' An efficient type, eh? ' Gisenius said slowly. ' Not over-zealous, I hope? '

Dänkel raised a deprecating hand. ' Anything but. The case is all that matters to him. The old boy couldn't care less about anything else. For instance, he simply investigated the sabotage business and named the guilty party without even setting eyes on him. When he's solved a case he just collects his fee and pushes off until the next one comes along. A machine couldn't be more objective, I assure you.'

' Good,' said Gisenius. ' He sounds as if he might do. Send him to see me as soon as possible—this afternoon, preferably. Let's say two o'clock.'

' I hope I can arrange it. The old boy's a bit choosy, as I told you, but I'll do my best.'

' Please do.' Gisenius glanced ostentatiously at his fob-watch. He always wore one, primarily out of a sense of tradi-tion, secondly because he admired its handsome chain, and thirdly so that he could glance at it ostentatiously when occasion demanded.

Dänkel remained seated, however, and his rubicund features registered slight embarrassment. ' I beg your pardon, Herr Gisenius,' he said diffidently, ' but you haven't given me any details yet.'

' I know. I shall give Herr Tantau any information he requires.'

' It's not usual, Herr Gisenius, really it isn't.'

' Perhaps not, but that's the way I want it.'

' Very well,' Dänkel replied, after a careful but not unduly prolonged show of hesitation. ' Seeing that it's you, sir, I'm prepared to accept. On the other hand, how can I estimate our fee if I don't know what's involved? '

' Work out a daily charge for Tantau's services.'

' I told you, he's not cheap. You'll have to reckon on a hundred marks a day plus expenses, all fees payable direct to me—my firm, I mean.'

' Agreed.'

Siegfried A. Dänkel was disconcerted by his client's swift acceptance. Obviously, he could have asked more. He felt a surge of curiosity as to what could possibly interest Conrad Gisenius so much that he was prepared to pay an exorbitant price for it.

But Gisenius said, this time with an air of finality: ' At the risk of repeating myself, I must ask you to regard this matter as strictly sub rosa. It involves a professional confidence which I'm in duty bound to respect.'

' I give you my word! ' Dänkel cried with a vehemence which belied the fact that he felt slightly cheated. ' I'd be the last person to betray a professional secret.'

Gisenius gave a satisfied nod. ' I shouldn't employ you otherwise.'

' I think I've discovered something rather odd here, sir.'

Kerze bent over the file marked ' Hotel Drei Kronen ' and examined the entry which Saffranski was indicating with his pencil-thin forefinger. It read ' DM 5000 '—a paltry sum by Kerze's standards but one which at once attracted his attention because the date opposite it read ' 6 January 1958 '.

' It caught my eye because it doesn't come under any of the normal headings,' Saffranski continued eagerly. ' It doesn't seem to have any bearing on the hotel's regular business transactions.'

' It might conceivably represent a private loan,' Kerze said slowly, watching the accountant closely as he did so. He was gratified to receive further confirmation that he had not been mistaken in Saffranski. The young man's spider-like mind had evidently grasped what Kerze had merely hinted at—that the entry might conceal a personal withdrawal, presumably on the part of the manager. If that were so, the implications could be serious. Careful checking and double-checking was indicated.

' I'll certainly follow up that line of inquiry, sir,' Saffranski promised. His pale eyes regarded Kerze with dutiful admiration.

Kerze glanced at his watch. There were another eight or ten minutes to go before he need leave for Gisenius's office—time enough to lavish a little attention on his home life. Raising his voice in a stentorian bellow he summoned his housekeeper, and Frau Brandstädter materialized like a genie.

' Where's Konstantin? ' he demanded.

'At school, sir.'

'What's he wearing today?' Kerze was generally indifferent to his son's appearance, as long as the boy looked clean and tidy, but questions like these were designed to demonstrate that there was nothing in Kerze's domain which his eagle eye did not alight on sooner or later.

'He's wearing his grey corduroy suit.'

'Excellent,' Kerze said. 'Corduroy's good value for money—quiet and sober-looking, too. Get another suit made in the same material, in brown this time. Where's my daughter?'

'Your daughter?' Brandstädter goggled at him as if he had asked for her name, age and occupation. 'But she's gone, sir. She left just over half an hour ago.'

'Left, did you say?' Kerze demanded alertly.

'Yes, by car, with a large suitcase. I thought . . .'

'I don't care what you thought,' Kerze said rudely. 'Stick to the facts, woman. Did she tell you where she was going?'

'No.'

'Did she say why she was leaving or when she was coming back?'

'No.'

'What did she have in her suitcase?'

'I don't know.'

'You don't know much, do you?' Kerze snapped furiously. 'What do you think I pay you for? It's your job to keep this place in order, keep your eyes open and run the household as I want it run. If you can't do that you might as well clear out!'

'Come on,' Bennicken said, 'it's time to go.'

'What's all the hurry?' demanded Frammler. 'If it's anything like the last get-together, we might as well save ourselves the trip. I've never heard such a load of rubbish in my life.'

'You're wrong there,' Bennicken said staunchly. 'It wasn't rubbish.'

'It was, you know,' Frammler persisted. 'Where dead bodies are concerned I'm in a better position to judge than anyone else—I'm an expert.'

Frammler described a fondly proprietorial gesture, which he was justified in making, since they were standing in the

132

nerve-centre of his establishment, the so-called embalming-room. There was an air of solemnity about the place which only Frammler appreciated. Those of his visitors who had a keen sense of smell gained a bewildering impression that they were in a cross between a tomb and a barber's shop.

'No one can teach me my own business, Bennicken—not even Gisenius.'

'A good man,' Bennicken said simply, adding, with an almost extravagant expenditure of words: 'One of the best.'

'Yes, but not in my particular field.'

This was an undeniable assertion which Bennicken did not attempt to contradict. He surveyed the appointments of the room with grudging admiration—the broad expanse of the waist-high slab in the centre, the shelves with their rows of chemist's jars, the two work-benches at window-level, each arrayed with the tools of the undertaker's trade: unguent-spoons, powder-puffs, ladles, razors and corset-like constructions of wire.

'Yes,' Frammler said, with smiling satisfaction, 'I know my business all right, you've got to admit that. Do you know what my latest innovation is? Double-skinned caskets!'

'Double-skinned caskets?'

'Yes, sir!' Frammler rubbed his hands delightedly, relishing the thought that he had managed to impress someone so stolidly unimpressionable. 'It's like this—everyone's rolling in money these days and a funeral's a one-time job. Consequently, they want it to be worthy of the occasion whatever it costs. Well, I've been improving the quality of my materials in the past few years—and putting my prices up too, of course. Clients now insist on guaranteed seasoned oak, not to mention Lyons silk and Holstein quilting inside, solid silver handles and fittings and all kinds of other fripperies. But even that's not good enough for them, Bennicken.'

'We ought to go.'

'I'm just coming, old friend, but let me finish telling you, just to show you how well I know my job. Well, I racked my brains for some way to satisfy my clients' burning desire to spend more money, and then I hit on a fabulous idea: double-skinned caskets—they're selling like hot cakes, too. That's what comes of knowing a bit about archæology. Follow me?'

'No.'

133

' Zinc coffins, man—lead coffins—any sort of coffin, supplied to order, just like the ancient Egyptians had. There's no real point to them, but they sell well. First cloth, then wood and now metal—that's progress for you. A few years back people were quite happy to be packed away in a cigar-box.'

Bennicken registered astonishment. ' So now you solder them into a can, like sardines? '

' Well,' Frammler said, his professional pride slightly injured, ' in a manner of speaking—yes.'

' Can I watch you? '

' Doing what? '

' Soldering someone in.'

' As a special favour to a friend—yes, all right.'

' I'd enjoy that.'

' Right,' said Frammler. ' We'd better go now. Gisenius is sure to be waiting for us. I'll tell you one thing, though. I'm not going to be dragged into anything, and I hope the same goes for you. When in doubt, stick with me.'

' A new guest has just booked in,' Gisela Wandel announced.

' Well? ' said Hirsch. ' What's so special about that? '

' Nothing, on the face of it, Herr Hirsch.' Gisela Wandel preserved her usual blend of icy calm and steely inaccessibility. ' But in this particular instance I thought it better to notify you personally of the guest's identity.'

' Who is it? '

' Fräulein Kerze. She's been given Room 117.'

Hirsch gripped the arms of his chair. ' It's lucky my nerves are good. You're not joking, I suppose? '

' I'm afraid not, Herr Hirsch.'

' When did she arrive? '

' About half an hour ago. I only heard just now. If you remember, you left standing instructions that the arrival of any guest resident in Rheine-Bergen was to be reported to the manager's office automatically.'

Hirsch strode out of the office and along the passage leading to the foyer, where he hurried over to the reception desk. He picked up the file containing registration forms, thumbed through them briefly and extracted one. ' There are a couple of points that need clearing up here,' he told the desk-clerk, who bowed and produced a stereotyped 'Certainly, sir.'

Folding the form in half, Hirsch strolled casually across the foyer and up the main stairs to the first floor. His stride quickened appreciably as he made his way along the corridor to Room 117.

Karen Kerze was in the act of unpacking her suitcase when he knocked and entered. She looked up in annoyance—the archetype of a pampered guest who resents being disturbed —but when she saw who it was her eyes sparkled like candles on a Christmas-tree.

'I was going to ring you in a couple of minutes,' she said. 'If you'd waited, you'd have been able to admire me in my new negligée.'

'What a pity,' Hirsch said grimly, closing the door carefully behind him. 'That would have enhanced the effect. I've a bloody good mind to give you a good hiding.'

'Aren't you glad I came?' The light in Karen's eyes started to fade.

'I'm enchanted,' Hirsch said, 'but I'll be even more enchanted when you've gone.'

'I'm not budging,' she said stubbornly, sitting down on the bed with an air of defiance. 'I'm a guest.'

'You're wrong,' he retorted. 'Your stay is at an end.'

'I'm paying for this room,' she said, her eyes flashing furiously. 'It's mine.'

'Wrong again,' Hirsch replied. 'For one thing you haven't paid yet, and for another, even if you had, it wouldn't alter my decision to turn you out. For your information, my girl, a hotel isn't legally obliged to provide anyone with board and lodging. We only accept the people we want, and the people we don't want we don't accept. You belong to the second category, so get cracking. Pack your bag and I'll send someone up to collect it in ten minutes' time.'

'You can't do that, Martin!' Tears came into Karen's eyes. 'You can't simply throw me out. I need your help— I've no one else to turn to. Everything's gone wrong.'

Hirsch's manner conveyed adamantine resolution, but he secretly prepared himself for the need to make a few minor concessions. In the first place he was pressed for time—the others were probably waiting for him by now—and in the

135

second place Karen had brought up one of the heaviest guns in the feminine armoury: she started to cry.

'Now listen,' he said warningly, 'I'm not going to let you manœuvre me into an awkward situation. You're not staying here, and that's final. You see this registration form? I'm going to tear it up.'

Hirsch suited the action to the word, watching Karen as he did so. 'You're going to pack your bag and wait for me here. I'll be back in about an hour's time. We can discuss any further points then. Is that clear?'

Karen nodded humbly. It was a gesture which conveyed utter sincerity, but she avoided looking at him. Sniffing pathetically, she groped for a handkerchief and dabbed her eyes with it.

'Don't do anything stupid while I'm gone,' he said sternly. 'You've made enough trouble as it is.'

Dänkel switched off the ignition and got out. He squeezed through the narrow gate and into the garden, where a small gnome-like figure was bent double over a seed-bed, rooting around among some diminutive plants with single-minded concentration.

Dänkel approached the little man with the caution of a bomb-disposal expert approaching a land-mine. 'Forgive me if I'm intruding.'

Tantau raised his head, looking strangely like a dachshund preparing to burrow his way down a rabbit-hole. 'You're not intruding, Herr Dänkel. I never allow myself to be disturbed if I don't feel like it, so there's no need to apologize.'

Dänkel glanced round the garden. Tantau had been living in his little cottage on the edge of the woods for some years now. It stood in peaceful isolation on the outskirts of a small village which did not appear on any road-map.

'Did you come for a chat?' Tantau inquired.

'Of course not,' Dänkel said. 'I've got a job for you.'

Tantau nodded thoughtfully. He rose to his feet with a faint groan and inspected his earth-stained hands. 'You've certainly learnt one lesson in the past few years,' he said. 'You've stopped beating about the bush when you want something out of me. It's a welcome change. Well, what can I do for you?'

Although he was twice Tantau's size, Dänkel shuffled from foot to foot like a schoolboy. ' I told you, it's a job. Not a very big one, but important.'

' How long will it take ? '

' Two or three days, I should think. Fifty marks a day, guaranteed—plus a generous allowance for expenses.'

' Not bad.' Tantau stared pensively at his little cottage. ' All the same, two or three days' donkey-work doesn't sound particularly attractive. I prefer gardening, frankly. On the other hand, my roof needs repairing and the fence is falling down. All right, I might be interested.'

' That's grand! ' Dänkel sounded relieved and grateful. ' I'll run you into Rheine-Bergen right away, then. It's very urgent.'

' Steady on,' Tantau protested. ' Give me a chance to wash my hands and put a suit on. In any case, I'd like to hear what it's all about first.'

' Just an investigation—the client wants us to trace a man in Rheine-Bergen.'

' Go on.'

' That's all I know, believe me.' Dänkel looked abashed. ' There's no need to look so suspicious, Herr Tantau, I haven't been given any details.'

' Come now,' Tantau said gently, ' you're not telling me you accepted the job sight unseen? '

' I had no choice. It's for a special client of mine—Conrad Gisenius, the lawyer—and he expressly stipulated that I shouldn't do the work myself. He wants to deal with you direct—you're to report direct to him.'

' And you agreed? ' Tantau's pale-blue eyes widened slightly. ' That reminds me. I could do with a new garden hose—and a set of interchangeable nozzles.'

' We can discuss that later.' Dänkel was not disposed to quibble about trifles. ' Come along with me now—that's the main thing.'

' Very well,' said Tantau. ' This business is beginning to interest me. I look forward to meeting the man who can twist you round his little finger with such apparent ease, Dänkel—without obligation, of course.'

' I'm glad you could come, gentlemen,' Gisenius said briskly.

'We have some important matters to discuss. I assume you're all acquainted with the latest development in this unfortunate affair?'

'We're acquainted with it,' Frammler said, 'but that doesn't mean we accept it as gospel. Dead is dead, and a double schnapps can't alter the fact. Which raises an important point, Gisenius: you're not going to leave us sitting here with our tongues hanging out, are you?'

'For the moment, yes,' Gisenius said firmly. 'I shall be glad to offer you a drink when we've settled all outstanding business.'

'Why not offer us one straight away?' Frammler persisted.

'There's nothing to settle.'

Gisenius glanced appealingly at Schulz, who was still the titular leader of No. 2 Section and could be relied upon to speak with authority when occasion demanded. 'Pipe down for a couple of minutes, Frammler,' he said. 'Gisenius has the floor.'

Frammler relapsed into silence and Gisenius gave Schulz an appreciative nod. 'You're all in the picture, then,' he continued. 'It's no longer a question of whether one of us was mistaken. We've got to take precautionary measures.'

'Against a handful of bones?' Frammler demanded.

'I've told you once, Frammler,' Schulz said reprovingly. 'Gisenius has the floor, so let's have a little discipline, shall we? Go on, Gisenius.'

'I'm genuinely dismayed by your attitude, gentlemen,' Gisenius pursued. 'No one seems to be fully aware of the implications of what has happened. Don't you realize what this could lead to if things went wrong?'

'Things mustn't be allowed to go wrong,' Kerze said.

Some members of the party nodded, but although no one openly dissented, Gisenius was quite correct in his assumption that no one was unduly worried.

'Our conscience is clear, friends!' Schulz cried spiritedly. 'Let's not talk ourselves into feeling guilty about anything. If someone wants to make trouble, all I can say is, let him try —we'll show him! He'll be lucky if he gets away in one piece.'

'Bravo!' said Bennicken.

'That's the ticket,' Hirsch said acidly. 'If anyone questions your integrity, part his hair with a meat-axe.'

Karl Schulz looked perplexed. 'What do you mean by

138

that, Martin? You don't seriously believe anyone could accuse us of not having done our duty? '

' People's conception of duty varies from one day to the next,' Hirsch said, ' though I must admit that the more militant approach is in the ascendant again.'

' Gentlemen,' Gisenius implored, ' our one danger lies in doing what we're doing now. We must stop bickering and pull together.'

' We've always worked as a team when it came to the pinch,' Schulz said stoutly.

' That's the position we're in now,' Gisenius insisted. ' It's not merely a question of our consciences, which are—as Schulz has so rightly said—entirely clear. No, I'm afraid we've got to take something quite different into account—namely, the fact that an ill-founded suspicion, once voiced, could affect each and every one of us in the most unpleasant way. Think it over for a moment.'

Gisenius gave the old comrades ample time to ponder the point in so far as they deemed it necessary. Some of them shared Frammler's craving for alcoholic refreshment, but they could see that Gisenius would not satisfy it until he had concluded his exposition.

' While we're on the subject,' he resumed, ' I'd like to draw your attention to a few recent cases. A respectable citizen of Munich was arrested at his office desk on suspicion of having seduced a minor. The charge proved to be unfounded, but he spent several weeks in gaol. Shortly afterwards another equally respectable individual was remanded for questioning and subsequently sent to a lunatic asylum for observation because he was suspected of having abetted perjury. He spent months behind bars before the charge was dropped. Another innocent man with a spotless record was forced to spend two years in prison . . .'

' For God's sake! ' Frammler interposed in tones of horror. ' Give the subject a rest and bring out the schnapps! '

' Appalling, really appalling,' Kerze muttered, shaking his head.

' It's amazing how many human lives have been sacrificed on the altar of justice, so-called,' Martin Hirsch said, ' and yet I'll bet there are still some people who claim that everything done in the name of justice is justified.'

139

'Me, for one,' Bennicken said.

'Let's get down to practical details,' Gisenius suggested. He was not displeased with the way the meeting had progressed. Everything had gone as he had foreseen—it could hardly have done otherwise. 'So far, all we've established is that someone may be trying to meddle in our private affairs.'

'Let's do him!' growled Bennicken.

Gisenius dismissed the suggestion with a curt wave of his hand, and Bennicken subsided. He had the strong man's respect for intellectual ability. Gisenius went on: 'We don't know if it really is Meiners, but there's a possibility that it may be his brother. Can anyone shed any light on this point?'

There was a buzz of conjecture, but no one produced any concrete evidence.

'It's not the sort of thing they put in an army paybook,' Schulz said. 'Who's interested in whether a man's got brothers, after all?'

'We are,' Gisenius gently corrected him, 'at least in this instance. Let's assume that it really is Meiners's brother. The question then arises: how does he know what happened? Who told him? In the nature of things, it could only be one of us.'

The other five, Hirsch excluded, looked shocked. In at least three cases, shock was succeeded by the sort of anger which always sets in when those who are convinced of their own essential righteousness sense that they have been basely betrayed.

'The bastard!' grunted Bennicken.

'If it really was one of us,' Kerze said robustly, 'he deserves to be shot.'

'I'd refuse to bury him,' Frammler declared, 'even if his widow went down on her knees and begged me to.'

Schulz wagged his head sorrowfully. 'A friend wouldn't do a thing like that.'

Hirsch raised one eyebrow. 'I've known friends do worse.'

'Then they weren't real friends,' Schulz said stoutly.

'Precisely,' Gisenius continued. 'That being so, I appeal to each of you to examine his own conscience. If any of you feels he might have been responsible—whether accidentally or through carelessness—I beg him to come forward. Let him tell us, in all sincerity, what happened, and we will do our best to understand. And let him do so here and now, before it's too late. Gentlemen, I appeal to you to be frank. If any of you have anything to say, please speak up.'

Seconds passed, but no one spoke. The stony silence was broken only by the ticking of the grandfather clock in the corner of Gisenius's office. The old comrades covertly eyed one another, mutually assessing their capacity for perfidy.

It was Karl Schulz who terminated this uncomradely proceeding. ' It wasn't one of us,' he announced.

' What makes you so sure? ' Gisenius asked softly.

' I'm certain it wasn't.' Schulz looked round challengingly. ' Anyone disagree? '

If anyone did, he declined to say so.

' I can assume, then,' Gisenius said, ' that none of us would wish to prevent this issue from being cleared up. May I further assume that you have sufficient faith in me to allow me to take the appropriate steps? '

' You may,' Schulz said, speaking for them all.

' May I also count on the full support of everyone present? '

' You may.'

' Even if it involves practical assistance and financial backing? '

' Yes.' It was Willy Kerze who spoke this time, aware that the key-word ' financial ' was aimed primarily at him.

' At your service day and night,' Bennicken said, meaning himself and his taxi.

' Petrol from me,' Schulz chimed in promptly, '—any amount you like. Just phone, that's all.'

Frammler grinned. ' My establishment is also at your disposal day and night.'

' What about you, Hirsch? ' Gisenius demanded.

'Count me in,' the hotelier said, ' but I'll refrain from telling you what I think of the operation.'

' We can imagine,' Kerze snapped.

Gisenius refused to tolerate any budding altercation at this crucial stage of the proceedings. ' Then it only remains for me to thank you for the confidence you have shown in me,' he said hastily. ' I shall place this matter in the proper hands. Our first objective is to find the man who looks like Meiners. Steps are being taken to trace him. I shall keep you up to date with developments, and I expect your fullest co-operation in return. If you require anything to drink, gentlemen, you'll find it in the outer office.'

'My name is Tantau,' said the little man, 'Heinrich Tantau.'
'What do you want?' the chief clerk inquired distantly.
'Nothing,' replied Tantau. 'I'm not here because I want anything. Someone wants something from me.'
'From you? Who, may I ask?'
'Herr Gisenius.'
The chief clerk looked sceptical. 'He sent for you?'
'So it seems,' Tantau said. 'That's what Herr Dänkel told me, anyway.'
'One moment.' The chief clerk suppressed a sneer. He rose with extreme deliberation, cast another incredulous glance at the shabby little figure and knocked on the door of Gisenius's office. He found his employer alone and, as usual, fully occupied. Gisenius appeared to be engrossed in a pile of documents.
'There's a man outside who says you want to see him, sir. His name is Tantau. Herr Dänkel sent him.'
Gisenius glanced up from his work with a look of satisfaction. 'So soon? That's what I call quick work. I wasn't expecting Herr Tantau until later, otherwise I should have notified you. Kindly show him in.'
'Certainly, sir.' The chief clerk opened the door and asked the man his employer had called 'Herr' Tantau to step inside.
Gisenius rose to greet him with a mechanical smile which froze on his face when he saw his visitor's appearance. This state of affairs lasted barely a second, however. Gisenius had too many years of profitable experience behind him not to realize that it was unwise to judge by externals.
Accordingly, he did what he had already planned to do on Tantau's arrival. He went over to his visitor, extended a welcoming hand and deftly manœuvred him into the most comfortable chair. 'A cigar?' he asked. 'Something to drink?'
'No, thank you,' Tantau said. 'I have other vices.'
His voice had a peculiar timbre, like that of an inquisitive but good-natured child—an agreeable voice, Gisenius thought. His hands, too, resembled those of a child. They were small

and slightly ingrained with garden soil, and he folded them carefully on his lap like a model pupil of advanced years.

'I'm told you were a member of the police force, Herr Tantau.'

'I was.'

'A chief superintendent, if my memory serves me?'

'Yes. I'm just an old-age pensioner now.'

Gisenius noted with satisfaction that Tantau appeared to set no particular store by his past glories, which would facilitate matters considerably.

'Would you be prepared to do some work for me?'

'That's why I'm here.'

'And may I count on your absolute discretion?'

'You may.'

Gisenius strove hard to detect some special quality in Tantau. He looked odd, certainly, but there was nothing about him to suggest that he possessed exceptional ability. The face was seamed and wrinkled like a wrung-out flannel, the mouth scarcely discernible and the hair silvery-white, sparse and stringy. The eyes, which were a faded blue, had a weary look suggestive of lack of sleep. All in all, the man seemed totally unremarkable.

'Very well,' Gisenius said finally, after some moments of indecision, 'we'll get down to details, if you're agreeable.'

'I'm agreeable.'

'The job I have in mind may not be particularly complicated, Herr Tantau,' Gisenius said gravely, 'but it requires careful handling. It must also be carried out with a maximum of tact and discretion. I should like to emphasize that.'

'You were coming to the details,' Tantau interposed.

'Well,' Gisenius said, firmly banishing all his misgivings, 'what it boils down to is this: I need a certain address.'

'Have you thought of consulting a telephone book?' Tantau inquired amiably.

Gisenius endeavoured to conceal his displeasure at what he felt to be an inappropriately flippant remark. 'There's more to it than that. The man in question is only staying in Rheine-Bergen temporarily. That's what we're assuming, at least.'

'May I ask who " we " refers to?'

'That is immaterial, Herr Tantau. Please assume that

I'm asking you to trace this person on behalf of one of my clients.'

' Very well.'

' Do you think you'll be able to trace the man's whereabouts? '

' It's possible.'

' Then you'll undertake the job? '

' I didn't say that,' Tantau said politely. ' I'm not averse to undertaking such a commission, if only because of the proposed fee, but I'd like some more detailed information first —as much information as you can provide. Much as I hate to admit it, I'm not a mind-reader.'

After taking a few moments to digest what he had just heard, Gisenius came to the conclusion that Tantau might, for the first time, have revealed a hint of what he was said to be made of. The man was shrewd. He had a streak of mild irony and he had made it plain that his approach to his work was thorough and conscientious. Gisenius found the general picture reassuring. ' What do you want to know? ' he asked.

Tantau smiled as though he took the lawyer's acquiescence for granted. Then he said: ' The name of the party concerned.'

' Meiners, Michael Meiners.'

' Date of birth, place of origin, occupation? '

' I'm afraid I can't supply any of those particulars,' Gisenius replied. ' The only thing that seems relatively certain is that he must have been born in about nineteen twenty-four—perhaps even later.'

' Do you know him personally? ' Tantau inquired. ' I only ask because I need at least a rough description of his personal appearance.'

' Well,' Gisenius said slowly, ' he's about six foot two, slim, bony, pale-complexioned, has unusually large blue-grey eyes and fair hair, and speaks without any regional accent. That's more or less all I can tell you about him.'

' And you don't know where he lives or what he does for a living? '

' I've no idea. I'm not even certain whether he exists.'

Tantau's eyes looked pale, watery and unseeing as ever. ' What if I do manage to find this Michael Meiners? ' he mused.

' Then your job will be done,' Gisenius said firmly. ' You

144

will merely inform me of his whereabouts and leave the rest to me.'

'It's not much of a job,' Tantau observed, shaking his head, 'not much compared to the fee you're paying.'

'Let me worry about that,' Gisenius replied. 'If the job seems straightforward, so much the better. The fact remains that it's of the utmost importance to me—my client, I mean. Don't let the size of the fee prey on your mind.'

'I won't,' Tantau assured him. 'May I at least inquire what steps you've taken so far?'

'Virtually none, Herr Tantau. It's a job for an expert.'

'If that's your opinion, Herr Gisenius, I see no reason to doubt it. But to recapitulate: you're looking for a man named Michael Meiners, whom you believe to be staying here in Rheine-Bergen. How long has he been in town?'

'Five or six days. That was the first time anyone saw him —or thought they saw him.'

'And yet you don't even know if he exists? That's what you said, wasn't it?'

Gisenius nodded gravely. It was clear that Tantau's hearing functioned well. He not only caught the gist of what he was told but registered it in detail, word for word. It followed that he must have a serviceable memory and also that, despite his age, his deductive faculty was still intact. The man had his points.

'He may be a man named Michael Meiners. On the other hand he may be someone else of the same name, or even someone who merely resembles Meiners.'

Tantau smiled like a child with a new toy. 'It's an intriguing case,' he said. 'I'll take it on.'

'Good.' Gisenius experienced a sense of relief. 'How do you intend to proceed?'

'The essential point, as I see it, is this: someone is convinced that he saw a man who might have been Meiners. Let's start from there. Who is this someone? What exactly did he see? When and where did he see it?'

'I'll take you to see Herr Hirsch, the manager of the *Hotel Drei Kronen*. He'll be able to give you further particulars.'

'Get me today's papers,' Kerze commanded the clerk at the reception desk of the *Drei Kronen*.

'Right away, sir.'

'And then inform Herr Hirsch of my arrival. He's expecting me. I'll wait for him in the foyer.'

'At once, sir.'

Kerze approved wholeheartedly of the way guests were treated in the *Drei Kronen*. He was fully aware of the value of meticulous service in an age when lack of staff was universal and courtesy at a premium. It was yet another token that Hirsch had the establishment well in hand. If he, Kerze, decided to enter the hotel business, he might conceivably allow Hirsch to keep his job, always provided the man showed a genuine readiness to toe the line.

Kerze busied himself with the *Rheine-Bergen News*. It was a newspaper which appealed to him, not only because he knew the owner but also because Gisenius wielded considerable influence over its editorial policy. He was flattered but not unduly surprised, therefore, to find the third page devoted to a long article on the Building Exhibition. It was dominated by a photograph three columns wide which featured the tasteful Stabilator stand as its central motif and bore the caption: 'Long-term planning and constructive achievement are the main features of this highly successful exhibition.' Without false modesty, Kerze credited the remark to his personal account.

Indeed, why should he not take pleasure in his achievements and successes? Feeling a sudden urge to drink his own health, Kerze beckoned to a waiter who was standing in the doorway of the dining-room.

The waiter, who happened to be Paul, hurried over obediently, bowed and said in a discreet undertone: 'Is the Herr Direktor looking for Fräulein Kerze?'

Kerze lowered his newspaper and regarded Paul in some surprise. 'What makes you think that?'

'I believe Fräulein Kerze has gone out,' Paul volunteered.

'Gone out?' Kerze muttered, looking perplexed.

His mind quickly digested the information. If Karen had gone out, the logical inference was that she had been in, that she was staying on the premises—possibly, even, that she was installed in Hirsch's private quarters. Kerze ground his teeth at the thought. It was just the sort of thing that evil unscrupulous woman-chaser would do!

'Can I get the Herr Direktor anything?' Paul inquired politely, relishing the effect of his information upon Kerze.

'A large brandy,' Kerze said hoarsely.

The large brandy and Hirsch arrived in quick succession. Kerze downed the brandy but did not at first notice Hirsch. He sat there brooding darkly on the possible implications of what he had heard. A man like Hirsch would be quite capable of seducing the daughter of a prospective major shareholder in Europa Hotels Limited simply in order to preserve his lucrative job. Human nature was like that—Kerze was an expert on the subject.

'Sorry to have kept you waiting,' Hirsch said with an unsuspecting smile. 'I had to sort out a couple of problems in the office.'

'You've got a bloody nerve,' Kerze said belligerently, raising his voice, 'grinning at me like that after what you've been up to!'

'Not so loud, please,' Hirsch said. 'You're not in your factory.'

'If you don't like my tone that's just too bad,' Kerze growled. 'I don't like your behaviour, so we're quits.'

'I suggest we go to my office.'

'Why not your flat?' Kerze demanded. 'Or have you got something up there you don't want me to see? No one pulls the wool over my eyes, Hirsch—you ought to know that by now.'

'Very well,' Hirsch said, anxious to cut short a distasteful scene which was already raising a few eyebrows, 'let's go to my flat.'

Kerze sprang to his feet and hurried to the main stairs. As Hirsch followed him he passed Paul, the waiter. The man's suppressed smirk told him all he wanted to know.

'Did you serve Herr Kerze just now?' he asked in passing.

'I did, sir,' Paul said, 'to the Herr Direktor's entire satisfaction, I venture to say.'

Kerze had already reached the landing and was steering an unerring course for the manager's private apartment. He wrenched the door open and flung it wide. Then he stood in the doorway and peered in. His empurpled features grew slightly less contorted when he saw nothing to confirm his suspicions.

'If you expect to find your daughter here,' Hirsch said quietly from behind him, 'I'm afraid you're in for a disappointment.'

'What do you mean?' Kerze demanded rudely. 'You don't deny she's here in the hotel, do you?'

'In the hotel, yes, but not in here.'

'It amounts to the same thing.'

'No it doesn't,' Hirsch said. 'Look, let's sit down for a moment. Why do you think I invited you over?'

'To tell me a pack of lies, probably. You won't get anywhere, though, I'm not buying it. Kindly produce my daughter at once, Hirsch. I'm taking her home.'

'I couldn't be more delighted.'

Kerze involuntarily accepted Hirsch's invitation to sit down. He felt bemused. 'Hirsch,' he said with a note of supplication, 'don't try to hoodwink me.'

'Your daughter presented herself at the reception desk at about midday today and booked a room,' Hirsch explained patiently. 'When I heard about it I urged her to leave again. That's all there is to it.'

'The little slut!' Kerze growled. 'Where can I find her?'

Hirsch hesitated for a few moments. 'Room 117,' he said.

Kerze loped off down the corridor like a bloodhound on the trail. He examined each door in turn until he came to a halt in front of No. 117. The door resisted his furious onslaught. It was locked.

Looking somewhat disconcerted, Hirsch hurriedly produced a key-ring from his hip pocket, selected a pass-key and opened the door. The room, though empty, was obviously in occupation. Articles of clothing which unmistakably belonged to Karen were strewn about, and her suitcase stood empty on the rack.

'What does this mean?' Kerze fumed.

Hirsch picked up the telephone and asked for the desk. 'Room 117 seems to be still occupied,' he said. 'What's the position?' He listened in silence for a moment, and what he heard did not appear to rejoice his heart. Replacing the receiver, he turned to Kerze with an air of exasperation. 'Karen hasn't kept her side of the bargain. She wrote out a new registration form, paid a week's rent in advance and then drove off in her car—destination and time of return unknown.'

'If this is another of your tricks, Hirsch,' Kerze said menacingly, 'you'll regret it. You needn't expect any quarter from me, I warn you!'

'Ah, I'm glad I've found you at last,' said Gisenius.

Kerze frowned. 'How did you know I was up here?'

'It was Hirsch I wanted, really, but since you're both here so much the better.'

'You're in luck,' said Hirsch. 'One of us nearly ended up in hospital just now.'

'And it wouldn't have been me,' Kerze retorted.

Gisenius took in the situation at a glance. The two men were sitting in Hirsch's apartment looking as if they might fly at each other at any moment. It was a sight which Gisenius had witnessed more than once in the past. Ordinarily, he wouldn't have minded, but under present circumstances it was an unnecessary complication.

'A joke's a joke,' Kerze said angrily, 'but this is going too far. You may find it hard to credit, Conrad, but this swine persuaded my daughter to come and live here with him at the hotel.'

'It's not true,' Hirsch rejoined.

'It can't be true,' Gisenius said with quiet conviction.

'What's that?' Kerze demanded indignantly. 'You mean to say you're taking his side?'

Gisenius sat down between them. 'It's not a question of taking sides. I'm merely stating the obvious. If I say I'm convinced that Hirsch didn't induce your daughter to come and stay here, it's because I refuse to believe that he'd be stupid or careless enough to indulge in such a risky course of action.'

Hirsch looked relieved. 'That's the first word of sense I've heard in the last half-hour.'

'I must admit it sounds logical,' Kerze conceded reluctantly.

Gisenius nodded, gratified that his reasoning had found such a ready response. 'I've brought along the man who's going to trace Meiners for us—or whoever he is. He's waiting downstairs in the foyer. He wants to take a look at a photograph of Meiners, and you're the only person who has one, Hirsch.'

'Yes, and I wonder why,' Kerze said pointedly. 'Why did you keep that photo, Hirsch?'

'I not only kept it. I've got it hanging on my bedroom wall.'

'Because you find it edifying?'

'Because it's a reminder, because it makes me sleep badly, because it stops me glamorizing my memories of the war, because I'm a sentimentalist or because I want to hide a mark on the wall—who knows?'

'All that matters at the moment,' Gisenius said, 'is that the photograph exists. The man wants to see it, so let's show it to him.'

Martin Hirsch disappeared into his bedroom and emerged a few seconds later with the photograph in his hand. He gave it to Gisenius, who studied it intently. Kerze craned over his shoulder.

'Odd how long ago it all seems,' Gisenius mused.

Kerze sniggered. 'We were a funny-looking lot in those days—especially you, Hirsch.'

The photograph seemed to hail from a remote and forgotten world. Faded by the light of five thousand days, it was the sort of amateur snapshot which contrives to look informal and a little stiff at the same time. It depicted a farm-yard in Central Germany. Ranged between barn and cow-shed, squinting slightly as they looked into an invisible sun, stood seven soldiers of varying age but generally youthful appearance. The broad-shouldered figure in the centre was that of Sergeant Karl Schulz. On his right, equally bulky and imposing, stood Grenadier Kerze. On his left and slightly behind him was Lance-Corporal Gisenius, inconspicuous but not insignificant. Flanking the central trio like two massive pillars were Lance-Corporal Frammler and Corporal Bennicken, legs planted firmly apart and thumbs hooked into their belts. On the extreme left, next to Hirsch but half a pace to his rear, stood Grenadier Meiners, a gangling, adolescent-looking figure with large, rather timorous eyes.

'He hasn't changed much,' observed Kerze. 'I'd know those moon-calf's eyes anywhere.'

'Meiners was a nice lad and a courageous one,' Gisenius

felt impelled to state. 'He also happened to be unlucky, but we can hardly be blamed for that.'

He tucked the photograph under his arm and got up. 'Come on,' he said. 'This man I've engaged may want to ask you some questions, and I don't think we ought to keep him waiting—he's expensive. Besides, Tantau doesn't strike me as the sort of man one can keep hanging around like a chauffeur.'

'Just a moment, Gisenius.' Hirsch caught the lawyer by the sleeve. 'What did you say his name was?'

'Tantau,' Gisenius replied, somewhat surprised by this unexpected show of interest, 'Heinrich Tantau, if my memory serves me correctly.'

'Is he a little old gnome of a man who used to be in the police?'

'That's right. I'm told he was actually a chief superintendent at one time.'

Hirsch looked grim. 'Have you any idea who you're dealing with?'

'If you don't mind!' Kerze snapped. 'We all trust Conrad's judgment implicitly. He knows more about these things than a hotel manager, so pipe down!'

They were still standing shoulder to shoulder in the doorway. Hirsch, who seemed bent on blocking the exit, stuck stubbornly to his guns.

'It so happens that I've met Tantau,' he said, '—three or four years ago, when he was working here in the hotel on behalf of the company. There'd been some cases of theft.'

'Well?' Gisenius asked, a trifle impatiently. 'Did he solve them?'

'Inside two days.'

'What's wrong with that?' Kerze demanded, smiling triumphantly at Gisenius. 'It's always the same with you, Hirsch, you're never happy unless you're carping at someone.'

'He not only solved the thefts,' Hirsch persisted, 'he uncovered a few other things as well—proved that one of our guests was a would-be blackmailer and another a receiver of stolen property. He also asked a lot of awkward questions which put the staff's back up and annoyed some of the guests.'

'Splendid,' declared Kerze, secretly relishing the thought

151

that Hirsch, in his capacity as manager of the hotel, must have sweated blood. 'Just the man we need.'

Gisenius, who habitually sought the cause of every effect and did not seem quite as ready to dismiss Hirsch's misgivings out of hand, asked: 'Was Tantau's sphere of action clearly specified in advance?'

'That was just the trouble,' Hirsch said. 'The board's brief was far too vague. Instead of putting him on one specific case, they temporarily employed him as a sort of hotel detective —for simplicity's sake, I suppose. That gave him carte blanche, and he took full advantage of it. He was directly responsible to the board, so I had no control over him. If they hadn't called him off when they did the hotel would have been empty inside a week.'

Kerze was enchanted. 'He must have stirred things up! No wonder you hadn't got a good word to say for him.' He chuckled maliciously. 'Put the fear of God into you, did he?'

'You may have good reason to fear him yourself, Kerze, only you're too stupid to realize it.'

'Now, now, gentlemen,' Gisenius said reprovingly. 'I think I'm clear on the general picture, Hirsch. Caution is never misplaced, but I've already covered your main point. I've given Tantau a specific and clearly defined brief, and I shall ensure that he follows my instructions to the letter. You'll see—engaging Tantau will turn out to be the best possible way of serving the ends of justice.'

Hirsch said: 'That's what I'm afraid of,' but the other two were already in the corridor.

'I intend to proceed methodically,' Tantau announced. 'I realize my methods may seen naive, but please bear with me.'

'Don't worry,' Gisenius assured him. 'Results are all we're interested in.'

The old detective smiled. 'Oh, I'll certainly be able to provide you with a result of some kind.'

They were standing in the *Café de Paris*. Tantau had given no specific reason for wishing to see the place, but his request had been granted immediately. Gisenius had shown a positive eagerness to accompany him, and Hirsch and Kerze seemed equally willing.

Preparations for the evening were under way. Quahnke, very much the artistic director, held sway upon the stage. Quahnke always exuded drive and enthusiasm when Hirsch was in the offing.

Hirsch and Kerze were sitting with Marlene Sonnenberg at a table near the bar. Marlene, who seemed more than usually vivacious, had been summoned, together with the pianist, to rehearse under Quahnke's supervision. Quahnke was planning some novel artistic effects—exotic background music topped by a *bouche fermée* vocal in the Duke Ellington manner (supplied by Marlene), and, in the foreground, a sort of tropical babe in the wood (Brigitte), who was to wander through the jungle, frolicking and admiring her reflection in imaginary pools, until, overcome by heat and solitude, she grew sleepy and started to divest herself of her clothes. If the final outcome of the new presentation was the same as the last, it at least gave Brigitte scope for novel contortions.

Brigitte had just appeared, childishly innocent but fleshily feminine, virginal-looking yet sensual as an adolescent's day-dream. Gisenius forced himself to look away. At the table near the bar, a genial Kerze was deep in conversation with Marlene Sonnenberg while Hirsch watched Gisenius and Tantau with a dubious expression.

' This photograph you've given me,' Tantau was saying, '—it's extremely interesting.'

' I don't imagine you'll want to keep it, will you? '

' You can have it back, but first I'd like to get a photographer to make a blow-up of Meiners's face. I'll be needing a picture of him.'

' I hope, Herr Tantau,' Gisenius said sternly, ' that we're fully agreed on the nature of your assignment. I would remind you that its scope is strictly limited. We require a certain address—nothing more.'

Tantau nodded. ' I understand entirely. You'll get your information and nothing more, but the methods I use are my own business.'

' I'm sure you know your job.'

Tantau seemed to accept this confirmation of his abilities as a matter of course. He blinked slightly, like an old dog warming himself in the sun. ' If you'd like an opportunity to see the sort of methods I generally use, I'll be happy to explain why I decided to begin my inquiries here as opposed to somewhere else.'

'Quite unnecessary, my dear Herr Tantau.' Gisenius looked a trifle distrait. As if by chance, his eyes had again wandered to the stage, where Brigitte was disporting herself under Quahnke's supervision. 'I have the fullest confidence in you. There's no need to divulge any professional secrets.'

'There's very little mystery about my job,' Tantau said, registering the direction of his companion's gaze. 'Contrary to widespread belief, police methods are disappointingly straightforward. It's just that every detective has his own particular approach. One of my idiosyncrasies is that I like to give clients a chance to get to know my technique.'

'Admirable,' Gisenius said, casting another brief glance at the stage. 'An excellent basis for mutual trust.'

Tantau's slight inclination of the head allowed of various interpretations. 'I'm starting my inquiries in this room because the party in question spent some time here. Therefore, he must have been seen by a number of people who had the time and opportunity to take a closer look at him.'

'And what do you hope to achieve, Herr Tantau?'

'Accurate descriptions, pointers—perhaps a definite lead: the monogram on a lighter, for instance, or details of clothing, or distinguishing marks, or a match-box advertising the name of a particular firm. It's even possible that someone has seen the man in question on an earlier occasion, or that he's been seen since. I was once lucky enough to trace someone's whereabouts within fifteen minutes, thanks to an observant waiter. The man had been fiddling with a key. The tab not only bore the name of the hotel where he was staying but his room-number as well.'

'I can see you know your business,' Gisenius said approvingly. 'Perhaps you'll forgive me if I rejoin my friends now.'

'Of course,' Tantau assured him. 'But may I beg a small favour first? Please ask Herr Hirsch to send me the waiter who was serving this table last night. I'd like his assistance and that of any other employees I may have to interview. I'm sure Herr Hirsch will know how to ensure their fullest co-operation.'

Tantau stood there blinking for a moment longer before

vanishing, like a ferret down a rabbit-hole, into the gentlemen's lavatory—presumably to inspect the rear exit.

Gisenius stared after Tantau with a certain measure of satisfaction, then turned on his heel and made for the table occupied by Hirsch, Kerze and Marlene Sonnenberg.

'Well, gentlemen,' he said on arrival, 'I don't think I was mistaken. That man knows his business.'

'What's his line?' Marlene Sonnenberg inquired.

'I think Herr Quahnke wants you, Fräulein Sonnenberg,' Hirsch interposed. 'Duty calls, I'm afraid.'

'What a shame,' she pouted, getting up. 'I was so enjoying our little talk.'

'Never mind,' Kerze said gallantly, 'we'll look forward to welcoming you back when the rehearsal's over.'

'I shan't be long,' Marlene promised. She threw out her bosom, smiled at the three men and departed in the direction of the stage.

No one spared her undulating hips a glance, not even Kerze, because Gisenius was already recounting the details of his conversation with Tantau. He passed on the little man's message to Hirsch.

'Fundamentally,' Hirsch said, 'what Tantau is doing is pretty simple.'

'Simple things need expert handling,' Gisenius replied. 'I'm sure we've found the right man for the job.'

Meanwhile, raised voices could be heard coming from the stage, where differences of opinion between Quahnke and Marlene Sonnenberg showed signs of erupting into a fracas of the first order. The three men at the table welcomed the distraction, especially Hirsch. Gisenius was intrigued, and Kerze, belligerent by nature, adored arguments even when he was not directly involved in them.

'You're asking me to prostitute my art!' Marlene exclaimed furiously. 'That's what it amounts to!'

'Fräulein Sonnenberg,' Quahnke replied with hauteur, 'let's not quarrel about art or whether you've got any to prostitute. The fact remains that you're under contract to sing here.'

'Yes, as a soloist!' Marlene retorted with equal hauteur.

' I wish to be employed as such—not as a fog-horn in the background, designed to drown the flat-footed shuffling of your snotty-nosed little protégée over there! '

Brigitte uttered a shrill squeal of rage and Quahnke's majestic features turned crimson with anger as he groped for a suitable riposte. It was a difficult task rendered more difficult by three factors: his own relationship to Brigitte, Marlene's influential friends and the presence of the manager.

Kerze gave a low whistle of admiration. ' That's what I call spirit! '

' It's a little hard on the girl,' Gisenius said. ' She's only a child, after all.'

' Children of that age are fully-fledged competitors in the entertainment world,' Hirsche corrected him. ' The Sonnenberg woman realizes that and she's behaving accordingly. You can't blame her.'

Kerze was still lost in admiration. ' What a woman! ' he breathed. ' I'd like to let her loose on my housekeeper.'

Hirsch, who had been watching Kerze intently, bent forward. ' Perhaps you ought to engage her to perform for you in private,' he said casually.

' It must be hard to make your way in the world at her age,' Gisenius mused, meaning Brigitte, not Marlene.

At this juncture Quahnke came hurrying up. ' My heartfelt apologies, Herr Hirsch. To think that such a thing should have happened in your presence! '

' It's all right,' Hirsch said, rising. ' I'll deal with it.'

Quahnke bowed. ' I'm deeply obliged.'

' Are you coming? ' Hirsch asked the other two. ' I'm going to have a little chat with Fräulein Sonnenberg.'

' Lead the way! ' Kerze said with alacrity.

Gisenius shook his head. ' You carry on. I'll wait for you here.'

Gisenius watched Hirsch and Kerze depart, temporarily on better terms, in the direction of the dressing-rooms. Then he glanced over his shoulder towards the rear of the room. As he had anticipated, Tantau was already at work interrogating a waiter—rigorously, judging by the look on the man's face. Satisfied, Gisenius devoted himself to his more immediate neighbours, among them Brigitte. Quahnke was sitting beside her, endeavouring to soothe her ruffled feelings.

Gisenius picked up Hirsch's glass of Anjou rosé and sipped it cautiously. To his untried palate it tasted sweet but not without a certain potency. As he drank, it seemed to tinge his skin with dawn light and bathe the room in gentle shades of pink. Draining the glass, he got up and walked over to Brigitte.

At the same moment, Quahnke departed on some seemingly urgent errand, leaving the chair beside the night-club neophyte conveniently vacant. Gisenius sat down on it gingerly, and it was some time before he essayed a remark. ' Regrettable,' he said ponderously, ' most regrettable.'

Brigitte, who had seen him coming but decided to feign maidenly surprise, gave a start and stared at him wide-eyed. It was an effective look. Although her face was slightly tear-stained, her robust gamine's charms could stand rough treatment. ' It was mean of her, wasn't it? ' she said hopefully. ' How could anyone say I've got flat feet? Do you think I have? '

She extended her legs—both of them—in his direction. Gisenius recoiled an inch or two but inspected the offending limbs gravely, much as he would have studied an important brief.

' You could have avoided all this,' he said. ' You should never have allowed yourself to get into this position.'

' But it wasn't my fault,' Brigitte protested. ' That Sonnenberg creature started it.'

' What I meant was, a girl like you doesn't belong in a place like this,' Gisenius said emphatically.

' Ah! ' sighed Brigitte, who had a child's instinct for reacting as she was expected to react. ' It isn't the best job in the world, but what's the alternative? A girl's got to live somehow.'

Gisenius was temporatily spared further girlish platitudes because he saw Tantau coming and instinctively drew away from Brigitte.

' I hope I'm not intruding,' Tantau said, contemplating the floor as if it were a source of vital information. He slowly raised his head and regarded the two figures before him— the teen-aged girl and the middle-aged man—with veiled

157

eyes, trying to make up his mind which was the tougher nut.

'Of course not,' Gisenius assured him.

'I've finished here.' Tantau studied Brigitte's legs as if they were part of the furniture.

'Any results?'

'A few leads,' Tantau said vaguely. 'One of them may turn out to be useful. A waiter here has twice run into the man elsewhere, each time in the same place. I shall continue my inquiries there. If I may, I'll accept your suggestion and enlist the help of your taxi-driver friend—Bennicken, isn't it?'

'By all means,' Gisenius replied. 'Bennicken is an extremely reliable man.'

'I'm glad to hear it.'

'You will keep me informed, won't you, Herr Tantau? For the time being, all I can do is wish you luck.'

Tantau blinked at the brightly-lit stage. 'Allow me to reciprocate, Herr Gisenius.'

6. *Memory Dies Hard*

Martin Hirsch opened his record cabinet and flicked through the albums. He did not take long to find what he was looking for. After listening to the first few bars of Bach's Brandenburg Concerto No. 4 he lay down on the divan without taking his shoes off and stared up at the ceiling.

Somehow, even Bach failed to have its customary effect. The notes flowed over him but left him unmoved.

He had spent years cultivating a casual approach because he believed it was the best way of taking life in his stride. He had done his best to ignore obstacles, shun responsibility and avoid trouble. And now, everything he had so far managed to dodge with such blithe self-assurance was rapidly closing in on him.

His train of thought was rudely interrupted by a brisk knock at the door. Welcoming the distraction, he propped himself on one elbow and called: ' Come in! '

Gisela Wandel entered.

' Splendid! ' cried Hirsch. ' You're just in time to hear a little good music. Come over here, I'll make room for you.'

' I've no wish to become involved in your private life,' Herr Hirsch,' Gisela Wandel said coldly.

' I should close the door in that case,' Hirsch retorted. ' Do you want everyone to see you sneaking into my lair—and me lolling on my couch? It's the perfect set-up for someone like our friend Paul.'

Gisela Wandel hurriedly closed the door. Leaning against it, she regarded him gravely and said: ' Fräulein Kerze's back. I thought you might be interested.'

' You're right, but why did you have to bring me the news in person? I have a 'phone, you know.'

' You may need me.'

' How do you mean? '

' Well,' Gisela Wandel's voice had regained its calm,

incisive, business-like tone—'Fräulein Kerze's in her room, but she's not alone.'

'What's that?' Hirsch demanded, once more the professional hotelier with long years of experience behind him. 'Do you mean she's got a man in there?'

Gisela Wandel smiled faintly. 'Your assumption is correct. Fräulein Kerze has a young man with her.'

Hirsch did not hesitate. Pausing only to straighten his tie, he squared his shoulders and strode out of the room. 'Give me some covering fire, Fräulein Wandel,' he called over his shoulder. 'Dig out the floor-waiter—he's probably having his afternoon nap—and tell the commissionaire to stand by as well.'

He hurried down the passage to Karen Kerze's room and burst in without knocking.

The sight that met his eye came as no surprise. It was the cl..sic hotel bedroom scene, a jumble of naked limbs, hurried discarded articles of clothing and rumpled sheets. The curtains were drawn, bathing the room in purple gloom, and the atmosphere was a compound of scent, cigarette-smoke and sweat.

'Get out, blast you!' a man's voice shouted indignantly.

'Oh!' Karen said, sitting up. There was a note of pleasure in her husky voice. 'It's you!'

Hirsch didn't bother to check whether the door behind him was closed or not. He switched on the centre light and wrenched the curtains apart, flooding the room with bright afternoon light. The stars of the bedroom farce disentangled themselves from each other.

'What's the idea!' the youth blustered with a mixture of rage and belligerence.

Hirsch scrutinized him as he sat on the edge of the bed like a boxer squatting in his corner. He was a surly young hunk of beefcake, bursting with the arrogant self-confidence that stems from a sense of physical superiority. A prolonged tussle with him would reduce Room 117 to matchwood. Hirsch knew his type.

'Hey, you!' The youth slowly got to his feet. 'Are you looking for trouble? Take my advice, Grandad—shove off and close the door from the outside.'

Hirsch did what seemed unavoidable, and he acted with

all due speed and dexterity. He opened with a left to the jaw, followed it up with a right to the solar plexus and brought his knee up into the boy's belly—all in rapid succession.

The result was surprising, not least from Martin Hirsch's point of view. The youth's eyes rolled in boundless amazement and he folded up in slow motion, slumping to the floor and staying there, mute and motionless as a broken doll.

'Encore!' Karen said with admiration in her voice.

Hirsch leant giddily against the wall. As though in a dream, he saw the commissionaire appear, escorted by the floor-waiter and supervised by Gisela Wandel. Astonished faces stared at him, a limp body was swathed in a sheet and dragged out, and the room swam before his eyes.

'You were wonderful!' Karen sighed.

'And you,' Hirsch growled, still panting, 'are an irresponsible little slut. Where have you been?'

'All over the place.' Karen extended her arms in a gesture which seemed to encompass, if not the whole human race, at least the male sex. 'What do you expect me to do? I'm looking for someone to love me, but no one will.'

'Rubbish!' Hirsch snapped.

'Does that mean you do? If only you did! I couldn't ask for anything better.' She grinned impudently. 'Tell me —did you beat him up for my sake?'

'For friendship's sake.'

Karen stretched out her arms. 'Come and get your reward, then.'

'Get up and get dressed,' Hirsch said. 'Pack your bag and come with me. I'm going to deliver you to your father.'

Karen pouted. 'Straight away?'

'Straight away—and stop acting like a common tart. You don't convince anyone, least of all me.'

'You don't love me, either,' Karen said sorrowfully, 'and you're the only person in the world I've ever trusted.'

'Hurry up!' Hirsch's tone was deliberately brutal. 'Your father's waiting for you. It'll be a real pleasure to hand you over in person.'

'Your best plan is to forget the whole thing,' Gisela Wandel said. 'You'll see—men have short memories when it's a question of anything unpleasant.'

161

'I'm pretty disappointed with that Martin Hirsch of yours,' Karen complained, ' even if he does pack a punch.'

' He's not " my " Martin Hirsch.'

' But you're fond of him, aren't you? '

Gisela smiled wrily. ' Do I give that impression? '

' Yes.'

Gisela bent lower over the suitcase which they were packing together. Karen had evolved a convenient method of packing. She simply piled her things in an untidy heap, leaving Gisela to fold them neatly and lay them in the suitcase. They worked in silence for a while.

' Every secretary's in love with her boss, isn't that what they say? ' Karen's shoulders jerked with laughter. She retired to the bathroom, leaving the door ajar, and began to paint her lips carefully.

Gisela zipped the suitcase and walked over to the door. ' If you've finished making up, Fräulein Kerze, shall we go? '

Karen smiled brightly. ' As soon as you like.'

' In that case I'll go and tell Herr Hirsch you're ready to leave. That'll give you about ten minutes to kill. If you haven't any other plans, perhaps you'd do me a favour.'

' Do you a favour? '

' Not me personally—the hotel, and Herr Hirsch in particular.'

' What is it? '

' It's quite simple,' Gisela said casually. ' Ring down for a waiter named Paul—I think you've come across him before—speak to him nicely, and ask him if he can get hold of your registration form, just for a few minutes. Tell him you want to look at it or make an addition of some kind. Offer him twenty marks to get it for you—thirty if he haggles.'

' Is that all? ' Karen shrugged and walked over to the telephone.

Gisela Wandel left the room looking manifestly pleased with herself. She walked along the corridor and down the main stairs to the foyer, where she went over to the chef de reception and asked him to accompany her to the office. They disappeared down the side passage just as Paul emerged into the almost deserted foyer.

Leaving the chef de reception busy checking the list of

arrivals for the previous week, Gisela went into the manager's office.

Karen Kerze's young man, still irate but slightly the worse for wear, was sitting in the visitor's chair. Behind him loomed the burly figure of the commissionaire, thirsting to display his reserves of physical energy, and in front of him, leaning nonchalantly against the edge of his desk, stood an alert Martin Hirsch.

'Ah, just the person I was looking for!' Hirsch called. 'You were a witness. Did this young man assault me or did he not?'

'He did,' Gisela said. 'The best thing we can do is 'phone the police and get them to remove him.'

'Why the police?' the commissionaire demanded stoutly. 'Leave it to me, sir—I'll be only too happy to chuck him out.'

'No,' said Hirsch, 'we'll do things properly. I'm thinking of charging him with trespassing.'

'And obscene behaviour,' Gisela put in.

The youth looked impressed despite himself. 'Listen,' he protested, 'what is all this? It was the girl who picked me up and brought me here—she even said something about paying me.'

'Better still,' Hirsch said. 'If that's true, it lays you open to a charge of male prostitution. You can go to gaol for that.'

The youth stared round in bewilderment. His position, which he was quite incapable of assessing logically, seemed to be becoming increasingly embarrassing and precarious.

'Well?' Gisela demanded. 'Who shall I notify first, our solicitor or the police?'

Karen's pick-up blustered and protested his innocence for a minute or two longer, but finally subsided into pleas for understanding and forbearance.

Martin Hirsch dictated an impromptu statement to Gisela Wandel in which the undersigned apologized for having disturbed the smooth running of the *Hotel Drei Kronen* in such a grossly inconsiderate manner. In return for this sincere expression of regret, the management would refrain from taking any legal action. Thankfully, the boy scribbled his signature at the foot of the sheet and made a hasty exit.

'I owe you a debt of gratitude,' Hirsch told Gisela when they were alone again.

163

Gisela said simply: ' If it's all right with you, I'll take you up to Fräulein Kerze now.'

They found Karcn waiting for them in Room 117. She was looking bored and subdued, but Gisela Wandel's eyes lit up when she saw that there was a registration form lying beside her on the pale-green quilt.

' All right, let's go,' Hirsch said. ' Your father's waiting for you. We got rid of your young man, by the way. What on earth made you pick on a bird-brained lout like that? '

Karen shrugged indifferently. ' If your needs are basic enough you don't bother about refinements.'

' Don't be an idiot! ' snapped Hirsch.

' May I draw your attention to something? ' Gisela interposed. ' Fräulein Kerze seems to be in possession of her registration form.'

Hirsch looked surprised. ' Is that so? ' He turned to Karen. ' How did you get hold of it? '

' I imagine one of the staff must have got it for her,' Gisela said, glancing significantly at Hirsch.

' Is this true? ' Hirsch picked up the form and studied it with mounting interest. ' Who was it, Karen? '

' Someone or other,' Karen said petulantly, '—that impudent creature Paul, if you must know.'

' This is splendid.' Hirsch eyed the slip of paper reverently, fully aware of its implications. Paul, the unwelcome snooper, had shot his bolt. What Hirsch was holding in his hand constituted clear legal grounds for dismissal.

' That ought to do the trick,' Gisela Wandel said.

Hirsch nodded gratefully. ' I won't be long,' he replied, and hurried out of the room with a look of anticipation.

' It was a deliberate trap, that's what it was! ' Paul fumed.

' I'm only interested in facts,' Hirsch said. ' You filched a registration form from the reception desk.'

' I didn't filch it,' Paul whined, ' I borrowed it for a guest.'

' Oh yes? And how much did she pay you? '

It dawned on Paul that he had lost the game, if not the rubber. Hirsch held the whip-hand. He had been caught fair and square, and there was ample evidence to back up the charge.

'It's a put-up job,' he burst out furiously. 'You laid a trap for me just because I know too much—because I've seen too much. It's a dirty rotten trick!'

'You're wrong,' Hirsch said quietly. 'It's a reward for your dirty rotten behaviour in the past.'

Paul turned on his heel and walked out without a word, without a parting flourish and without sparing Hirsch another glance. He even omitted to slam the door.

Hirsch interpreted Paul's behaviour as an unmistakable threat. Although he had not anticipated any other reaction, he decided to take out a little insurance in the form of three telephone calls.

The first was to Gisela Wandel, who was still upstairs with Karen in Room 117, as instructed. He told Gisela to make a detailed summary of the circumstances surrounding the purloining of the registration form, and to file it with statements from Karen and the chief receptionist. He further requested the presence in his office of Herr Lehmgruber, together with an up-to-date record of what he owed the hotel.

Hirsch's second call was to the managing director's office at the Stabilator works. Hirsch informed Kerze that Karen had returned to the hotel and was ready to come home. If Kerze agreed, he would drive her back personally, thereby bringing an unpleasant episode to what he hoped was a satisfactory conclusion.

Willy Kerze's tone was relieved and appreciative. He invited Hirsch to join him at home for what he described as a modest evening meal, *en famille*. Councillor Bartosch would also be present, if Hirsch had no objection. Hirsch announced that he would be delighted to accept.

Finally, Hirsch called Conrad Gisenius. After inquiring if there had been any new developments in the Meiners case and receiving a polite answer in the negative, he asked whether Gisenius was still interested in Lehmgruber. This query elicited a cautious affirmative, qualified by the words 'under certain circumstances'. Hirsch informed Gisenius that financial considerations required him to put pressure on the said Lehmgruber, which meant that he would almost certainly be in urgent need of money—about five hundred marks, to be more precise. The lawyer's response was positively enthusiastic. 'Send him along by all means, and thanks for the tip!'

'I'm not particularly interested,' Gisenius declared, leaning back in his chair. 'What have you got to offer?—Vague allegations, I suppose, but what's the good of vague allegations? I haven't the least intention of indulging in unwarranted slander. My sole concern is to further the ends of justice.'

'Conclusive evidence,' Lehmgruber said eagerly, '—that's what I'm offering you.'

A look devoid of illusion passed between the two men in Gisenius's office—an experienced politician endowed with legal ability, and an international frontier-jumper who knew the tricks of his trade: two dealers in the spirit of their age.

'Where do the dossiers come from?' Gisenius asked, stifling a yawn.

'They were compiled from reliable sources,' Lehmgruber assured him. 'It's not just hearsay. There are some very interesting items of evidence—receipts, photostat letters, affidavits and so on.'

Gisenius decided to cut the proceedings short. The plum was ripe for plucking. 'Show me them.'

'You want to buy my material, then? What are you prepared to offer?'

'I never buy a pig in a poke,' Gisenius said curtly. 'I'll look through your dossiers and name my own price.'

Lehmgruber nodded, conscious that the game of blind-man's-buff was over. He opened his not unduly bulky brief-case with an almost ceremonious air and quickly flicked through the contents. Finally, he withdrew five slim files and proffered them to Gisenius with a little bow.

'Five cases, all from your area.'

Gisenius took the files, placed them on the desk in front of him and opened the top one. Running a careful eye over the papers inside, he at once recognized their probable source of origin. They almost certainly derived from the East German State Security Service. Gisenius knew this because he had seen similar documents in the hands of officials of the West German State Security Service, with whom he worked from time to time.

'All originals or certified copies, as you can see,' Lehm-

166

gruber affirmed, watching Gisenius hopefully. 'They came into my hands quite by chance, but I'm prepared to let you have them.'

Gisenius said nothing, but lowered his head again and thumbed through the papers in silent concentration. They were all Lehmgruber claimed. The evidence was damning and complete. Some of it was already familiar to him, at least in outline.

The first dossier concerned a minister in the provincial coalition government and contained a detailed and fully-documented list of facts: the purchase of real estate at a suspiciously favourable price; a series of government contracts awarded to a firm whose board of directors included the minister's son-in-law; regular increments in the said son-in-law's salary immediately after the placing of each contract; large discrepancies between donations accepted on behalf of a certain political party and the actual sums credited to its account; the purchase of an allegedly second-hand car for about thirty per cent of its current list price. The final and most important factor from Gisenius's point of view was that the minister was not a member of his party.

The second and third dossiers referred, respectively, to a provincial councillor who belonged to his own party and a member of the Federal Parliament. The transgressions listed were of the sort that often recurred among public servants, e.g., malpractice, embezzlement of public funds, deliberate misinformation and purloining of official documents. Finally, there was evidence that they were in contact with the East— a particularly damning point, in Gisenius's opinion, but hardly sensational.

The fourth dossier concerned the editor-in-chief of a Rheine-Bergen newspaper and laid a whole series of revolting misdemeanours at his door. What made this all the more interesting was that he frequently indulged in biased, scornful and derogatory comments on sundry political figures of Gisenius's acquaintance. The dossier, which painted him as a brazen libertine and a seducer of under-age girls, contained two photographs, seven names and addresses and four affidavits —easily worth a thousand marks by themselves, Gisenius calculated.

He faltered when he read the name that leapt out at him

from the cover of the fifth file. He read it several times, but it refused to disappear. The name was that of Bartosch, Johannes Bartosch, Councillor Bartosch, strong right arm of the provincial president, darling of the authorities, confidant of senior diplomats, future son-in-law of Willy Kerze—and an almost ideal subject for prosecution under Paragraph 175 of the Penal Code, subtitled ' Homosexual Offences '.

Gisenius closed the last file with a decisive snap which conveyed total indifference. He stacked the dossiers carefully on top of each other and looked across at Lehmgruber with pale-blue, expressionless eyes. ' Quite interesting,' he said finally. ' I'll give you five hundred marks for the lot.'

' Oh, come! ' Lehmgruber looked shocked. ' I'd counted on a thousand at the very least.'

' I never haggle.' Safe in the knowledge that Lehmgruber needed money urgently, Gisenius felt confident of success. Five hundred marks would be riches to Lehmgruber in his present predicament, so why pay more than was absolutely necessary?

Lehmgruber capitulated. ' All right,' he said, looking beaten. ' Done. Five hundred for these five and an additional five hundred for the sixth.' He paused. '—Yours, Herr Gisenius.'

' You're insane.' The lawyer's eyes had become glacial. ' There can't be a dossier on me. My conduct has been absolutely above reproach. I've never violated any law currently in force. If there really is such a file it must be forged.'

' Quite possibly,' Lehmgruber conceded with a sly smile, savouring the thought that, at long last, he could afford to behave with a touch of condescension. ' But can't a fake dossier containing forged evidence prove just as dangerous as a genuine one, under the right circumstances? Think it over, and take your time. In any case, I didn't bring your file with me—it's tucked away somewhere safe. Just pay me five hundred for a start. The rest can follow in due course.'

' I'd like to have a talk with you,' Tantau said meekly. ' It's in your own best interests.'

' I decide what my best interests are,' the man retorted.

Tantau gave a melancholy smile. 'Ah, if only we all could, but we can't, I'm afraid.'

'Go away and stop wasting my time,' the man said contemptuously.

'You didn't mind wasting time in the *Café de Paris* the other night, did you?'

Tantau had picked up the man's scent without excessive difficulty, and now he was face to face with him. The only trouble was, his name wasn't Meiners but Siegert.

They were standing in a shabby bed-sitting-room, long and narrow like a section of underground railway. It was scantily furnished, and such personal effects as were visible —articles of clothing, eating utensils and a few technical books —showed signs of long and intensive use. It was more a cave than a room, and one which bore witness to long years of loveless occupation.

'The other night,' Tantau pursued, 'you drank a considerable quantity of beer and schnapps in the *Café de Paris*.'

'So what?' the man demanded belligerently. 'Whose business is it if I did? I got drunk, and I had a bloody good reason for getting drunk. It's not a crime, is it?'

Tantau's voice remained unvaryingly mild and patient. 'You left by the back door.'

'Yes, I did. Some bloody fool came up and started talking to me. I didn't feel like company. It made my gorge rise. Now get out—unless you're saying I didn't pay for my drinks? Is that why you're here?'

'Did you pay for your drinks?' Tantau inquired with gentle insistence.

'Yes I bloody well did, after each round—and I tipped the waiter, too.'

Tantau studied the man who called himself Siegert. He compared the face before him with the face of a man called Meiners, whom he only knew from a photograph. There was an undeniable resemblance, but that meant little.

'Let's assume there's been a mistake,' Tantau said cautiously.

'Assume anything you like, but push off!'

'Does the name Michael Meiners mean anything to you?'

'You're getting on my nerves!' shouted the man who called himself Siegert.

To Tantau, this statement carried the ring of truth. Siegert had blurted it out without a moment's hesitation—not that it was incontrovertible evidence that his name was not Michael Meiners. Undeterred, Tantau asked: 'How did you enjoy the Building Exhibition?'

'Why should I be interested in that crap?' Siegert demanded rudely. 'I work for the municipal cleansing department—on the administrative side,' he added.

'Since when?'

'I've worked there for years. And now get out of here before I do you an injury. All I can tell you is, I paid for my drinks, and if anyone says different, I'll bust his face in for him.'

'One last question,' Tantau said. 'Have you taken the bus to Rheine-Bergen from Babenberg recently?'

'Hop it!' Siegert yelled. 'I always travel by train—on principle!'

'You're the ideal driver for a detective,' Tantau said appreciatively. 'You're patient, you're reliable, and you don't ask questions.'

'If you say so,' Bennicken replied, laconic as ever.

'Stop at the next public call-box,' Tantau said.

Bennicken drove on down Kaiserstrasse to the corner of Parkallee, where he pulled up. 'Over there,' he said, jerking a thumb.

Tantau did not get out at once. He reached into his briefcase and extracted a picture of Schulz's section. It was one of three prints which he had taken the precaution of obtaining.

'Take a look at that.'

'I've seen it,' Bennicken said after a brief glance.

'You've hardly changed at all,' Tantau remarked, 'but then men with strong personalities seldom do.' His attempt at a winning smile made no impression on Bennicken, but he was not disheartened. Instead, he tapped one of the figures in the group with his forefinger. 'I can't say I'd have recognized Herr Gisenius.'

'That,' Bennicken said, 'is Frammler.'

'Ah.' Tantau's eyes narrowed slightly, a symptom of satisfaction. 'So that's Frammler.'

He got out and walked over to the 'phone booth, where

he flipped open the directory at 'F' and looked down the rows of names. A brief check showed that there was only one Frammler in the book. Tantau was not smiling now, and his expression remained unaltered even when he noted the unusual profession of the new man on his list.

The next five minutes were devoted to a telephone call to the personnel manager of the municipal cleansing department.

'To the petrol station,' he said, when he had rejoined Bennicken in the taxi.

'Which one?'

'The first one that occurs to you.'

'Schulz's, then,' Bennicken said tersely, treading on the gas.

'A loving father and a devoted friend communing together in perfect harmony,' said Karen Kerze. 'What a touching sight! It gladdens my heart.'

She defiantly slipped her arm through that of Johannes Bartosch and descended the stairs leading into the drawing-room of the Villa Kerze, where her father and Hirsch were sitting over their after-dinner brandy.

'You sound cheerful tonight,' Willy Kerze called jovially. 'That's what I like to see!'

Bartosch gave a graceful bow. 'Your daughter wishes to make an announcement—a pleasant announcement, I venture to hope.'

Karen stared past her father at Martin Hirsch. 'We're getting engaged.' She spoke as if she were proclaiming her intention of buying a new pair of shoes.

'Is this true?' Kerze demanded.

'Subject to your consent,' Bartosch said with a diplomatic smile. 'Please don't think we're in any way taking your approval for granted.'

Kerze feigned boundless amazement.

'Did I hear correctly?' He shot a brief but triumphant glance at Hirsch, who was refilling his glass. 'Are you serious about this?'

'I venture to say we are,' Bartosch replied.

'In that case, accept my heartiest congratulations!' cried Hirsch, draining his glass.

Kerze made a righteous endeavour to play the solicitous

parent. 'Are you fully aware of the significance of the step you're taking? You realize that this is the most momentous decision of your lives?'

Bartosch cocked his head a little on one side and regarded Karen with an air of possessive pride. Then he looked back at Kerze and said, with disarming candour: 'Speaking for myself, sir, I've carefully weighed my decision. It's the fruit of long consideration. That's why I trust you won't take it amiss if I officially request the hand of your daughter in marriage.'

Kerze gave a portentous nod. He had been picturing this scene for days and now that it had arrived he was delighted to find that it entirely matched his expectations.

'Karen,' he said in measured tones, 'my dear girl—you know how much your happiness means to me. Tell me in all sincerity: is this what you want?'

'Of course,' Karen said a trifle impatiently, still looking at Hirsch.

'In that case,' Kerze declared solemnly, 'who am I to stand in the way of your happiness?' He extended his arms in a dramatic gesture. 'My children! My dear, dear children!'

As protocol demanded on such occasions, Karen was the first to embrace him. She laid her burning cheek against her father's, looking over his shoulder at Martin Hirsch with wide, inquiring eyes. Hirsch regarded her sorrowfully but said nothing.

Johannes Bartosch was next in line for Kerze's paternal embrace. He too caught Hirsch's eye, but only because his rather constricted position left him no alternative. He survived Kerze's bear-like hug and Hirsch's coolly appraising stare with equal fortitude, confident that he had embarked upon one of the most propitious ventures in a promising career.

'I can't tell you how delighted I am, sir,' he assured Kerze.

'I think we understand one another,' Kerze replied.

Leaving the other two immersed in mutual congratulation, Karen walked over to Hirsch. She halted when their faces were only a few inches apart. 'One word from you, Martin,' she whispered imploringly, 'and I'll blow the whole thing sky-high.'

'You're wasting your breath. I'm not getting mixed up in your crazy schemes. If you don't know what you want, why should I make up your mind for you?'

'Just tell me you love me and I'll come with you.'

Hirsch frowned. 'I don't love you, but you can come with me anyway if you like. No conditions, though. One piece of stupidity doesn't cancel out another.'

'You're like all the rest of them!' Karen burst out wildly. 'All you can do is talk, talk, talk! I give up!'

'It never fails to amaze me how mistaken people can be,' Tantau remarked.

'You may be right,' Schulz conceded. 'I'm not well up on these things, but I suppose you've had a lot of experience.'

'I have indeed, some of it entertaining but most of it bitter. I've more than once seen witnesses take the oath conscientiously and then give evidence which bore no relation to the truth.'

'I can well believe it,' Schulz said gravely. 'But what's the answer? If people think about things for long enough they become convinced of them. What is the whole truth and nothing but the truth, anyway? I've often wondered.'

Tantau leant against a petrol-pump and regarded Schulz with mounting approval. The man appeared to be a decent, honest specimen of contemporary humanity, even if his naivety might have its dangerous side.

'Where were you when you thought you saw this man Meiners?'

Schulz did his best to describe the incident in a few concise sentences. He pointed out his own position and that of the bus and then, at Tantau's request, gave an objective account of weather conditions and visibility. Meanwhile, Bennicken slouched in his taxi looking manifestly indifferent to the whole proceedings.

'I'm not being a nuisance, I hope?' Tantau asked finally.

'Of course not.' Schulz looked genuinely surprised. 'If you're trying to help us, why shouldn't I give you all the help I can?'

Tantau put a hand on Schulz's arm and drew him aside, away from Bennicken, the petrol-pumps and the curious stares of his garage-hands. Looking Schulz in the eye, he

173

asked: 'Are you absolutely convinced that it was Michael Meiners you saw?'

'I was at the time, but I'll admit I may have made a mistake.'

'You can't say for certain?'

'No,' Schulz said, feeling a little helpless. He wanted to be helpful but he didn't know how.

'As far as I've been able to ascertain,' Tantau said, 'Michael Meiners has been seen three times so far: once at a petrol-station, i.e. by you, Herr Schulz; once at the Building Exhibition by—who was it again?'

'Kerze,' Schulz amplified, 'Willy Kerze.'

'Correct,' said Tantau, his eyes narrowing slightly. 'And a third time in the *Café de Paris* by Herr Hirsch. However, these three incidents don't hang together. I've already traced the man in the *Café de Paris*—it wasn't particularly difficult. Unfortunately, he isn't the man who was seen here at the petrol-station, nor the one who visited the Building Exhibition.'

Schulz looked dumbfounded. 'But that's extraordinary!'

'I know,' Tantau mused. 'There's been a mistake somewhere.'

'I'd greatly appreciate a look at your list of employees,' Tantau said courteously. 'Could that be arranged?'

'I'm only too happy to be of assistance, of course,' the manager of the *Café de Paris* assured him, even more courteously, 'but I'm afraid our books are confidential.'

Tantau's voice took on a note of quiet menace. 'As you're fully aware, sir, I'm conducting some inquiries here at Herr Hirsch's request and on his behalf. It was his personal wish and that of Herr Gisenius that I should be called in. Are you proposing to obstruct my activities here, and if so why?'

The manager blushed. 'Of course not! Please don't misunderstand me. I'll get you the personnel file at once.'

Tantau watched him as he scurried off, reflecting sadly that most people had something to hide.

The *Café de Paris* was only moderately full. On stage, Marlene and the band were making noises appropriate to the early hour. The body of the auditorium was occupied by a few scattered couples and three prematurely merry gentlemen

174

seated at a table on their own. A number of depressed-looking waiters hovered round them.

The manager hurried up carrying a file in his hand. He placed it in front of Tantau and inquired politely if he required anything. ' A beer, a double schnapps, and a chat with a man named Quahnke,' Tantau replied.

The manager bowed and pattered off again. Tantau opened the file and found what he had expected: a list of the staff, complete with their home addresses. Their occupations covered the range common to such establishments: office staff, kitchen staff, barman, cloakroom attendant, bouncer, waiters, cigarette-girl, band, singer, artistes.

' You wished to speak to me? '

Tantau looked up to find Quahnke standing beside him with an obsequious smile on his tragedian's face. He seemed disposed to be polite. At least it would facilitate the opening stages of an interview which might turn out to have its embarrassing moments.

' Please sit down.'

Quahnke obediently complied. His manner was deferential, but his eyes regarded the shabby little man who had struck such evident terror into the manager with faint amusement. What, he asked himself, was a gauche, inartistic, impoverished-looking creature like this doing in a night-club?

' A man sits alone at a table,' Tantau said. ' He drinks nine beers and nine double schnapps. Why? '

' To get drunk, I suppose.'

' And why should he want to get drunk? '

' Anger, sorrow, habit—who knows? There's usually a woman at the bottom of it.'

' True,' Tantau agreed. ' It might, of course, be due to a number of other reasons—business worries, melancholia, illness, mental instability—but seventy to eighty per cent of all abnormal behaviour is attributable to so-called affairs of the heart.'

' In a place like this—ninety-nine per cent.'

Tantau smiled. ' So the man sits here drinking and staring into space. But he doesn't sit just anywhere—he parks himself at this very table, where he has a view of the whole room. Why? '

Quahnke tried to look co-operative, but he couldn't alto-

175

gether conceal his surprise at what he deemed to be a thoroughly pointless conversation. 'Well, perhaps so that he can watch the woman in the case.'

'Perhaps. Let's assume you're right. Now there are two categories of women in this place, guests and members of the staff. It's the last category I'd like to examine more closely.' Tantau started to read through the staff list. He did so with meticulous care, while Quahnke sat and fidgeted.

'There appear to be eight female employees,' Tantau said finally, 'the manager's secretary, the cook, a hat-check girl, a cigarette-girl, a barmaid, a singer and two dancers. Have I missed anyone out?'

Quahnke bowed his leonine head in thought. 'No, that's the lot. Do you want to interview each one individually?'

'Good gracious, no!' Tantau exclaimed. 'Even my yearning for female companionship has its limits. For the time being, I'd just like a little chat with you about them. Let's start with the secretary.'

As Tantau had anticipated, Quahnke proved to be such a mine of information that it was not long before the majority of the female employees could be banished from further consideration.

'What about the singer, Marlene Sonnenberg?' Tantau inquired, eyes twinkling. 'She's a friend of the management, I suppose?'

'You're absolutely right,' replied Quahnke, 'except for one detail: the woman can't sing.' He frowned. 'But how do you know all these intimate details?'

'I can read,' Tantau said modestly. He omitted to explain that he possessed an excellent memory and had noted that Marlene Sonnenberg's address was identical with Karl Schulz's. 'Do go on, though. What about—' he consulted the list again '—Brigitte?'

'Brigitte is the solo dancer here—a personal discovery of mine.'

'Ah!' said Tantau.

'Please don't jump to any conclusions!' Quahnke said quickly. 'The young lady has—how shall I put it? —friends in high places. Please don't press me for details, though. My natural discretion wouldn't permit me to answer.'

Tantau refrained from putting Quahnke's discretion to the

test, at least for the moment. All he said was: ' Please send the cigarette-girl across, and tell the manager to come and see me in ten minutes' time.'

' Certainly.' Quahnke retired without further comment. His brief interview with Tantau had been enough to inspire him with grudging respect for the curious little man.

' Cigars or cigarettes, sir? '

Scrutinizing the girl closely, Tantau noted that her figure was good but her skin a little coarse and unhealthy-looking. She had a sweet, rather vacuous face. He guessed her to be about thirty.

' Tell me,' Tantau asked casually, ' what have you been doing to poor Herr Siegert? '

' Oh, him! ' the girl said irritably. ' I wish he'd lay off me. Did he send you? Are you his father? '

' God forbid,' Tantau replied. ' How long have you known him? '

' Years.' The girl grimaced. ' He goes on chasing me, but he's not my type—not any more. Anyway, what's it got to do with you? '

' I'm acting on the management's behalf, as you're probably aware. Our attention has been drawn to your friend's behaviour.'

' I couldn't care less what he's been doing.'

Tantau smiled. ' He's hardly congenial company, I must admit. I've already made his acquaintance, though not as thoroughly as I should like. Please tell me a little more about him—and be as frank as possible.'

' Not a care in the world—that's you,' Martin Hirsch said. ' I envy you, Karl. You obviously find life pretty uncomplicated.'

Schulz grinned self-consciously. ' Maybe I'm a bit dense. They say it simplifies things.'

' Nonsense! It's the people who think they're clever who are the fools.'

Hirsch had arrived at Schulz's flat late in the evening. He found him alone. Eva was at the cinema and Marlene Sonnenberg, Schulz's lodger and current interest in life, was at the *Café de Paris*. Thrown back on his own resources, Schulz was conscientiously improving his mind by reading a newspaper which Gisenius had recommended for his edification.

'Shouldn't Eva be home by now?' Hirsch inquired.

Schulz shook his head. 'It's one of these spectaculars. They usually last longer.'

'You're not worried?'

'Why should I be?' Schulz gave a complacent laugh. 'The cinema's only on the next corner, and she's not a child any longer.'

'Glad to hear you admit it,' Hirsch said promptly. 'She's getting quite grown-up these days, don't you think so?'

'She certainly seems to be.' As always, Schulz swelled with pride when he spoke of his sister. 'Funnily enough, I've found her particularly grown-up in the past week or so.'

Hirsch raised his glass to Schulz and drank, taking his time.

'You know,' he said suddenly, 'I've lived a pretty easy-going sort of life. I've had a lot of fun, one way and another, but the sands are running out.'

'Stop talking as if you had one foot in the grave,' Schulz chaffed. 'You've got years ahead of you. You're not forty yet.'

'Thirty-eight,' Hirsch said, '—and I feel like an old man sometimes.'

'Come off it! You're in your prime. Any girl who gets you can congratulate herself.'

'You mean that?'

'Of course I do.'

'I'm happy to hear it.'

'What do you mean?'

'Well,' Hirsch said, 'I've been doing some serious thinking recently—about myself and the way I live—and I've come to the conclusion that it's time for a change.'

'Go on.'

'The long and the short of it is, I want to get married.'

Karl Schulz's blue eyes widened. He crouched a little in his chair like a big dog about to spring. 'Who to?' he asked tensely.

Hirsch did not hesitate. 'Your sister.'

Schulz sat there for several seconds, his brows furrowed in thought. Then he drew a deep breath and stood up. Hirsch

178

followed suit, resigning himself to the idea that his friend was about to knock him down.

'Martin,' he said at last, breathing heavily, ' I'm delighted, absolutely delighted.'

They were slapping each other on the back when Hirsch sensed a sudden stiffening in Schulz's manner.

' What about Eva? ' Schulz demanded, looking at him searchingly. ' Have you done any—' he paused, embarrassed, '—any spade-work in advance? '

' No,' Hirsch said gravely, ' Eva doesn't know anything about it yet.'

Schulz scratched his head. ' Well, that's very gentlemanly of you, Martin, but isn't it a bit unwise? '

' You don't think I'd go behind your back, do you? '

' No, no—it's very decent of you.' Schulz smiled. ' Anyway, I've no objections . . .'

' That's the main thing.'

' Well, not exactly. It's my sister you want to marry, not me.'

' But I have your consent? '

' And my blessing, provided Eva'll have you—not that there's any reason why she shouldn't.'

Hirsch smiled confidently. ' I hope not.'

' But get one thing straight, old friend: no more womanizing for you from now on. You've sowed your last wild oat.'

' Agreed! ' Hirsch gaily extended his hand and Schulz wrung it until it hurt. ' You know what? ' he went on, massaging his fingers, ' We ought to crack a bottle of champagne to mark the occasion.'

' We ought,' Schulz agreed, ' but I'm afraid I don't keep any on the premises.'

' In that case, I've got a suggestion to make. The film must be just about over, so let's go and meet Eva. Afterwards we can all go over to my place and have a chat over a bottle of champagne. How does that strike you? '

' You're in a hurry, aren't you? ' Schulz said with a wink.

They left the flat, clattered down the stairs and emerged into the darkened street, laughing as they went. They strolled along to the corner. The street-lamps shed a friendly glow on the asphalt, but the cinema entrance was in semi-darkness.

'Hello!' Hirsch exclaimed with a trace of surprise. 'Is the show over already?'

'Not a bit of it,' Schulz declared. 'They're just cutting down on electricity. I know the owner. He buys his petrol from me, and he's an old skinflint. He always douses the lights before time.'

'I hope you're right, Karl.'

The nearer they got, the more apparent it became that Schulz was wrong. The foyer and exterior lights had been extinguished, and a small, portly man was in the process of pulling a steel grille across the swing doors. A full-busted screen idol smiled inanely down on them from the poster above the entrance, the gloom of night finally settling upon her mascara-rimmed eyes.

Schulz walked up to the plump man with Hirsch at his heels and asked: 'Finished for the day?'

'They came out half an hour ago.'

'No one left inside?'

'The cinema's empty. Looking for your sister, Herr Schulz?'

'Not exactly.' Schulz had no intention of giving any outsider an insight into his private life. 'I just happened to be passing. Have you seen her, by any chance?'

'I'll say,' the fat man replied. 'A pretty girl like your sister, Herr Schulz? She's the sort you look at twice.'

'Ah well,' Schulz said with laborious unconcern. 'I expect she's gone for a stroll.'

'I don't blame her,' the fat man replied gallantly. 'It makes you want to be young again, a lovely spring night like this. The air's like milk, and what's nicer than a spot of courting?'

'Than a spot of what?' Schulz growled.

'I'm sorry!' the fat man said, retreating a step. 'Forget what I said—I may be wrong, anyway, but the young man your sister was with looks a very nice young chap, very nice indeed.'

'Come on,' Hirsch urged, taking his friend's arm and propelling him gently down the steps. Schulz complied, looking slightly dazed. 'I didn't know a thing about it, Martin,' he murmured, 'I swear I didn't.'

'It may not mean anything,' Hirsch said. 'Perhaps she bumped into an old school friend.'

'I doubt it,' Schulz said stubbornly. He brooded in silence for a moment or two, and when he next spoke his voice had taken on a belligerent note. 'She can't do this to me! Vanishing into the night with some fellow or other—who does she think she is!'

'Let's take a walk round the block,' Hirsch suggested. 'Don't worry, she'll be back.'

'No,' Schulz said ominously, 'this is my affair. I'd prefer to handle it myself, if you don't mind. Please go home now. I'll let you know what happens tomorrow—if there's anything to tell.'

Hirsch, who was sitting behind his desk when Tantau entered, tried to muster a smile for the benefit of his belated visitor.

'I never fail to be fascinated by the hotel business,' Tantau said.

'Your enthusiasm seems to have unfortunate results. My secretary tells me you managed to create an uproar in the *Café de Paris* this evening.'

'I wouldn't go so far as to say that,' Tantau replied modestly.

'Herr Tantau,' said Hirsch, 'I hope you haven't forgotten your terms of employment.'

'Far from it,' Tantau assured him. 'In any case, you're to blame for my being here. I'm here because I'm intrigued by you. A few years ago, when I was working for a firm of inquiry agents in Frankfurt—just for my own amusement, of course—I was sent to Rheine-Bergen on a job.'

'Don't remind me! You turned the hotel upside down. Worse still, you annoyed my guests so much that they started leaving in droves.'

'A couple of your guests were given the choice between prosecution and departure, and they chose what they considered to be the lesser of two evils. However, the assignment cost me my job because Europa Hotels lodged a complaint with my employers, and I was dismissed.'

'I'm sorry,' Hirsch said.

'I was dismissed,' Tantau continued cheerfully, 'so I retired to a little village some kilometres from Rheine-Bergen. I like it there. In fact, I intend to spend the rest of my days there, keeping the wolf from the door by taking the occasional job.' He gave a quick, goblin smile. 'But I'm digressing. The immediate reason why my employers in Frankfurt fired me was a report on my activities from the manager of the *Hotel Drei Kronen*—in other words, from you, Herr Hirsch.'

' I know,' Hirsch said with genuine regret, ' but I didn't mean to get you sacked.'

' I read your report at the time, and I must confess that it was first-rate—from a purely objective point of view. It was articulate, excellently thought out and convincingly put. And that, Herr Hirsch, is why your present attitude intrigues me so much.'

' As far as I'm aware,' Hirsch interposed, ' your job is to find a man called Michael Meiners. Have you found him yet?'

' You mean,' Tantau corrected him gently, ' my job is to find a man whom various persons—yourself included—have identified as Michael Meiners.'

' Isn't that the same thing? '

Tantau stroked his chin. ' I'm afraid not.'

Hirsch looked disconcerted. ' What do you mean? Do you distrust me? '

' Not you, necessarily, but your powers of observation. That's what worries me a little. Allow me to explain. Do you know how I'd sum up the little group of interested parties to which you belong? A peculiar combination—solid citizens all, some of them influential and others merely respectable, but a peculiar combination for all that. Three of them think they've seen Meiners. It is three, isn't it? '

' Yes,' Hirsch said warily.

' Let's take a closer look at them. First, Herr Schulz: an honest man, I'd say—simple, upright and trustworthy. Then there's Herr Kerze: an efficient business man, determined and a trifle impulsive. Finally, there's you, Herr Hirsch, the least prejudiced of the three, sceptical by nature, prone to cynicism and utterly realistic. This being so, I ask myself: why should you of all people have made a mistake unless you wanted to make one? Don't you see what I'm driving at? '

Hirsch frowned and shook his head. ' I haven't a clue.'

' Do I have to spell it out for you? ' Tantau blinked in apparent bewilderment. ' What I mean is: if you, of all people, make a mistake, you must have some very special reason for doing so. To be blunt, your mistake may have been deliberate. Now do you understand? '

' Even less than before.'

' I'll try to explain. You allege that you saw Michael Meiners—you even tell your friends about it. Now it so happens that the man you saw is called Siegert. He works for the municipal cleansing department and he's been living in Rheine-Bergen for years. In fact, he's visited the *Café de Paris* on several occasions. He's interested in your cigarette-girl.'

' I didn't know that.'

' But you insisted that he was Michael Meiners. Why? '

' Because I was convinced he was.'

' I beg leave to doubt that.' Tantau spoke with elaborate courtesy. ' I'm quite ready to accept that your motives for such a deception were valid, but you'll have to explain them —either to me or your friends. It's up to you, but you must make up your mind quickly. The man named Siegert—the man you identified as Meiners—is sitting in the *Black Cat* at this moment. You can go and take a look at him if you like, or you can inform your friends—or, alternatively, you can confide in me, either now or tomorrow, but no later please. The decision is yours.'

Shortly before midnight two telephone calls were made, each of which was to have certain repercussions. An attempt to reconstruct them at a later date elicited conflicting versions of what was said, although their actual content sounded reasonably innocuous.

First conversation: Hirsch to Gisenius

Time: 11.44 p.m.–11.46 p.m.

Hirsch: ' Gisenius? I've got something to tell you. It's urgent.'

Gisenius: 'I'm busy. What's on your mind? '

Hirsch: ' The man I thought was Meiners is in the *Black Cat* at this moment, so Tantau tells me. The only trouble is, he's not Meiners. His name appears to be Siegert.'

Gisenius: ' Thanks for calling me. I'll think it over.'

Second conversation: Gisenius to Frammler

Time: 11.47 p.m.–11.51 p.m.

Gisenius: 'Frammler? Something's come up. I need a competent man with an open mind.'

Frammler: 'That's me.'

Gisenius: 'I've just been told that the man Hirsch identified as Meiners is in the *Black Cat*. He goes by the name of Siegert, apparently. Like to take a closer look at him?'

Frammler: 'Would I! The *Black Cat* is just the place.'

Gisenius: 'Give Bennicken a ring. He can drive you there.'

Frammler: 'Good idea.'

Gisenius: 'Try to draw him out. He may have some reason for masquerading as Meiners. Someone may have put him up to it.'

Frammler: 'I'll worm it out of him, don't worry.'

'You can knock off now,' Frammler told the landlord of the *Black Cat*. 'It's closing time,' he added jovially.

'You must be joking,' the landlord protested. 'I don't close till one.'

'It's one now,' Frammler announced, tapping his wrist-watch, which read twelve-fifteen. 'You can turn this miserable-looking crew out into the street now—all except one, that is. I'll point him out to you.'

'Listen,' said the landlord, 'anything to oblige an old friend, but I need every pfennig I can squeeze out of this place.'

'Never mind that. It's closing time,' growled Bennicken, who was standing behind Frammler, looking as massive and powerful as a steamroller.

'You won't suffer,' Frammler said persuasively. 'I'll foot the bill for any loss of business. What's more, I'm going to swell your profits by giving a private party here.'

'That's different, of course,' the landlord replied. He hitched his shirt-sleeves an inch or two higher and made as if to spit on his palms.

Frammler checked him. 'Just a moment. Let's give your customers the once-over first.'

Frammler and Bennicken inspected the occupants of the bar, who ignored their scrutiny. Ten or a dozen customers still lingered in the smoke-filled parlour, seated at wooden tables which looked as if they had not been scrubbed for a twelvemonth. The walls around them, also faced with wood were hung with beer show-cards, pennants and group photographs. The *Black Cat* was the periodical rendezvous of drinking clubs such as ' The Jolly Farmers' and ' The Nature-Lovers '.

' That's him,' Bennicken said, raising his square jaw like a mastiff taking scent.

Frammler gave a low whistle of surprise. ' Well, I'm damned. He really does look like Meiners. He can't be, though.'

' We'll see,' said Bennicken.

Frammler nodded and turned to the landlord of the *Black Cat*. ' Now listen. Get rid of your customers. The only one who stays is the one we'll be sitting with. Licensing hours don't apply to him, understand? '

The landlord scowled. ' I hope you're not going to make trouble for me, Frammler,' he said. ' You're not up to any funny business, are you? '

' Get moving,' Frammler replied amiably. ' Or do I have to remind you of one or two little things? '

The landlord needed no further prompting. During the Occupation, he and the undertaker had collaborated on a number of joint ventures for which ' funny business ' was a comparatively mild description. Thanks to Frammler's black-market haulage service—for which his hearse provided an excellent front—the *Black Cat* had been kept well-supplied with liquor purloined from Allied military stores. Things like that put a man under an obligation.

Followed by Bennicken, Frammler made for the table in the corner. Like many fat men, he had incongruously small feet which seemed to twinkle as he walked. Bennicken, by contrast, stalked along ponderously as though wading through an invisible snow-drift. They sat down on either side of their quarry. He certainly bore a resemblance to Michael Meiners, though his pale face and melancholy expression might have been occasioned by the quantities of beer and schnapps with which he had evidently been plying himself.

' You don't mind, do you? ' Frammler asked, when he was safely ensconced.

The man hardly bothered to look up. His attention was centred exclusively on the half-empty glasses in front of him.

185

'What did he say?' inquired Bennicken.

Frammler chuckled. 'He says we're very welcome. He's extraordinarily pleased to make our acquaintance, and he's itching to have a chat with us.'

Bennicken nodded indulgently. 'Why not?'

The man's pale-blue eyes suddenly focused on his visitors with a look of surprise and annoyance. 'What do you want?' he demanded, stumbling over the words.

Frammler stared at him closely for a moment, then bowed and said: 'Allow me to introduce myself. Ludwig Frammler's the name.'

The man drained his beer. 'So what?'

'And this gentleman here,' Frammler continued in dulcet tones, 'is Herr Bennicken.'

'Yes,' Bennicken rasped, 'that's me.'

'Why don't you bugger off?' the man said scornfully. He picked up his schnapps glass and drained that too. 'Landlord!' he called hoarsely. 'The same again!'

Frammler sat back in his chair, and his little porcine eyes began to gleam. Bennicken also eased his frame an inch or two backwards, and the chair on which he sat groaned at every joint. The brief glance that flashed between the two men was enough to reassure them that they were at one. It was just like the old days.

Frammler inspected the bar-parlour. As he had anticipated, the landlord had done his work well. All the other customers had disappeared except two, and they were already making for the door. An acrid stench of stale beer and spirits filled the room, and the air was still thick with drifting clouds of tobacco-smoke.

'Bring our friend whatever he wants,' Frammler told the landlord briefly. 'A little pick-me-up won't do him any harm.'

'Find a table of your own,' the man mumbled. He was too drunk to notice the abrupt change in the atmosphere. 'There's enough room now, God knows.'

'Not very friendly, is he?' Frammler remarked.

'Give him time,' said Bennicken.

The landlord brought the beer and the double schnapps and set them on the table in front of the man, together with two heavy beer-mugs and two large bottles of Dortmund export beer—a beverage which Frammler always favoured when transacting business of a special nature.

'If I know you,' Frammler told the landlord, 'you'll be wanting to do your books now. Better go next door—no one'll disturb you there.'

'All right.' The landlord retired, only too happy to leave the three men alone. Glancing over his shoulder, he saw a scene of snug conviviality: three boon companions with their heads close together, apparently immersed in friendly discourse. One of them was pretty far gone, but the general atmosphere was harmonious—the landlord was ready to swear to that if called upon. He switched out a few lights before ducking behind the bar and vanishing into the adjoining room.

Frammler and Bennicken pulled their chairs still closer, effectively hemming Siegert in.

'You're after something, aren't you?' he muttered.

'You don't miss a thing,' Frammler said, looking amused. 'What's your name—Hawk-Eye?'

It slowly dawned on Siegert that he must try to pull himself together. 'What do you want, blast you?' he said, more violently this time.

Frammler folded his hands contentedly over his paunch. 'In the first place,' he said, 'we'd like to know your name. You evidently didn't notice that we introduced ourselves in a civilized way. The gentlemanly thing would be to return the compliment. Don't you care whether people think you're a gentleman or not? We're deeply hurt.'

'Deeply,' Bennicken confirmed.

'All right,' the man said in a tone of exasperation. 'My name's Siegert. Now push off and leave me in peace.'

'Did you hear that, Bennicken?' Frammler inquired, looking enchanted. 'Our friend's name is Siegert.'

Bennicken nodded. His grim nutcracker countenance registered satisfaction.

Frammler cocked his head on one side. 'You never use the name Meiners, I suppose?'

'Don't start all that bloody nonsense again!' Siegert shouted. 'I'm getting sick of people calling me that.'

'But you've been calling yourself Meiners, haven't you?'

'Have I hell!' Siegert made as if to rise. 'You can go and . . .'

'Steady!' Frammler reproved him. 'Kindly control yourself. You'll offend our sensibilities.'

Siegert had only moved a few inches when Bennicken struck. The taxi-driver scarcely moved the upper part of his body and his face remained expressionless, but his arms moved like pistons, swift, powerful and rhythmically precise. One of his palms caught Siegert on the back of the head and the other slammed against his face five or six times in succession. Siegert's head danced like a ball on a pintable.

'Help!' he gurgled. His face had turned paler than before and his eyes reflected the fear that had suddenly permeated his fuddled brain.

He opened his mouth again, and again Bennicken struck. This time the heel of his palm contacted the crown of Siegert's head with a noise like a muffled pistol-shot.

Siegert slumped in his chair, wide-eyed with astonishment. His head fell forward on to the table, knocking over his glass, and lay there motionless in a puddle of beer.

Frammler raised his eyebrows. 'You're in form.'

Bennicken said modestly, 'Nothing to it.' Reaching past the inert head, he delicately picked up Siegert's glass of schnapps, which had remained intact, and drained it.

'Just like the old days,' Frammler mused.

'Practice makes perfect.' Bennicken contentedly wiped the schnapps from his lips with the back of his hand. His eyes glinted.

'One small point,' the undertaker said. 'Please don't make a mess of his face. It's not just a question of æsthetics. Obvious signs of violence always give rise to awkward questions —I speak from experience.' He took a swig of beer. 'See if he's got any papers—a wallet or something.'

Bennicken took Siegert by the hair and pulled his head back. The man hung there, breathing stertorously with his mouth agape. Still holding him upright with one hand, Bennicken groped in the breast-pocket of his open jacket with the other and withdrew a battered black wallet.

'That'll do for the time being,' Frammler said. He deftly opened the wallet and removed the contents, item by item: an identity card, a pay-slip, a driving licence, two private letters, a few bank-notes and a small packet of visiting cards. He examined each in turn with close attention.

'There's nothing like a German for thoroughness,' he said contentedly. 'Nine-tenths of the people who pass through my hands carry full identification with them. It's in the blood. Running a funeral business in a country like ours is a pleasure, believe me!'

'Well?' Bennicken's tone did not betray undue curiosity. 'Is his name Siegert?'

Frammler nodded. 'Siegert it is. Works in the transport section of the municipal cleansing department. Been in Rheine-Bergen for three years. Lived somewhere in the Zone before that. Nothing in common with Meiners as far as I can see, except a certain resemblance to a sheep.'

'So what?'

'It's just what I expected,' Frammler said complacently. 'People ought to pay more attention to my advice.'

'Shall we leave him here?'

'Not so fast,' replied Frammler. 'We still haven't got an answer to the most important question of all. Why did he pass himself off as Meiners?'

'Did he?' Bennicken demanded.

A thoughtful look came into Frammler's eyes. 'Well, he let someone mistake him for Meiners. Why should he have done that? For fun? I doubt it. He must have had some definite object, but what could it have been?'

'Maybe Hirsch knows.'

'Bennicken,' Frammler said solemnly, 'take a good look at that man. Would you have mistaken him for Meiners?'

Bennicken picked up Siegert's head and examined it. 'Not on your life,' he said firmly.

'But Hirsch did,' Frammler observed. 'Or perhaps I should say, Hirsch acted as if he did.'

'You mean?' Bennicken's brows contracted. 'I don't believe it!'

'Wake him up,' Frammler said decisively, indicating Siegert. He massaged his hands as though putting on gloves. 'Come on, Bennicken. We don't want to be here all night.'

Bennicken picked up Frammler's beer-glass and projected the contents into Siegert's face with a brisk flick of the wrist. Siegert opened his eyes almost at once, but it obviously took him some moments to remember where he was, who was with him and what had been happening.

Frammler's manner was tolerant—considerate, even—and Bennicken did his best to emulate him. When Frammler smiled gently, Bennicken grinned broadly. They gave Siegert ten or fifteen seconds to recover.

'Why,' Frammler inquired mildly, 'did you masquerade as Michael Meiners?'

'I didn't,' Siegert replied with an effort, '—I swear I didn't. I don't know what this is all about.' Hastily, he added: 'I don't know anyone called Meiners. I've never heard of him, believe me I haven't.'

'He's not only impolite,' Frammler said, looking aggrieved, 'he's trying to lie to us. I don't like that at all. I don't expect you do either, my dear Bennicken. Am I right?'

Bennicken rose deliberately and stood towering over Siegert. Siegert, evidently fearing the worst, shrank back against Frammler. 'If I knew anything I'd tell you,' he pleaded.

At a nod from Frammler, Bennicken's hand shot out with the speed of lightning and fastened on Siegert's collar. Pulling him to his feet he simultaneously brought his knee up into the region of the man's stomach and then released his hold. Siegert slumped back into his chair with a moan.

'What do you want me to say?' he gasped finally. 'What in heaven's name do you want me to say?'

Frammler leant forward. 'You don't know who we are, do you?'

'No,' Siegert said apathetically, all resistance gone.

'And you've never heard names like Schulz, or Gisenius, or Kerze, have you?'

'No.'

'But you do know the name Hirsch, don't you? Shall I jog your memory? Hirsch, manager of the *Hotel Drei Kronen* and the *Café de Paris*—do you know him or don't you?'

'I know him,' Siegert said dully.

'I thought so.' Frammler winked at Bennicken and sank back with a sigh of satisfaction. He pulled out a handkerchief and ceremoniously mopped his palms.

Bennicken resumed his seat. 'Well then,' he said, regarding Siegert with something approaching affection, 'why didn't you say so straight away?'

' Landlord! ' Frammler called genially. ' Drinks all round. We've earned them! '

The landlord emerged from the back quarters. ' Hello! ' he said, staring at Siegert's face. ' Did the gentleman fall over or something? '

' You've hit the nail on the head,' Frammler declared. ' Our friend here had a drop too much. He tripped and fell before we could stop him. Isn't that so, Siegert? '

' That's so, isn't it? ' Bennicken insisted.

' Yes,' Siegert said submissively, ' I fell down.'

The landlord looked relieved. ' Ah well, these things happen.'

That night, Tantau had an idea. It was one of those ideas which he regarded as the product of an endeavour to look for the simplest solution to any problem.

Tantau was well aware of the form that solution should take. He had recognized it from the outset, but he had shirked putting the simplest of all solutions to the test. There were several reasons for this. For one thing, he took an almost childish delight in making detours of an entertaining nature. For another, whenever a new case came into his hands he felt a compulsion to lay bare the mental processes of other people and watch their emotions come into play. The third reason was that he was growing old and spent too much time alone. One of his few remaining pleasures was the elucidation of trivial problems. He had grown modest in his demands and his hopes of stumbling upon a complex crime had dwindled, but he had never abandoned them entirely.

Feeling an urge to see if the elementary rules of detection still held good, he took a map of Rheine-Bergen and spread it out on the table.

' The man came from the direction of Babenberg,' he muttered to himself, tapping the map with a pencil, ' destination: Rheine-Bergen. He was still in the bus when it stopped at the filling-station. There are no more stops between there and the terminus. Bennicken junior reports that he got out at the cattle-market carrying one bag and a briefcase. There's no indication that he took a taxi from there, so it's more than likely that he booked into a hotel in the neighbourhood of the market—judging by his appearance, a second- or third-class hotel.'

Tantau reached for the town guide that went with the map. He opened it at the hotel section and ran his eye down the list, concentrating on the cheaper category. There were five hotels classified as 'inexpensive' in the general vicinity of the cattle-market. Having jotted their telephone numbers down he pulled his purse out of his pocket and extracted ten ten-pfennig pieces—the wherewithal for five local calls.

Rising to his feet with a faint groan that told of advancing age, weariness and the lateness of the hour, he wrapped a scarf round his neck, clapped a battered hat on his grizzled head and shuffled cautiously out of his lodgings. Once in the street, he made for the near-by public call-box which he had come to regard as his private property.

He inserted two coins and dialled the first number on his slip of paper. His inquiry was couched in succinct terms: ' Have you a Herr Meiners staying in the hotel—Herr Michael Meiners? '

The reply, equally succinct, was in the negative.

A call to the second hotel on his list elicited a similar response. When he came to the third, which was the *Gasthof zur alten Post*, the response was no less succinct, but this time it was in the affirmative.

INTERIM REPORT NO. 3

STENOGRAPHIC RECORD OF A POLICE INTERVIEW

WITH LUDWIG FRAMMLER

*conducted by Chief Inspector Sand
on 1 May 1961
in connection with the events of 20 April 1945*

After being informed of the subject of the interview and cautioned, Herr Frammler made the following statement:

My name is Ludwig Frammler. I am forty-four years old and the proprietor of a funeral parlour.

What exactly do you want? I've got no statement to make of any kind. I run an expanding business—that's all I'm interested in. Anyway, what do you mean—sixteen years ago? Can you remember precisely what you were doing last Wednesday? Of course you can't. What do you think I am, then—an electronic brain?

You want the truth from me? Don't make me laugh! The truth as I see it? That's a bit more like it. I might have a go at that, but I warn you, I'm not a clairvoyant, nor a historian.

Take my time, did you say? I will.

We moved into Steinwiesen on the evening of April 19th. The atmosphere was quite pleasant, I might add, at least in the farm where we installed ourselves. Homely and countrified, it was, with a warm stove and the smell of fresh bread everywhere. We perked up as soon as we set eyes on the place and marched into the farmyard as though it was the Promised Land—with Hirsch three paces to the fore, as usual. He had a sixth sense for a soft billet.

Mind you, the farmer tried to make difficulties at first— you'll notice I said at first. He wanted to cut our quarters down to the bare minimum and even tried to refuse us his hospitality altogether—until we talked to him, that is. Bennicken always hit on the right tone to adopt in situations of that sort.

Why do I mention that? Because it provides a clue to what happened later on. There were these fat-arsed, bread-baking civilians sitting there with nothing to do but wait for the war to end, with the Russians only a few kilometres away, setting fire to everything inflammable and laying every-thing in skirts. Finally, in between, there were us soldiers—hungry and exhausted. You can't blame us for wanting a little comfort and relaxation.

To cut a long story short, we told the civilians where they got off and then we drank a glass together, and another glass, and another after that.

That took the edge off our thirst, so to speak. Having got pleasantly stewed, we started feeling like something else. I'll give you three guesses what it was. You've guessed already—I can see it on your face. Well, the idea came easily enough, but putting it into practice presented a few problems. We were seven men, and the only talent available was a worn-out farmer's wife, a spotty-faced school-girl and a refugee woman and her daughter.

The last two had most to offer—I'm not ashamed to admit it. The mother was a very Nordic type in her mid-thirties, a little on the plump side but sexy in a cow-like sort of way. The daughter took after her. She only had a half-ration of everything her mother had, but quite a few people go for that sort of thing. There was only one thing to do under the circumstances and that was to get stuck in!

The only trouble was, Hirsch was sitting between them, and Hirsch always went down big with the ladies. By the time he'd started on his third bottle, he had his arm round one of the only two acceptable females in the place—the mother—while young Meiners sat there making sheep's eyes at her less well-developed daughter.

Question:
You didn't have a high opinion of Meiners?

Answer:
It wasn't my job to judge him as a man, only as a soldier. As a man he was an unknown quantity, but I'd known him as a soldier for several weeks.

Question:
Was he a good soldier, in your opinion?

194

Answer:

He wasn't an experienced soldier—I know that much. He was a bit of a passenger.

Question:

Can you quote any examples of his inexperience?

Answer:

I was just going to. As I say, we arrived in the billet, found these two women there and warmed them up, and they started ticking over nicely. Hirsch piled in first as usual, but the rest of us weren't averse. You know how it is—beggars can't be choosers. And what does Meiners do? He gawps at the girl as if she's the Virgin Mary! When she took a stroll outside, three of the party scampered after her like dogs after a bitch. Not Meiners, though—he just mooned at her and didn't lift a finger.

We made a few cracks about it, of course. Meiners blushed like a beetroot. For one moment I thought he was going to weep with rage, but he didn't dare open his mouth. What we found hardest to understand was that he finished up by refusing to drink with us. He didn't know he'd been born, that lad. Gazed at the girl with his heart in his eyes but couldn't think what to do about it—not to begin with, anyway.

It wasn't a particularly enjoyable evening, all things considered, but it was bearable. At least there was plenty of liquor. All I know is, I woke up where I'd fallen asleep, except that I was under the table instead of at it.

Question:

So you don't know what happened during the night of April 19th–20th?

Answer:

Much as I hate to admit it—no, I don't. I'd have been tickled to know how everything turned out—who did what with whom, and so on—but I was drunk, gloriously drunk. In actual fact, it was the best thing that could have happened. The mother was too old for me, to be quite honest, and the daughter was too young. I'm more of a middle-of-the-road man, myself. The lid's got to fit the pot, whatever anyone says. I always knew what I liked, even in those days.

As I told you, we all woke up feeling like the wrath of God. That's why I find it so damned hard to remember any details. I only know it was light already when I pulled on my boots. The other thing I remember is hearing this refugee woman screaming like a banshee—nerve-racking it was. She'd found her daughter in the barn, dead as mutton.

Question:
Can you give me any details?

Answer:
Can I! Corpses have always been a speciality of mine, though I thought of them more as a hobby than a profession in those days. As to the cause of death, I can only tell you this: the back of her head had struck a metallic object with great force—or, to describe the situation more graphically, someone had thrown the girl on her back in the hay. It wasn't hard to see why—the state of her clothing made it pretty obvious. Unfortunately, there was an old harrow beneath the hay. You know what a harrow is, don't you? A gadget like a bed of nails, only much bigger, for breaking up soil and levelling it. One of the spikes had gone into her skull.

Question:
Was the mother's reaction consistent with the tragedy of the situation, or did you feel she was only play-acting?

Answer:
You're being too subtle for me. Some women scream on principle, whether you lay them or not.

Anyway, Schulz gave me the job of looking after her, which I did. It took some psychology, too, I can tell you. Instead of beating her own breast and reproaching herself for not taking better care of her daughter, the stupid bitch promptly tried to pin the blame on someone else. Women always oversimplify things, and this one was no exception. She actually started accusing us—us!

I was furious, of course, but I soon showed her the error of her ways. 'Let's have a name,' I said, '—one name, not seven!' Then I asked her to stop and think a bit. There were other men in the house, and the countryside was swarming with them. Then again, it might have been an accident. The girl had had a drop or two herself—couldn't even sing the *Deutschlandlied* properly.

I had a lot on my plate that morning, what with one thing and another—not that I begrudged the time. I'm a humane man, as I told you. It was pretty late by the time I'd finished with the mother and rejoined the rest of the section, who were

196

already in position. Schulz hustled me up to the edge of the wood, but just as I got there the balloon went up. The Russians opened up with everything they had, and the whole of the edge of the wood started boiling like a bloody cauldron.

We had no alternative but to retreat in good order.

Question:

What about Meiners?

Answer:

Got himself clobbered by the Russians, poor devil. There was nothing we could do.

Question:

Which of your party devoted most time to the Boddanski girl the evening before, and who seemed most concerned when she was found dead the following morning?

Answer:

I thought I'd made that clear—Hirsch, for one, but he went for anything in skirts. Then there was Meiners, staring at her the whole time as if he'd like to eat her alive—not that it meant anything. I fancied her myself, up to a point, and so did we all. That's the thing about war. The closer you are to death, the stronger your natural urges become. It just so happened that liquor appealed to me more at that particular juncture, you follow me?

7. *The Secret Game*

'Chief Superintendent!' Sand exclaimed as Tantau shuffled into his office. 'How splendid to see you again after all this time!'

Tantau smiled. 'You can dispense with ceremony. I'm a private individual now, you know.'

'To me,' Sand replied solemnly, 'you'll always be the man who taught me my job.'

Tantau chuckled soundlessly for several moments. 'I know, I know,' he said at length, manifestly amused, 'I did teach you a few things in the far distant past, but you stopped being a pupil of mine years ago—in fact you never really were one, luckily for you. We're the product of two entirely different generations, you and I. I belong to a dying race—the intuitive poets of criminology; you're a straightforward technician.'

'What's wrong with combining both approaches, Chief Superintendent?'

'Tantau,' the old man corrected him. 'I regard the successful blending of imagination and scientific method as a pipe-dream. No one individual can ever possess both to the full.'

Motioning Tantau into the best chair in the office, Sand selected a small upright chair for himself as though to perpetuate the master-pupil relationship.

'I'm most intrigued,' he said, regarding Tantau with veneration.

'What about?' Tantau asked absently.

'You never accept a case unless it interests you. Something quite out of the ordinary must have happened, otherwise you wouldn't be here.'

'My dear Sand,' Tantau said indulgently, 'times change, as you know, and our habits and inclinations change with them. I can remember a time—how many years ago would it be now?—about fifteen, I suppose—when my whole energies were focused with passionate intensity on obtaining a loaf of bread or a sack of potatoes or a few grammes of fat. These days I occasionally work for various agencies, as you're probably aware, but only as a means of supplementing my modest pension.'

'A touching story, sir,' Sand said with a twinkle in his eye, 'but I don't believe it. You'd never be satisfied with mere routine.'

'You seem to forget I used to be a stickler for routine, as you call it.'

'Yes, but only when it helped you to get your man.'

'This isn't Berlin, Sand.'

Sand threw up his hands. 'Don't I know it! No one could be sorrier than I am. Anyone in the force who lands up here is doomed to rot.'

'So your dearest ambition is a nice complicated little murder, eh?'

'Isn't it yours?' Sand leant forward confidentially. 'When I heard you were here my first reaction was to wonder what had been happening in my patch. To be quite frank, I'm still in the dark.'

'So am I.'

Sand sat back, looking incredulous and disappointed. 'I don't understand,' he said slowly, 'not yet, anyway.'

'You still won't understand if I tell you why I'm here.'

'Why are you here?'

'I need your help,' Tantau said simply. 'Could you instruct the officer who checks hotel arrivals at Rheine-Bergen Central to supply me with any information I may require?'

'Well?' Sand demanded impatiently. 'What else?'

'That's all.'

'In that case, I'll see to it at once. But why rope me into this? You could get all the information you need without my help. You know the tricks of the trade.'

Tantau grinned. 'Why should I use tricks when I've got connections?'

Sand's expression ceased to be that of the devoted pupil. He felt cheated and provoked. Once more, with an intensity that had not waned in twenty years, he sensed the humiliating natural superiority of this strange little man, who had plunged so resolutely from one tangled case to the next. It had been a traumatic experience, working under such a man, and Sand had taken a long time to shake off his inferiority complex. Now he felt it creeping back again.

'There's something behind all this,' Sand insisted. 'What is it?'

'If I knew that I doubt if I'd be sitting here,' Tantau said meekly. 'But let's agree on our phrasing first: let's prepare ourselves for the possibility that there really is something behind all this.'

'They 'phoned to say you were coming. I didn't have time to hang out any flags, I'm afraid.'

Sergeant Brahmvogel greeted Tantau like an old and honoured acquaintance. Although he wasn't fully acquainted with the old man's background, Sand's instructions had been most explicit. 'I've been given orders to do everything possible to help you,' he continued.

'For the moment,' Tantau said politely, 'I'd just like to look through your file of hotel registration forms, if I may.'

'Of course,' Brahmvogel replied. He ushered Tantau into the records office under the respectful gaze of one or two younger policemen. 'What's it to be? All the hotels in the area, or just one? How far back do you want to go, or are you looking for a specific name?'

Tantau beamed. 'Wouldn't you like to know! I imagine you'll be giving the worthy Chief Inspector a full report on my activities afterwards, eh?'

'Precisely, sir,' Brahmvogel agreed, amused at his visitor's knowledge of the official grape-vine. 'I'm sure you'll find plenty of ways to throw me off the scent, though.'

'For instance?'

'Well,' Brahmvogel said, bending forward confidentially, 'if you're only interested in one hotel you'll act as if you were interested in several, and if you're looking for one particular man you'll make inquiries about four or five. Correct?'

'Perfectly,' said Tantau. 'Would you mind looking out the registration form of a man called Michael Meiners. He booked into the *Gasthof zur alten Post* a few days ago.'

'That's a new dodge,' Brahmvogel said admiringly, pricking up his ears. 'What about letting me in on it?'

'Later, perhaps,' Tantau replied with a smile. 'Can I have the form now?'

'Right away.' Brahmvogel launched himself at the filing-cabinet. His expression was sceptical, but he soon found what Tantau—allegedly—was looking for.

Tantau took the form and read it through with meticulous care, imprinting it on his mind word for word. Then he asked politely: 'Could you warn the porter to expect me and ask him to supply me with a little information?'

'Ah!' exclaimed Brahmvogel, his brow clearing. 'I see it all now. You're making inquiries about one man so as to cover a whole hotel. Not a bad idea at all. Of course I'll 'phone the porter. You carry on—he'll be gushing like an oil-well by the time you get there.'

The porter turned out to be as elderly as the hotel and its décor. Far from gushing like an oil-well, he was a reticent old man with an air of patriarchal dignity.

Tantau displayed consummate patience—always one of his greatest assets. He skimmed through the hotel records, apparently without any definite end in view, chatting about this and that, picking guests' names at random and questioning the porter about them in a perfunctory way. The only name he temporarily omitted to mention was that of Meiners.

Tantau's visit to the police station had provided him with all the relevant details save one—the man's room number—but a quick glance at the porter's list showed him a '21' opposite the name Meiners. Tantau's eyes narrowed almost imperceptibly: the key to Room No. 21 was not on its hook.

'Is it customary for your guests to surrender their keys when they leave the premises?' he inquired casually, still leafing through the books.

'It is indeed,' the porter said. 'It's one of our rules, as a matter of fact.'

'I see several gaps on your board there—18, 21 and 34, for instance. Does that mean the guests are in their rooms at this moment?'

'It does.'

'Isn't that unusual at this time of the morning?'

'It is,' the porter replied promptly, relishing the chance to display his expert knowledge to an attentive audience. 'It's unusual, but not as unusual as all that, especially when you know the guests' habits as well as I do. It's part of a

201

porter's job. For instance, the gentleman in No. 34 won't be up till noon. Between you and me, he went to an all-night party last night.'

'And No. 18?'

'A lady visiting her husband. He's working here temporarily with a team of post office engineers. The lady hardly ever leaves her room. Her husband gets back towards evening. It's a double room, you understand.'

Tantau feigned lively interest. 'No one can say you don't know your job,' he said with well-modulated admiration in his voice. 'What about No. 21?'

'A very nice gentleman,' the porter hastened to assure him. Tantau had a fair idea of the attributes a guest had to possess in order to rate as ' nice ' in the eyes of hotel staff. The inference was that Meiners was a quiet and undemanding guest, probably on demi-pension, a reliable tipper and a regular exchanger of polite good mornings.

'Why should he still be in his room? Was he out on the tiles too?'

'He's probably working up there—quite a lot of our guests do, particularly the commercial gentlemen. Most of them use their rooms as a temporary office.'

'Do you happen to know what the gentleman in No. 21 does for a living?'

'Not an easy job, sir,' the porter volunteered. 'I think I understood him to say that he's come here to collect some old debts.'

Shortly afterwards, Tantau met the man named Michael Meiners.

To engineer the encounter, all Tantau had to do was wait. The key hung on its hook, midday was approaching, and a smell of cooking pervaded the hall. Tantau whiled away the interval by chatting to the porter at length, but nothing he said, even now, was without its underlying purpose. His choice of words amounted to a carefully planned diversionary manœuvre.

Tantau calculated that the porter would be questioned by Brahmvogel, and the latter by Sand. Accordingly, he asked a series of precise but, from his point of view, wholly meaningless questions about three guests picked at random from the porter's list.

Then, almost on the stroke of midday, Tantau saw Michael Meiners descending the narrow stairway into the hall. He recognized him instantly.

The man's appearance matched the photographic enlargement in Tantau's pocket with almost disconcerting accuracy, allowing for the inevitable changes wrought by the passage of the years. There was a network of fine lines round the eyes, the lips had grown thinner and the skin had lost the bloom and elasticity of youth, but the eyes were astonishingly unaltered—large melancholy eyes the colour of a blue summer sky veiled by a leaden haze.

' Good morning, Herr Meiners,' the porter said affably.

' Good morning,' Meiners replied. His voice sounded hoarse and toneless, almost as if he found it an effort to speak at all. Glancing casually in his direction, Tantau saw that his neck was traversed by a broad scar, the relic of what must have been a very deep wound. Still pink and fissured, it ran obliquely downwards from the left ear, past the jugular, and disappeared beneath the edge of his shirt-collar.

' No mail, I'm afraid,' the porter said regretfully, taking the proffered room key.

' I wasn't expecting any,' Meiners's manner was polite but not exaggeratedly so. He stared past the porter and Tantau, smiling faintly in a way which somehow recalled the melancholy of a lonely child.

Tantau watched him go. He noted that Meiners had a slight but perceptible limp which caused him to lean to the left, and his left arm hung slack at his side.

' A very nice gentleman,' the porter remarked.

' I'm sure you're right,' Tantau said meditatively, ' but one should never go by appearances.'

' Tell me the truth! ' Karl Schulz demanded. ' Come on, out with it! I'm your brother, aren't I? '

Schulz believed this to be his most potent argument, and he brought it into play repeatedly. He had been pressing Eva for an explanation ever since she arrived home late the night before, but the response had been absolutely nil.

He had let a night go by in the hope that she would reconsider her attitude, but the result was still failure. His promptings bore no fruit.

'My dear Eva,' he said, as mildly as he could manage, 'I know what human nature is—you mustn't think I don't understand. There's nothing I'd like better than to see you happily married one day.'

'That's all right, then.' Eva beamed at her brother gratefully. 'Perhaps I can get down to some housework now. Shall I make you a cup of coffee?'

'Listen to me, girl!' he insisted angrily. 'It takes two to make a couple. I know you well enough to feel certain that everything's straightforward and above-board on your side, but what about him? Do I know him?'

'You will do as soon as everything's sorted out.'

'As soon as what's sorted out?'

Eva gave a smile which Schulz found suspicious in the extreme.

'Who is he? Is he respected and looked up to? Does he make good money? Has he got a future? You know me— I'm not a snob. His occupation doesn't matter, nor his income, and I couldn't care less about his family background. But is he a decent chap?'

'I think so, Karl.'

'What do you mean, you think so? You've got to be certain, you've got to have proof! All right, who is this youngster you've been gallivanting about with after dark?'

'I love him,' Eva said, 'so you're bound to like him.'

'Is he in love with you?'

'I'm sure he is,' she replied with quiet confidence, 'but it's just possible he hasn't realized it yet. That's why I mustn't rush him into anything. He's got to be given time.'

'Listen, Eva,' Schulz said, 'let's put this thing on a proper footing. No hole-in-the-corner business, no nocturnal gadding about. I tell you what—invite him home. I'll treat him like a member of the family, I promise you. What about it?'

'No,' she said with gentle obduracy, 'not yet.'

'Damn it all!' Schulz exploded. 'What's the matter, are you ashamed to show him off?'

Eva shook her head. 'He's rather sensitive on the subject of family life because his own doesn't seem to have been too happy. That's why we'll have to be patient with him. I've got plenty of patience, I'm happy to say.' She walked to the door. 'I'll get your coffee now.'

Karl Schulz rose abruptly and barred her path. 'It all sounds highly suspicious to me,' he said. 'I don't like the sound of it and I'm going to put a stop to it. From now on, you won't leave this house after dark unless you're accompanied by me or someone I can trust—Martin Hirsch, for instance. If this young—young man wants to see you he can report to me first.'

Eva regarded her brother with a faint smile. 'You can't ever have been in love, Karl.'

'Of course I have!' Schulz declared stoutly. 'I was more careful, that's all.'

'What's love got to do with being careful?'

'Plenty, and I'll prove it to you. I love you, but I'm careful enough to want to run an eye over your boy-friend —which I will do sooner or later, take it from me. And God help him if he turns out to be a bastard! I'll break every bone in his body and send the pieces home to his family in a sack, or my name's not Karl Schulz!'

'You've been so kind to me,' sighed Brigitte. 'I don't know how to thank you, really I don't.'

'My dear child,' Gisenius said in his most fatherly voice, 'you've no need to thank me. It's quite natural for a man to take an interest in his fellow-beings, especially when he feels that it's worth while.'

He eyed the girl benevolently as she sat perched on the edge of a chair not three feet from him. Her girlish but ample bosom filled her grass-green pullover to perfection.

It went without saying that Gisenius had received her in his office, this being the most neutral territory he could think of. Misunderstandings were less likely to arise there than anywhere else, or so he imagined.

He had been unable to banish Brigitte from his mind. The very first time he saw her on the stage of that dubious establishment, the *Café de Paris*, he had felt an urge to take her under his wing, to spare her the necessity of exposing her virginal charms to the lecherous leers of the common herd.

'The function of society is to safeguard human dignity,' he went on, 'and the best form of government is one which leaves the individual free to develop his or her personality. That, I venture to say, is the whole object of life.'

' How nice,' she breathed.

The sight of her warmed his heart. Confidently, but only for a few seconds, he laid a hand on her knee.

' We must try to find a suitable method of moulding your future and channelling your activities in a pleasant and worthwhile way.'

' That would be lovely,' she said, inching closer. ' I don't know why, but I feel I can trust you.'

Gisenius cleared his throat. ' It's not unnatural. After all, I could be your father.'

' But you're not.' Brigitte spoke with disarming directness.

Gisenius nodded noncommittally—the only rejoinder which occurred to him on the spur of the moment—and again laid a hand on her knee. This contact, to which she submitted without demur, lasted considerably longer than the first. ' Let's think what we can do for you, my child. Have you any ideas? '

' Well,' Brigitte said eagerly, ' you could speak to Herr Hirsch and ask him to give me a permanent engagement or increase my fee—to twenty marks a night, say.'

' Of course.' Gisenius could not quite conceal his disappointment. ' But I wasn't thinking so much of material things. I'm more concerned with your—your moral welfare, let's say. I feel you ought to start all over again, my dear child.'

' Oh, I will, if that's what you want. The only trouble is, I've never learnt anything. All I can do is dance a little. I know it's not much, but at least it's a living. What else could I do? '

' There are any number of possibilities, my child, provided you're willing to place yourself in my hands.'

' Oh, yes! ' Brigitte assured him in heartfelt tones. " You're the sort of man a girl can trust—I can feel it.'

' Let me think, then,' Gisenius said, seemingly overwhelmed by so much innocent trust. ' Well, you could try working here in my office, for instance, under my personal supervision. How would that appeal to you? '

' I don't know exactly,' said Brigitte, bowing her head. ' I'm afraid I'd be too stupid.'

Gisenius stroked his chin. ' There are other alternatives, of course.'

' What I'd like best would be to learn housework and study

books—in a little flat of my own, if possible. That would be useful, wouldn't it? '

'We'll see,' Gisenius said, glancing at the clock on his desk. It was high time he left for the Stabilator works, or he would miss Willy Kerze's finest hour. Taking the girl's hand —a firm, warm, determined little hand—he said: ' I feel you have faith in me, my child. You won't regret it, I assure you.'

'Oh, no,' Brigitte said, 'I'm sure I shan't.'

'Am I speaking to Frau Kerze,' Tantau inquired in tones of deep respect, 'Frau Direktor Kerze? '

'Afraid not,' Brandstädter said distantly, 'I'm only the housekeeper here. There isn't any Frau Kerze.'

'I beg your pardon. I thought . . .'

Needless to say, the news that there was no Frau Kerze came as no surprise to Tantau, who made a habit of familiarizing himself with the personal background of all his clients. He also knew that Kerze himself was at his factory, which was precisely why he had told Bennicken to drive him to the villa.

'What a pity,' Tantau said, subjecting her to an appealing gaze from his dachshund's eyes. 'I'm conducting some inquiries for Herr Kerze, you see. My name's Tantau, Heinrich Tantau.'

Brandstädter's curiosity was whetted by the word 'inquiries.' 'You'd better come inside. I'll make you a cup of coffee, if you like.'

'I'm sure you brew magnificent coffee,' Tantau said eagerly. 'You give that impression, and I never could say no to a good cup of coffee.'

Two minutes later Tantau was ensconced in the kitchen. Chatting without any apparent end in view, Tantau found Brandstädter an attentive listener. From this he deduced that opportunities for conversation in the Villa Kerze were limited, a welcome circumstance which gave promise that Brandstädter would prove as eager to talk as listen. To prepare the ground, he set to work to create an atmosphere of mutual trust.

Tantau's tactics were twofold. First, he conveyed to Brandstädter that he considered her exceptional, both as a housekeeper and as a person. Secondly, he made it clear that he was well-informed by speaking of Gisenius, Karen Kerze and Hirsch in an allusive fashion which hinted at an intimate knowledge of their personal affairs.

'Ah, yes,' Brandstädter sighed, and Tantau could almost hear the ice crack as her wintry countenance broke into a smile. 'Young people are a worry, there's no denying it. Poor little Karen could have done with a mother.'

'All the same,' Tantau put in, 'she had you, didn't she, my dear Frau Brandstädter?'

'What could I do for the child?' lamented Brandstädter. 'She spent most of her time with strangers. It was all I could do to run the house. And Herr Kerze never thinks of anything but his work—I'm afraid he's not a family man by nature.'

'But he's a man for all that,' Tantau said, smiling, 'and everyone has an occasional fling.'

Brandstädter bridled. 'I wouldn't know about that.'

'Of course you would,' Tantau replied, with the easy intimacy of an old friend. 'You can speak quite frankly to me—you'll find me a discreet and sympathetic listener.'

'What do you think of this suit?' Kerze inquired. 'I picked midnight-blue because it looks smart but not too funereal.' A sudden doubt struck him. 'Or do you think I ought to have chosen something else?'

'Stay as you are,' Gisenius advised. 'You've developed an admirable social sense in the past few years, Willy. I congratulate you.'

They were standing in the managing director's office of Stabilator Limited. A proportion of the firm's share capital was ostensibly held by outsiders, but it was, in fact, a limited company whose effective ownership was limited to Kerze himself. And now, at last, he was on the threshold of one of his greatest moments: the Minister was about to invest him with the Federal Order of Merit.

'It's not going to be cheap, this business,' Gisenius said judicially.

'It's not going to be particularly expensive, either,' Kerze replied, tweaking his tie into position. 'The biggest potential expense was paying the workers to attend the ceremony in the firm's time, but I've solved that problem pretty neatly. With Bartosch's help, I've persuaded the Minister to inspect the works, which means, of course, that production must be going at full blast. The tour of inspection will last until the official lunch-break, and that'll be the signal for everyone to stream into the main hall and join in the festivities.'

'Bravo!' cried Gisenius. 'That's what I call organization. You should save a tidy sum, which may make it easier for you to fall in with a small request I have in mind.'

Kerze's complacent expression vanished in a flash. 'I might have known you didn't turn up early just to pass the time of day,' he grumbled. 'You're here to tap me again, that's what. Well, get this straight, Conrad: I can't go on laying golden eggs indefinitely. I'm already paying for this wild-goose chase of yours. What's come of it, anyway?'

'Nothing,' Gisenius said tersely, 'virtually nothing, but in my opinion that's a good sign.'

'You mean it's a false alarm?' Kerze registered a degree of relief. 'Good—all the better.'

'The only fact that's been established so far is that Hirsch tried to hoodwink us.'

'Typical of him!' Kerze snapped.

'It seems he deliberately raised a false alarm. Tantau tracked down the man he identified as Meiners in the night-club, and Frammler and Bennicken conducted a few inquiries on their own initiative. The man turns out to be a harmless fellow who bears a vague resemblance to Meiners. On the other hand, he does admit to knowing Hirsch.'

Kerze was outraged. 'Bloody hell! What does Hirsch think he's playing at?'

'I'm beginning to wonder myself.'

'I tell you this much,' Kerze said harshly. 'If he's up to any tricks I'll settle his hash once and for all. I'll have him thrown out on the streets and make sure no one gives him another job. I've already got enough evidence on him to put him inside.'

The lawyer's eyes narrowed. 'Is that so?'

Kerze stalked over to the telephone and asked to be put through to his home. 'Finish checking those books today, Saffranski,' he told the accountant, 'and get the contract with Europa Hotels ready for signature. I want to settle the whole business by tomorrow if possible.'

'Excellent,' said Gisenius, who had been listening intently, 'but if I were you I should only look upon the steps you've just taken as a possible basis for future action against Hirsch.

Don't do anything for the moment. We'll discuss it when the time comes.' He glanced at his fob-watch. 'Now to the matter in hand. Do you really intend to announce your daughter's engagement to Bartosch this evening?'

'But of course!' Kerze boomed. 'It's all settled—mainly thanks to you, my dear Conrad.'

Gisenius did not disclaim credit where credit was due. 'I realize that their engagement will bring a series of material advantages in its train.' He paused for effect. 'For all that, we should do our utmost to eliminate any potential obstacles to the match—anything which might endanger it.'

Kerze's brows contracted. 'What are you driving at?'

'I've just had an opportunity of examining a dossier. Its origin is of secondary importance, but its contents . . .' He paused again. 'The dossier contains a mass of convincing evidence against Bartosch—genuinely convincing. You know you can trust my judgement in that respect. The weight of evidence is positively overwhelming and extraordinarily well-documented. I don't need to tell you what it's about.'

'God Almighty!' Kerze's usually florid face acquired a sudden pallor. 'You can't be serious!'

'Keep calm,' Gisenius said. 'It's quite possible that the documents are forgeries, but that doesn't make the dossier one wit less dangerous. You'll have to buy it if you want to avoid trouble.'

Gisenius omitted to mention that the dossier was already in his possession. He wasn't a welfare organization. If Kerze had been a poor man in dire straits he wouldn't—so he assured himself—have hesitated to hand over the file as a sort of advance wedding present. But Kerze was a rich man, so it was only right and proper for him to provide a quid pro quo. To Gisenius, the secondary fact that he proposed to use Kerze's contribution to buy his own dossier from Lehmgruber was no more than a natural corollary of the first proposition. He was not over-anxious about the smarmy little informer's file on himself, but it would be safer in his own hands than someone else's.

'All right,' Kerze said at length. 'I'll buy the muck for the sake of peace. How much is it worth?'

'A thousand marks,' Gisenius replied, mentally crediting the hundred-per-cent profit to his personal welfare account.

'Done,' Kerze said grimly, adding in reproachful tones: 'How could Bartosch do this to me?' He took a few hesitant steps towards Gisenius and halted abruptly. 'I'll deduct it from Karen's dowry, you mark my words. Bartosch will be lucky if he gets a pfennig out of me.' He passed a hand across his brow. 'But let's think about something pleasant for a change. The Minister should be here any minute now.'

'It'll be a shame if you miss Herr Kerze's great moment,' Tantau said.

'I know, but I've got such a terrible lot to do,' sighed Brandstädter. 'It's a real responsibility, running a house like this.'

The housekeeper was still entertaining Tantau at the kitchen table, all her inhibitions dispelled by a consuming urge to communicate. There was no sign of the responsibilities that weighed so heavily on her shoulders. The cold buffet for Kerze's personal guests had been delivered ready-prepared by a delicatessen shop in Rheine-Bergen, the drinks had been set out since midday, and a maidservant was busy polishing glasses.

'I'd like to, really I would,' Brandstädter continued, preening herself, 'especially as the Herr Direktor personally asked me to be present.'

'Then what are you waiting for?' Tantau said coaxingly. 'I'll be glad to escort you, if you'll permit me to—my car's outside.'

Brandstädter gave a coy smile. 'Well, if you really think I ought to be there . . .'

'Of course, it'll be a pleasure to accompany you,' Tantau assured her shamelessly. 'Come on, we mustn't miss the first act.'

Before Brandstädter complied with Tantau's suggestion she launched herself into the role of mistress of the house, leaving Tantau to smoke one of Kerze's privately imported Havanas. As he sat there, he idly noted everything Brandstädter did. It was not particularly difficult to follow her movements because she left the kitchen door wide open and adopted the strident and autocratic tone which she invariably employed when Kerze was not at home.

First, Brandstädter addressed someone in the drawing-room,

evidently the maidservant. She deplored the presence of smears on sundry glasses and demanded a greater expenditure of elbow-grease. She announced her intention of attending the Herr Direktor's investiture at his personal invitation and warned the maidservant not to improve the shining hour by sneaking off to see her boy-friend, who apparently worked as a mechanic in the garage two hundred yards down the road.

Secondly, Brandstädter went into a room leading off the long front corridor and conversed with a man of indeterminate age whom she courteously addressed as 'Herr Saffranski'. Tantau heard her ask him if he wanted anything, and Saffranski replied: 'No thank you, Frau Brandstädter. I'll be finished here in another five or ten minutes, and then I'm going to the works. I mustn't miss the ceremony, must I!'

Thirdly, Brandstädter emitted a stentorian bellow of 'Konstantin!' A few moments later, Tantau heard a small boy's timid voice asking politely what Frau Brandstädter wanted. Brandstädter made inquiries about some homework which the boy admitted was still unfinished. There followed a stern reprimand from Brandstädter and an injunction to make up for lost time.

These three exchanges, which Tantau noted automatically, acquired special significance later on.

For the moment, Tantau's entire attention was centred upon the edifying spectacle of Frau Brandstädter in ceremonial garb. She had donned a Persian lamb coat which, though not of the choicest quality, at least demonstrated that employment in the Kerze household was not without its material rewards.

Bennicken hardly looked up when Tantau handed his female companion into the vehicle which he had described as 'my car'. The taxi-driver switched on and awaited instructions.

'To the factory,' Tantau said gaily.

'The Minister's on his way, sir,' announced the commissionaire of the Stabilator works, replacing the receiver. 'He should be here in about seven minutes.'

Everything had been brilliantly organized. Kerze had seen to that by entrusting all the administrative details to his sales manager, Herr Sängerwald, a shrewd man who had repeatedly proved his business acumen by selling off obsolete

Stabilator stock as the latest adjunct to modern building techniques. He received salary and commission, drove a gleaming American sedan and was treated with comparative respect by Kerze himself.

'Inform the managing director at once,' Sängerwald told the commissionaire. Turning to a group of nervous figures hovering near the works entrance, he called in tones of quasi-military command: 'Corps of drums ready? Floral tribute ready? Works committee ready?'

'Ready, sir!' several voices replied with alacrity.

This was the signal for the sales manager's plan of action to commence. He had left nothing to chance, meticulously checking and double-checking each detail to ensure that everything dovetailed neatly. Sängerwald had never enjoyed the benefits of military training. Discipline ran in his veins.

Sängerwald took final stock of the arrangements for the Minister's reception. On the left of the entrance stood the works band—popularly known among employees with a military turn of mind as 'the corps of drums'—and on the right the works committee, selected after joint consultation with the Christian-Democrat and Socialist trade unions. In front of these worthies stood a small girl—the commissionaire's daughter—carrying a sheaf of flowers.

At this juncture the managing director appeared, escorted by Conrad Gisenius. The sales manager hurried up to Kerze and reported that all was in readiness for the Minister's reception, as instructed. Kerze rewarded his trusty henchman with a handshake and Gisenius followed suit while the workers looked on with interest.

Reaching his allotted place, Kerze graciously suffered the secretary of the works committee to press his hand and utter a few well-chosen words of congratulation. This done, he indulgently chucked the commissionaire's daughter under the chin and nodded with equal benevolence at the works band, whose leader returned the compliment by coming smartly to attention.

Almost at the same moment the Minister's car hove into view. It was followed, contrary to all expectations, by another vehicle which proved to be a taxi containing the incongruous figures of Bennicken, Tantau and Frau Brandstädter. Temporarily, however, all eyes were fixed on the first vehicle, a Mercedes 300 of traditionally sombre hue.

In response to a word of command from Sängerwald, the works band struck up the march *Old Comrades*. The commissionaire's daughter skipped up and down with excitement and the secretary of the works committee cleared his throat. Willy Kerze's features moulded themselves into a cordial smile of welcome.

Hermann Bocksdorff, provincial minister of finance, descended, escorted by Councillor Johannes Bartosch. Both men advanced on Kerze, and those present could hear, above the frenzied endeavours of the works band, ' welcome . . . a very great honour . . . trust you will be pleased . . .'

The Minister smiled, nodded, smiled, shook hands with Kerze, Gisenius, the sales manager and the secretary of the works committee, smiled, chucked the commissionaire's daughter under the chin, smiled, acknowledged the works band with a wave of the hand, and smiled again.

' First item on the agenda:' announced Sängerwald, ' a tour of the Stabilator works, personally conducted by Herr Direktor Kerze.'

Outside the gate, Bennicken had began to sound his horn loudly and continuously. Thrusting his bullet-head through the window of the cab, he bellowed: ' Open up, blast you! '

Konstantin Kerze sat in his room, hunched over the table with his head between his hands, staring at his homework.

He didn't look round when the door behind him opened.

Saffranski closed the door carefully and stood there motionless with his long bony hands pressed together at chest-height. It was a solemn pose which matched his earnest expression, now utterly devoid of deference or humility.

Saffranski remained like that for several seconds, with his cold sad eyes fixed on the seated figure of the small boy a few feet away from him. He studied the blonde hair on the drooping head, the curve of the neck, the hunched, slender shoulders. It was a picture composed of broad, flowing brush-strokes rather than sharp contours, a complex of gentle curves. Saffranski's lips parted slightly as he moved soundlessly towards the boy.

Konstantin continued to stare at the exercise-book in front of him, trying to concentrate on the figures that swam before his eyes—whole armies of them, separated by rivers of white paper

214

connected by plus and minus signs and ending in the twin horizontal lines which cried out for the solutions he found it impossible to supply.

As he looked, he saw a shadow move across the page. He flinched away from it instinctively, and a tremor ran through his body. His head jerked round and his startled eyes met Saffranski's.

Saffranski started to smile.

'Oh,' Konstantin said with a sigh of relief, 'it's you, Herr Saffranski.'

'Are you frightened?'

'Not of you.'

'But you were frightened, weren't you?' Saffranski insisted.

Konstantin smiled shyly. 'Well—yes, you gave me a start.'

Saffranski's eyes were almost closed now, but his smile deepened. Slowly unlacing his long bony fingers, he extended his right hand and passed it across Konstantin's hair. It glided almost imperceptibly down the boy's neck to his shoulders, where it rested, lightly but without tenderness, as though it had suddenly become inanimate. 'So you're afraid,' he said in a low persuasive voice.

'No I'm not,' Konstantin replied defensively, 'not now. Why should I be?'

'Have you ever been by yourself in a wood, where there's nothing but undergrowth twining itself round your feet and trees looming over you? Have you ever crept through an empty house in the dark, with the rain rattling at the window-panes and the wind whistling round the eaves? Have you ever lain in bed at night and felt the cold and darkness and silence flooding in on you? Didn't your heart ever thump and your knees tremble and your stomach twist itself into a knot? Haven't you ever felt like that?'

'I don't know,' Konstantin said, wide-eyed and open-mouthed. 'Perhaps I have.' It was almost as if he could sense all that Saffranski had described—the limpness of limb, the thunderous beating of the heart, the sudden contraction of the stomach.

'Then you've been afraid,' Saffranski sounded pleased, and for a moment he closed his eyes entirely.

'But I'm not afraid when you're there,' Konstantin insisted bravely.

'That's good.' The hand resting on Konstantin's shoulder seemed to come to life again. It grew heavier and slid tentatively downwards. 'You can trust me.'

'I do!' Konstantin protested vehemently, as though doubt had been cast on one of his better traits. With the abrupt inconsistency of youth, he added: 'Could you help me with my sums, Herr Saffranski?'

'Of course.'

Saffranski stationed himself close behind Konstantin and bent over the exercise-book. He laid both hands on Konstantin's shoulders as if to steady himself, and his chest brushed the boy's back. There was a long silence, broken only by the sound of Saffranski's heavy breathing.

Eventually he said: 'There's nothing very difficult about these. We'll polish them off inside ten minutes. Perhaps we can go for a little stroll in the garden afterwards. If you really aren't afraid, Konstantin, it means you must be brave. Are you brave?'

Konstantin looked dubious. 'I think so.'

'Well,' Saffranski said softly, 'you may have a chance to find out—soon.'

Sängerwald's voice rang through No. 3 Bay: 'Eyes front, men! The Minister's coming!'

The call heralded a further stage in his carefully planned programme. The curtain was about to rise on the final act, the investiture of the Federal Order of Merit, and the factory's main bay was thronged with appropriately awestruck spectators. Stabilator Ltd. was on the threshold of its finest hour.

The 'men'—also referred to as operatives—fell silent. Some of the older ones among them stood to attention, and many of the younger generation entered into the spirit of the occasion with equal enthusiasm. A sea of heads turned to watch the Minister's entrance.

The Minister himself appeared to be in the grip of deep emotion. As the initiated were aware, he had a special talent for surveying his surroundings as if nothing but grandeur met his eye. Even the provincial premier had been struck by this

216

happy facility, which had led to the Minister's being entrusted with many enviable responsibilities.

The works band struck a chord and the works choir embarked—in accordance with Item 1 of Part 2 of the official schedule—upon the noble and uplifting anthem *Hail to Thee, Land of Our Fathers*. The Minister strode down the chalked-off aisle towards the platform, escorted by a group consisting of Kerze, Bartosch, Gisenius, Sängerwald and the secretary of the works committee.

A flower- and bunting-bedecked chair of honour stood ready for him, and beside it another, evidently reserved for Kerze. These were flanked on either side by further chairs destined for guests of honour, senior employees, privileged local dignitaries, friends and dependents. The common herd remained standing.

Comfortably installed in one of the chairs reserved for friends and dependents sat Tantau. His eyes were half-closed and he wore a contented smile. Bennicken, burly and impassive as ever, stood to one side but within call. Seemingly uninterested in what was going on around him, he merely waited—it was hard to tell what for.

Tantau leant towards Frau Brandstädter, who was preening herself beside him, and asked: ' Who's the gentleman walking behind the Minister and Herr Kerze? '

' That's his son-in-law to be, Councillor Bartosch.' Frau Brandstädter knew everything, and she imparted everything she knew to Tantau the moment he expressed an interest in it. The little man had gained her confidence. Telling herself yet again that she had never encountered a more attentive listener, she whispered a few more details into his politely inclined ear.

Meanwhile, Item 1 of Part 2 of the official schedule (' Arrival of the Platform Party ') had been completed. The sales manager's order of the day stipulated that Item 3 was to consist of an address of welcome delivered by a representative of the firm. This turned out to be Sängerwald himself. Mounting the podium in his new capacity, he spread out his notes and started to read them. Duration: seven minutes dead, as prior timing with a stop-watch had proved.

And so to Item 4, the Minister's address apropos of the investiture of the F.O.M., followed by the investiture itself.

What the Minister actually said was unimportant. Anyone who was interested could have read it in any newspaper report of any investiture held anywhere. It didn't matter who was investing whom with what—the phrasing seldom varied.

Willy Kerze's reaction, on the other hand, might have been described as one of humble gratitude. He stood there with massive head bowed, fingers aligned with trouser-seams, heels clamped together and toes pointing outwards at an angle of twenty-five degrees.

'Once learnt, never forgotten,' murmured Tantau, but Frau Brandstädter was too overcome by emotion to hear. She sobbed audibly, momentarily becoming the loyal and devoted retainer of a great man whose finest hour she was privileged to witness. The faint aura of reflected glory proved too much for her. Her breast heaved convulsively and she hurriedly groped for a handkerchief.

Bartosch beamed like the hero of the hour, Gisenius's smile radiated Christian charity, and even Bennicken yielded to some nameless stirring of the senses. Sängerwald surveyed the crowded hall with an air of triumph, and the spectators murmured their approbation.

Finally, Willy Kerze ascended the podium. His midnight-blue suit looked decorative in the extreme, and his words derived a certain force from the fervour with which they were delivered. He declared that he felt proud and grateful, not least to his loyal and trusted colleagues, and by colleagues he meant everyone from senior executives to the humblest operative in the slab-moulding shop, from accountants to clerks, cleaning-women and messenger-boys. 'That,' he concluded, 'is why I shall be wearing this decoration on behalf of you all!'

'I'm sure I've heard that somewhere before,' Tantau murmured. He was enjoying himself hugely.

At a nod from the sales manager the works band struck up *Now thank we all our God*, eagerly supported by the male-voice choir. One or two of the workers also appeared to know the words, and the general effect was deafening.

'Much more of this and the Almighty may need ear-plugs,' mused Tantau, but his words were lost in the enthusiasm which reigned near the platform. The walls resounded and one of the overhead lights flickered and went out, but the short-circuit did not, Tantau was sorry to note, quench the singers' ardour.

'Big boys aren't afraid,' Saffranski observed with a slow, meditative smile. 'Are you a big boy?'

'I'm not afraid,' Konstantin said vehemently, 'really I'm not!'

'Have you ever laid your hand flat on a table and brought the point of a knife down between your fingers, faster and faster? Have you ever done that?'

'No,' Konstantin admitted, looking surprised. 'Do people do that?'

Saffranski gave an emphatic nod. 'They do if they're not afraid—if they're big boys.'

'Shall I try it?' Konstantin asked. He sounded compliant but not particularly enthusiastic.

Saffranski put an arm round Konstantin's shoulders and drew him close, laughing silently. Feeling constricted, the boy tried to free himself from the embrace, but Saffranski's grip grew tighter.

They were still in Konstantin's room. The boy's home-work was finished, thanks to Saffranski's expert assistance, and the sums now marched across the pages of his exercise book with military precision. Konstantin had emerged from a slough of despond eager to show his gratitude.

'Have you ever jumped over a bare scythe?' inquired Saffranski.

Konstantin looked intrigued. 'How do you mean?'

'It's quite simple,' Saffranski explained. 'One person takes a scythe and swishes it backwards and forwards at knee-height, and the other has to jump over it each time.'

'Isn't it dangerous?'

'Of course, but only if you're scared—not if you're brave and good at jumping. Are you good at jumping?'

'I think so,' the boy replied doubtfully. Then, with a sudden access of courage, he added: 'Shall we try? We could go into the garden. There's a scythe in the tool-shed. Do let's!'

Saffranski gave a short laugh. 'If you're as keen as all that, why not? Let's go into the garden.'

Konstantin seemed overjoyed to be able to leave the room

at last. He skipped out of the door and down the stairs with Saffranski following slowly in his wake. The accountant's long bony face wore a look of dark, brooding satisfaction. His eyes, which never left the boy, registered every detail of the coltish grace of his scampering form.

Saffranski halted suddenly with one hand held to his chest in an attitude of pain, listening for sounds of movement in the silent house. He pushed open the kitchen door, then peered into the drawing-room, but there was no one to be seen. He called for the maidservant and Frau Brandstädter, but his summons brought no response. After waiting for a few moments longer, nervously clasping and unclasping his fingers, he hurried out into the garden.

' Come on! ' Konstantin called excitedly. ' I want to show you something.'

Saffranski followed him across the lawn, lush and green with the first growth of spring, to the pool whose surface gleamed between the budding birch-trees and dense shrubbery that surrounded it. There, beside the pale-blue water, stood Konstantin.

' I've got a hide-out here.'

' I know,' Saffranski said, moving closer.

Konstantin frowned. ' I didn't think anyone knew.'

' No one does,' Saffranski replied softly, ' except us two.'

Konstantin stared at Saffranski with joyous disbelief. He had developed an intense liking for this tall thin young man who treated him so considerately, spoke to him as an equal and helped him with his sums. No one had ever been as good to him before.

' It's terrific here,' Konstantin said eagerly. ' There isn't another place like it.'

' You're right,' Saffranski agreed. ' It's a good place.'

The long strip of water was bordered by tangled clumps of undergrowth. Paths skirted it on two sides, but elsewhere the banks were screened by dense thickets which grew to the water's edge. The pool was further shielded from view by the luxuriant yew hedges in the background. Silence reigned, save for the sound of dark water gurgling away down the waste-pipe.

' Where's the net? ' Saffranski asked.

' Which net? '

'I was watching you a few days ago,' Saffranski's eyes had left the boy and were examining the surface of the pool, which looked blackish-brown at close quarters. 'You went into the tool-shed and came out with that big fishing-net of your father's. Then you crawled off into the bushes with it.'

'You know about that?' Konstantin said, wide-eyed.

'I know about that,' Saffranski replied softly, 'and a lot of other things as well. Where's the net, Konstantin?'

'It fell into the pond,' the boy said. A glint of fear had come into his eyes—fear not of Saffranski but of his father. The whole weight of his father's wrath, which he dreaded beyond all measure, would come thundering down on his head. Dejectedly, he asked: 'You won't tell him, will you?'

Saffranski shook his head, but his pale blue eyes remained fixed on Konstantin's face. He clasped his hands together once more. His lips parted slightly. 'We ought to get that net out of the pond,' he said, 'don't you think so? Right away, before your father finds out.'

'Yes, but how?'

Saffranski bowed his head as though obeying some inner compulsion to watch his hands. 'We'll get undressed and dive in.'

'Now?' Konstantin inquired in boundless astonishment. 'Isn't it too cold?'

'What's the matter?' Saffranski asked, not looking at the boy. 'Are you scared?'

'No,' Konstantin replied in a small voice.

Saffranski raised his head and stared steadily at Konstantin before he spoke again. 'Then get undressed.'

'A most successful function,' the Minister assured Kerze. 'I should like to extend my heartiest congratulations.'

Kerze coughed deprecatingly. 'Thank you, sir,' he said, stressing the 'you'. 'It's your presence which has lent lustre to the occasion.'

They had now reached Part 3 of Sängerwald's schedule relating to 'The Investiture of the Managing Director with the F.O.M.', a post-ceremonial celebration in the form of refreshments.

While the bulk of the factory workers and junior staff trooped into the main hall of the works canteen, there to regale themselves on two free beers and a plate of frankfurters and potato salad, selected invitees and senior members of the staff assembled in the senior executives' canteen, where beer and wine flowed freely and guests were plied with mountains of cold meat and piles of substantial-looking open sandwiches. Although the Minister and Kerze formed the undisputed focus of the whole gathering, the ' post-ceremonial celebration ' was really aimed at the press, which was represented by reporters from each of the three local papers. However, Sängerwald found it hard to wean the gentlemen of the press from their open sandwiches. Despite his efforts, all three declared themselves sufficiently well-informed. One of them went so far as to tell Sängerwald, through a mouthful of sandwich: ' The Minister won't say anything we haven't heard him say before.'

Gisenius threaded his way, smiling affably to left and right, towards two figures who were standing in the background. Tantau was leaning comfortably against the wall and Bennicken was imbibing beer straight from the bottle—his usual method.

' Herr Tantau,' Gisenius said in formal tones, ' may I inquire the purpose of your presence here? '

' A good question,' Tantau conceded politely. ' I'm looking for something, though if you were to ask me precisely what, I'm not sure I could put my finger on it.'

Gisenius looked stern. ' Are you sure you aren't wasting your time? '

' I don't think so,' purred Tantau. ' Actually, I want to have a talk with Herr Kerze. He happens to be next on my list.'

' But you can't see him today,' Gisenius protested. ' He's far too busy.'

' All days are one to me,' said Tantau, ' and all occasions equally suitable. Since you happen to be here too, Herr Gisenius, perhaps you can give me a little information? '

' Later,' said Gisenius. He glanced round, apparently sensing that the Minister required his presence, and retired in haste.

Tantau smiled indulgently and turned his attention to Bennicken. The cab-driver was taking vigorous gulps, barrack-room fashion, from his bottle, which he held to his lips like a bugler preparing to sound the charge. ' Good stuff? ' inquired Tantau.

'The best,' Bennicken said dourly, between swallows. Meanwhile, the party was growing noisier. The members of the works committee laughed heartily at some witticism on the Minister's part. Bartosch raised his glass to Sängerwald, who regarded this as a signal honour in view of the Councillor's budding personal relationship with his managing director, which was no secret to him. Gisenius whispered something to Kerze, and both men looked in Tantau's direction, but at that moment the Minister readdressed himself to Kerze. Having spoken earlier of exalted subjects such as State and nation, economics, science and religion, the Minister turned to the more intimate domain of house, home and family life.

'I'm told, my dear Kerze,' he said confidentially, 'that you intend to crown your day of official celebration with an announcement of a more personal nature.'

'I do indeed, sir,' Kerze replied, no less confidentially. 'The Minister is exceedingly well-informed.'

The Minister permitted himself a complacent smile. 'It's my job to be. May I inquire where the prospective bride is? I'd so much like to congratulate her. I didn't see her during the ceremony.'

Kerze frowned. It suddenly occurred to him that he hadn't clapped eyes on Karen all day. Devoid of filial respect as she was, she might at least have attended the ceremony and feigned a little interest. For that matter, she ought to have been there to greet her fiancé, if not out of affection, for form's sake. Obviously, she was on the loose again, but where?

'I quite understand,' the Minister said, fully in command of the situation. 'She's at home, playing the little housewife and waiting to welcome her fiancé.'

Kerze's brow cleared. 'Exactly, sir.'

'Ah, well,' the Minister sighed indulgently, 'love is all!'

'What are you afraid of?' Saffranski said, bending down. 'Aren't you going to take your shirt off?'

'My shirt as well?' Konstantin asked.

'Take everything off,' Saffranski told him. 'You can't get into the water with your clothes on, can you—and that's what you'll have to do if you want to find that net.'

'I've forgotten exactly where it fell in.'

'We'll look for it,' Saffranski replied. His lips twisted in a strange smile. He, too, seemed to sense the chill that rose from the waters of the pool, because his hands began to tremble. 'We've got to find that net. You know what'll happen if your father finds out you've lost it.'

'But he won't find out, will he, Herr Saffranski?'

'Never,' Saffranski said. 'He won't know a thing about it.'

'That's all right, then.' Konstantin looked up at his new friend with an expression of fervent devotion. He was so determined to prove his gratitude that he forgot about the cold and began to unbutton his shirt.

'Come here,' Saffranski said evenly, 'I'll help you.'

'Thanks, I'll manage. It really is cold, though.'

'Come here,' Saffranski repeated. He helped Konstantin to pull the shirt over his head, tugging at it fiercely until the boy's naked body was revealed. 'Don't be frightened.'

Saffranski fell silent, but his mouth remained open and the whites of his eyes gleamed dully, like soiled snow. He laid his palms against the boy's thin chest. 'You're cold, child,' he said in an almost inaudible voice.

'No I'm not,' Konstantin replied faintly, assailed by a sudden and inexplicable pang of fear.

'I can feel you are,' Saffranski murmured. 'Come closer —come really close. I'll warm you.'

His hands enveloped the small body and clasped it to him. He felt the child struggle violently and buried the open mouth against his chest, and the convulsive movements of the small, weak, writhing body sent a thrill of savage ecstasy down his spine. He let out a bubbling groan of pleasure.

Mirrored in the oily brown waters of the pool, the thick bushes and tree-tops resembled strangely-shaped walls and watch-towers guarding some realm of silence. Below them, two entwined shadows danced wildly on the water, reeling and swaying, until one detached itself and fell, silent as a dead leaf, into the void.

The surface of the pool splintered like glass. Concentric ripples passed across it, obliterating the scene as though it had never been.

'To mutual understanding, our nearest and dearest, and the Fatherland!' said the Minister, raising his glass.

'Hear, hear!' Kerze responded, following suit.

Sängerwald cautiously insinuated himself into the ministerial group and whispered in Kerze's ear. 'You're wanted on the 'phone, sir.'

'Not now, my dear chap!' Kerze hissed indignantly.

The sales manager looked apologetic. 'They said if was important.'

Gisenius nodded at Kerze. 'No need to tear yourself away, Willy. I'll deal with it.'

Kerze, who had embarked on a conversation of some moment with the Minister, was highly reluctant to abandon it. He had just learnt that ' they ' were considering an extension of the road system, a project which might have an important bearing on the future development of Stabilator Ltd. For all that, he felt vaguely apprehensive. He stared past the Minister to where Gisenius was taking the call on his behalf in the far corner of the senior executives' canteen. The lawyer's expression, nonchalant at first, slowly froze into one of deep concern, but by the time he rejoined Kerze and the Minister a few moments later he was his usual bland self again.

'I beg your pardon, Minister,' he said deferentially, 'but I wonder if I might steal Herr Kerze from you for a few minutes.'

'By all means,' the Minister replied, adding with a hint of curiosity: 'Not bad news, I hope?'

'Far from it, sir,' Gisenius assured him briskly. 'A minor problem of administration, that's all.'

Kerze availed himself of the Minister's permission without delay and bore Gisenius off into a corner occupied by platoons of empty bottles. 'What's up?'

'A call from the central police station in Rheine-Bergen. They've picked up your daughter and they'd like you to collect her.'

'God Almighty!' Kerze cried dramatically. 'How could the shameless little bitch do such a thing to me—today of all days!'

'Not so loud!' Gisenius urged.

'I'll tan her hide for her, the slut!' Kerze said angrily. Then it occurred to him that he had no idea how Karen had got into the hands of the police in the first place. 'What's she been up to?'

'Drunken driving', Gisenius announced. 'I'm told she's completely written off a car—her own, I'm happy to say.'

'What am I to do?' asked Kerze. 'I can't simply walk out of here.'

'I'll handle it, if you like.'

'That's one solution,' Kerze conceded. His deductive faculty had started to function again. 'But there must be a better one. The Minister would notice your absence and I'd have to provide him with a convincing explanation.'

'We could think one up,' Gisenius said. 'All the same, it might create complications if I turned up here later with Karen in tow. Besides, I want to hear what the Minister has to say about this road extension—there's too much at stake. What about sending Bartosch?'

Kerze seemed to derive a perverse pleasure from the idea. 'It might do him good to get to know his future bride properly,' he muttered, but his unerring sense of the practical did not desert him. 'Bartosch is essential here, he's one of the Minister's party. Anyway, I'm going to see him safely engaged to Karen today, come hell or high water. Who does that leave?'

'Tantau,' said Gisenius. His brow cleared abruptly. 'That's it—Tantau!'

'You think he'd deal with it?'

Gisenius gave an emphatic nod. 'For a fee, of course. This sort of thing is just up his street. What a piece of luck, his being here! Tantau knows the ropes, believe you me. He'll know just how to handle the police.'

'All right,' Kerze said with relief. He was longing to re-enter the Minister's orbit. 'Be a good chap and arrange it for me, Conrad.'

Kerze hurried off and Gisenius went over to Tantau, who was staring out of the window with Bennicken at his side.

'I'd like a word with you, Herr Tantau,' Gisenius said briskly.

'By all means—two or three, if you like.'

Gisenius ignored Tantau's little pleasantry. 'Would you be prepared to undertake an additional job of a rather different nature? It's to do with Herr Kerze's daughter, Fräulein Karen Kerze. The police are holding her in Rheine-Bergen on a charge of drunken driving.'

'Interesting,' Tantau replied impassively. 'What do you want me to do about it?'

'Deal with the formalities,' Gisenius said in business-like tones. 'Give her all the assistance she requires and stop her saying anything stupid. Then take her home. Give me a full report—consult me by 'phone if necessary. It'll be worth an extra day's pay to you.'

Tantau nodded thoughtfully. 'I'll take it on,' he said, 'but only if I'm allowed to handle it in my own way.'

'You have my full authority to act as you think fit,' Gisenius replied, 'but act quickly. Fräulein Kerze's presence is urgently needed at home.'

'Where is she?'

'At the central police station in Rheine-Bergen.'

Tantau looked pleased. 'Good, that may simplify things considerably. Would you be good enough to 'phone and tell them to expect me. It might be best if you spoke to Sergeant Brahmvogel and made it clear that I'm acting on behalf of Herr Kerze and yourself.' He turned to Bennicken. 'Come on, Jehu, let's see how much speed you can get out of that chariot of yours!'

'Nice to see you again,' Sergeant Brahmvogel said affably. 'You're becoming quite a regular visitor.'

Tantau was inside Rheine-Bergen Central. Having left Bennicken at the wheel of his taxi, on the principle that anyone not directly concerned with the matter in hand had better be excluded, he now stood facing Brahmvogel across the counter, his frail frame contrasting strangely with the burly, broad-shouldered figure of the police sergeant. Two or three constables sat at their desks looking busy and listening hard.

'Take a walk, you lot!' Brahmvogel called to them. 'And when you've done that, go and dust the filing cabinets.'

The constables rose, grinning. Brahmvogel's word was law in Rheine-Bergen Central, and had been for years.

'So you're working for Messrs Gisenius and Kerze, are you?' Brahmvogel said when they were alone.

'Do you disapprove?'

'No, but you've bitten off more than you can chew this time. That girl in there is a proper handful.' He jerked a thumb over his shoulder. 'We had to lock her up.'

'What did she do?'

'Ploughed into a newspaper kiosk—to avoid a head-on collision, so she says. A constable brought her in. She was pretty high, I can tell you.'

'Did she agree to a blood-test?'

'No,' Brahmvogel sounded aggrieved. 'She refused. What's more, she raised merry hell. Talk about a fish-wife!' He scratched his close-cropped head ruefully. 'What's the matter with the girl, anyway? She actually seemed grateful when we locked her up. Any idea why?'

'A vague one,' Tantau grinned. 'She's supposed to be announcing her engagement this evening. Her father's very keen on the idea.'

'And she isn't?'

'So it would appear.'

Brahmvogel gave a sympathetic wink. 'In that case, maybe she'd better spend the night here. Wouldn't that be the best thing?'

'It's no good, I'm afraid,' Tantau said. 'Herr Gisenius is Herr Kerze's legal adviser, and I've no doubt he's pretty well-informed on the extent of police powers.'

'True,' Brahmvogel agreed. His voice took on an almost sorrowful note as he added: 'Poor little thing!'

'I'll do my best to help her—in my own way,' Tantau went on. 'The first step is to get her out of here.'

'That won't be too easy,' Brahmvogel said. 'She's as stubborn as a mule, and there's a little matter of resisting arrest to be taken into account.'

'If my memory serves me rightly,' Tantau replied, 'road accidents which don't involve any personal injury or flagrant abuse of traffic regulations can often be settled out of court, so to speak—as long as the party concerned is prepared to pay full compensation for any damage caused.'

'True,' Brahmvogel conceded, 'but that doesn't apply to this little vixen. It was all three of my men could do to hold her. She won't listen to reason.'

'May I try?' Tantau asked.

'You don't seem to have any idea what your new protégée is like, my dear Herr Tantau.' Brahmvogel smiled significantly and took a bunch of keys off a hook beside the inner door. 'However, if you insist, I'll go and ask the young lady whether

228

she'll condescend to accept your offer of help. It may take a minute or two—five or six, more likely.'

Brahmvogel grinned at Tantau, jingled the cell keys at him and disappeared down the passage with purposeful tread, leaving the old man alone in the charge-room. As usual, Tantau tried to occupy his time as agreeably and profitably as possible. Brahmvogel's reference to five or six minutes had been quite explicit, so he slipped across to the duty-sergeant's desk where, as he well knew, the charge-sheet and daily reports would be neatly inserted in a file cover. Opening it, he started to leaf through the contents in search of the report on Karen Kerze's accident. Only someone in full possession of the details of a charge could refute it with any reasonable hope of success.

While in quest of the report on Karen, Tantau caught sight of a name he knew: Siegert. He started, peered at the sheet more closely and began to read it. Siegert had lodged a complaint against two unidentified men who had committed an apparently motiveless assault on his person.

Tantau hastily closed the file just as Brahmvogel, ostentatiously stamping his feet, re-entered the room. The sergeant glanced keenly at the duty-sergeant's desk. Then, with a contented chuckle, he announced: ' She says you can go to hell.'

' There you are—I told you she'd see me.'

' On your own head be it,' Brahmvogel said, as he led Tantau down the narrow stone-flagged passage with its white-washed walls and stout plank floors. He inserted a key in a lock, turned it with an air of ceremony and flung the door wide, taking cover as he did so. Promptly, a tin plate sailed into the passage and clattered against the opposite wall.

Tantau walked in without flinching. Being familiar with such premises, he knew that their stock of ballistic missiles was strictly limited. Apart from that, he was still quite quick on his feet.

He remained standing near the door, which Brahmvogel prudently shut behind him, and made a leisurely inspection of the girl who was sitting on the wooden bed with her legs drawn up under her. His first impression was of an extremely attractive young woman whose pretty but petulant face had none of the vixenish quality he had been led to expect. Karen's expression was one of righteous indignation rather than shrewish ill-temper.

' What do you want? ' she snapped. ' Get out of here, or I'll chuck the stool at you! '

' Carry on,' said Tantau. ' Try it, if you want to, but I should pick it up by the seat, not the feet. That way you control the centre of gravity and get more accuracy.'

' Who the hell are you? '

Tantau formally introduced himself with an attention to detail which obviously surprised her. He withheld nothing that might be of interest to her, telling her where he came from, who had sent him and what his mission was. ' If there's anything else you'd like to know you only have to ask.'

' Leave me alone! ' Karen said passionately. ' That's all I want—to be left alone.'

She shrank back like a cornered animal when Tantau took a few paces towards her, but he merely picked up the stool, set it down beside the bed and cautiously lowered himself on to it.

' You know,' he said with a wary smile, ' this isn't my first visit to a prison cell. I've seen dozens in my time, though I must confess that few of their inmates were as pretty as you.'

' Flattery will get you nowhere,' Karen said scornfully.

Tantau's eyes twinkled. ' I'm afraid I'm not quite your type.'

Karen stared at him with a trace of surprise, but all she said was: ' Stop talking rubbish. Go away and leave me alone.'

' Have you ever stopped to think how many people have suicidal tendencies? ' Tantau inquired equably. ' I'm not talking about people who turn the gas on or fill themselves with sleeping-pills—they're poor unimaginative creatures. No, my dear, there are plenty of others who die a little more every day—youths who sublimate their natural urges in amusement arcades and kill their time on earth in fun-fairs, girls who go without food and sleep because of unrequited love or jump into bed with the next man that comes along.'

' You're being a bore,' Karen said bitterly.

' I know, I know,' Tantau agreed, equable as ever, ' there's nothing so boring as the truth. It's the exact opposite of the dream-world conjured up by pop records, paperbacks and sentimental films. The only trouble is, dream-worlds become more and more real, until everyday life, which mainly consists of work and loneliness and responsibility, becomes so appallingly boring that people try to duck out—preferably at someone else's expense.'

' Brilliant! ' Karen exclaimed scornfully. ' You ought to write for the Sunday papers.'

' My dear girl,' Tantau continued, undeterred, ' I've seen more dead bodies in my life than you have strange beds. I've known people who died simply because they didn't read to the end of a letter, because they didn't dare ask a question, because they couldn't be bothered to wait another three minutes.'

' What's that got to do with me? '

' You want life to give you just what it can never give you —a formula, a system, a book of rules. That's nonsense! Life is full of surprises. Everyone has to live his own life and make the best of it. It's no use ramming the next newspaper kiosk with your foot hard down and hoping you'll find an answer in the wreckage.'

' Oh my God! ' Karen groaned, settling herself more comfortably on the bed. ' They've sent me a father confessor.'

' You could use one,' Tantau replied. ' You're wrong, though. I'm more in the nature of a business man—I don't expect something for nothing. You don't want to get engaged, do you? Well, that might be arranged.'

' How? ' Karen demanded with sudden interest.

' Certainly not by smashing up your car. Who stands to lose most by doing a thing like that? You, of course! Who stands to gain? No one! All right, then, let's try to clear up that mess for a start.'

' And you guarantee I won't have to get engaged? '

Tantau regarded her steadily. ' Is it really such a bad idea? '

' Bad? ' She gave a bitter laugh. ' It couldn't be worse. I don't want to, I simply don't want to—can't you understand that? '

' I can understand anything if it's said with enough conviction.'

' Then help me! '

' I'll do my best, but there are one or two conditions to be fulfilled first.'

' Like what? '

' The first step is to get you out of here, my girl. It shouldn't prove too difficult if you take my advice. Will you? '

' All right,' Karen replied with sudden decision. ' I trust you,' she added quietly. ' I must trust someone—anyone—otherwise there'd be no point in going on.'

Tantau looked distressed. ' You shouldn't talk like that. I'll do what I can, but I don't promise anything. Every human being has to come to terms with himself in the end. It may sound trite, but it's true. You've got to be able to trust yourself—that's half the battle.'

' What a wonderful ceremony! ' sighed Frau Brandstädter. ' Inspiring, it was—really inspiring! '

' Yes indeed,' Kerze replied impatiently, ' yes indeed.'

' So solemn, too—almost like a church service.'

' Yes, yes,' said Kerze, his irritation mounting.

The privileged few had extricated themselves from the milling throng of merry-makers at the Stabilator works, installed themselves in a waiting cortège of cars and driven in state to the Villa Kerze. The villa's festively decorated reception rooms were now the scene of a distinguished gathering which included the Minister, one of his government colleagues, Councillor Bartosch, Gisenius, the local member of the Bundestag, one of the provincial party chairmen and a newspaper editor sympathetic to the cause. Also in evidence was Marlene Sonnenberg, clad in a startling brick-red creation. Kerze noted without undue pleasure that the singer was closely attended by Hirsch and Schulz. The guests' gay laughter rang through the house and their figures could be seen in blurred outline against the frosted glass doors that led into the ante-room where Kerze and Frau Brandstädter were standing.

Pleading the duties of a host, Kerze had temporarily deserted the party, and Brandstädter, still half-intoxicated by the solemnity of the investiture, had seized the opportunity to impress on him how deeply she admired and respected him, and, consequently, how worthy she was of his trust and esteem.

' Now listen, you! ' he interrupted her, delighted to have

found a receptacle for his pent-up spleen at last. 'Why didn't you tell me Karen had gone off again?'

'How was I to know, sir?' Brandstädter protested. 'Fräulein Karen left the house at midday, but I thought she was going to meet her fiancé or have her hair done for the ceremony.'

'And what about Konstantin?' Kerze pursued with undiminished fury. 'Didn't I leave express instructions that he was to be in the hall when the guests arrived—in his blue suit and white shirt?' He had a sudden vision of his son standing there with scrubbed hands and hair neatly combed. What more charming welcome could the Minister and his other guests have had—what more delightful token of the Kerze family idyll? 'Well, where is he?'

'I don't know.'

'You don't know?' growled Kerze. 'You make it your business to know all about my personal affairs, and you don't know where my son is! You're slipping, woman!'

'I can't find him, sir. He must be hiding somewhere.'

'Then go and look for him! I intend to present him to my guests in fifteen minutes' time, so you'd better get cracking!'

Kerze stared contemptuously after Frau Brandstädter's retreating figure for a moment before turning to check the reserves of liquor on the sideboard. He listened to the noise coming from the drawing-room and was gratified to hear that the party was going with a swing. Then, glancing quickly into the hall to assure himself that no one was in sight, he swiftly uncorked a bottle of whisky, poured out half a tumbler and drained it at a single gulp.

'I need a place where I can talk quietly,' Tantau said. 'Is there any room in the house which isn't being used for the party?'

'There's Herr Kerze's study,' suggested Frau Brandstädter.

'Lead the way,' Tantau said. 'After that, you might like to do me three small favours: take a pot of strong coffee up to Fräulein Karen's room, get Herr Bennicken some beer and sandwiches and then tell Herr Kerze and Herr Gisenius that I must speak to them—both of them. Be discreet about it, though.'

'What about you, Herr Tantau?' Brandstädter inquired eagerly. 'Don't you want anything?'

'No, thank you,' Tantau replied. 'Just sluice your face in cold water, that's all. I can see you've been crying. If you feel like talking to someone about it, we'll have a little chat later on, when I've finished my other business.'

Brandstädter looked relieved and grateful. 'It's a treat to meet a sympathetic person like you. Anyone can tell your heart's in the right place.'

'It doesn't make my job any easier,' Tantau said drily.

He allowed Brandstädter to conduct him to Kerze's study, where he switched on all the lights and opened the window wide. This done, he selected the most comfortable chair in the room, manhandled it into a commanding position and sank into it, stretching his legs out in front of him.

Tantau's eyes closed, but his face acquired—as it almost invariably did when he was alone—a look of peculiar animation. Furrows traversed his brow, merged, diverged, and finally disappeared. His mouth twisted into a grimace of impish glee and he chuckled silently at some anonymous but vastly entertaining thought.

Abruptly he opened his eyes and sat up. His expression became impassive and his body seemed to shrivel. Only the gleam in his eye betrayed his keen sense of anticipation.

He made no move to rise when Kerze and Gisenius entered the room, but merely regarded them expectantly as they advanced on him and halted in front of his chair.

'Well, is it all settled?' asked Kerze. 'Where's my daughter?'

'Your daughter's in her room,' Tantau announced. 'I advised her to have a cold shower and some black coffee and then tidy herself up.'

'Go on,' Kerze demanded.

'One moment, Willy,' Gisenius interposed. 'I think we might sit down for a moment. There's no point in rushing things.'

Tantau sat back with an air of satisfaction. 'The facts are as follows: Fräulein Kerze was driving down Kantstrasse at 4.35 p.m. in the direction of Promenadeplatz. About a hundred yards north of the Municipal Theatre she lost control of her vehicle, allegedly because a car coming in the opposite direction tried to overtake in defiance of traffic regulations.'

Kerze uttered an exclamation of triumph, but Tantau's cool stare reduced him to silence again.

'Fräulein Kerze thereupon mounted the pavement and collided with a newspaper kiosk,' Tantau continued. 'Her car was severely damaged, as was the newspaper kiosk, but no physical injury was sustained.'

'Not bad so far,' Gisenius remarked judicially. 'Is that all?'

'I'm afraid not. A police constable who happened to be in the vicinity reported that Fräulein Kerze was not only exceeding the speed limit but, in his opinion, unfit to drive.'

Kerze swore under his breath.

'There's worse to come,' Tantau went on. 'Fräulein Kerze not only declined to assist the police in their inquiries but offered violent resistance. She used abusive language to one policeman, assaulted two others and finally had to be taken into custody by force. In other words, she was locked up in a cell.'

'For God's sake!' groaned Kerze. 'How could she do this to me!' he added in heartfelt tones.

'A highly distressing affair,' Gisenius conceded. However, having observed Tantau closely throughout, he realized that his report was only a preamble. He had a distinct feeling that Tantau was making for some predetermined objective. 'I assume you managed to clear the air a little?" he hazarded.

'I did,' Tantau said. 'Fräulein Kerze's car sustained severe damage—three thousand marks' worth, at a rough guess —but her insurance should cover that. Damage to the newspaper kiosk is estimated at between eight hundred and a thousand marks, but the proprietor has agreed not to take any action provided that full compensation is paid within three days. The police are not going to prefer charges of speeding and drunken driving because of insufficient corroborative evidence.'

'I congratulate you!' Gisenius exclaimed with genuine admiration.

'Furthermore,' announced Tantau, 'the police are prepared to be broad-minded on the subject of resisting authority, obstructing an officer of the law in the performance of his duties, using abusive language and so on.'

'Excellent!' Kerze cried. 'That's what I call a first-rate job.'

Tantau modestly brushed the compliment aside. 'There's bound to be a minor charge of driving without due care, of course, but the usual fine is between sixty and a hundred marks, not more.'

'Very good,' Gisenius said thoughtfully, 'but is that all?'

'It's enough for me,' declared Kerze, who had regained his cheerful self-assurance. 'Let's not waste any more time— we can settle any details tomorrow. We mustn't forget our guests. The Minister's waiting, and there's an announcement to be made before the evening's out.'

'All the same,' Tantau said quietly, 'there's one minor point to be settled first.'

Gisenius stiffened. 'Well?'

'What more is there to say!' Kerze cried spiritedly. 'Everything's settled already, thanks to your excellent work, my dear Herr Tantau.' He turned to Gisenius. 'Let's go up and fetch Karen, Conrad. I'm sure everyone's anxious to congratulate her.'

But Gisenius would not be distracted. 'You were going to tell us something, Herr Tantau. A minor point, I think you said.'

'That's what I called it,' Tantau replied, 'and from my own point of view that's all it is, though it's possible you may not see it in the same light.' He paused. 'My only means of clearing up this whole business—which might have had serious consequences, I may say—was to enlist Fräulein Kerze's personal support. It wasn't an easy matter, to say the least. However, I had your full authority, Herr Kerze. I was at liberty to offer financial and other inducements, was I not?'

'Of course,' Kerze said grandiloquently. 'Never haggle over a few pfennigs—that's my motto. Success is all that counts, and no one can say you haven't been successful.'

'I only succeeded because I made Fräulein Kerze a definite promise,' Tantau replied. 'I told her that she needn't announce her engagement this evening.'

'What!' Kerze exclaimed in consternation. 'Impossible, utterly out of the question! You must be joking!'

'I gave my word,' Tantau said with quiet finality.

'Rubbish! She couldn't have taken you seriously. It was just a dodge on your part—a trick, that's all.'

'It was a promise,' Tantau insisted. 'If I hadn't given it, the whole arrangement would have been impossible. It was the only way.'

'Now listen to me!' Kerze exploded. 'Who the devil do you think you are? Your job was to clear the air, not meddle in my private affairs. You must be out of your mind! What the hell have your promises got to do with me? Damn all —I'll tell you that for free! No one gave you permission to make promises in my name, so why should I feel bound by them? Count me out!' He turned to Gisenius. 'Come on, Conrad, we've wasted enough time here as it is.'

'Just a moment,' the lawyer said warningly. Leaning towards Tantau, he asked: 'This promise of yours—do you propose to hold us to it?'

'Not necessarily,' replied Tantau, 'but I'd point out that it takes two to make a bargain. If you try to override me and dismiss my promise to Fräulein Kerze as irrelevant and immaterial, what's to prevent me from breaking my undertaking to you?'

'Come to the point,' Gisenius said tensely.

'Well, I promised Fräulein Kerze that she needn't get engaged if she did all she could to help me sort things out, and I promised you to trace Michael Meiners and inform you of his whereabouts. If you refuse to honour my word in one case, why should I feel bound by it in another?'

'What's this?' bellowed Kerze. 'Blackmail?'

Gisenius impatiently signalled him to be quiet. 'Does that mean you know where Meiners is, Herr Tantau?' he asked keenly.

'I do,' Tantau said. 'He's alive, and I know exactly where to find him.'

'He's alive,' Kerze repeated in a dull voice. He turned to Gisenius for help, but Gisenius was staring unblinkingly at Tantau.

'That being so,' Tantau continued, 'I have a proposition to make: if you honour my word to Fräulein Kerze and allow her to call off her engagement, I'll tell you where you can find Michael Meiners. Before I do, however, there's one other condition to be fulfilled: you must tell me what you intend to do with the man. I insist on knowing.'

'What infernal cheek!' Kerze fumed.

Gisenius adopted a more cautious approach. 'Aren't you being a little presumptuous, Herr Tantau?'

'I don't think so,' Tantau said firmly. 'It's my job to trace people, not lead them like lambs to the slaughter. I traced a man called Siegert for you, and someone beat him up. A curious coincidence, don't you agree?'

'Let's not go into that now,' Gisenius replied curtly. 'Herr Kerze has decided not to announce his daughter's engagement this evening—isn't that so, Willy?'

Kerze looked dazed. 'Are you serious, Conrad?'

'I strongly advise you to postpone the announcement.'

'All right,' Kerze said, breathing hard, 'if you really think so.'

'We can iron out any further points later,' Gisenius concluded. 'I shall expect you at my office tomorrow morning, Herr Tantau. Things may seem clearer to you after we've had another little talk.'

'Where on earth can Konstantin have got to?' Kerze boomed with spurious joviality. 'I wanted to introduce him to you all.'

'Yes indeed,' said the Minister, who was in high good humour, 'there's nothing I like better than the sight of a happy home. I love shaking hands with children and patting their heads. I know gestures of that kind are dismissed as vote-catching stunts, but to me children are more than a living reminder of the future which it is our duty to safeguard.' He cleared his throat, and a misty look came into his eyes. 'When I look at them, memories of my own happy boyhood come flooding back. Yes, by all means let us meet your son, my dear Kerze.'

'The young scamp seems to have gone to ground,' Kerze said gaily, trying not to grind his teeth. 'Too shy to show his face, I suppose.'

'I've looked everywhere, sir,' Frau Brandstädter whispered in his ear.

'Then go on looking, Frau Brandstädter.'

The Minister bent over Marlene Sonnenberg and laid a

discreet hand on hers. 'Don't you adore children, dear lady?' he asked earnestly.

'I'm crazy about them,' Marlene replied, matching her tone to his.

Although disturbed by Tantau's news and infuriated by his demands, Kerze was not utterly cast down. His private party promised to be a complete success. The Minister and his entourage were in splendid form. Marlene Sonnenberg made a magnificent centre-piece, as he had known she would, and Martin Hirsch's social expertise had won general and ministerial approval. Karl Schulz contributed to the good cheer by bustling around filling glasses.

'What about your charming daughter?' asked the Minister. 'Isn't she going to honour us with her presence either?'

'She's not feeling too well, I'm afraid,' Kerze's voice rang with regret. 'She was involved in an accident this afternoon —nothing serious, I'm happy to say, but the doctor has ordered her to rest.'

'How disappointing,' said the Minister, but he did not succumb to disappointment for long, consolation in the shape of Marlene Sonnenberg being ready to hand.

Johannes Bartosch, however, looked concerned. 'Forgive me,' he said, manœuvring Kerze into a corner, 'I don't quite understand. What's the trouble?'

Kerze simulated cheerful optimism. 'Nothing that a night's rest won't cure, my dear chap. It can't be helped.'

'But is it really nothing serious?'

'Don't worry.' Kerze assumed his most fatherly manner. He was determined to avoid further complications and equally determined to hang on to Bartosch at all costs. 'Please don't alarm yourself—it simply means we'll have to postpone the official announcement for a couple of days at most.'

'As you wish,' Bartosch replied with dignity.

Kerze patted him on the back and hurried off to inspect the liquor bottles in the ante-room, his favourite brand of whisky among them. He badly needed another pick-me-up.

Frau Brandstädter appeared in the doorway of the study, where Tantau was still taking his ease in the arm-chair. 'Are you sure there's nothing I can get you?'

239

'My needs are very simple these days, Frau Brandstädter. By the way, how's Fräulein Karen?'

'She's lying on her bed listening to trashy music.'

'Good.'

Brandstädter eyed Tantau compassionately. It was obvious to her that the poor, tired old man needed looking after. 'I'll get you some coffee.'

'No, thank you,' said Tantau, 'it would only wake me up. If you really want to do me a favour, could you find me some sweets?'

'Sweets?' Brandstädter looked perplexed. 'You mean chocolates and so on?'

'Precisely.' Tantau gave a slightly shamefaced smile. 'Chocolates, candies—it doesn't matter what.'

'I'll see what I can do,' Brandstädter said, shaking her head. 'Fräulein Karen may have some in her room.'

She stumped out, and Tantau took advantage of her absence to make himself even more at home. He placed a cushion behind his back and wriggled deeper into the chair, smiling at himself indulgently. Even in the old days he had made a habit of keeping an ample supply of confectionery in his desk, and his consumption always increased in proportion to the complexity of a case.

Brandstädter returned with a large box of candies which Tantau fell upon without delay, chewing vigorously. Although he was tempted to sit back and close his eyes in rapture, Brandstädter's evident need for consolation deterred him.

'What's worrying you, Frau Brandstädter?'

'It's Konstantin,' she sniffed. 'He still hasn't turned up, and we've looked for him everywhere.'

'How do you mean, everywhere?'

'All over the house,' she said, throwing up her hands in despair. 'We've searched every room from the attic to the cellar, but he's nowhere to be found.'

'When boys of his age vanish,' Tantau said, munching, 'the first thing to do is to check their friends' homes.'

'Konstantin hasn't got any friends!'

Tantau regarded Brandstädter with incredulity. 'Surely he must have some?'

'Konstantin is a very well brought up child,' Brandstädter said proudly. 'He never tears around with other boys. The

240

only time he leaves the house is to go to school, and even then he's usually accompanied by the chauffeur.'

Tantau deposited a piece of half-eaten chocolate on the table beside him as though his appetite had suddenly deserted him. ' Has this often happened? ' he asked. ' I mean, doesn't he ever go off by himself for an hour or two? '

' Never! ' Brandstädter replied indignantly. ' He wouldn't dare to! He's a very obedient child, and he does exactly as he's told. He plays in the garden sometimes, but never outside. I've never known him to run off and hide before.'

Tantau reluctantly abandoned his indolent pose and sat up, shoulders slightly hunched and head cocked on one side as if listening for distant sounds. ' Who saw Konstantin last, and when? '

' I did—this afternoon, just before we left for the ceremony. I spoke to him. He was doing his homework.'

Tantau nodded, recalling that he had overheard the conversation from the kitchen. ' And you've searched the house from top to bottom? Did you look in the servants' rooms as well as the attic and the basement? '

' We looked everywhere! ' Brandstädter cried in desperation. ' It's terrible—he's simply vanished! '

' Have you looked in the garden? '

' No, but he can't be out there now. The nights are too cold still. We called him, of course, but there was no answer. We looked in the garages and the green-house, too, but there was no sign of him.'

' Fetch me a torch or a lantern,' Tantau said crisply. ' Switch all the outside lights on and tell Bennicken to leave his beer and come with me. But no fuss, mind you! I don't want anyone to be alarmed—I'm just going for a little stroll in the garden.'

' What are we looking for? ' Bennicken demanded.

' Not fairies, I'll tell you that much,' Tantau said tersely.

' I was in the middle of my supper.'

Tantau paused on the terrace for a moment to get his bearings and then shuffled resolutely across the lawn towards his first objective, the pool. At his heels plodded Bennicken, uttering occasional grunts expressive of resentment. As far as could be deduced, he was complaining that he had been engaged to drive Tantau around, not to accompany him on nocturnal jaunts.

Tantau derived no particular pleasure from the monologue going on behind him. ' Ever seen a dead body? ' he called over his shoulder with a deliberate note of challenge in his voice.

Bennicken sounded unimpressed. ' Plenty of times.'

' Ever handled any? '

' Dozens.' Nothing seemed to shake Bennicken. ' Is that what we're looking for? '

' You never know,' Tantau replied evasively. He scrutinized the edges of the pool closely, but could see nothing in the pale starlight except a blurred black line where the banks merged with the smooth and seemingly bottomless ribbon of oily water. He switched on his torch, and its beam sliced the darkness. Individual bushes emerged from the amorphous gloom of the night with startling clarity.

' Why here? ' asked Bennicken.

' We've got to start somewhere,' Tantau said. He sounded pensive.

' But why here? '

As if by accident, Tantau let the beam of his torch play briefly on Bennicken's face, but all he could detect was an expression of sullen scorn. He switched off again.

' Let's talk about death,' he said, hoping to crack the man's hard and leathery shell. ' There's something disgustingly tactless about death, especially when people take its presence for granted—in war-time, say. As soon as it becomes generally accepted, corpses get strewn around at random—in broad daylight, in the middle of the road, in flower-beds, market-places, ditches, woods—anywhere you like.'

' No need to tell me,' Bennicken said professionally, ' I know.'

' But in normal times, so-called, even death conforms to certain rules. It stops being so repulsively casual and becomes more discreet. Corpses become a rarity, at least in public. People normally do their dying in private, either at home or tucked up in a hospital bed. On that basis, where should anyone who suspects the existence of a dead body look first? In nooks and crannies, trunks and cellars, woods and ponds.'

' Sounds reasonable,' observed Bennicken.

Tantau abandoned any further attempt to explore the by-ways of his companion's mind. He switched on the torch again, got down to his knees and started to crawl through the bushes parallel to the bank and about a yard from the water's edge. It was not long before he was wheezing from his unaccustomed exertions.

'Here, let me go first,' Bennicken suggested.

Tantau accepted the offer with alacrity, and Bennicken's massive body began to cleave a path through the undergrowth. Clamping the torch between his teeth, he forged relentlessly ahead like a human bulldozer. Before long, he was panting too, but his rate of progress remained so rapid that Tantau found it hard to keep up with him.

'Here's something!' Bennicken called at last.

Tantau crawled forward hurriedly, disregarding the twigs that whipped and stung his cheeks. Still crawling, he saw that Bennicken was shining the torch on some articles of clothing, obviously belonging to a boy.

'Well?' Bennicken said. His eyes glinted with satisfaction.

Tantau took the torch from him. Its beam explored the clothes that lay scattered on the ground, then travelled slowly across the trampled grass of the little clearing to the bank, which also showed marks of feet. Reaching the water, it lingered there, probing the greenish depths. At one point, the oily surface seemed to glow a trifle more luminously, as though something pale and elongated lay beneath.

'There's something down there.' Bennicken made the statement as unemotionally as if he were telling one of his fares what was on the clock. Deliberately, he started to remove his jacket. 'I'll take a look,' he added, as he kicked off his trousers.

Tantau trudged back to the house. 'Get me a blanket,' he told Frau Brandstädter in a strangely flat voice. 'Then notify the police. Konstantin is dead.'

8. Crime Sometimes Pays

'You're an early bird,' said the porter of the *Gasthof zur alten Post.*

'Perhaps I haven't been to bed at all,' Tantau rejoined. 'You never can tell.'

'You don't look the all-night-party type.'

'I'm getting on,' said Tantau. 'I don't need much sleep. Old men get plenty of time to look around before they close their eyes for good.'

The porter, also an elderly man, seemed a little disconcerted. 'You've a strange way of putting things,' he said, flicking an imaginary speck of dust off the counter. He wasn't in the mood for dissertations on death so early in the day. None of the hotel guests had even breakfasted yet.

Tantau appeared to have unlimited time on his hands. He leant against the porter's desk, a pale, rumpled, dwarfish figure. 'Ever heard of the black file?' he asked.

The porter shook his head. His persistent visitor's macabre line in early morning conversation was getting on his nerves.

'The black file,' Tantau explained, 'contains details of mysterious cases—inexplicable phenomena which the police have failed to elucidate, unsolved murders whose full circumstances are unknown to anyone—except the murderer, of course.'

The elderly porter looked slightly bewildered. 'I don't see that that's got anything to do with me.'

'Quite a few people take that attitude,' Tantau said affably. 'The most unlikely individuals fall prey to self-deception. They only see what they want to see—like the doctor who issued a death certificate to a family he'd known for years. He certified the cause of death as heart failure. When the body was exhumed later, at my insistence, it turned out that the dead man had been shot and the bullet-hole camouflaged with sticking-plaster.'

'Terrible,' commented the porter. He glanced round

244

almost desperately for someone to rescue him from further morbid revelations, but no one came.

'That's the sort of case you find in the black file. A large number of crimes are never solved, of course. It makes you think, doesn't it? You may have rubbed shoulders with a dozen murderers in your time.'

'Excuse me,' the porter broke in hastily. 'I'll have to leave you now. I'm needed in the kitchen.'

Tantau smiled. 'Don't let me detain you.'

The porter vanished. Tantau's talk of the hereafter had achieved the desired effect, and the road to the hotel bedrooms was now clear. He mounted the narrow stairs without undue haste. When he reached the door of Michael Meiners's room he paused to listen. The oppressive hush was broken by the sort of noises habitually made by someone beginning the day—the plash of running water, the brittle clatter of tooth-brush against mug, the muffled gurgle of ancient plumbing. Tantau knocked at the door.

Silence fell again for a few seconds before he heard the sound of bare feet padding across linoleum and floorboards. A moment later the door opened to reveal Michael Meiners, dressed in an open shirt and hastily-buttoned trousers.

'Good morning,' Tantau said politely.

'Good morning.' Meiners frowned with the effort of recollection. 'Didn't I see you downstairs with the porter yesterday?'

Tantau gave a courteous smile. 'You did, but you don't know who I am.'

He walked past Meiners into the bedroom. It looked like a thousand other bedrooms in a thousand other cheap hotels, with clumsy utilitarian furniture and grimy covers and curtains. There was an imitation oak bedstead against the wall and a wash-basin in one corner. It was a shabby room, devoid of any special features.

'Don't you want to know why I'm here?' Tantau asked.

Meiners closed the door and came slowly and diffidently towards him. His neck and a large expanse of thin chest were clearly visible through his gaping shirt. The skin was criss-crossed with jagged scars, broad and angry-looking, and the hands that hung at his sides trembled slightly—though this might have been due to the chill of the grey April morning.

245

Tantau indicated the scars with his forefinger. 'War souvenirs?'

Meiners nodded.

Tantau looked vaguely aggrieved. 'You don't seem particularly upset at my bursting in like this. Most people would have thrown me out by now.'

Meiners stared pensively at the old man with resignation in his large melancholy eyes. 'I detest violence,' he said quietly.

'But you're prepared to tolerate it?'

Meiners leant wearily against the wall. 'Have I done something to you—am I indebted to you in some way? Why are you here?'

'I've come to ask you a few questions,' Tantau said cautiously. 'However, I think you ought to know why I propose to ask them. To be brief, my name is Tantau and I work for an agency—an information service, if you like. I've been told to find out if there's a man named Michael Meiners staying in Rheine-Bergen and, if so, why he's here.'

'If that's all you want to know, there's no reason why I shouldn't tell you. My name's Michael Meiners and I'm here on behalf of my firm, collecting debts.'

'You've been here for some days, haven't you?'

'Yes, working for my firm.'

'And throughout that time you've devoted yourself entirely to business matters? You haven't pursued outside interests of any kind? You've made no personal contacts?' Tantau gave Meiners an encouraging smile. 'You haven't, for instance, felt tempted to call on any of your war-time companions?'

Meiners detached himself from the wall and walked with an apparent effort to the bed, where he sat down and regarded Tantau with a look of inquiry. 'Is that why you're here?' he asked.

'Would it worry you if I said yes?'

Meiners shook his head. 'It's all so long ago,' he said slowly. 'Why should I force my presence on them? I've almost forgotten what happened.'

'If several people are involved in something, it isn't enough for one of them to forget about it.'

'I don't want to be reminded!' Meiners protested. 'It's

246

over and done with as far as I'm concerned—you can go and tell them so, if they're interested.'

Tantau wagged his head sorrowfully. ' I'm afraid it isn't as easy as that. Let's assume you really mean what you say: you don't want to be reminded—you want to forget. What guarantee is there that you won't change your mind? Isn't it conceivable that something might occur to alter your present attitude? '

' I don't understand and I don't want to understand.' Meiners straightened up with a jerk and a look of pain flitted across his face. ' All I want is a chance to finish off my work here. I'll be through in two or three days, and that'll be the last anyone sees of me.'

' Until next time? ' Tantau inquired mildly.

' There won't be a next time.'

' I'm prepared to believe that, but my opinion is of secondary importance.'

Meiners clenched his teeth and eyed Tantau with suspicion. ' Are you forcing me to ask who sent you? '

Tantau smiled. ' I imagine you've guessed that already.'

Meiners rose to his feet and began to pace up and down between the window and the door. At length he paused and confronted Tantau with a look of torment on his face.

' Sixteen years is a long time, Herr Tantau,' he said, ' especially for someone in my position. For me, those years have been filled with sickness, imprisonment and loneliness. I've only been back in this country for two years. I don't live luxuriously, but at least I make a living. I've found a little peace at last, I earn a little money and I do my job— that's all I ask. For me, the past is dead and buried.'

Tantau bowed his head in thought. ' Your stay here is purely coincidental, then?'' he asked casually.

' Entirely.'

' A strange coincidence, though, wouldn't you agree? '

' Yes,' Meiners conceded without hesitation. He walked over to the bed and sat down again, this time perching on the edge as though to be nearer his visitor. Clasping his hands round his knees, he said: ' I work for a debt-collecting agency in Frankfurt. I'm a field representative, which means I'm always moving about from place to place—anywhere where there's a concentration of bad debts or hire-purchase instalments to be collected. Last week I was in Ravensbrück, and this week I was sent here. It was a complete coincidence. My firm decides where I go, not me.'

'And you've spent your whole time collecting debts?'

'I visited the Building Exhibition once.'

Meiners made no further comment, and Tantau felt it wiser not to press for details. He merely said: 'Would you be prepared to show me your credentials, Herr Meiners?'

Meiners hesitated briefly. Then he reached for a bulky briefcase lying on the bedside table and opened it. Removing one bundle of papers after another, he handed them to Tantau. They included written instructions to the debt-collecting agency from large firms, mostly mail-order houses, written instructions from the agency to its field representative, i.e. Meiners, daily report forms, receipt slips, daily payment records and an officially attested and frequently renewed form of authority made out in Meiners's name.

Tantau found nothing to arouse his suspicions. The daily report forms spoke of hard and unremitting work. Meiners's visit to Rheine-Bergen appeared to be wholly coincidental.

'Entirely convincing,' the old man said slowly.

Meiners looked relieved. 'There you are! I'll be finished here in two days' time—three at the outside. Then I'll move on.'

'What about moving on straight away?'

Meiners stared at Tantau in dismay. A bewildered look came into his eyes, and it was some moments before he spoke. 'I can't—I'd lose my job if I did. I'm not one of our top representatives, you see. I can't afford too many failures— that's why I have to work really hard at the job. I never learnt a proper profession. I didn't have a chance to. It could be very awkward for me if I packed up now without settling everything—I mean, without completing the firm's business.'

'Look,' Tantau said, 'I'd like to have a long talk with you, but my time's limited at the moment. I'm expected at a meeting. To be quite frank, they're expecting a report from me.'

Meiners hung his head.

'The gist of my report,' Tantau continued gently, 'will be that a man named Michael Meiners is staying at the *Gasthof zur alten Post.*'

'And I felt you wanted to help me,' murmured Meiners.

Tantau gave him a friendly nod. 'Please bear with me. I was just going to offer you a piece of advice. I never submit a report that doesn't accord with the facts, but facts change from hour to hour. In plain language, my friend, move out of here and book into another hotel. It's as simple as that.'

'You think it's the right thing to do?'

'It's the practical thing to do. Simply omit to leave a forwarding address with the porter. I'd be grateful if you kept in touch, though.' Tantau produced a notebook, tore out a sheet and scribbled some figures on it. 'You can reach me at this number between midday and one o'clock.'

'I don't know what to do,' Meiners said helplessly. 'I can't think straight any more, but somehow I feel you may be able to help me.'

'I'm glad,' Tantau said, getting up.

'Why are you doing this?'

Tantau smiled. 'I'm a fun-loving old man and I'm inquisitive by nature, as you've probably gathered. I've got any number of vices—I see that more and more clearly the older I get—and my greatest vice is what some people call a sense of fair play. It'll be the ruin of me yet.'

'Things can't go on like this,' Karl Schulz said accusingly. 'If there's one thing I can't stand, it's dishonesty.'

Eva looked her brother in the eye. 'That makes two of us, Karl.'

Marlene Sonnenberg, busy varnishing her nails, said: 'You've been talking at cross-purposes for days now. Eva's old enough to have her little secrets.'

'Secrets—from me?' Schulz stood in the middle of the kitchen like a rock defying the raging elements.

Marlene gave a knowing chuckle, and Eva had the depressing feeling that she had been misunderstood. 'I'm sorry if I've caused any unpleasantness.'

'Unpleasantness, did you say?' Schulz's righteous indignation mounted. He took it for granted that Eva ought to have unlimited faith in him. 'Treachery would be a better word!'

Marlene laughed again. 'Oh come, Karl, Eva's a big girl now—or hadn't you noticed?'

Schulz ignored the remark. He felt as if the world—his world—were rocking on its foundations.

249

'I'm not easily upset by things,' he said. 'They used to call me the man in the iron mask sometimes, in the war, but what I've had to put up with in the past few days has really got under my skin.'

'And on my nerves,' Marlene murmured to herself.

'I'll never forget the sight of Bennicken carrying that poor little devil Konstantin into the house—wrapped in a rug, and water dripping all over the place.'

'It was an accident, Karl,' Marlene said soothingly, but Schulz appeared to be re-living every detail of the incident with painful clarity.

'His hair was full of mud and his little arms and legs looked so thin—like a bird's legs, they were. It reminded me of bodies I'd seen in the war—all shrunken, somehow. Poor little chap!'

'Don't talk about it any more,' Eva said gently. 'You mustn't take it to heart so.'

Schulz cast a brief expressionless glance at his sister. 'It's been years since I saw anything like that. I could hardly get a word out. All I wanted to do was go home and forget about it.' His voice rose abruptly to a fierce bellow. 'And what did I find at home? Nothing! Nobody! My sister was out on the tiles again!'

'Everybody has to grow up some time,' remarked Marlene.

'I don't think you're qualified to discuss this subject, Marlene,' Schulz said in tones of reprimand.

'Our attitudes differ on lots of subjects.'

'You're telling me!' retorted Schulz. 'It was a disgrace, the way you behaved at Kerze's last night.'

'You make me laugh!' cried Marlene.

Dismayed, Eva stared in turn at her irate brother and his indignant girl-friend. 'Please don't quarrel on my account.'

'On your account!' Marlene stood up. 'Don't flatter yourself! A man who's incapable of summoning up a spark of human understanding isn't capable of love either. I object to being treated like a piece of furniture.'

And with that she gathered up her aids to beauty and flounced out.

'Good riddance!' Schulz yelled after her, but when she had gone he flopped on to a kitchen chair as if his legs had given way. ' I don't know,' he mumbled, ' everything's gone haywire.'

Eva leant towards her brother, eyeing him with a mixture of sorrow and affection. ' Don't be sad,' she said, laying her hand gently on his arm.

Schulz shook it off impatiently and brooded in silence for some moments. ' What's the matter with us? ' he demanded. ' We lived a nice peaceful life, didn't we? Weren't we happy —didn't we have every reason to be satisfied with the way things were? '

' I'm so sorry, Karl,' Eva said softly, ' but what can I do? '

Schulz stared at the floor. ' There's something odd going on,' he said darkly. ' Things have been going wrong for days now. Some of my friends avoid me, others lie to me, others try to pull the wool over my eyes or talk me into doing things I disapprove of—it's enough to make a man sick! People tear up old friendships like lavatory paper, unpleasant surprises crop up at every turn, an innocent child dies a ghastly death, and to cap it all my sister goes roaming around like a bitch on heat! '

' You're wrong, Karl.' Eva spoke without resentment.

' Maybe,' Schulz said, trying to be fair. ' But I don't understand you, Eva. There's never been anything between us which you felt you couldn't tell me.'

' I've got something to tell you now, Karl,' Eva said bravely. ' I think I'm pregnant.'

' You're what? ' Schulz exclaimed. ' Did you say pregnant? '

' Yes.'

' Are you sure? '

' Pretty sure.'

' Eva, Eva! ' Schulz cried in dismay, but his indignation suddenly evaporated. He felt an unexpected surge of joy. ' It can't be true! '

' We'll soon know one way or the other, Karl, but I'm fairly certain.'

She held out her hands to him and he took them in his. Rising, he clasped her to his broad chest and gently patted her slender shoulders. ' My poor little girl,' he said huskily, breathing hard.

Suddenly he stiffened and held her at arm's length, ' What about the father? ' he demanded, looking into her eyes.

Eva smiled. 'He doesn't know anything about it yet, and I don't want him to for the time being. I've got to break him in gently.'

'You mean you still won't tell me the man's name?'

'That's just what I do mean,' Eva said.

'I trust you've a full report for me at last,' said Gisenius.

'There isn't much to tell,' Tantau replied.

Willy Kerze, who was standing behind Gisenius's chair, said: 'Yesterday evening you gave the impression that you had something definite to report.'

'First, Herr Kerze,' Tantau said soberly, 'I should like to express my sincere condolences. I had no chance to do so last night, in all the confusion.'

'Thank you,' Kerze said in measured tones.

Tantau treated Kerze to a blandly disarming look. 'Since you happen to be here, Herr Kerze, perhaps you could satisfy my curiosity. I should be interested to know if the police have instituted any inquiries, and if so with what result.'

'Two officers called last night after you left,' Kerze said with some repugnance. 'They turned up again today—at an unearthly hour, I might add.'

'Do you know what conclusion they reached?'

'They said it was an accident.' Kerze sounded indignant at this invasion of his private domain. 'But that's what they said last night. I should have thought one visit would have been enough for them.'

'Well,' said Tantau, 'it was dark last night and the police are a thorough lot. Full inquiries always have to be made, even in the case of an accident. There's always the possibility of negligence, you see.'

'Negligence?' Kerze shot a worried glance at Gisenius. 'What does that mean?'

'Merely a routine term,' the lawyer reassured him. 'There's no need to be alarmed. It hasn't any bearing on this case.'

'I'm not alarmed,' Kerze retorted. 'I can't be held to blame. It was an accident—an act of God.'

'A peculiar accident, though,' Tantau said deliberately. 'Don't you think so?'

'If you don't mind!' Gisenius sat back in his chair with

a jerk. 'The only thing that strikes me as peculiar, Herr Tantau, is that you've managed to sit here for a quarter of an hour without uttering a word about the matter under discussion.'

'There isn't much to tell,' Tantau repeated, looking exasperatingly genial. 'But as I think I told you yesterday, before I inform you of Herr Meiners's present whereabouts I should appreciate an answer to a certain question.'

'Are you making conditions?' Kerze demanded.

Gisenius frowned at the ceiling. 'Herr Tantau,' he said suavely, 'as I trust you are aware, we engaged you to do a job for us, and you undertook to carry it out promptly, without provisos of any kind. However, since it would distress me to think that you felt you were associated with something which wasn't absolutely above-board, I'll do my best to answer your question. What is it?'

'What will happen to Michael Meiners if I give you his address?'

'We'll have to talk with him, that's all. We'd like to meet him again.'

Tantau smiled faintly. 'Some interviews are conducted with an excess of enthusiasm, wouldn't you say?'

'Do you know what he's driving at?' Kerze demanded, staring bemusedly at Gisenius.

The lawyer nodded. 'I believe I do,' he said gravely. 'But believe me, Herr Tantau, it was a mistake—a regrettable error. It won't occur again, take my word for it. Does that answer your question sufficiently?'

'It does if it's true,' said Tantau. 'It would be extremely serious if it weren't,' he added mildly. 'I'm sorry to have to labour the point, but I'm not a butcher.'

'Very well,' Gisenius said hastily. He obviously found the conversation embarrassing and was anxious to bring it to an end. 'And now may I have your report?'

A trifle ostentatiously Tantau produced a notebook. It was virtually empty, but he opened it and pretended to read, watching his audience over the top of the page. 'Michael Meiners, date of birth 15 March 1924, place of birth Immenstadt, now resident at 17 Fasanengasse, Frankfurt am Main, currently visiting Rheine-Bergen.'

Gisenius folded his hands on his chest—a symptom of

intense concentration. Quietly but with great emphasis, he asked: ' Where is he staying? '

' At the *Gasthof zur alten Post,*' Tantau announced. ' He's been there for nearly a week.'

Kerze exhaled sharply with a sound like a tyre bursting, but Gisenius asked: ' Did you manage to find out why he's here? '

Tantau bowed his head in assent. Then, quite deliberately, he selected a word whose dangers were not lost on him. ' Ostensibly,' he said, ' Michael Meiners is here to collect debts for a debt-collecting agency.'

' A pretext! ' Kerze exclaimed promptly.

Gisenius raised a restraining hand and gave Kerze a brief but unmistakable look of warning. ' Well, Herr Tantau,' he said civilly, ' that completes your duties. Thank you for your prompt and expert assistance.'

' It's been a pleasure,' Tantau replied, making no move to rise.

' That's that, then,' Gisenius said impatiently.

' And my fee? '

' You'll receive it in due course.'

' For the whole of today as well? '

' We're not mean, Herr Tantau. You must have noticed that.'

' Yes indeed,' Tantau agreed, ' and I'm sure you have your reasons for being generous. The only trouble is, I suffer from what is known as professional integrity. It may sound strange, but I'm afraid I dislike receiving something for nothing. I prefer to give my clients their money's worth.'

' Submit a full written report, if you insist.'

Tantau shook his head thoughtfully. ' That would be a waste of time.'

' Then call it a day.'

' Most generous of you,' Tantau murmured, ' but please don't put temptation in an old man's path.'

' What do you want, then? ' Gisenius was growing slightly restive. ' Your job's finished and we've nothing else for you to do.'

' Ah, there's always something to do, even for an old has-been like me.' Tantau's smile was almost diffident. ' If it's all right with you, I'd like to solve a problem which has been puzzling me. What could have prompted a boy to take

254

his clothes off on a cold April day and fall into a pond? I should be most intrigued to know the answer.'

' Who knows what goes on in a child's mind? ' Gisenius said vaguely.

' Let him carry on,' Kerze interposed, glancing at Gisenius in a way which denoted that it was one method of getting rid of the old fool. ' It can't do any harm.'

Gisenius shrugged. ' If you think so . . .' He too found the idea of diverting Tantau's attentions not unattractive.

' In that case, gentlemen, many thanks,' said Tantau, ' I shall do my best to justify your obvious faith in me.'

' I'll be glad when we've seen the last of that man,' Kerze said, when the door had closed behind the old detective.

' We ought never to have got involved with him,' Gisenius acknowledged reluctantly. ' He knows too much, and that could be dangerous.'

' Never mind,' Kerze said with a touch of complacency, ' we've got Meiners's address at last—that's the main thing.'

Gisenius sighed and pressed one of the buttons on his desk. ' You look as though you need a drink. What'll you have? '

The chief clerk, who could ape the manners of a ducal butler when he considered it appropriate, appeared promptly and stood waiting in the doorway.

' Brandy,' said Kerze.

' Brandy it is,' Gisenius confirmed, turning to the chief clerk. ' Have a bottle and a glass sent in, and when you've done that ring the reception desk at the *Gasthof zur alten Post* and ask if there's a Herr Meiners staying there. There's no need to mention my name. That will be all.'

The chief clerk retired with dignity.

' One can't always dodge difficulties, Conrad,' Kerze said. ' The thing is to overcome them, and that's what we're doing now.'

' Your optimism never fails to amaze me,' Gisenius said indulgently, ' but in this particular instance I'm afraid I'm unable to share it. I've too many misgivings.'

' Tell me about them.'

' Very well,' Gisenius replied. ' Let's think back to that day on the edge of the wood. Meiners was in a very exposed position, if you remember.'

'It was a job for a suicide-squad,' Kerze said reminiscently. 'No use disguising the fact.'

Gisenius raised his eyebrows in reproof. 'My dear fellow, please try to avoid using such—such highly-coloured language. It creates the wrong impression.'

'Fair enough.' Kerze was quite prepared to give ground on this point. 'Meiners was in an exposed position.'

'Precisely,' said Gisenius, 'a position which almost immediately came under concentrated enemy fire. However, we escaped.'

'That's just it!' Kerze broke in. 'We all escaped—all of us, Meiners included.'

'That's not the way to look at it,' Gisenius said promptly. 'We may feel justified today in assuming that Meiners escaped, but there seems little doubt that he was in a moribund condition. He was seriously wounded—left for dead. We don't yet know what became of him. It may have taken him years to get on his feet again. He may have spent the interim in a P.O.W. camp or suffered some permanent physical disability—he may even be a cripple.'

'All the same, he's alive,' Kerze said harshly. 'At least nobody can be held responsible for his death.'

'That still leaves the business of the girl the night before. If you remember, we decided that Meiners was the only one who could possibly have been responsible.'

'Blast it all!' Kerze burst out. 'How soon are we going to be able to forget the whole thing, that's what I'd like to know?'

'My dear Willy,' Gisenius said solemnly, 'as I've already emphasized, our first concern is to clear those of us who are genuinely innocent. There's only one way of doing that, I'm afraid, and that is to find the party or parties responsible.'

'How do you propose to do that?'

Gisenius inclined his head, an extremely effective gesture conveying humility and resignation. 'It distresses me to draw the only possible conclusion from the facts available to us, but who did, in fact, bear the responsibility, the sole responsibility?'

'Schulz?' hazarded Kerze.

Gisenius nodded gravely. 'He was the unit commander. He was in charge. What happened could only have happened with his knowledge and consent. Militarily and from a practical point of view, the responsibility for every decision was his alone. Consequently, he alone is answerable for everything that happened. I'm genuinely sorry to have to say it, but I can't find a more reasonable or logical inference.'

'So it's Karl Schulz,' Kerze said in an almost business-like tone.

'And let's not shirk the distressing business of the previous night, either. If we're honest, we can only come to one conclusion. Practically speaking and in the very nature of things, only one man fills the bill. I might almost call it psychologically inevitable that he should be regarded as the only possible suspect. His general behaviour and dubious moral character single him out for the role. You know who I mean, of course.'

Kerze did not hesitate. 'Hirsch.'

'A logical and inescapable deduction,' declared Gisenius, visibly gratified by Kerze's powers of comprehension. 'All this is just between the two of us, of course, but don't forget that it represents our insurance policy in the last resort.'

At this juncture the chief clerk re-entered the room and stood stiffly in the doorway. At a nod from Gisenius, he reported that a man named Michael Meiners had been staying at the *Gasthof zur alten Post* for the last few days, but had left for an unknown destination about an hour before.

Gisenius raised one hand and the chief clerk withdrew.

'What does that mean?' Kerze inquired anxiously.

Gisenius seemed unperturbed. 'There are two possible explanations,' he said. 'In the first place, Meiners may have left town altogether for reasons of his own. That wouldn't be a bad solution—in fact, it might be the best of all. On the other hand, it could be a fortunate coincidence—too fortunate for my taste.'

'What's the other alternative?'

'That he's moved out of his hotel but not left town.'

'You mean he's trying to give us the slip?'

'Precisely. And because we can't ignore that unpleasant possibility, I'm rather afraid we must prepare ourselves for the worst.'

'How could it have happened!' wailed Frau Brandstädter. 'I did everything I could for the boy—treated him like my own—and what does he do the moment my back's turned? He goes bathing!'

'Bathing?' An alert gleam came into Tantau's eye. 'Who said he went bathing?'

'The police,' Brandstädter replied without hesitation. 'The doctor said so too. Heart failure caused by sudden immersion in cold water—that's what he called it. But what could have put the idea into the poor child's head?'

Tantau had been asking himself the same question, but unlike the police and the doctor he found it impossible to accept the easy answer. He admitted that boys of Konstantin's age were unpredictable but he also knew that they were normally averse to exposing themselves to pain or discomfort without good cause. This meant that a boy like Konstantin might well venture into icy water, but only if there were some specific reason, e.g. because he wanted to show off, because he was looking for something, because someone had dared him to, or, finally, because someone had pushed him in.

Tantau meditated on the possible alternatives at his leisure as he sat in the kitchen listening to Frau Brandstädter's explanations with half an ear.

'It was an accident,' she complained, 'but why should it have happened to Herr Kerze of all people—dear kind man that he is?'

'People call death the great leveller, and in my experience they're right,' Tantau said, rising to his feet. 'Do you mind if I take a look around? Herr Kerze gave me permission.'

'I'll be glad to show you anything you want to see.'

'To start with, perhaps you'd be kind enough to take me to the boy's room.'

Brandstädter nodded, her moon-face clearly conveying that it was a pleasure to be of service to a man of Tantau's infinite charm. She stumped up the stairs ahead of him and led him along the first-floor corridor until she came to a door at the far end. 'This is Konstantin's room,' she said, opening it.

'Thank you,' said Tantau, 'but you mustn't let me keep you from your work. I realize how precious your time is. You're always on the go.'

Brandstädter nodded graciously at the old man and returned to the kitchen.

Tantau stood in the doorway and surveyed the room which

had once been Konstantin's. In some respects it looked as he had expected it to look, but one feature struck him immediately. Neatness reigned supreme. The boy's shoes stood in an orderly row in one corner. There were no articles of clothing strewn around, and even the school-books on the desk near the window were stacked in symmetrical piles.

'Too tidy,' Tantau muttered to himself. 'Probably had no choice, poor little devil!'

After cursorily examining the contents of the chest of drawers he walked over to the wardrobe, wagging his head as he did so. He inspected the suits inside one by one, paying special attention to the trousers. There was scarcely a stain, tear or darn to be seen.

Sadly, Tantau concluded that Konstantin had been a quiet boy. His clothes bore no marks that might have been produced by climbing, sliding or scuffling. He decided to exact a suitably high price for the life of this small and solitary child. He shuffled wearily towards the window and paused with drooping shoulders in front of Konstantin's desk.

A bright shaft of light fell on the top, clearly illuminating every detail. Tantau noticed that all the exercise-books were neatly stacked except one, an arithmetic book, which lay open in the middle of the desk. Beside it lay a pen. Splash-marks on the blotter indicated that it had not been put down carefully but cast light-heartedly aside. Beside it stood an ink-bottle of the type carried by schoolchildren in their satchels, squat in shape and equipped with a dipping device and a screw-top. The top, Tantau noted, had not been replaced—another small point, but one which was inconsistent with the order which reigned elsewhere in the room.

Tantau picked up the open exercise-book and examined the last page of calculations. He read them through thoroughly and worked them out before turning back the page and checking the penultimate page and the two before that. It was a task which took him some time and taxed his rusty knowledge of mathematics, but he persevered.

He replaced the exercise-book and straightened up with a sigh. After a final glance round the room, he hurried downstairs again to the kitchen, where he found Brandstädter busy cleaning silver. Her manner conveyed possessive pride in the opulence of the household over which she presided.

'Konstantin was a nice child, by all accounts,' said Tantau, sitting down near Brandstädter and eyeing the gleaming silver with apparent interest.

'He was a very obedient child, I'll say that for him.'

'Was he athletic—tough?'

'Not exactly,' Brandstädter replied with mild surprise. 'He was more of a brainy type, if you know what I mean.'

Tantau leant forwards and ran an appraising eye over the article of silver which Brandstäder was polishing so diligently. Catching sight of his face reflected in a cake-knife he sat back again with a grimace of distaste. 'Are you good at arithmetic, Frau Brandstädter?'

'How do you mean?' Her surprise deepened. 'I'm given a monthly housekeeping allowance by Herr Kerze, and I account for that down to the last pfennig. I'm never out, either.'

'I'm sure you're not,' Tantau said soothingly, 'but that's not quite what I meant. I was just wondering if you ever helped Konstantin with his sums.'

'Good gracious no! Herr Kerze would never have stood for anything like that. Konstantin always had to finish his homework by himself before he was allowed to leave his room. Anyway, even if I'd wanted to, the stuff they do in school these days is so complicated that I can never make head or tail of it.'

'Tell me,' Tantau inquired, 'when we went to the ceremony at the factory yesterday, who stayed behind?'

'Konstantin, of course—more's the pity!'

'Was he left here by himself, or did someone else stay behind?'

'Of course he wasn't left by himself,' Brandstädter said. 'Herr Kerze would have disapproved strongly. Anna—that's the maid—she was here, getting the drawing-room ready and polishing glasses.'

'I'd appreciate a word with Anna,' said Tantau, adding gallantly: 'If you've no objection, dear lady.'

'Of course not,' Brandstädter assured him.

She waddled out into the passage emitting repeated and imperious cries of 'Anna!' In less than a minute she was back again with the maid at her heels. Anna lingered in the doorway, a robust young creature with good-natured bovine eyes which shone with a mixture of curiosity and apprehension.

'Tell me, Fräulein Anna,' Tantau said with quiet insistence, 'how long were you out of the house yesterday afternoon?'
'Who says I was?' Anna replied defiantly, glaring at Frau Brandstädter as if she were the ultimate in infamy. 'Who's been snooping on me, I'd like to know? I do my work—what more do they expect?'
'How long?' Tantau persisted.
'An hour, that's all. What's wrong with that?'
'Nothing, as far as I'm concerned,' Tantau replied with a smile, but Frau Brandstädter gave an outraged snort.
'I like that!' she snapped. 'You mean to say you left your work without so much as a by-your-leave and went off cuddling with that young man of yours? You haven't heard the last of this, my girl, I promise you!'
'Never mind,' Tantau said soothingly. 'That's not the point.'
'I won't stand here and be insulted!' Anna hissed. 'I do my work here, like I'm paid to. Why shouldn't I take a few minutes off when I've finished what I've got to do?'
'Do you mind if I say something now?' Tantau cut in. 'We've established that you went to see your young man, Fräulein Anna. It's quite immaterial to me whether you were allowed to do so or not. I'm only interested in knowing when you left the house.'
'It was just after Frau Brandstädter left for the factory.'
'I knew it!' Brandstädter cried. She appealed to Tantau. 'You've only got to turn your back on these girls for two minutes and they're rolling in the grass with their skirts over their heads.'
'You've got a dirty mind!' Anna said belligerently.
'Now, now, Fräulein,' Tantau implored. 'Frau Brandstädter left the house, and you went off to see your mechanic immediately afterwards. Am I right so far?'
'Yes.' Anna eyed the old man at the kitchen table with some surprise. 'How did you know he was a mechanic?'
'I've got ears,' said Tantau, winking at her covertly. 'Before Frau Brandstädter left, I heard her talking to you. She warned you not to sneak off to the garage down the road. I thought at the time that it was unwise of her to put the idea into your head.'
'You're a sly one and no mistake!' the girl said admiringly.

'It didn't take much working out,' Tantau replied. He gave Anna a sympathetic nod of dismissal and she flounced out, slamming the door behind her.

Brandstädter snorted with fury. 'I'll give that creature what for! She obviously doesn't know who she's dealing with!'

'I'm sure she does,' Tantau ventured boldly, drawing on his reserves of credit with the housekeeper. 'A strong personality like yours couldn't fail to make a deep impression on anyone. But tell me, Frau Brandstädter—you talked to three people just before we drove to the factory, if I'm not mistaken: Konstantin, Anna and someone called Saffranski. Who is he?'

'A very nice gentleman,' Brandstädter declared, her expression softening. 'A well-mannered gentleman. He's been working in Herr Kerze's study for the past few days.'

'That makes two people who stayed behind,' said Tantau, '—Konstantin and Herr Saffranski.'

Frau Brandstädter shook her head. 'No, Herr Saffranski left the house about ten minutes after we did.'

'How do you know?'

'He told me so—didn't you hear him? His work was nearly finished and he wanted to attend the ceremony at the factory.'

Tantau's next question followed swiftly, but with a total lack of emphasis. 'Do you know whether Herr Saffranski actually attended the ceremony?'

'Oh, yes, I saw him there—I even spoke to him. Such nice manners, he has.'

'So you mentioned,' Tantau said courteously. 'You say you saw him and spoke to him. Would you mind if I took a look at the study?'

Brandstädter not only conducted Tantau to Kerze's study but showed him where Saffranski had sat and pointed out the file which had been occupying his attention.

This document seemed to exercise a magical fascination over Tantau. Smiling like a child indulging in some harmless game, he sat where Saffranski had sat and, miming Saffranski, picked up the file and opened it. He noted that it was marked 'Europa Hotels Limited' and referred to a hotel with which he was only too familiar: the *Drei Kronen*. Furthermore, the documents inside suggested that Kerze was contemplating some kind of financial transaction. He was obviously taking a deep interest in the running of the *Drei Kronen*, which was managed—for the moment at least—by his war-time comrade Martin Hirsch.

'Well, well,' Tantau said thoughtfully, closing the file again, 'it's not often a man's hoist with his own petard.'

'I don't follow you,' said Frau Brandstädter, looking puzzled.

'I'll explain later,' Tantau replied guilelessly. 'By the way, it occurs to me that I forgot to ask the maid if she's good at arithmetic.'

'Her—good at arithmetic?' Brandstädter gave a contemptuous sniff. 'She can hardly write her own name!'

'Excellent,' Tantau seemed pleased. 'It's not that I don't appreciate the value of a good grounding in mathematics, but in this particular case I can't help welcoming the generally low standard of mathematical knowledge in this house.'

Martin Hirsch perched on Schulz's desk with his legs dangling. 'What about running into town with me, Karl?'

Schulz looked dubious. 'I oughtn't to, really. These chaps aren't fit to be left on their own. Still, if you'd really like me to.' He put his head round the door and shouted: 'I'm going into town for half an hour to see the builders about repainting the frontage. You can clean the windows while I'm gone—and don't miss any!'

They climbed into Hirsch's car and drove off in the direction of town, skirting the centre and avoiding the main road.

'Where are you taking us?' Schulz demanded with a sudden air of suspicion. 'I thought we were going to have a drink together, or something.'

'You'll see,' Hirsch said. They had negotiated the northern outskirts of town, leaving the new housing estate on their right, and Hirsch was now piloting the car down a side street leading to Schulz's neighbourhood.

'You aren't going to my place, are you?'

Hirsch did his best to look innocent, but he concentrated on the road and refrained from meeting Schulz's eye. 'I've got a book here, Karl. I thought Eva might enjoy it.'

Karl Schulz started fidgeting. 'I hadn't bargained for this,' he said nervously. 'We'd better not call in now, Martin.'

'Why ever not, my dear fellow?' Hirsch protested, glancing at him with affectionate concern. 'I thought we'd agreed that Eva and I should get to know each other better. There's nothing wrong with taking you along, is there—or would you prefer me to sneak round and see her behind your back?'

'You couldn't even if you wanted to,' Schulz said bitterly. 'I've locked her in. I hadn't any choice.'

Martin Hirsch braked to a halt and stared at Schulz in outrage. 'Damn it all, Karl, your sister's a grown woman. You can't do a stupid thing like that!'

'Rubbish!' Schulz said roughly. 'I've got my reasons. And now, if you want my advice, take the next turning on the right and let me out.'

'I'm coming with you, Karl. I won't be brushed off like this.'

'All right, we'll both get out and walk the rest of the way, and while we're at it I'll pass on an item of news which may give you something to think about. But don't tell me afterwards I ought to have spared your feelings.'

Obediently, Hirsch took the next turning on the right and parked within sight of the cinema round the corner from Schulz's flat. They set off side by side, with Schulz dragging his feet reluctantly.

'Well, what's this revelation of yours?' Hirsch demanded.

Schulz looked gloomy but determined. The street was almost empty.

'All right, I'll come straight to the point,' Schulz said grimly. 'Eva's been meeting a young man, as you know.'

'Yes, I know,' Hirsch said. 'She's young and pretty. She has a right to a little fun occasionally.'

'A little fun? That's rich!' Schulz laughed harshly. 'She's going to have a child.'

Hirsch stopped in his tracks. 'No,' was all he could say, 'no—it can't be true!' Instinctively, he glanced round for potential eavesdroppers, but the street was still deserted except for an old woman, a child and a young man, now only some seventy or eighty yards ahead. The young man looked vaguely familiar. 'Who's the father?' he said at length.

Karl Schulz shrugged contemptuously. He was too overcome with shame and anger to look his friend in the face. They had turned the corner by now, and Schulz's eyes travelled over the smooth frontage of the block of flats in which he lived, a box-like edifice built of regular concrete slabs and pierced at equally regular intervals by windows like blind eyes. Looking across the street, he saw that the young man had stopped outside. He too had a fleeting impression that he knew him, but his attention was temporarily claimed by the need to find an answer to Hirsch's question.

'The father?' he said. 'God knows. The whole thing was probably an accident, but it's too late to do anything about it now. Eva refuses to tell me his name.'

Martin Hirsch looked shaken. 'Poor girl, she must be in a frightful state.'

'That's not the impression I get,' Schulz growled.

Hirsch laid a hand on his friend's arm with the air of one who has reached an important decision. 'Look,' he said, 'let's not lose our heads over this. After all, what difference does it make? It doesn't make Eva a less delightful or desirable girl. Is it her fault she's going to have a child?' He paused. 'What's the matter, Karl? You're not listening to a word I'm saying.'

'Take a look at that youngster over there,' Schulz said ominously.

Hirsch followed the direction of his gaze. 'I noticed him earlier,' he said impatiently. 'It's young Gisenius, isn't it?'

Schulz gave a meaningful nod. 'Exactly, but what's he doing on this side of town?'

'Taking a walk, I imagine.'

'Why is he so interested in my flat, then?' Schulz snorted like a restive horse. 'I don't like it, Martin. There's something funny going on here!'

Shaking off Hirsch's restraining hand, Schulz stalked across the street as though drawn by a magnet. The two men saw Claus Gisenius enter the main hall, and as they followed suit they caught sight of his legs disappearing up the stairs.

By the time they reached the first-floor landing, Claus was standing outside Schulz's front door with his thumb on the bell. He then proceeded to knock until a faint voice was heard, evidently Eva's. Her exact words were inaudible but their meaning was clear.

'Damn and blast it!' Claus exclaimed finally. 'I've a bloody good mind to kick the door down.'

'Don't bother,' Schulz said menacingly over his shoulder, 'I've got a key here.'

'My reputation is unassailable,' Gisenius declared with conviction. 'If you're wise, you'll remember that.'

'No one would dispute that,' Lehmgruber replied readily. 'You're reputed to be a man of the highest integrity—far be it from me to deny it.'

The two men were sitting in Gisenius's office: in the visitor's chair, Lehmgruber, possessor of important documents; behind the massive desk, Gisenius, intensely interested in Lehmgruber's documents but shrewd enough not to show it.

'There are just a few minor points to settle,' Lehmgruber continued, 'but we shouldn't find it hard to reach a mutually satisfactory arrangement.'

'I thought we'd already agreed on a figure. Let's see—' Gisenius pretended to search his memory '—five hundred marks, wasn't it?'

Lehmgruber sat back, tenderly caressing the briefcase that lay across his knees. 'Today's prices aren't necessarily the same as yesterday's,' he murmured.

Gisenius knit his brows. 'Do you realize what you're saying?'

'Of course,' Lehmgruber replied briskly.

'Then you must also realize that you're playing a dangerous game.' Gisenius's voice took on a note of menace. 'One word from me and the security services would be on to you in a flash.'

'I've no doubt,' Lehmgruber agreed, 'but wouldn't that be a little unwise? They might find your dossier on me.'

'This is blackmail,' Gisenius said flatly. 'Nevertheless, I'm prepared to offer you a thousand marks.'

Lehmgruber gave a delighted smile, like an art collector contemplating a new acquisition. 'It's one of the disadvantages of democratic government that the Opposition sometimes wields influence,' he observed with ill-concealed satisfaction. 'For instance, a lot of local councils follow quite a different political line from the government. This produces a form of competition, and the logical object of competition is to put the other firm out of business at all costs.'

'A thousand marks,' Gisenius said, undeterred, 'and that's

my final word on the subject. A thousand—not a pfennig more.'

'What if I said two thousand?'

'I'd have you thrown out.'

'All right, two thousand. What about it?'

'Certainly not.' Gisenius pressed a buzzer on his desk.

'I can't believe that's your last word,' Lehmgruber said with a smile. 'And please don't tell me it's more than you can afford. I know all about your private resources.'

'They're not unlimited, take it from me!' Gisenius warned. 'I advise you not to harbour any illusions on that score. I don't lay golden eggs, so think it over and let me know what you decide as soon as possible.'

'I leave the decision to you, sir,' Lehmgruber said politely.

'I'll wait until tomorrow, let's say, but don't make it any later.'

'After you!' Schulz's manner was grimly affable. 'Don't be shy, lad!'

Claus Gisenius looked unperturbed. 'I came to see your sister. I trust you've no objection?'

'Who said he had?' Martin Hirsch said pleasantly.

Karl Schulz, determined to remain in command of the situation, opened the door to reveal his sister.

'I wasn't expecting you, Karl,' Eva said, looking slightly taken aback.

'Maybe you were expecting him!' Schulz snapped, shoving Claus Gisenius ahead of him.

Closely watched by the other two, Eva and Claus greeted each other as though it had been months since they last met. They exchanged a smile, and Claus said quietly, as they shook hands: 'Everything all right with you?'

'It is now,' Eva replied with equal restraint.

'Then I'll go,' Claus said, turning to leave.

'You're staying!' Schulz growled. He propelled Claus into the flat, followed by Hirsch, who could not conceal his apprehension. He glanced at Eva, but Eva, he noted sadly, seemed to have eyes for no one but Claus.

Schulz herded them all into the kitchen, clearly intent on having a show-down. 'Sit down all of you,' he commanded.

'Karl,' Eva implored, 'please don't make a scene.'

'Eva's right, Karl,' Hirsch said. 'Take it easy.'

Schulz subjected them to a challenging stare. 'I'm master in this house.'

'Maybe,' Claus broke in, 'but that doesn't give you the right to keep your sister under lock and key.'

Schulz stiffened. 'Don't take that tone with me!'

'That's the lawyer talking,' Hirsch said gloomily. 'He takes after his father, from the sound of it.'

'He does, does he?' Schulz took a step towards Claus.

'I couldn't care less whose son I am or whether you know my father. All I'm interested in at the moment is what gives you the right to incarcerate members of your family. It's barbaric, I tell you—medieval!'

'Did you hear that, Martin?' Schulz fumed. 'The bloody impertinence of it!'

'Yes, I heard,' Hirsch said, 'and I must confess the boy has a point. However you look at it, you shouldn't have locked Eva up.'

'What!' yelped Schulz, outraged at what he felt to be a stab in the back. 'I try to protect my sister, and you tell me off for it—you of all people!'

Eva adopted what was, under the circumstances, the simplest and most effective course of action. Taking advantage of the altercation between her brother and his friend, she extended her hand to Claus and bade him a cheerful but firm farewell. Then she turned to Hirsch, who gave Claus a nod of dismissal.

Schulz stared from one to the other, correctly gauging that a concerted effort was being made to by-pass him. 'What's all this!' he exclaimed darkly, but Claus Gisenius had seized his chance. Raising a hand in farewell, he departed, closing the door behind him.

'Bored, are you?' chuckled Frammler. 'I suppose you're looking for someone to entertain you?'

Tantau gave a faint smile. 'And you think you're the man for the job?'

'Everyone comes to me sooner or later,' Frammler said complacently, '—especially later.'

The undertaker had shown Tantau into the embalming-room.

'Take a look round,' he said with proprietorial pride.

'Functional, modern, practical and completely hygienic, but not without dignity.'

The embalming-room's pretensions to dignity appeared to rely chiefly on its lighting. Although it was broad daylight outside, the place was illuminated by electric lights disguised as altar-candles. The cupboards containing chemicals and accessories shone with cleanliness. The work-bench at the side, which also served as a desk, was meticulously tidy. The mortician's table in the centre of the room under its now extinguished bank of lights was covered by a snow-white sheet, and beneath it could be seen the outlines of a small body.

'You seem to have a strong stomach, Herr Tantau. Isn't your nose in working order?'

'I'd like a hundred marks for every hour I've spent in a mortuary,' Tantau said. 'All the same, I can't say I've ever come across anything as elegant as this. What a pity your clients aren't in a condition to appreciate it.'

Frammler's laugh was subdued—it was one of his principles to maintain an air of solemnity in business hours—but his little eyes twinkled alertly. 'You're very flattering,' he observed. 'I wonder why. Are you planning to pump me?'

'Not at all,' said Tantau. 'Everything's settled. I've already found Meiners.'

Frammler drew himself up sharply and stood motionless for a few seconds before replying. 'You mean you've found his grave,' he said at length.

Tantau shook his head. 'Michael Meiners is alive. He's in town at this moment.'

'You're crazy,' Frammler said bluntly. 'You're mixing him up with a man called Siegert. We had a word with him —he's quite harmless.'

Tantau smiled at this gratuitous clue to the identity of Siegert's assailants, but for the moment he had other fish to fry. 'Strange how positive you are that Meiners is dead.'

'I have my reasons,' Frammler said evasively, 'but I intend to keep them to myself.'

'You're mistaken, I'm afraid. He's alive.'

'I know my business,' Frammler insisted. 'There's not much I don't know about dead bodies.'

'Does your expert knowledge extend to Konstantin Kerze?'

Frammler cast a brief glance at the diminutive form under the sheet. 'What do you mean?' he demanded. 'There's no mystery about that, surely?'

'Do your observations tally with the findings of the police?'

Frammler stared at Tantau with total incomprehension 'I'm an undertaker, not a coroner,' he growled. 'The report says it was accidental death due to heart-failure.'

'And you find the report satisfactory?'

The undertaker frowned. 'What are you driving at? I saw Meiners's body. He was as dead as the boy over there is, that's all I know.'

'Let's assume that Konstantin's accident had left him horribly mutilated,' Tantau said thoughtfully, '—for instance, that he was involved in a road accident which completely crushed his head.'

'It sometimes happens,' Frammler remarked judicially.

'Well then. If someone showed you the mangled body of a boy and said: this is Konstantin Kerze, what would you do? You'd check to see if it really was Konstantin Kerze and not someone else, wouldn't you?'

Frammler was temporarily reduced to silence. He opened his mouth and then shut it again, breathing like an asthmatic.

'How do you know what happened?' he said at last. 'Who's been talking to you? What bastard gave you the idea that I made a mistake about Meiners's body? Which sod was it? Come on, out with it!'

'You're forgetting your grave-side manner,' Tantau said mildly. Glancing round the room, he walked to the door and drew the black curtain aside, revealing a set of switches. He pressed the only one that was off and the lights over the embalming table glazed into life, harshly illuminating the linen sheet and the contours of the small body beneath it. Tantau pulled the sheet away.

As he stared down at the puny, naked body of Konstantin Kerze, a strangely abstracted expression came over the old detective's gnarled and wrinkled face, setting it in a rigid grimace.

'What's the matter?' Frammler inquired with a touch of uneasiness. 'Feeling queasy after all?'

Tantau shook his head. His face lost its rigidity and

came to life again. ' Tell me, Herr Frammler,' he said slowly, ' when you look at a dead man, do you try to picture the circumstances surrounding his death? '

' No.' Frammler sounded faintly revolted by the idea. ' Why should I? '

Tantau's eyes remained fixed on Konstantin's body. ' Do you ever stop to wonder why people die at all? '

' Good God, man! ' Frammler exclaimed, looking bewildered. ' What do you take me for? Everyone has to die some time—it's the most natural thing in the world.'

' Not always. Not everybody dies of senile decay. Some people die because they've lived too hard, others rot to death from inactivity and others are mown down by the wheels of progress or the march of civilization, but quite a number of people owe their death to outside intervention.'

Frammler gave an indifferent shrug. ' Murder, you mean.'

' No,' Tantau replied, slowly shaking his head. ' Murder is a disease as old as mankind itself. I'm talking about something more sophisticated, something far more insidious— something which occurs with a frequency which surpasses our wildest imaginings. I call it indirect murder.'

' Indirect murder? ' Frammler looked genuinely puzzled. ' What's that? '

' A woman who systematically nags her husband to death, a business man who ruins a competitor by underhand means, a man who drains his wife's life-blood by brutality and lack of affection, a father who drives his children to despair, a boss who bullies a sensitive employee to the brink of suicide, a person who takes advantage of a trustful, guileless boy and hounds him to the point of no return. No court in the world has jurisdiction over acts like these, Herr Frammler, but they're still an indirect form of murder—and if there's one thing I abhor, it's that.'

' Peculiar ideas you have,' Frammler commented, raising his eyebrows. ' I don't know where we'd be if everyone thought the way you do. The world's a tough place, Herr Tantau. A man has to be tough to survive. The weak always go to the wall—it's the law of natural selection.'

' It's the law of the jungle,' Tantau said quietly. ' I've no desire to live in a world where only the brainless and heartless have a guaranteed chance of survival, Herr Frammler.

That's why, whenever I look at a dead body, I always ask myself whether anyone was to blame, even indirectly.'

Frammler looked mystified. 'In that case, you'd better blame the water in the pond for being so cold that it gave the boy heart-failure.'

But Tantau was not listening to the undertaker. He had bent low over Konstantin's body and was scrutinizing the neck, shoulders and hips. He even put out the forefinger of his right hand and ran it over the boy's skin.

'Don't go underestimating the quality of my work,' Frammler said quickly. 'Children aren't easy subjects, you know. You'd be surprised how much easier it is to make older people look like angels.'

'There are some pressure-marks on his throat,' remarked Tantau.

'You're telling me,' the undertaker replied. 'It wasn't easy to get rid of them. I even had to work on them with paraffin. But that's children all over—no sense of personal hygiene, scratches and grazes and spotty skin and dirt under their finger-nails. They don't take care of their bodies.'

'He's got some abrasions on his shoulders, too.'

'I shouldn't be surprised.' Frammler dismissed Tantau's comments as purely self-assertive. 'Ponds like that are full of rubbish—sharp stones, broken bottles, and so on.'

'And mud,' added Tantau. 'You can't find anything much softer or more yielding than mud, and these scratches and abrasions are comparatively fresh. Haven't you ever heard of the Kehlmann Effect? According to Kehlmann, any wound—whatever its nature—remains unaltered from the moment of death onwards—and these abrasions, Professor Frammler, are fresh. They must have been caused at the time of death or immediately prior to it.'

Frammler remained studiously unimpressed. 'Well, what does that prove?'

'Nothing very much,' Tantau said softly. 'It merely confirms what my instinct has been telling me all along: it wasn't an accident.' In a still quieter and less audible voice, he added: 'It was murder.'

'I suppose you're playing the guardian angel again,' chuckled Sergeant Brahmvogel, extending his hand.

Tantau shook it warmly. 'Just trying to rescue another poor innocent from the clutches of the police, that's all.'

'I'm afraid you'll have to wait a few minutes. Your poor innocent is fortifying herself at the moment.' Brahmvogel winked confidentially. 'Fräulein Kerze's in the bar on the corner, if you're interested.'

'I see.' Tantau knew that Karen had been told to present herself at Rheine-Bergen Central to put the finishing touches to her statement about the crash. From what Brahmvogel said, he guessed that she had taken a taxi to the police station and popped into the nearest bar for a dose of Dutch courage. The inmates of a police station almost invariably used the nearest café as their 'local', so she had probably been seen by a constable fetching sandwiches or beer for his colleagues.

Tantau raised a valedictory hand and walked to the door. 'I should be back here with Fräulein Kerze in a few minutes. Then perhaps we can wrap this thing up.'

'Fair enough,' said Brahmvogel. 'You know something, Herr Tantau? I wouldn't lose any sleep if everyone reduced their cars to scrap-iron. The pity of it is, they tend to smash other people up in the process.'

Smiling, Tantau made his exit from Rheine-Bergen Central. He walked up the street to the bar on the corner, peered through the window for a moment and then entered.

The place was almost deserted at this hour. A bored-looking barman lolled against the counter and two patrons were talking business in the furthest corner, but Karen was sitting by herself drinking cheap brandy out of a large glass.

'What are you up to?' she called to Tantau. 'Playing the nanny again?'

'Sergeant Brahmvogel called me a guardian angel just now,' the little man replied, approaching with some diffidence, 'though I fully realize that not everyone would agree with the description.'

'Never mind, sit down.' Karen made a sweeping gesture of invitation. 'I don't know what you must think of me,' she continued, and for a moment or two her oval, doll-like face looked grey and weary. 'We only seem to meet when I'm at the end of my tether.'

'Some people never feel like that. It's them I'm sorry for.'

'Aren't you sorry for me, then?'

273

'Why should I be?' Tantau blinked like a friendly old dog. He picked up Karen's glass, sniffed it briefly and poured its contents into the capacious ashtray on the table between them. 'We all come a step nearer the grave each day. Do you consider it absolutely essential to accelerate the process?'

Karen's eyes flashed. 'Do you get a kick out of tormenting me?' she cried passionately. 'You're insufferable sometimes!'

'I'm sorry if I upset you.' Tantau reached for her hand and she involuntarily surrendered it.

'All right,' she went on, ' so you've staved off my would-be fiancé temporarily and got me out of trouble with the police. What else do you propose to do for me?'

'Nothing,' Tantau replied. 'Anyone who tries to insulate a person from the world may be robbing him or her of valuable experience. Some people live from one party to the next and others from one bed to the next, but they're all making a big mistake. Variety is the spice of life, my dear. Everything's grist to the mill.'

'Konstantin's death included?'

Tantau studied Karen closely. To him, no one personality resembled another, and each living soul was a psychological landscape in itself. No character could be gauged with mathematical precision. On the other hand, no human mind was entirely inaccessible. 'How much do you know about Konstantin?' he asked.

'He was my half-brother,' Karen replied in a low voice. 'We had the same father. He was a nice boy, but that's as far as my knowledge of him goes.'

Tantau's head drooped until his chin rested on his chest. 'Don't try to sound as if you're incapable of loving anyone.'

'That's just what I do mean!' Karen said vehemently. 'I've never known what family life is—if it exists at all outside novels or church sermons. My mother cleared out when I was a child, my brother didn't mean much more to me than a household pet, and my father's a walking factory. All he can think of is selling his synthetic slabs. When I told him I couldn't sleep at night, he talked about bricks. When I told him I was worried about men, he made a song and dance about the state of the building industry. God, how I hate him!'

'But that isn't all, is it?' Tantau blinked as though in response to a sudden twinge of pain. 'Along comes Bartosch, whom you detest, and Hirsch, who doesn't want you. Finally, your young brother dies, and you begin to wonder if you're responsible in some way.'

'I am responsible, I don't deny it,' Karen conceded. 'I've been asking myself what difference it would have made if I'd devoted more time to Konstantin, if I'd stayed at home a bit more instead of careering around all over the place—if I'd shown a spark of affection for the poor boy.'

'Remorse is a healthy sentiment as long as it isn't carried too far. However—' Tantau's eyes narrowed to the point of near invisibility '—that isn't all that's worrying you, is it? I suspected it as soon as I saw you, and now I'm certain. You can't bring yourself to believe that Konstantin's death was an accident, can you?'

Karen looked startled. 'How did you know?'

'Simple deduction,' Tantau replied with a smile. 'You were on your way to the police station, as arranged. You knew that all you had to do was sign a statement, and yet you felt you needed a large brandy. Why? Not to help you sign a statement, I imagine, but because you were nervous about asking the police to make further inquiries into Konstantin's death. Well, I'll tell you something. I don't believe it was an accident either.'

'Then take on the case!' cried Karen. 'You will, won't you?'

'I've already taken it on,' Tantau said, 'but now I feel properly authorized to do so. May I consider you my client?'

'Oh yes, do!' Karen's face had lost some of its tension. 'I can't talk to anyone else the way I talk to you,' she said gratefully. 'Why couldn't my father have been more like you?'

'You've got to help me.' Bennicken looked enormously trustful. 'I'm in a proper mess.'

'My dear Bennicken, you know I'm always glad to be of assistance,' Gisenius assured him, '—when it's within my power, of course.'

'If you can't help me no one can.'

The lawyer indulged in a faint but gratified smile. He found it particularly pleasing to see Bennicken in his office,

275

cap in hand, on this day of all days. 'What's the trouble, my friend?'

'A complaint.' Slightly shamefaced, Bennicken perched uncomfortably on the extreme edge of the visitor's chair.

Gisenius leant back in his chair and smiled encouragingly. 'Well?'

'The police came round,' Bennicken ventured, 'about the punch-up.'

'The police?' A sudden shadow crossed the lawyer's brow. 'What—er—punch-up?'

'With Siegert.'

'What's that? You mean the police know you assaulted him?'

'No,' Bennicken said tersely.

Gisenius shook his head as though to dispel a momentary attack of deafness, but his reserves of patience were inexhaustible. 'Tell me the whole story,' he said, 'from the beginning.'

Bennicken made a manful attempt to do so, but his vocabulary was unequal to the demands of detailed and comprehensive narration. Gisenius had to ask him several questions before a reasonably clear picture emerged.

It appeared that, after undergoing treatment at the hands of Frammler and Bennicken, Siegert had drunk himself into a state of total insensibility. Next morning he had turned up late for work at the municipal cleansing department, with the result that three dust-carts remained idle for lack of instructions. His superior had hauled him over the coals, and Siegert, searching for an excuse, announced that he had been attacked and beaten up in the vicinity of the *Black Cat* at about one o'clock that morning. He had refrained from mentioning names or giving personal descriptions, even when his enraged superior called in the police.

An official complaint was lodged and the usual routine inquiries began. Nothing concrete came to light at first. Siegert still avoided implicating Frammler or Bennicken directly. His sole concern was to placate his boss and provide an excuse for his belated arrival at work. Then came one of those ridiculous coincidences: a constable on the beat had noticed a familiar vehicle parked at the scene of the alleged assault at the precise time it was said to have occurred, to wit,

Bennicken's taxi. The police had called on Bennicken, and Bennicken had called on Gisenius.

'They didn't get any change out of me,' the taxi driver declared stoutly. 'I didn't say a word—just told them I hadn't seen a thing.'

'But they'll continue their inquiries. It's quite possible they'll find more evidence and come back again. What if you're brought face to face with the man?'

'You're here,' Bennicken replied trustfully. 'You'll deal with it.'

'That remains to be seen.' Gisenius subjected his humble friend to a long stare, as though making a careful assessment of his value. 'What if I can't help you this time?' he asked at length.

Bennicken's usually impassive features registered dismay and bewilderment in turn, but a moment later he shrugged indifferently. 'I'll be up the creek, that's what.'

'But you won't be alone,' Gisenius pointed out. 'Frammler will also be implicated, and I may be as well. After all, it was I who suggested the interview with Siegert—you could always tell them that.'

'No,' Bennicken said dourly, 'I'll see this through on my own.'

Gisenius rose and laid his right hand on the shoulder of his staunch friend and former comrade-in-arms, a gesture which Bennicken received as if it were an accolade.

'My dear fellow,' Gisenius said, 'men like you are the cement that binds society together.'

'I'd risk my neck for you,' Bennicken said hoarsely, 'you know I would.'

'And I,' Gisenius replied with ill-concealed satisfaction, 'will gladly do everything in my power for you. Just sit down again and make yourself at home, my dear chap. I'll be back in a minute.'

Leaving Bennicken, Gisenius retired to the chief clerk's office and asked to be put through to Frammler.

'Listen, Frammler,' he said urgently, 'I've just been told that this man Siegert has had the impertinence to lodge a complaint alleging assault and battery—against persons unknown, for the time being. The trouble is, Bennicken's taxi was seen at the precise place and time of the alleged

277

assault, and the police have questioned him. What's your reaction?'

Frammler's first reaction was a prolonged chuckle. Then, as the undertaker's strange access of mirth subsided, Gisenius heard him say firmly: 'He must be off his rocker—Siegert, I mean. He's got no witnesses, so it's just his word against ours. Apart from that, the landlord at the *Black Cat* can testify that everything was in order.'

'I'm happy to hear it,' Gisenius commented. 'In that case, the best solution would be for Siegert to withdraw his complaint—present himself at the police station and explain that he was mistaken. Could you arrange that?'

'Leave it to me.'

Gisenius hung up and proceeded, at his leisure, to sign a few of the letters that were lying ready for him on the chief clerk's desk. It wouldn't do Bennicken any harm to think he was fighting the good fight on his behalf.

A quarter of an hour passed before Gisenius returned to his office, wearing an optimistic smile.

'Bennicken, my friend,' he said, 'your worries are almost over. I've dropped a word here and there and straightened one or two things out. As far as I can see, matters are as good as settled.'

'How can I thank you?' Bennicken said, breathing heavily.

Gisenius waved his protestations aside and seated himself at his desk again, looking studiously self-assured. Suddenly, a bright idea seemed to strike him. 'If you really want to be helpful,' he said, 'there is something you could do for me.'

'Name it,' Bennicken replied promptly.

'To begin with, perhaps you'd be kind enough to find Herr Tantau for me. I must speak to him as soon as possible.'

'I'll find him. What else?'

'A rather delicate matter.' Gisenius made a show of reluctance, but his smile radiated appreciation of his friend's assistance. 'It's to do with someone called Lehmgruber, an unscrupulous man who needs careful watching. All I want you to do for the moment is to take a look at him as unobtrusively as possible, just so you'll know what he looks like—so that you won't mix him up with someone else if the occasion

278

arises. Lehmgruber—make a note of the name. He's staying at the *Drei Kronen.*'

'Anything you say,' Bennicken replied. 'Don't worry, I'll take a good look at him.'

'The investiture was superbly organized,' Tantau said gravely. 'Am I right in assuming that it was your work? '

'You are,' Sängerwald replied with equal gravity. 'May I inquire if you're a member of the Kerze family? '

Tantau smiled wrily and shook his head. 'My loss was the family's gain.'

'Strange,' said Sängerwald, ' I'm sure I saw you in the reserved seats during the ceremony. Unless I'm mistaken, you were sitting in the front row next to Frau Brandstädter, Herr Kerze's housekeeper.'

'Congratulations,' said Tantau. 'You obviously have an excellent memory.'

The sales manager looked modest. ' I'm always in training. A man in my job has to keep his eyes open. For instance, I know everything there is to know about our most important customers, down to the dates of their wives' birthdays.'

'What about the firm's employees? Are you as well-informed about them? '

'More or less,' Sängerwald replied with a self-assured smile. 'Herr Kerze occasionally calls on me to stand in for him. What did you want to know? '

'A couple of things.' Tantau stared at the sales manager keenly. 'For a start, what sort of status does an accountant have in your firm? '

'Senior status, I'd say.' Sängerwald smiled. 'Herr Kerze is the apex of our organization. Immediately under him come the production manager, the chief engineer and your humble servant, the sales manager—not that I've listed us in order of precedence. Under us, in official order of seniority, come the stores manager, the head of the dispatch department, the personnel manager and the three accountants, Kisskalt, Wenninger and Saffranski.'

'So the accountants also had reserved seats during the investiture? '

'Of course. We're a conservative firm in that respect. It's one of our principles to observe protocol.'

'In that case,' Tantau said meditatively, 'there were three main groups in the hall during the ceremony: first, guests of honour and members of the Kerze family; secondly, senior members of the firm, including the three accountants; and, thirdly, the hoi polloi.'

'You could put it like that,' the sales manager conceded, 'though I'd prefer to use different terminology myself.'

This paved the way for further inquiries. In the old days, Tantau would have entrusted these to a staff of detective-inspectors, sergeants and constables, but now he had to pursue them in person. Patiently and perseveringly he roamed from one office and factory bay to the next, interrogating senior employees. His question was the same in each case: 'Who were your immediate neighbours during the investiture?'

After several hours of this, Tantau had reconstructed an accurate seating plan of the first few rows. There was only one person missing, and that was Saffranski, Siegfried Saffranski.

Glancing at his watch, Tantau left the Stabilator works and set off on foot to Kerze's villa. On arrival he looked at his watch again and found that he had covered the distance in twelve minutes of fairly leisurely walking.

Inside the Villa Kerze Tantau encountered Frau Brandstädter, as he had expected. Without allowing himself to be drawn into a prolonged bout of kitchen gossip, he said: 'You told me you saw Herr Saffranski at the factory yesterday. Are you sure of that?'

'Absolutely positive,' Brandstädter said firmly. 'I spoke to him.'

'When?'

'Just after the ceremony. He was standing near the door. Such a modest man, Herr Saffranski.'

Tantau's calculations only took a few seconds, but their outcome perturbed him. Viewed from one angle, they amounted to a death sentence.

'How nice of you to come and pay your respects,' Tantau told his visitor. 'I'm quite touched.'

Chief Inspector Sand gave an ingratiating smile. 'I didn't serve under you for nothing.'

Tantau removed some books from the only chair in the

room and made a sweeping gesture of invitation. Sand sat down, subjecting Tantau's temporary quarters to keen scrutiny as he did so. He looked vaguely saddened.

Tantau interpreted Sand's reaction correctly. 'I know what you're thinking—a shabby furnished room in a lodging-house! Don't worry, my boy, I could have stayed at the *Drei Kronen* if I'd wanted to, all expenses paid, but I prefer to stay here when I'm in Rheine-Bergen. The house belongs to the widow of a policeman called Wernicke. He used to be my driver—got himself killed while he was working for me.'

'I'm sorry,' Sand said quietly.

'No sentimentality, please! I strongly advise you not to model yourself on me. I'm a misfit. I was born at the wrong time—that's all there is to it.'

'You mean you've never got used to the idea that there's murder and murder?'

'I lived to see the day when a government resorted to crime, and since I was paid to catch criminals I automatically fell foul of the government. It nearly broke my heart, Sand, but not quite. The age we live in now is doing its best to finish me off. It hasn't dissociated itself firmly and consistently enough from a regime which committed every kind of crime including mass murder. That depresses me, Sand. I don't like living among people who still pride themselves on having been accessories to murder.'

Sand pulled his briefcase towards him. 'I've brought you a little present—I hope you don't mind. It's nothing much, just some Merano candies.'

Tantau groped in the bag and fished out a particularly handsome chunk of glazed white marzipan. He examined it with rapture for a moment or two and then bit into it.

'Marvellous,' he said, eying his visitor quizzically. 'All right, I've taken my bribe. What do you want?'

'It's a minor matter,' Sand said. 'At least, that's how it seemed until you started taking an interest in it, Chief Super-intendent—I'm sorry—Herr Tantau.'

'I take an interest in a lot of minor matters, my dear Sand. Which one are you referring to?'

'The accident at the Kerze house—young Kerze's unfor-tunate death. Two C.I.D. men from the local station looked into it and found nothing suspicious, so they closed their file on the case. Then it became known that someone was making further inquiries.'

' Someone called Tantau? '

Sand nodded. ' The local sergeant got nervous. He rang his opposite number at Rheine-Bergen Central—Brahmvogel —and asked if he knew anything about you. Needless to say, Brahmvogel at once got in touch with me.'

' Whereupon you raced off to the nearest sweet shop.'

' More or less.' Sand gave an ingenuous smile. ' If any ordinary mortal had started nosing around I'd have said: let him carry on. But when it happens to be the ex-chief of a homicide division—well, I'm bound to feel a bit perturbed, aren't I? '

' Not necessarily,' Tantau said. ' For instance, you could sit tight and wait until the case reaches you via official channels —if it ever does.'

Sand's jaw-muscles tightened. ' Is that what you want me to do? ' he asked evenly.

' Even if I said it was, you wouldn't leave it at that,' Tantau replied with a smile. ' Some of my curiosity must have rubbed off on you during the years we worked together.'

' Then there is something wrong! ' Sand burst out. ' I knew it the moment I heard your name mentioned. Well, Herr Tantau, may I count on your support? '

' You want me to do your homework for you? '

' Herr Tantau,' Sand said with pride, ' this is the first time I've ever made such a request, and you're the only man I'd ever consider asking.'

' You're wasting your time, Sand. I'm not a policeman any longer. I'm only interested in seeing that justice is done.' The old man proffered the bag of sweets, and Sand took one without thinking.

' I gather you don't believe Konstantin Kerze's death was accidental.'

' Correct,' Tantau said equably. ' And if I know you, you'll discover the truth for yourself with comparative ease. It shouldn't take you longer than twenty-four hours to solve the case, which gives me about twelve hours' start. That ought to be enough.'

' Enough for what? '

' To make sure that my idea of justice prevails.'

'Herr Tantau,' Sand said with deep and evident concern, 'tell me what you have in mind, I beg you. I should hate it if circumstances compelled me to work against you.'

'You work for the law,' replied Tantau. 'I work for justice. If there's any difference between the two, then we're on opposite sides of the fence.'

'I've a good mind to go on leave,' Sand said bitterly.

'Don't worry—the urge won't last.' Tantau gave him a sympathetic smile. 'Look, just for old time's sake, here's a tip. I know you'll find out everything I've found out in due course, but there's one detail that may elude you: Konstantin Kerze's murderer was good at figures.'

Conrad Gisenius retired to his study and made two telephone calls.

First telephone call: 7.47 p.m.–7.52 p.m.

Gisenius: 'Well, my dear Bennicken, I think the time is ripe.'

Bennicken: 'For what?'

Gisenius: 'Have you found out what Lehmgruber looks like?'

Bennicken: 'I'd know him anywhere.'

Gisenius: 'Lehmgruber will be leaving the *Drei Kronen* in about twenty minutes. When he calls for a taxi, can you make sure he gets yours?'

Bennicken: 'Of course.'

Gisenius: 'He'll be carrying a briefcase. It's the contents I'm interested in.'

Bennicken: 'I get you.'

Gisenius: 'There are two alternatives. Either Lehmgruber will ask you to drive him straight to my office, in which case the contents of his briefcase will already be complete, or he'll make a detour. If so, it will mean he wants to pick something up first. Is that clear?'

Bennicken: 'As daylight.'

Second telephone call: 7.53 p.m.–7.56 p.m.

Gisenius: 'Well, Herr Lehmgruber, I think the time is ripe.'

Lehmgruber: 'I hope we're not talking at cross-purposes, Herr Gisenius. My price hasn't changed.'

Gisenius: 'Two thousand marks, as agreed, cash on delivery.'

Lehmgruber: 'I'm delighted to hear it. Those papers are worth every pfennig, I can assure you.'

Gisenius: 'I'll expect you at my office, then. It's just before eight o'clock now. Shall we say in about half an hour?'

Having completed his calls, Gisenius hurried out into the hall and graciously permitted the maid to help him on with his overcoat, remarking in casual tones that he was going out to get a breath of fresh air.

Strolling along as though absorbed in thought, he gave a polite good evening to almost everyone who passed, doffing his hat and studiously turning his face to the light of the street-lamps.

Crossing the road, he walked down Wilhelmstrasse towards Bismarckstrasse, where he turned first up one side street and then another until he reached a small backwater called Liebiggasse. There, surrounded by other equally tall and gloomy houses, he found Number 37.

Enveloped in a smell of stale onions and mouldering cabbage, Gisenius climbed the worn and battered stairs until he came to a door on the third landing. He rang three times.

A moment later the door opened to reveal Brigitte. Her eyes registered delighted surprise when she saw who it was.

'I wanted to see how you were getting on,' Gisenius said, not without dignity. 'Tell me if it's inconvenient, and I'll come back some other time.'

'Oh, no!' Brigitte assured him. 'Please come in, you're very welcome.'

'Perhaps you oughtn't to receive gentlemen callers at this hour,' Gisenius observed cautiously. He pulled out his handsome fob-watch and glanced at it. 'It's after eight o'clock already,' he added, presenting the massive gold chronometer for her inspection.

'You're welcome any time,' Brigitte declared.

'I'm happy to hear that,' rejoined Gisenius. 'There are times in life when we all need someone we can trust.'

Bennicken waited at the head of the rank until Lehmgruber appeared in the brightly-lit entrance of the *Drei Kronen*. Then he let in the clutch and drove across to where Lehmgruber was standing. ' Taxi, sir? ' he asked briskly.

Lehmgruber gave a curt nod. Bennicken hardly had time to open the rear door before he pushed past him and settled himself in the back seat. ' The station! ' he called. He was not carrying a briefcase.

Bennicken drove off in the direction of Bahnhofstrasse. He crouched behind the wheel like a racing driver, the set of his bull neck and broad shoulders expressive of intense concentration, but he drove with extreme care, never exceeding the speed limit and keeping an eagle eye on the traffic.

' The station,' he said, gently braking to a halt.

Lehmgruber jumped out. ' Wait here, I'll be back in a few minutes.' So saying, he hurried off and disappeared through the main entrance.

Bennicken got out and sauntered after him.

Lehmgruber's first port of call was the yellow ' Departures ' board. After studying it for a moment he walked across to the counter and bought a ticket. Bennicken was on the point of swearing blue murder and launching himself at what he suspected to be a dud fare when his slow-motion intellect warned him just in time that it might be a blunder.

Lehmgruber pocketed his ticket and hurried over to the left-luggage office, where the clerk produced a briefcase. Bennicken's bovine features broke into a broad grin of satisfaction. He trotted back to his taxi and held open the rear door with the deferential air of a perfect chauffeur. Lehmgruber climbed in and gave the address of Gisenius's office.

Bennicken put on a convincing show of incomprehension. He pretended not to have heard properly and asked Lehmgruber to repeat the address. Lehmgruber did so, his expression clearly conveying what he thought of the taxi-driver's level of intelligence.

The taxi got under way again, this time at an even more leisurely pace. Bennicken circumnavigated the station yard, passed the entrance to Bahnhofstrasse and made for the so-called station close. This was a long narrow strip of ground near the railway lines, dotted with ornamental trees and surrounded by dense hedges of lilac.

' You there! ' Lehmgruber called over Bennicken's shoulder. His tone was noticeably condescending. ' You! If you think you can push the fare up by making detours, you've got another think coming. I wasn't born yesterday! '

' Road works,' Bennicken said, grinning to himself. ' Temporary diversion.'

' I'll check up on that,' Lehmgruber retorted, confident that he could brow-beat a half-witted provincial cab-driver. ' If you've misinformed me, you'll find yourself in hot water.'

' I can hardly wait,' Bennicken murmured with relish.

The taxi emerged from the station close, crossed a main road and started to bounce along a track near the goods yards. Bennicken knew the area well. He left the main loading bays on his right and turned into a disused siding. It was a world of deserted warehouses, empty platforms, overgrown railway lines and rusty barbed wire fences of bizarrely irregular shape.

Bennicken braked sharply and the taxi jolted to a halt. Turning round, he said cheerfully: ' Well, this is it.'

' You're crazy! ' Lehmgruber protested furiously. ' This isn't the address I gave you—you must be out of your mind! Get me out of here or I'll make trouble for you.'

Bennicken looked positively elated. ' You—make trouble for me? I'd like to see you try! ' He got out and opened the rear door. ' All right,' he purred. ' Out! '

It dawned on Lehmgruber that he had landed himself in a highly unenviable predicament. Not only was the taxi-driver looming over him built like a gorilla, but the area looked dangerously deserted. There was not a soul in sight, and any cry for help would have been drowned by the clatter from the goods yards and the hum of traffic from the main road not far away.

' How much longer are you going to be? ' Bennicken demanded, losing some of his good-humour. ' Out, I said! '

' I warn you! ' Lehmgruber said nervously. ' Don't try anything, or you'll regret it! '

' I'll teach you to try and rob an honest cab-driver! ' snarled Bennicken.

' What's that? ' Lehmgruber exclaimed in bewilderment. ' What am I supposed to have done? '

' You tried to rob me,' Bennicken replied with awesome calm. ' You've already done several poor sods like me, but you've picked the wrong one this time.'

He craned forward into the car, his hands in their heavy

leather driving gauntlets groping for Lehmgruber like a pair of mechanical grabs, but Lehmgruber, his face chalky-white with terror, shrank back. He held his briefcase in front of him with one hand, shield-fashion, and fumbled in it desperately with the other.

'Stand back!' he screamed, pulling out an automatic. 'Stand back or I'll shoot!'

'Don't make me laugh,' Bennicken said grimly, and at the same moment his leather gauntlets descended in a vicious chopping movement. They smacked against metal and thudded against Lehmgruber's body almost simultaneously.

There was a sharp, dry report, and an acrid scent of burning powder filled the interior of the car. Sounds from the goods yard and the arterial road flooded with unnerving clarity into the oppressive stillness that followed the shot. Lehmgruber and Bennicken might have been turned to stone. They watched and waited, each wondering if the other had been hit.

Then, nimble as a stoat, Lehmgruber dived for the open door and attempted to squeeze past Bennicken's bulky figure. Bennicken's fists came down like pile-drivers, and Lehmgruber collapsed and lay there, inert as a bundle of rags.

The taxi-driver straightened up. He was panting slightly and his face shone with sweat, but he emitted a contented chuckle as he extended his leather-encased hands and ceremoniously smoothed the wrinkles from his gauntlets. He had just looked round to assure himself that there was no one in the vicinity when Lehmgruber began to twitch and groan.

Wagging his head with evident delight, Bennicken stooped over Lehmgruber and seized him by the collar. With almost leisurely deliberation, he picked him up and carried him effortlessly across the siding. There he propped his slowly recovering victim against the edge of the disused platform, much as he might have propped a ladder against a wall.

'Now, you bastard,' he growled. 'Pin your ears back and listen.'

Lehmgruber quickly abandoned a shortlived attempt to evade Bennicken's iron grasp. The punishment he had already received had convinced him that to court a renewed onslaught at the hands of this maddened gorilla would be tantamount to suicide. 'What do you want?' he moaned.

'You lured me here,' Bennicken said persuasively. 'You attacked me. You fired at me, but I was too quick for you. Got it?'

'Why are you doing this?' Lehmgruber cried desperately. 'What's your game?'

'Shut up!' recommended Bennicken. 'You fired at me. There was a struggle and you beat it.'

'I what?'

'You beat it,' Bennicken said tranquilly. 'Taxi-thieves pinch the takings and then beat it.'

Bennicken stood away from Lehmgruber's wilting form. He put out one fist as though gauging the range and then, with lightning swiftness, drove the other into Lehmgruber's belly. There was a dull thud. Lehmgruber doubled up with a grunt and started to slide down the fence just as Bennicken's left smashed into the side of his head. He slumped almost vertically to the ground.

Bennicken turned on his heel without waiting to see the effect of his punches. He had no need to. He strode over to his taxi with the slow and reminiscent tread of one who has feasted royally and switched on the interior light. On the floor lay an automatic—a 7.65 mm. Walther—and beside it the briefcase, stuffed with papers. With a complacent nod he switched off the light and returned to his victim.

Lehmgruber saw him coming and tried to crawl away, stark terror written in every movement, but was brought up short by the edge of the platform.

Bennicken planted himself in front of Lehmgruber with arms akimbo. He stared down, savouring the sight for a moment. Then he said with a cheerful grin: 'Now listen to me. I'm off to the police now, to tell them you pulled a gun on me. There's a bullet-hole in the cab to prove it, so get going and keep going. The police'll be here in half an hour. If they find you, you've had it. Understand?'

Bennicken breathed heavily. It was years since he had indulged in such conversational exertion, but he had done a thorough job. Conrad Gisenius, his friend and comrade-in-arms, would be proud of him.

INTERIM REPORT NO. 4

STENOGRAPHIC RECORD OF A POLICE INTERVIEW

WITH KARL SCHULZ

conducted by Chief Inspector Sand
on 1 May 1961
in connection with the events of 20 April 1945

After being informed of the subject of the interview and
cautioned, Herr Schulz made the following statement;

My name is Karl Schulz. I am forty-one years old and
a garage manager by occupation.

Yes, I commanded No. 2 Section of No. 3 Platoon. This
consisted, on the 19th of April 1945, of a sergeant—myself—
and six men. Five of them were experienced soldiers and the
sixth had only been assigned to the section three weeks earlier.
His name was Meiners.

At 1815 hours on April 19th 1945 the company reached
a village called Steinwiesen, and my section was billeted in a
farm on the outskirts. We moved in, cleaned our weapons
and checked our equipment. At 1900 hours I held a kit
inspection.

At 2000 hours Lieutenant Kronshagen, our company
commander, called an N.C.O.s' conference. Lance-Corporal
Gisenius went along with me. Lieutenant Kronshagen told
us that the situation was serious and fixed the company's
time of departure for 0600 hours the next morning.

Half an hour after receiving these instructions I was back
in the billet. Hirsch informed me that a consignment of
drink had arrived. I didn't ask any questions because I knew
that the normal ration wasn't more than a quarter of a litre
per man. When my men suggested asking the farm people to
a little get-together, I agreed. I always made a point of
keeping on good terms with civilians.

After I'd cleaned and checked my own equipment, I went
to visit one of my fellow-sergeants in the house down the road.
I stayed there for just under an hour, and by the time I got

back to our billet the party was in full swing. I joined in for a while—there was no reason why I shouldn't—but by about 2300 hours I was ready for bed, so I told them to have a good time and turned in.

Question:

What exactly did you mean by ' a good time '?

Answer:

What I said. I hoped they'd enjoy themselves without making too much of a din.

Question:

You say you left the party at about 2300 hours. Who was present at that time?

Answer:

All the rest of the section, as far as I can recall. They were sitting around in a circle with the civilians. It was a standing order that members of the armed forces were to treat the civilian population like members of their own families, male and female alike.

Question:

Who was sitting between Frau Boddanski and her daughter?

Answer:

Hirsch.

Question:

And who was sitting on the other side of Fräulein Boddanski?

Answer:

Meiners. Frammler was next to Frau Boddanski and Bennicken and Kerze sat opposite—but there wasn't anything significant about the arrangement. It was accidental.

I spent the night in an upstairs room—alone. On the dot of 0500 hours next morning—April 20th, that was—I was awakened by the platoon runner. Shortly afterwards, while the men were still asleep, Lieutenant Kronshagen turned up and ordered me to take my section and move to a position on the edge of Copse 307. Our job was to block the road at the point where the road-bridge crossed the Barzenbach about a hundred yards from the wood.

At 0510 I roused the section. At 0515 I made a preliminary check, and by 0545 we were ready to move off. We did so at 0600 hours, as instructed.

Question:

Where were your men when you went to wake them?

Answer:
Where I'd left them—in the farmhouse kitchen. I found all six of them there when I went to wake them.
Question:
Did you notice anything unusual, or did everything seem quite normal?
Answer:
I don't know what you're driving at. A soldier's entitled to a bit of fun sometimes—provided he does his duty as his superiors see it. With us, it was a case of eat, drink and be merry for tomorrow we die. But that's only by the way. If you want a straight answer, the men's behaviour when I woke them was quite normal.
Question:
You mean all of them were suffering equally from the effects of alcohol?
Answer:
Some people can take more than others. Bennicken could drain a bucket without turning a hair. It only took a thimbleful to put young Meiners under the table. Gisenius hardly touched the stuff, but Hirsch had a pretty good head and so did Frammler. I'm not much of a drinking man myself. It's not the sort of thing you can lay down any universal rules about.
Question:
When did Frau Boddanski inform you that her daughter had been found dead in the barn?
Answer:
At about 0600.
Question:
What was your reaction?
Answer:
I didn't believe her story at first, but then I went and checked up on it. After a chat with my second-in-command, I got Frammler to tackle the job. Frammler was used to dealing with dead bodies, and the rest of us had more important things to do.
Question:
Do you mean to say it never occurred to you that a member of your section might have been responsible?
Answer:
Not for a moment. Anyway, while Frammler was trying to

cope with the unpleasant details, I marched the rest of the section off to our allotted position. We began by clearing a field of fire and dealing with things like air-cover and camouflage. Then we got the M.G. into position.

Question:

Who was manning the M.G.?

Answer:

Bennicken and Meiners to start with. I told Frammler to join them later.

Question:

What about the others?

Answer:

The others were detailed to block the road close to the edge of the wood. Hirsch, Gisenius and Kerze were in that party.

Question:

What did you do?

Answer:

I divided my time between the two parties, lending a hand wherever I was needed.

Question:

How far apart were the groups?

Answer:

Somewhere between a hundred and two hundred yards.

We could hear tanks coming nearer and nearer the whole time, but we soon got used to it. I sprinted across to a neighbouring section, which was also operating independently, and tried to borrow a bazooka. They couldn't spare one, but we didn't let it get us down.

Frammler reappeared just after 0700. He reported that Frau Boddanski was still in a terrible state and refused to calm down. There was some talk of Meiners being involved because he was the last one to be seen with the girl, but I thought this was probably a coincidence, and Frammler agreed. He said the woman was hysterical.

After receiving this report—I was with the road-block party at the time—I sent Frammler off to join the other two on the M.G. and went on helping to fell trees. It was a tough job, but as an N.C.O. and section commander I felt it my duty to set an example. While I was still at it, heavy firing broke out.

Question:

Can you give any more details?

Answer:
Well, the enemy fire was converging from several points, not
only from tanks but grenade-throwers and infantry weapons
as well.
Question:
What happened then?
Answer:
I watched the shells falling fair and square on the edge of the
wood. I heard a frightful scream, and then Frammler came
running through the trees towards us, shouting: ' The M.G.'s
out of action—Meiners has copped it! '

Just then—or so I seem to recall—Gisenius came running
up. He had intercepted a company runner who had been
detailed to bring me a message from Lieutenant Kronshagen.
According to Gisenius—and I had no reason to doubt the
word of an experienced soldier—the message was simply:
' Withdraw! '

I shouted to the section to fall back on Steinwiesen, but by
the time we were able to withdraw as ordered it was a question
of every man for himself.
Question:
When did the engagement end?
Answer:
Somewhere between 0900 and 1000 hours, I'd say, though it's
hard to tell for certain. When the pressure lifted I found the
section had completely dispersed. The odds against us had
been too great.
Question :
Wasn't there anyone left?
Answer:
Yes, Hirsch. He was lying beside me.
Question:
What about the rest of the section?
Answer:
I thought they were dead or missing. The ground round
us looked like the surface of the moon. Hirsch and I passed
the farm where we'd spent the night. It was a pile of rubble.
We crossed a series of fields and worked our way round the
edge of a marsh until we came to the next village, where we
found the remains of our company. Lieutenant Kronshagen
was there, and so was Frau Boddanski.

The company commander asked me where my section was. He took my report like a man. It wasn't the first unit he'd lost that morning. Then he asked for my opinion on the death of Fräulein Boddanski. I told him the truth: I said I knew nothing about it, except that the last person to be seen with the girl was Meiners, who had been killed.

Question:

Were you certain that Meiners had not survived?

Answer:

Absolutely positive.

Question:

What made you so sure?

Answer:

Circumstances in general, also the fact that Frammler had made a statement to that effect. Hirsch took it for granted, too. The concentration of fire was simply terrific. It wouldn't have surprised me if the whole section had been wiped out.

9. *Laying the Ghost*

'Thank you,' said Gisenius, when Bennicken had delivered his report on the previous night's encounter with Lehmgruber. He caressed the unopened briefcase on his knee. 'If I hadn't realized before how implicitly I could rely on you, my dear friend, this would have convinced me.'

'Any time,' Bennicken replied, gripping the lawyer's hand. 'I'd do anything for you, anything at all.'

Gisenius seemed equally affected. 'I know you would. Let's hope the need never arises.' His voice took on a less emotional note. 'There was one more thing, though. Did you manage to locate Tantau?'

'Got him with me,' Bennicken replied with a grin. 'I'd almost forgotten—I dug him out of bed. He's waiting outside in the cab.'

'I've been trying to get hold of you since noon yesterday,' Gisenius said irritably. 'Where have you been?'

Tantau looked vague. 'All over the place. You'd be surprised how I get around.'

Sensing that he had started off on the wrong foot, Gisenius hastened to offer his visitor a chair.

'Herr Tantau,' he said deliberately, 'that information you gave me yesterday was incorrect. Michael Meiners is not staying at the *Gasthof zur alten Post.*'

'No? Are you sure? He was there all right when I spoke to him yesterday morning.'

'Possibly, but he moved out immediately afterwards. Why?'

'Maybe the bed was too hard or the room too expensive or the view too depressing—how should I know? Has he changed hotels or did he leave town altogether?'

'Why ask me? It's your business to find out.'

'You mean the job still stands?'

'Of course. My instructions to you were to find Meiners's present whereabouts. Those instructions are still in force. Do you think you'll be able to trace him?'

'It's quite possible.'

'Good. By the way, what did you discuss with Meiners when you saw him?'

'The weather, the smells in the hotel, registration forms—all kinds of things.'

'Did you discuss the past?'

'We may have done. Would it worry you if we had?'

'You're very inquisitive.' Gisenius rose and walked to the window. 'Aren't you, Herr Tantau?'

'Let's say I like to be well-informed.'

'I underestimated you at first.' Gisenius swung round to face his visitor. 'I realize now that it's no use playing blind man's buff with you.'

'I'm delighted,' Tantau said encouragingly.

'Doing a job isn't enough for you—you like to fill in the background. I presume, therefore, that you already know why I'm so keen to have Michael Meiners's present address.'

'Perhaps.'

'I want to talk things over with him,' said Gisenius, 'not only in my own interests but on behalf of several of my friends. We're anxious to clear up a certain episode in the past—once and for all, if possible. Meiners must be made to realize that we're ready and willing to do so, and the only way of ensuring this is to have a full and frank discussion with him.'

'Very well,' Tantau said. 'I'll try to find him and persuade him to talk to you. But don't cherish any false hopes, Herr Gisenius. My impression is that Meiners hasn't the slightest desire to speak to you or your friends.'

'Do your best, anyway—and please hurry. Time is running short.'

Tantau gave a remote smile. 'I get that feeling too.'

'Who are you?' Saffranski said resentfully. 'What do you mean by barging in like this? You didn't even wait for me to say come in.'

'There wouldn't have been much point—I didn't knock.' Tantau eyed Saffranski equably. 'Just in case you decide to eject me with an equal lack of formality, I'd better tell you that we have something in common—not much, but something. We both work for Herr Kerze.'

'Why didn't you say so straight away?' Saffranski's indignation dispersed like morning mist. 'Please take a seat. I was just doing my exercises.'

'Thank you.' Tantau selected a chair beside the bed and surveyed his surroundings. There was something light, clean and angular about the room, the predominant colours being white and clear green. But, although the general effect was one of almost Prussian severity, it also contained an element of untidiness. Books and clothes were strewn about and a number of cheap prints had been cut out and pinned to the walls.

Studying the prints, Tantau saw that they were all of Greece, a dream-world of blue skies, sun-bleached stone, white-washed villages, wine-dark seas and noble sculpture.

Saffranski's eyes lit up. 'Are you interested in Greece?'

'I'm interested in most things.'

'That's real art for you.' Saffranski straightened up, his thin chest heaving under the skin-tight singlet. 'They've distorted human ideals these days—perverted them completely. You don't find true greatness anywhere any more.'

'You've got some scratches on your shoulder,' Tantau said abruptly.

'From my last cross-country run, I expect.' Saffranski reached for a towel and draped it round his neck. 'You said you worked for Herr Kerze, but you don't belong to the firm.'

'No, I'm doing a job for him—a confidential assignment, you might call it.'

Vaguely perturbed by the reference to scratches on his shoulder, Saffranski drew up a chair and sat down facing Tantau with a distrustful expression. 'A confidential assignment?' he said defiantly. 'Anyone could say that. Can you prove it?'

'Perhaps you'd find it instructive if I told you what you yourself are working on at the moment. Herr Kerze has told you to check the books of the *Drei Kronen* with a view to acquiring an interest in Europa Hotels Limited.'

Saffranski raised his eyebrows. 'What else do you know about me?'

'A couple of things. For instance, I know you're good at figures.'

'Well, what's the matter with that?'

'Nothing at all.' Tantau blinked lazily in Saffranski's direction. 'Your cross-country run seems to have been quite a performance. Those scratches on your shoulder look pretty deep.'

'I must have brushed against some thorns.'

'Or finger-nails?'

Saffranski started infinitesimally, but he regained control of himself with lightning speed. Displays of emotion were exceedingly rare with him. He had only lost control of himself once in his life.

'You're talking about a woman, I suppose,' he said scornfully. 'Do you find it entertaining to dwell on that sort of thing?' He gave a sour smile. 'There's nothing more degenerate than a bourgeois imagination. I can quote you an example. I was brought up by an aunt, and when I turned sixteen I was allowed to spend one evening a week at the gym. One night there was a bit of a scuffle, and I came home later than usual, covered in bruises. My aunt accused me of having been with a woman—love-bites, that's what she thought they were!'

'Presumably your aunt was a woman of experience,' Tantau said drily. 'Bruises can result from a variety of causes—it's very hard to differentiate between them after the event. Scratches are different, though. They not only leave traces on the recipient. They leave them on the donor as well.'

Saffranski's eyes narrowed. 'I don't know what you mean.'

'I think you do,' Tantau replied with unnerving calm. 'Anyone who scratches someone—and the scratches needn't be as deep as yours—scoops up tiny fragments of skin beneath his nails. These fragments, however minute, can be identified with ease and certainty, even when they're recovered from the nails of a corpse which has been buried for weeks—or immersed in water for hours.'

Saffranski preserved a stunned silence.

'But you needn't let a little thing like that worry you,' Tantau continued softly. 'I can produce some even more convincing evidence. There's one of your foot-prints beside the pool, for instance—not that that's the end of the world. It may be three or four days old. Then there are your finger-prints in Konstantin's room—but what do they prove? Only that you were up there some time.'

'What are you after?' Saffranski burst out. 'What do you want?'

'I merely wish to draw attention to certain miscalculations on your part, Saffranski,' Tantau said with a thin smile. 'Fatal miscalculations. For example, you overlooked a witness: the maidservant.'

Saffranski opened his mouth to speak but thought better of it.

'I expect you looked round for the girl and failed to find her. Why not? Because she was in the lavatory, of course. A little while later she saw you and Konstantin walking down to the pond together.'

'I was at the investiture!' Saffranski cried wildly. 'I can produce witnesses who saw me there.'

Tantau coolly waved the objection aside. 'Don't delude yourself,' he said. 'The time of death has been accurately established. You didn't put in an appearance until half an hour afterwards. It's only a twelve-minute walk from the house to the factory gates, and you didn't enter the hall until after the ceremony was over. I've got two witnesses to prove it. Any more questions?'

'Are you from the police?' Saffranski spoke with an effort.

'No. If I were, our little chat would have taken quite a different turn. It won't be long before the police get here, though. They're already on your track, and you must have a pretty fair idea of what'll happen when they pick you up.'

'Stop torturing me!' Saffranski cried in horror.

'Who's torturing you? Once upon a time they used to stretch men on the rack—and I can't imagine a more convincing example of human stupidity. Methods like those were brutal and primitive. Things are quite different today. There'll be day and night interviews, systematic interrogations, articles in the press. You'll be stripped bare and driven naked through the jungle known as public opinion. People always take a keen interest in sex-murderers.'

' Is that what you think I am? ' gasped Saffranski. ' Do you really mean all you've said? '

' Every word of it. What's more, you haven't a hope in hell of pleading diminished responsibility and getting yourself consigned to an institution—take it from me.'

' Isn't there anything I can do? ' Saffranski moaned, writhing like a worm. His face had gone deathly pale. ' Isn't there any way out? '

' The best means of killing a rat,' Tantau said softly, ' is rat poison.'

' I've been wondering when you'd come,' Michael Meiners said impatiently. ' I told you yesterday where to find me.'

' I haven't been entirely idle since then,' Tantau replied with a melancholy smile.

Meiners's new quarters were in the equally inexpensive but appreciably noisier Bahnhof Hotel. It was the least conspicuous form of accommodation in Rheine-Bergen and the hotel room in which they were sitting the most neutral rendezvous imaginable.

' Can I offer you a coffee or something? ' Meiners asked.

Tantau's smile broadened. ' You seem a little more communicative than you did last time.'

' I've straightened out my ideas since then. That's why I wanted to have a talk.'

' Good. If you're really feeling hospitable, perhaps you'd get them to send up a bar of chocolate for me. I haven't had any breakfast yet.'

' By all means.' Meiners looked a little surprised. ' What sort of chocolate do you like? '

' Coffee-cream or plain. Better ask room-service for a selection.'

The floor-waiter appeared with a tray. After careful deliberation, Tantau picked out three bars and started avidly on the first—Medium Plain.

' What form does your new approach take? ' he inquired.

' Well,' Meiners said, leaning back in his chair, ' I've always done my best to forget what happened. I simply didn't want to remember. It wasn't just that particular day, you see—it was the years that followed. But never mind all that —I tried to forget.'

'Until your firm sent you back here.'

'Yes,' Meiners said without hesitation. 'When the manager told me, I was absolutely flabbergasted for a minute or two. I felt like turning the job down at first, but then—probably because I didn't want to risk getting the sack—I told myself: all right, go there, make your calls and don't worry about anything else.'

'You can't go out in the rain and say: I'm not worried. You get wet just the same.' Tantau started on his second bar of chocolate. 'You could put it another way. No man lives in a vacuum, so he has to try and come to terms with his fellow-men. He hasn't any alternative. Even if his motives are purely selfish, he has to make some attempt to improve the human estate—to make mankind a little happier, or cleverer, or cleaner, or fatter, or healthier.'

Meiners brooded in silence for a moment. 'From the sound of it, the others haven't forgotten either. They still remember, and they're worried. But isn't that a sign of remorse on their part? Isn't it a good reason for calling it quits?'

'Not so fast,' Tantau warned, breaking off another square of chocolate. 'Some people can forgive and forget anything. They have an unbounded faith in human nature. I haven't anything against them, of course, if only because they're few and far between, but the point I want to make is rather different. You mustn't see people as essentially good or bad. You have to study them closely, analyse them objectively, do your best to sum them up—not love or despise them blindly.'

'Why tell me all this?' Meiners demanded. 'I was going to wash my hands of the whole affair, and now you've complicated it all.'

'It's a complicated business,' said Tantau. 'Take the question of remorse, for a start. You may think your friends have a healthy conscience, but wouldn't it have been more to the point if they'd demonstrated it sixteen years ago?'

'It was war-time.'

'And that excuses everything, I suppose! No, my friend, isn't it possible that this conscience of theirs has been dormant for years—that it's been sleeping more and more soundly as time has gone by, and that it's only just woken up again? I beg leave to doubt, incidentally, that conscience comes into

301

it at all. What you've aroused could just as easily be the instinct for self-preservation.'

'You're making things difficult for me,' Meiners said morosely.

'It would be wrong to do otherwise.'

'I wish I'd never come.'

'You're not the only one, my dear Meiners, but come you did. You were seen arriving on the bus. Did you recognize Karl Schulz?'

'Not for certain, but I had a feeling it might be him.'

'Why did you visit the Building Exhibition? Did you mean to run into Kerze?'

'It was an accident.'

'But you recognized him?'

'Yes. He hasn't changed much—except for his waist-line.'

'Did you see him coming towards you? Did you realize he wanted to speak to you?'

'Yes,' Meiners admitted, 'but I didn't want to speak to him—or anyone else in the section, for that matter. The thought of meeting him made me nervous. I was too much of a coward, that's probably what it was.'

Meiners walked to the window and rested his forehead against the cool glass.

'So far, I've been thinking entirely about myself,' he said after a long pause. 'That became very clear to me after our first conversation, Herr Tantau. When I told you I wanted to call it quits just now, I didn't give all my reasons.'

'I realize that.' Tantau eyed the remaining bar of chocolate with affection. 'Having acknowledged your own failings—for want of a better word—you were prepared to credit others with having done the same.'

'Wasn't I right? Wouldn't you have done so too?' Meiners left the window and resumed his seat beside Tantau. 'The others did something contemptible, but they were simply succumbing to human weakness. They were frightened, too. They acted in panic, surrounded by chaos. Their lives were at stake. Whatever they did, isn't it understandable that they did things under extreme pressure which they wouldn't normally have done? The situation was anything but normal.'

Tantau put down the last bar of chocolate and regarded

it pensively. Then he pushed it away and said: 'If you pursue that train of thought to its logical conclusion, the inference must be this: the actions of your so-called comrades-in-arms were attributable to human frailty, but because you also have your failings and made mistakes of your own, you want to let the matter drop—even though there's no comparison between the mistakes made on each side. Am I right?'

'Of course I made mistakes,' Meiners said eagerly, 'mistakes which explain a great many things. For instance, I was an inefficient soldier. I was shy and not particularly forthcoming. I kept myself to myself. It wasn't surprising they didn't like me.'

'In other words, you had the effrontery to be born, and if you died it was entirely your own fault. There's always some excuse if you look far enough. One man has to die because his pigmentation offends people, another because his nose isn't the right shape. You weren't sociable enough, so you had to go. There's always some explanation.'

'Herr Tantau,' Meiners said slowly, 'I'm not denying their guilt. It may be great, but it's not everlasting. Things were different then—it's hard to imagine how different. For my part, I'm prepared to forgive and forget. Tell that to your clients—or my former comrades, whichever you prefer.'

Tantau reached for the third bar of chocolate and stripped off the wrapper. 'Listen to me carefully, Meiners,' he said. 'Your reasoning is shaky. Guilt isn't a marketable commodity, nor is it dependent on human memory. It's a given quantity, a basic ingredient of existence. You can't alter it, diminish it or explain it away, which is why it's absurd to try and eliminate it by an act of will. There's only one way of doing that, and that is for the guilty party to recognize the full extent of his guilt, to acknowledge it and shoulder his responsibilities with genuine remorse. That's the only way of transforming guilt into something worth-while. Guilt exacts its own penalty. It can't be dispelled until that penalty is paid. That's your problem, Meiners, and you can't evade it.'

Meiners passed a hand over his brow. 'What ought I to do?'

'What you're afraid of doing,' Tantau said. 'Confront

303

your former friends and give them a chance to make a clean breast of it. Then you can call it quits.'

'It's time you looked through last week's figures,' Gisela Wandel said reprovingly. 'The monthly report to head office is due tomorrow.'

Martin Hirsch made a vague gesture. 'You deal with it. You know your way round the books quite as well as I do.'

Gisela frowned. 'It may not be my place to say this, Herr Hirsch, but I feel you've been neglecting your work recently.'

'Your intuition does you credit,' Hirsch replied cheerfully. 'If I ask you to write the report for head office, it only shows what a high opinion I have of you. I'm giving you a chance to display your rare abilities. Carry on, show me how efficient you are. I'm going out. I've got better things to do.'

'Will you be gone long?' Gisela's manner was studiously distant. 'The police are coming to ask some questions about Lehmgruber. He disappeared last night, if you remember.'

'It'll save him and us a lot of trouble if he never comes back. A man ought to be able to disappear occasionally. I'd like to go to ground myself—it wouldn't matter where, as long as there were no more reports to head office, no more voices from the dead, no more emotional women to cope with. If the police come about Lehmgruber, give them all the particulars they need. I told you, I've got more important things to do.'

Hirsch walked out of the office and drove off to the block of flats where Karl Schulz lived. He ran upstairs and rang the bell.

Eva answered the door, and Hirsch noted with delight that she smiled quickly as soon as she saw who it was. 'Karl isn't at home,' she said, opening the door wide. 'Please come in all the same, if you'd like to.'

Hirsch followed her into the kitchen and accepted a cup of coffee. After a few minutes' general conversation, he said: 'It's good to be here with you, Eva. I've known you ever since you were a child, and—' he hesitated '—well, I've always been very fond of you.'

'I'm fond of you too,' Eva said spontaneously. 'You used to be my ideal. Film stars and footballers always took second place with me.' She laughed softly. 'I remember telling Karl I was going to marry you when I grew up.'

'I'm nearly twenty years older than you are,' Hirsch said, torn between pleasure and embarrassment.

'Age doesn't matter.'

'Glad you think so, but I've led a pretty hectic life.'

'I know. We used to gossip about you at school.'

This time, Hirsch didn't know whether to feel pleased or embarrassed. 'It wasn't as hectic as all that,' he protested.

'Never mind,' said Eva. 'You have to live life to the full before you understand it, I realize that. Besides, it must have its advantages, being a man.'

'What makes you say that?' Hirsch asked sharply. 'Do you mean men are lucky because they can't get pregnant?'

Eva blushed and looked away in confusion. 'Yes, I suppose so.'

'A child is its mother's child, Eva,' Hirsch said softly. 'If you had one, it would belong to you, and only you.'

Eva's cheeks turned even pinker. She tilted her cup and studied the contents. 'You know about it, then?'

'I'm your brother's friend and I'm your friend too. Don't ever forget that.'

'Thank you.' Eva laid her hand on his. 'I always hoped you felt that way.'

Hirsch bowed his head. 'Do you understand, Eva? If your child ever needs a father, remember me.'

'You're pushing this case a bit, aren't you?' Chief Inspector Sand said peevishly.

Sergeant Brahmvogel looked aggrieved. 'But sir, it means we've got something definite at last on this villain who's been doing all the cab-drivers.'

'What makes you so sure the cases are connected?'

'Sir,' Brahmvogel said stubbornly, 'I realize you've put most of the division to work on the Kerze case, but isn't that more of a side issue? The papers have gone to town on this taxi-thief and we've got half a dozen reporters breathing down our necks. Don't you think we ought to do something about it?'

Sand's Achilles' heel was that of all senior policemen: lack of personnel. He could only do one thing at a time—never keep two or three balls in the air at once—and in this instance Brahmvogel was undoubtedly right. The taxi hold-up had priority.

Sand withdrew all except one member of his scanty C.I.D. force from the Kerze case and put them to work on what soon became known as the Lehmgruber case.

The first result was that Bennicken senior's statement relating to the events of the preceding night, duly taken down in writing at Rheine-Bergen Central, was confirmed. Examination of the taxi revealed a bullet-hole in the bodywork between the rear seat and the near-side door panel. A search of the area where the incident had occured brought to light a bullet embedded in the ground, calibre: 7.65, probable make of gun: Walther. Among the finger-prints found on the door-handle and frame were some which probably belonged to the assailant.

The second result was that interrogation of the other cab-drivers on the rank and their descriptions of the fare who had emerged from the *Drei Kronen* tallied exactly with the particulars given by Bennicken himself. Subsequent inquiries at the *Drei Kronen* made it possible to identify his passenger with a fair degree of certainty as a man called Lehmgruber.

The third result was that examination of the hotel room previously occupied by Lehmgruber disclosed numerous finger-prints which proved to be identical with some of those found in Bennicken's taxi.

Back in his office, Sand put down the 'phone with a sigh. ' All right,' he told his second-in-command, ' you can issue a warrant and put out a general call.' The wheels began to turn.

This should have been the signal for Sand to embark on the double-checking which was one of the basic rules governing the investigation of serious offences. It was his duty to re-examine every link in the chain of evidence, but he did not do so with his usual meticulous care, first because of his acute shortage of personnel and secondly because he refused to neglect the business of Konstantin Kerze.

Sand had no alternative but to wind up his inquiries into the Lehmgruber case at top speed. The West German F.B.I. was already requesting particulars in the hope that they might throw light on parallel cases, but Sand unhesitatingly reassigned one of his best men, a detective-inspector named Faltermeier, to the Kerze case. He gave him a slip of paper bearing the names Brandstädter and Saffranski.

'Concentrate on those two,' Sand told him. 'Both of them were at the Villa Kerze on the morning in question, and the Brandstädter woman should be able to supply you with some useful information.'

'What about Saffranski?'

'He's an accountant,' Sand replied non-committally, echoing Tantau, '—you know, good at figures.'

Leaving his puzzled subordinate staring at the slip of paper, Sand climbed into a waiting police car and drove to the *Drei Kronen*, where two more of his men were waiting for him. One of them had combed Lehmgruber's room without producing any startling results and the other had interviewed members of the hotel staff and collected all available documentary evidence of the vanished guest's sojourn at the *Drei Kronen* with—or so it seemed to him—a similar lack of success.

Sand took the sheaf of papers and studied it carefully before making his way to the manager's office.

'Go right in, Chief Inspector,' Gisela Wandel told him. 'Herr Hirsch is expecting you.'

Sand said: 'You don't seem overjoyed to see me.'

'No offence,' Hirsch replied without malice, 'but your men do make themselves rather conspicuous, don't they?'

'They don't have the polish of trained hotel staff, I grant you that. But let's get down to business. Do you know what this chap Lehmgruber did for a living?'

'I can't say. "Broker" was all he put on his registration form.'

Sand gave a thin smile. 'I suppose you're going to tell me he was just one guest like a hundred others, but wouldn't it be true to say that you devoted a little more time to him than you do to most of your patrons?'

'Who told you that? Fräulein Wandel?'

'Come, come,' said Sand, 'don't underestimate your subordinates.' He spread out his papers on Hirsch's desk and tapped a figure with his forefinger.

'I get it,' said Hirsch. 'I see you've an eye for figures, Chief Inspector. As a matter of fact, I did talk to Lehmgruber a couple of times. He was a poor financial risk.'

Sand appeared to find this interesting. 'Putting myself in your position, I can imagine asking this poor financial risk what guarantee of payment he could give—what security he could offer or what his prospects were.'

'What his source of income was, you mean?'

'Precisely. You see, what emerges from these particulars is, first, that the man had no money, secondly, that you gave him an ultimatum, and, thirdly, that he produced some cash. There's no record of his having received a draft from any bank or post office, and no mail arrived for him while he was here. Ergo, he must have got his windfall somewhere in Rheine-Bergen—but where? Who gave it to him? Did he really give you no indication?'

'No,' Hirsch said after a moment's reflection, 'not that I can recall.'

Sand waited patiently for a few seconds. Then, lingering over the words, he said: 'Never mind, it's just conceivable that the odd detail may come back to you some time or other. If so, please let me know at once. It could be important.'

'Well,' Frammler remarked in a low voice, ' that's one more job done. It went off perfectly, didn't it?'

'Spot on,' growled Bennicken.

'Yes,' Schulz agreed, 'it was really classy.'

Hirsch corrected him. 'Not classy, Karl—first-class.' He turned to Frammler. 'That is your most expensive category, isn't it?'

The subject under discussion was Konstantin's funeral, which had been undertaken by Frammler's Interment Institute. The décor included four candelabra with genuine beeswax candles, and the coffin and surrounds were draped in the satin and velvet which only funerals at the upper end of the price-range commanded. Lesser refinements such as incense-candles, strewn fir-branches, potted evergreens and artificial lilies in imitation Greek urns had been supplied free of charge by Frammler, for the sake of friendship and public relations.

'Grand, that's what it was,' declared Bennicken, blowing his nose loudly.

Hirsch said: 'I could use a drink.'

'Later,' Bennicken retorted firmly. 'Gisenius said we were to wait.'

They waited, resigning themselves to the fact that they still had, in any case, to express their condolences to their bereaved friend.

Kerze himself, a dignified picture framed by two large potted evergreens, was surrounded by an élite of mourners from industry, commerce and public life. Beside him stood Karen, clad in black, which suited her admirably, and beside her stood her would-be but not-quite fiancé, Johannes Bartosch, who had seized this opportunity of demonstrating his personal ties with the Kerze family. Behind Kerze, inseparable as a shadow, lurked Conrad Gisenius. The mourners filed by in a seemingly endless line.

'Eighteen minutes,' murmured Frammler, glancing at his watch. 'That's almost a record. Kerze'll have to pay overtime if he doesn't watch out.'

At long last the gathering broke up and the invited mourners dispersed. Karen, gallantly escorted by Bartosch, also made for the exit, but not before casting a reproachful glance in Hirsch's direction.

'Lucky dog,' said Frammler. 'She's the best thing Kerze ever manufactured in his life.'

'Shut up,' Bennicken said evenly.

Willy Kerze, accompanied by Gisenius, advanced on the little group with hand outstretched. The four old comrades squared their shoulders and prepared to express their condolences in wordless but heartfelt fashion.

'Thank you, my dear friends,' Kerze said ,producing a phrase which he had already used to good effect on the more eminent of his guests: 'It's only in our darkest hours that we really appreciate the consolation true sympathy can bring.'

Gisenius cleared his throat. 'Our friend Kerze would also appreciate it if we joined him for a small drink at the *Drei Kronen*. Can you arrange that, my dear Hirsch?'

'I've already booked the Oak Room,' Hirsch said.

'In that case, shall we go?'

They went. Kerze, escorted by Gisenius, climbed into his limousine. Next came Bennicken's taxi, containing Schulz and Hirsch, and Frammler brought up the rear in his hearse, partly because he had to get it back to town anyway and partly because it was valuable publicity for his firm.

'Friends,' said Kerze, when they were assembled in the Oak Room with their glasses duly filled, 'thank you once again. Need I say more?'

They drained their glasses, deposited them on the table and sat down.

'Well, that's the way it goes,' Frammler said meditatively. 'The call comes for us all sooner or later.'

'Too soon for some,' amplified Hirsch, 'and too late for others. Quite a few poor sods get helped on their way, and some people make a good thing out of it.'

Frammler glared at Hirsch furiously and then appealed to Kerze. 'Did I cheat you?' he demanded. 'Aren't my prices reasonable? I even gave you a discount, didn't I?'

'Certainly,' Kerze conceded, 'but need we discuss commercial matters at a time like this?'

'Hear, hear!' Karl Schulz said firmly, and there was more than a touch of the veteran N.C.O. in his tone as he added: 'Watch it, Frammler!'

'Gentlemen,' Gisenius interposed, 'however deeply moved we may be at this time by our friend Kerze's tragic bereavement, we mustn't entirely lose sight of our common problem. I refer to Michael Meiners.'

Everyone present turned to look at Gisenius—Martin Hirsch alert, Karl Schulz resigned and Frammler with evident misgiving.

'We must face facts,' Gisenius went on. 'Meiners is not only alive—he's actually here in town. We may come face to face with him at any moment. What then, my friends?'

'It entirely depends what Meiners expects of us,' Hirsch said, in response to the lawyer's challenging stare. 'You never know, he may only want to have a little chat about old times. Perhaps he'd like to discuss how and why he was supposed to have died sixteen years ago.'

'That's no subject for discussion,' Kerze said promptly. 'We mustn't let it come to that. And while we're about it, Hirsch, I wish you'd stop behaving as though the whole affair didn't concern you.'

'I was partly responsible for leaving him in the lurch,' Hirsch admitted. 'God knows I've regretted it since, but I had nothing to do with what actually happened and I wasn't in the barn, either . . .'

' I don't understand you lot,' Schulz complained. ' I
mean, what's the good of dodging our responsibilities? '

Frammler raised his eyebrows. ' Our responsibilities? '
he queried, reaching for the bottle. ' I was only a lance-jack
—the lowest of the low. I wasn't a sergeant like you, Schulz.'

' That's right, pass the buck! ' Hirsch burst out furiously,
noticing with distress that Schulz had turned as white as
a sheet.

Gisenius intervened. ' Unfortunately, gentlemen, the situation isn't straightforward from the legal aspect. To begin
with, there's the girl's death. We did suggest that Meiners
might have been involved, did we not? '

' It was the obvious solution,' said Frammler.

' Damn it all! ' Hirsch exploded. ' What do you mean,
we suggested? It was you who concocted the whole thing,
Gisenius. You put the others up to it.'

' I don't deserve that,' Gisenius said, looking hurt.

Kerze reacted promptly. ' That's a swinish thing to say! '

' Swinish! ' Bennicken chimed in.

' Fancy saying such a thing to someone who's done so
much for us all! ' Kerze puffed indignantly. ' If anyone's
stuck his neck out for us, it's Gisenius. How often have
I told him: Conrad, deal with it for us, I'll foot the bill—and
he's dealt with it. And what thanks does he get? I'm
ashamed of you! I refuse to have anything more to do with
you.'

' Is that a threat or a promise? ' demanded Hirsch.

Conrad Gisenius bowed his head as though to hide invisible
tears, but Karl Schulz rose to his feet.

' Lads! ' he said solemnly. ' I'm sorry about all this.
I'm only a simple chap, but I know where my duty lies and
I'm prepared to take the consequences.'

' Stop it, Karl! ' Hirsch said in a horrified voice.

Bennicken said: ' Let him speak.'

Schulz took a deep breath. ' As I see it,' he gulped, ' I
was your sergeant. I was in command, so I must bear full
responsibility.'

Hirsch groaned. ' What rubbish, Karl! '

' Who'd have thought it of you, Schulz? ' said Frammler.
' First-rate—that's what you are.'

Gisenius rose from his chair, clasped Schulz's hand and

shook it with feeling. 'You've set us a shining example, my dear Schulz. We all—' he glanced keenly round the table but failed to catch anyone's eye '—we all appreciate it more than we can say.' Almost briskly, he added: 'It provides each of us with a safeguard—not, of course, that we can accept.'

'I don't see why not,' Frammler said with unabashed candour. 'Wouldn't it be the simplest solution?'

Gisenius smiled. 'The simplest solution, perhaps, but not the only one. Schulz has given me an excellent idea. He feels that he ought to bear full responsibility on our behalf. But who, I now ask myself, bears responsibility for him—and so for us all? Well?—His superior officer, of course!'

Frammler gave an admiring whistle. 'Not bad!'

Gisenius warmed to his theme. 'It was Kronshagen who ordered us into action. Consequently, one might say that what happened to Meiners was his responsibility. Furthermore, all the reports of the girl's death were passed on to him—and that, my dear Schulz, provisionally disposes of your liability.' He raised his glass. 'Gentlemen, I believe we have every reason to congratulate ourselves on having hit upon an admirable solution to our difficulties. The toast is comradeship, coupled with the health of our friend Karl Schulz. May his exemplary sense of duty be an object lesson to us all!'

They all drank. While they were drinking, Gisela Wandel appeared.

'There's a man waiting outside to speak to you,' she said. 'His name is Meiners.'

'I sometimes wonder what goes on inside these old boys' heads,' Claus Gisenius said, tapping his brow disrespectfully.

'They're only fifteen or twenty years older than you are, Eva replied quietly.

Claus shrugged his shoulders. 'Maybe, but they're shot to hell, mentally. Hitler broke their backbone once and for all.'

They were standing in the hall of Karl Schulz's flat, exchanging caresses which lacked the usual carefree abandon.

'Things can't go on like this,' Claus said, gently detaching himself. 'We'll have to make these old fogies realize that times have changed since their young days. What did they mean by ganging up on us like that? Surely your brother could have done his own dirty work—or doesn't he feel safe unless Hirsch is backing him up? '

' Martin Hirsch happens to be a friend of my brother's, Eva said. ' For that matter,' she added diffidently, ' he's a friend of mine, too.'

' What! ' Claus exclaimed irritably. ' That superannuated Casanova! '

Eva's voice was soft. ' I've known Martin longer than I've known you, Claus—I've known him all my life.'

' Exactly. He's old enough to be your father and he enjoys playing the Dutch uncle. What is all this, anyway? Do you love me or don't you? '

' That's a silly question,' Eva said tenderly. ' Still, when I come to think of it, I love Martin Hirsch too—in quite a different way, of course.'

' Thanks a lot! That's a great comfort.'

' But Claus,' she said, touching his arm, which he abruptly withdrew, ' how can you help loving someone a little when he's prepared to do anything to earn your love? '

' What does that add up to? You don't mean he wants to marry you? '

' He'd marry me under any circumstances.'

Claus stared at her in bewilderment. ' Under any circumstances? '

' Yes—even if I were going to have a child by someone else.'

' And are you? '

' I may be,' Eva said quietly. ' Please don't ask me any more.'

Claus leant against the door. ' It's fantastic! ' he murmured. ' It can't be true! '

' You needn't believe me if you don't want to. The door's right behind you.'

' What did you say? You must be out of your mind! ' He gave a shaky smile. ' You're not going to chuck the father of your child out of the house, are you? '

He stretched out his arms. Eva nestled against him. They stood there for a long time, silent.

It was Claus who broke the silence. ' We mustn't stand

around like this,' he said. 'You've got to take it easy from now on, remember.'

'Oh, Claus,' Eva said happily, 'I'm afraid you've picked an awfully silly girl to be the mother of your child.'

Claus laughed. 'Don't worry, love. I'm sharp enough for both of us.'

'But what are we going to do?'

'The right thing, of course.'

'It won't be easy.'

'Maybe not, but it'll be fun.' Claus squeezed her hand. 'Even if we have to blow up the whole of the old comrades association in the process.'

There was a particular reason for Tantau's visit to the *Café Liedtke*. The proprietor, who hailed from East Prussia, was in possession of some excellent recipes for original Königsberg marzipan.

'I'm glad you've come,' Liedtke said genially. 'I'd like your opinion. You know how difficult it is to blend chocolate with marzipan? Well, I think I've found the answer at last.'

He bustled off and came back with a large plate of chocolate-filled marzipan balls.

Tantau tasted one with the tense expression of a scientist on the verge of an epoch-making discovery. 'Superb!' he declared, after testing a second piece. 'You certainly have found the answer. At a guess, I'd say you've blended almond essence with the chocolate instead of using a pure chocolate filling.'

Liedtke looked delighted. 'You ought to have been a confectioner.'

'Possibly,' Tantau said. 'It would certainly have spared me a lot of trouble—that, for instance.'

He indicated the entrance. Chief Inspector Sand had just come in and was scanning the tables. When he caught sight of Tantau he waved and came across.

'Better leave us alone,' Tantau told Liedtke, 'but don't dare take that marzipan with you.' He turned to greet Sand, who was looking troubled. 'Well, Chief Inspector, I gather you've found out who was responsible for Konstantin Kerze's death.'

'Yes,' Sand replied bitterly, 'just under an hour ago. If I hadn't been side-tracked by another case I'd have found out even sooner.'

'But not soon enough, presumably.'

'No, I expect you'd have beaten me to it in any case. All the same, I'd like to know when you first became convinced of Saffranski's guilt.'

'I guessed it after a few hours, my dear Sand. However, I don't have a C.I.D. team at my disposal, and I could never have proved anything even if I had.'

'My God, you're artful!' Sand said with reluctant admiration. 'You'd never admit that you've been working against us, would you?'

'Not against you, my dear Sand—merely a little ahead of you.' Tantau's tone was conciliatory. 'Remember, I was lucky enough to have several hours' start, but we passed the post almost together. You did a good job.'

'Maybe,' said Sand, 'but not a thorough job.'

'No?'

'No. Saffranski had a visitor early this morning—a man. His description fits you to a tee. Do you deny you were there?'

'Why should I? Yes, I did have a little chat with our peculiar young friend.'

'What about?'

'I'll make a bargain with you, Sand. You tell me Saffranski's version of our conversation and I'll give you my comments.'

'You're pretty sure of yourself, aren't you?' Sand said sourly. 'I ought to have known.'

'Quite,' replied Tantau, 'you ought to have known better than to play cat and mouse with me—I'm no stranger to such tactics.' He picked up another piece of marzipan. 'What you're trying to tell me—correct me if I'm wrong—is that Saffranski has made no statement about my conversation with him for the simple reason that he's incapable of making any statement at all.'

'Precisely,' said Sand, accepting defeat like a man, 'Saffranski's dead. He poisoned himself.'

'It was the best solution,' Tantau said quietly.

'But not a just one.'

'Please don't confuse justice with legality, Chief Inspector. The law is fallible. It once served the interests of a criminal

315

regime, and some of its erstwhile administrators are still in office. When the C.I.D. does their dirty work, as it often has to, it becomes an accessory after the fact.'

'The sort of danger you envisage doesn't arise in this type of murder case.'

'My dear Sand, you know perfectly well that I'm an opponent of the death penalty and always have been. Whenever the law has been licensed to kill it has killed innocent people as well as guilty, starting with the incurably sick and the incurably idealistic and ending with everyone who happens to disagree with the political system of the day. I loathe the death penalty, but what's to be done with a sex-maniac who murders children—who can't help murdering children? I don't concede the right of the law to kill, even in his case. Sex-murderers are sick—mentally deranged, if you like. If we want to protect society from them we should take them into protective custody and put them in special institutions; executing them solves nothing. On the other hand, I do concede their right to end their own abysmal lives, whether they do it out of self-abhorrence or fear . . .'

'So you drew Saffranski's attention to that alternative,' Sand observed bitterly.

Tantau pushed the plate of marzipan away with a sigh. 'The case is closed.'

Michael Meiners lingered in the doorway, as though afraid his intrusion might be resented. He was very pale, and the scars on the side of his face stood out like angry weals.

'Good afternoon,' he said diffidently, eyeing the figures round the table. They were all standing now, and six pairs of eyes stared back at him with a mixture of apprehension and mistrust.

'I hope I'm not intruding,' he continued in a subdued voice. 'Herr Tantau suggested that I should come.'

As ever, when the hour of decision struck, Conrad Gisenius was the first to spring into action. He walked over to Meiners with resolute tread, trying to inject some cordiality into his smile. 'Welcome, my dear fellow!' he cried, extending his hand. 'Do you recognize me?'

'Gisenius,' Meiners said in a flat voice.

'You remember. How nice!'

'Why shouldn't I!' Meiners took the proffered hand without undue hesitation.

Gisenius derived considerable relief from this conciliatory gesture. The ice seemed to have been broken.

'Yes,' said Gisenius, pumping Meiners's hand with ostentatious bonhomie, 'I'm Gisenius. Since we last met, I've become what I always wanted to be—a lawyer with chambers of my own.'

'You could tell that, even in the old days,' Martin Hirsch broke in. 'Gisenius always spoke as though he was addressing a jury. He's changed less than any of us.'

'It's Hirsch, isn't it?' For the first time, Meiners's face broke into a genuine smile. He put out his hand and Martin Hirsch shook it warmly.

'You probably remember my predilection for the good things of life. Well, I tried to make my day-dreams come true by going into the hotel business—and the only result is that I spend most of my time dreaming of quitting it.'

Karl Schulz left the table and advanced on Meiners. Looking him straight in the eye, he said: 'I'd like to shake your hand too, Meiners. I'm glad you're still alive. I always tried to be a good friend to you in the old days, and that's the way I'd like it to be now.'

'Thank you, Schulz,' Meiners replied.

'Karl's been promoted since you last saw him,' Hirsch explained. 'He manages a filling-station now. He earns three times as much as he did when he was a sergeant, but he only has a third as many people to bully.'

'Come off it!' Schulz growled cheerfully.

'I'm Kerze.' The industrialist tried to register a subdued pleasure appropriate to his role as a bereaved father.

'You haven't changed much either,' Meiners said.

'Nice of you to say so, my dear fellow,' Kerze replied. 'I've put on the best part of a hundredweight since we last met.'

'He's digging his own grave with a knife and foik,' said Hirsch. 'It's a great way to go, eating yourself to death, but I'm not sure he enjoys it to the full.'

Gisenius cleared his throat reprovingly. Terms like 'grave' and 'death' were unsuited to the occasion.

'Kerze has been the biggest success of us all,' he interposed hastily.

317

Kerze made a deprecating gesture. 'Materially, perhaps.'

'He built a whole industry out of nothing,' Gisenius pursued. 'I expect you saw his stand at the Building Exhibition, didn't you?'

Meiners made no reply. He was wrestling with one of the attacks of weakness that had troubled him on and off for years—a sense of total debility, a feeling that his bones were thin-walled and hollow, his flesh soft as a sponge. A pulse in his temple beat with the insistence of a metronome.

'If you ever need my help,' Kerze was saying, 'don't hesitate to call on me.'

'We all owe Kerze a great deal,' Gisenius put in. 'You can rely on him.'

'Thank you,' Meiners said weakly, taking Kerze's hand.

'What about me, old lad?' another voice broke in. 'Don't you recognize me? I always thought this mug of mine was unique. Some people say I look like a gorilla, but I take that as a compliment. There's nothing sadder-looking than a gorilla, and you've no idea what an asset that is in my business.'

'Frammler,' Meiners said.

Frammler looked gratified. 'Right first time! No. 2 Section's jack-of-all-trades—tailor, cook and barber—that was me. These days I bury dead bodies. I bet that surprises you, doesn't it? Frammler's Interment Institute—first-class service! Generous discount and commission available to personal friends.'

Michael Meiners shook hands and turned to face the only member of the group who had not yet greeted him.

'Bennicken,' growled the latter, without moving. 'Remember me?'

'Yes,' replied Meiners. He did not extend his hand.

'Why don't we all sit down?' Gisenius suggested quickly. 'Pull up a chair for Meiners. We mustn't keep our guest of honour standing around.'

While Schulz and Hirsch produced a chair and placed it between them, Frammler set a beer-glass in front of the new arrival and proceeded to fill it with kirsch.

'Tell me,' Schulz said incautiously, 'now that you've heard a bit about our doings, how about returning the compliment? What's been happening to you?'

'Let's drink a toast first,' Gisenius suggested.

The others prepared to comply, but Meiners did not seem to have heard. He stared at Schulz for a moment before replying. 'After I'd been left alone on the edge of the wood I came under heavy fire—from all sides, or so it seemed at the time. The ground round me was churned up. I lay there for a while, stunned and bleeding, and then I passed out. When I came to again weeks later, I was a prisoner of war in a camp hospital.'

'Appalling,' Gisenius remarked vaguely. 'Still, that's war for you,' he went on. 'I'm sure no one wants to revive painful memories, least of all you, Meiners. Am I right?'

'Yes,' Meiners replied with a hint of firmness. 'Let sleeping dogs lie.'

'Well spoken!' cried Gisenius. 'An admirable sentiment, if I may say so. We ought to drink to it. Don't you agree, gentlemen?'

They all drank except Meiners, which struck at least one member of the gathering as suspicious.

'What's the matter?' Kerze demanded bluntly. 'Do you bear us a grudge?'

'Why should he?' Gisenius said quickly. 'It's all water under the bridge—isn't that right, Meiners?'

'Yes,' Meiners murmured, 'that's right.'

'A commendable attitude—most commendable.' Gisenius glanced round the table. 'Never forget one thing, gentlemen: war isn't a child's game. The main thing is to emerge from it as creditably as possible. Isn't that so, Meiners?'

Meiners nodded weakly, and the lawyer's face glowed with triumph. Good sense had prevailed and perseverance had paid dividends. A major threat had been averted.

'You haven't let us down, my dear Meiners.' Gisenius raised his glass. 'A man must look to the future, not remain rooted in the past—you obviously realize that as clearly as we do.' He paused for a moment, but Meiners made no comment. 'Gentlemen,' he continued, 'this is a red letter day. We ought to celebrate it.'

Surveying the company, he saw a ring of acquiescent faces, one of which belonged to Meiners. The ex-members of No. 2 Section raised their glasses and crowded round Meiners with every sign of good-fellowship. With victory seemingly complete, Gisenius decided that he could afford to absent himself long enough to make a few telephone calls.

Frammler clapped Meiners on the back. ' You've done the right thing, old lad. I reckon you've changed for the better in the last fifteen years.'

'A man after my own heart,' Karl Schulz declared with feeling. His world was back on an even keel once more.

Martin Hirsch gave a wry smile. ' A nice accommodating man, you mean.'

' Meiners has behaved in the only possible way,' Kerze said with some asperity. ' Where would we be if everyone tried to turn his personal experiences into a universal criterion? It's unthinkable! '

' Unthinkable,' Frammler agreed, sipping at his kirsch.

Bennicken crouched motionless in his chair, but no one spared him a glance. Michael Meiners was such an undisputed focus of attention that even Gisenius's absence seemed to have passed unnoticed.

' Everyone has his troubles,' Kerze pursued. ' I've had my share, but do I moan about them? Certainly not, I do my best to overcome them. Anyone worth his salt presses on regardless and does his duty like a man.'

' Exactly,' said Frammler. ' Nothing in life is free. You can't fight a war without shedding blood—it's only natural.'

' It's fate,' Karl Schulz said ponderously.

' It's a convenient excuse, you mean,' Hirsch retorted, but Kerze was already speaking again.

' We've all made sacrifices,' he asserted in ringing tones, '—Meiners too, of course, but he wasn't the only one. Always bear that in mind, my dear Meiners, and you'll find some things easier to accept.'

' I don't quite follow,' Meiners said, frowning. ' You're not expecting an apology from me, are you? '

' Nobody's expecting or demanding anything,' Kerze replied emphatically, '—nobody, and I hope that goes for you too, Meiners. No friend worthy of the name tries to incriminate another. That's what you call fouling your own nest.'

' What! ' exclaimed Meiners. ' Don't tell me you're proposing to blame me for something you did yourselves! '

' What do you expect us to do,' Frammler demanded, '—go down on our knees and beg your pardon because you

320

were stupid enough to rape a girl and then stick your nut out of a slit-trench at the wrong moment? Don't make me laugh!'

'Take it easy!' warned Schulz, but Meiners ignored his plea.

'It's no good!' he cried excitedly. 'We can't settle things like this!'

'Shut your trap, then,' Bennicken said. His tone was menacing.

'I'm not going to take your foul insinuations lying down,' Meiners said in a shaking voice. 'I came here to patch things up, not to be insulted.'

'No one's insulting you,' Kerze assured him. 'You're just imagining it.'

'How dare you!' Meiners jumped to his feet, trembling with agitation and disappointment. 'I was prepared for anything. I'd have accepted any sort of apology or explanation, however unconvincing. But to be treated like a criminal as well as an idiot—no, that's going too far!'

'Steady on, fellows!' Schulz called imploringly. 'Remember the old team spirit!'

'You can't pull the wool over my eyes,' Meiners snapped. 'If this is what you call team spirit, I spit on it!'

Karl Schulz winced. The fact that Meiners had aimed his remark at the others eluded him. All he knew was that a comradely exhortation had been rudely rejected.

'So that's what he means by patching things up,' remarked Frammler.

Kerze burst out: 'Who the hell do you think you're talking to, Meiners? I insist on a formal apology.'

'I—apologize?'

'Certainly. No one spits on the hand of friendship and gets away with it!'

'Meiners will apologize,' Schulz said soothingly, 'won't you, Meiners?'

'No I won't! I wash my hands of you. I attributed your behaviour sixteen years ago to human weakness and your hesitation today to an understandable sense of shame. I was ready to let bygones be bygones. You may have thought it was I who died in 1945, but now I realize it was you who ceased to exist for me from then on. Do you hear? In my eyes, you're dead men!'

Karl Schulz hung his head, Martin Hirsch stared at Meiners wide-eyed and Frammler started to giggle foolishly, but Kerze roared: ' You ought to be ashamed of yourself! '

' It's enough to make a man sick,' Bennicken said grimly. ' You're right—it's sickening! ' Meiners cried, shaking with fury. He spun on his heel and headed for the door.

Gisenius had retired to make his telephone calls fully convinced that all was in order. He was still possessed by this agreeable sensation as he collided with Meiners and caught him by the shoulders. ' You're in a hurry, old friend! ' he said jovially.

' Stuff your friendship! ' Meiners shouted. He plunged wildly out of the room and slammed the door behind him.

For the first time ever, the others saw Conrad Gisenius totally at a loss for words. His mouth opened and closed several times, but no sound emerged. At length, as though the act of speech pained him, he asked: ' What was all that? '

Hirsch's tone was wearily ironical. ' Team spirit,' he drawled.

Two figures strolled through the mild spring sunshine which bathed Rheine-Bergen's municipal gardens. They were an oddly assorted couple. The man, short and elderly with the wrinkled features of an aged dachshund, was neatly but shabbily dressed, while the trim young girl beside him, pretty in an almost too doll-like way, was wearing an elegantly tailored costume.

' What am I going to do? ' Karen Kerze complained. ' The man I love won't have me and the man who wants to marry me doesn't suit me.'

Tantau gave a sympathetic smile. ' It's an old problem, my dear. Speaking off the cuff, I'd advise you to abandon them both. I'm only talking in general terms, though. I can't give a real opinion without knowing more details—not that I want to pry.'

' That's all right. I told you before—I trust you.'

' Well,' said Tantau, blinking in the sunlight, ' number one on your list is Martin Hirsch, isn't he?—Don't look so surprised, Karen, I'm not a mind-reader. My hearing's still good and I can put two and two together, that's all.'

' You're a marvel,' said Karen. ' I'm slowly getting

used to the idea that you know everything about everyone.'

'Did Hirsch ever give you any grounds for hope?'

'It seemed like it at first, but just when things were shaping nicely he bolted like a frightened horse.'

'I can imagine it,' Tantau grinned. 'Despite widespread rumours to the contrary, Hirsch doesn't strike me as being a professional lady-killer.'

'He has his weaknesses, but I'm not one of them, worse luck. I have an idea he's afraid of my father.'

'It's possible,' said Tantau, 'but I doubt it. In my opinion, Hirsch is one of those rare creatures who genuinely don't care about security or a settled existence. He could cut loose and make a fresh start any time he chose to.'

'Then why doesn't he do it, and take me with him?'

'Perhaps he knows more about your true feelings than you do yourself. After all, he's acquainted with your family background. I expect he senses instinctively that what you need is a father, not a lover.'

Karen came to a halt, and a look of surprise passed across her face. 'It's never occurred to me before,' she said eventually. 'Perhaps I ought to give it some thought. On the other hand, mightn't it be better to try and find out what Martin thinks about it?'

'Haven't you tried already?'

'Yes, but I see things more clearly now.'

Tantau chuckled. 'Well,' he said, patting Karen affectionately on the arm, 'I won't try to stop you. I couldn't even if I wanted to, I know. I can see you're determined to have it out with him.'

'Yes, I am. I want to make a fresh start too.'

'I'm sure you do, but what about Bartosch?'

'He wouldn't know what to do with a wife.'

'Are you speaking from personal experience?'

'I just know, that's all,' Karen said firmly. 'He looks like a thoroughbred stallion, he's intelligent and well-mannered and I'm sure he's got all sorts of other admirable qualities, but he's entirely lacking in one respect. I happen to attach a certain amount of importance to it. Is that very naughty of me, Herr Tantau?'

'This is disastrous,' Gisenius said, when Meiners had gone.

'The cheeky sod!' Bennicken growled contemptuously.

Frammler rubbed his hands together as though to warm them. 'He tried to put one over on us, but we told him where he got off.'

'Bunglers,' Gisenius said darkly. 'That applies to all of you!' he added with uncharacteristic bluntness.

'What more could we do?' Karl Schulz demanded. 'We did our level best to be friendly.'

'No one could have been friendlier.' So saying, Frammler prudently withdrew to a defensive position behind the kirsch bottle. When Gisenius was on the war-path, wise men took cover.

'Everything would have gone all right if Hirsch hadn't insisted on making his usual witty remarks,' fumed Kerze. 'He egged Meiners on.'

Bennicken emitted a furious snort.

'If that's what Bennicken thinks of Kerze's ludicrous insinuations,' Hirsch said promptly, 'I agree with him entirely. It was Kerze who systematically rubbed Meiners up the wrong way, not me.'

'Silence!' shouted Gisenius. None of his friends had ever heard him employ such a tone before, and it reduced them to stunned immobility. 'All attempts at self-justification are superfluous. Worse than that, they're a waste of time. Under the circumstances, it doesn't matter who's to blame for this catastrophe.'

'It wasn't me, anyway,' Kerze muttered.

'Nor me,' Gisenius said reprovingly. 'It may have been ill-advised of me to leave you alone with him for ten minutes, but how was I to know that would be long enough for you to ruin all my hard work?'

'You know,' mused Hirsch, 'I got the impression that Meiners was being sincere. He really wanted to bury the hatchet.'

'He looked as if he wanted to bury it in our skulls when he stormed out of the room just now!' Kerze snapped.

'I sympathized with him,' Hirsch replied calmly. 'I'll tell you something else: if you'd tried the same treatment on me, I'd have kicked your arses in turn.'

'Mine included?' Bennicken inquired menacingly.

'Yes. I'd have dug out my old jack-boots for your benefit.'

Frammler raised a placatory hand. 'I doubt if anyone would have tried it on with you, Hirsch,' he said, grinning, 'but that flabby-minded fool asked for it. He hasn't changed a day. Once a wet streak, always a wet streak.'

'Stop talking twaddle and concentrate on the facts,' Gisenius said sternly. 'To the best of my knowledge, they are as follows: Meiners arrived in town several days ago and started watching us. We put Tantau on to him and he promptly eluded us by changing his hotel. The only inference was an alarming one: he wanted to avoid a direct confrontation. However, Tantau traced him again and told him to come here, which he did, either because he had no alternative or because he thought the time was ripe. So he came and pretended to want a reconciliation—not that I entirely reject the possibility that his initial impulse may have been genuine. He then changed his mind—provoked into doing so by heaven alone knows what sort of irresponsible remarks on your part —and flounced out.'

'He can go to hell!' Kerze said furiously.

Gisenius looked grave. 'I'm very much afraid he may have other plans—a smear campaign in the newspapers, political pressure, legal proceedings—perhaps all three at once. It's disastrous, I tell you.'

'For all of us?' queried Kerze.

'For the man responsible, surely,' Frammler remarked with shameless self-assurance. 'Poor old Schulz will be the first to get it in the neck.'

'If you try to drop poor old Schulz in the shit I'll see you do more than soil your fingers, I promise you,' Hirsch said grimly.

Gisenius rapped the table with his bony knuckles until silence was restored. 'Gentlemen,' he said, 'don't forget this: Schulz may have been in command, but he was only acting on the company commander's behalf. We must get hold of Kronshagen. He's got to exonerate Schulz—and us, too—otherwise we're done for.'

Kerze looked round triumphantly. 'If the man's got an ounce of team spirit,' he said, 'he'll do it!'

Karl Schulz glowered incredulously at the unfamiliar figure that greeted him at his own front door. 'You here?' he said.

'That's all I needed. You've got a nerve, haven't you, showing your face round here?'

Claus Gisenius gave an affable grin. 'I've been waiting for you for hours.'

'Hop it, lad,' Schulz said wearily, 'it's lucky for you I've had a hard day or I'd break every bone in your body.'

Eva, who was looking over Claus's shoulder, smiled disarmingly. 'He's got something important to tell you, Karl.'

'Fix me a cup of coffee,' Schulz said. 'And either get rid of your boy-friend or I'll get rid of him myself.'

Claus looked unabashed. 'Strange family customs you have. Is it considered good form to chuck your future brother-in-law out of the house?'

'My what?' Schulz demanded. 'What are you talking about?'

'Me.'

Schulz shook his head vigorously like a horse tormented by flies. 'I'm not in the mood for cheap jokes, so watch it!'

Eva beamed at her brother. 'Claus means what he says, Karl,' she said happily.

Schulz stared from one to the other in bewilderment. 'Is this true?'

'Certainly,' said Claus. 'Eva and I are getting married. It's all settled, but if you insist on my making a formal request for your sister's hand in marriage—all right, I'll go through the motions.'

After a pause devoted to some heavy breathing, Schulz said gruffly: 'Just so we understand each other properly, lad—the fact that my sister may be having a child doesn't entitle you to marry her by force, understand? Getting a girl pregnant is one thing and loving her is another—and so is marrying her, for that matter.'

'You're quite right,' Claus said calmly, 'but they all go together with us.'

'We love each other, Karl,' Eva said.

'In that case,' Schulz replied, 'I won't stand in your way.' He took a step towards Claus and clapped him on the shoulder. Tears of emotion gleamed in his eyes as he caught hold of his sister and clasped her to his chest.

'You ought to be ashamed of yourselves,' he said hoarsely, 'upsetting me like this. Still, you've got my blessing, for what

326

it's worth. What about my cup of coffee, damn it—and fetch me a clean handkerchief first.'

Tantau entered the Oak Room in the *Hotel Drei Kronen* and sat down opposite Gisenius, looking wary. Bennicken remained standing by the door like a mute sentinel.

' You sent for me,' Tantau said. ' What can I do for you? '

' First, permit me to thank you for your speedy and efficient work so far.'

' You pay accordingly.'

' You traced Meiners and sent him to us, as instructed,' Gisenius said. ' Unfortunately, our interview with him didn't yield quite the results we'd hoped for, which raises a couple of important points. The first is: do you know his present whereabouts? '

' I do.'

' Excellent. The second thing I want to know is whether you've gained his confidence sufficiently to be able to exert any influence on his decisions.'

' And if I had? '

' I'd like you to arrange a sort of cease-fire—for twenty-four hours, let's say. Do you think you could do that? '

' Possibly, but what do you hope to gain? '

' Time, my dear sir, time for you to undertake a new assignment. Do your best to see that Meiners thinks very carefully before making any further move. Stave him off until midday tomorrow. That ought to be long enough for you to complete the inquiries I have in mind. What do you say? '

' I can't say anything until I know your exact intentions.'

' You're being very obstinate, Herr Tantau. I can only assure you that I intend harm to no one.'

' Not even to Meiners? '

' God forbid! Meiners's lot has been a tragic one. Who could fail to sympathize with him, even if he did lose control of himself and say some hard things? '

' Am I to assume that Meiners has quarrelled with you and your friends? '

' I'd prefer to call it a contretemps—a mutual misunderstanding. I might add that it took place while I was out of the room making some urgent telephone calls.'

' What hard luck,' Tantau said drily. ' But that's the

curse of being shrewd. You can't always protect others against their own stupidity.'

'How true, Herr Tantau!' Gisenius nodded sagely. 'Some people attract disaster like a magnet. It doesn't matter what they do, they always end up on the debit side. They're branded for life, and nothing can change that.'

'Except death.'

'Michael Meiners,' Gisenius said, 'was a victim of the demonic forces unleashed by war. He's as innocent as a new-born babe and completely defenceless against the more predatory members of the human species.'

'A poetic description of a very prosaic situation,' commented Tantau. 'What practical inference am I supposed to draw from that?'

'I'm not sure I follow you, Herr Tantau,' Gisenius said. 'However, I gain the impression that you've developed a certain liking for Michael Meiners.'

Tantau did not conceal his surprise. 'If I may say so, Herr Gisenius, you're a man of many parts. You carry out your plans meticulously and with the utmost single-mindedness, but that's not your only distinguishing characteristic. What makes you really exceptional is your ability to read people's thoughts and assess their state of mind. It's a rare talent. It also explains a great deal.'

'I don't know about that,' Gisenius said modestly, studying his finger-nails, 'but I'm certainly familiar with the nature of human weaknesses—my own included. Everyone has his faults, but no one is entirely devoid of positive qualities. One only has to detect and mobilize them.'

'Very well,' Tantau replied, 'it's true—I wouldn't do anything which might harm Meiners. If you're so aware of that, Herr Gisenius, why shouldn't I admit it?'

The lawyer's smile conveyed that he had seen through Tantau at last. 'Then we're agreed,' he said. 'On the other hand, it would be equally unjust if I and my friends were to suffer through no fault of our own. Let us try—Meiners, you and us—to prove that no blame attaches to any one individual and that anything which may have happened was attributable to a combination of highly regrettable factors. That, Herr Tantau, forms the basis of your next and most important assignment.'

' Can you give me some details? '

Gisenius glanced quickly at Bennicken's motionless figure, but there was nothing to suggest that the taxi-driver was taking any interest in the conversation.

' Our aim is to clear this whole thing up once and for all,' Gisenius said emphatically.

Tantau could not entirely disguise his sense of expectancy. ' I'm still waiting to hear what the job consists of.'

' Absolute clarity—that's the main essential,' Gisenius pursued, ' but the only way of achieving it is to retrace our steps with all due care. If Meiners is to achieve peace of mind, we must explore the chain of responsibility, as it were. This will mean getting hold of the man who gave the crucial order, even though he couldn't have been blind to its potential consequences. Make a note of that point—it's important. The name of the man is Kronshagen. He was in command of the company, so his testimony could be vitally important.'

' Where can I find him? '

' I heard he was living in Frankfurt, but I know practically nothing about him except that he qualified as a lawyer after the war. He may be a barrister or even a civil servant—who knows? Your job is simply to find out whether Kronshagen would be ready to make himself available if necessary. No need to go into details or acquaint him with the precise nature of the testimony which may be required of him—e.g., that the situation on April 20th 1945 was chaotic and that it would be impossible to reconstruct events or pin-point individual responsibility for anything. It will be quite enough if you secure his general consent to help members of his old unit. Could you manage that? '

' I can't guarantee results, of course, but I'll certainly speak to him.'

' Good. Your job is twofold then. Point one, you persuade Meiners to mark time. Point two, you travel to Frankfurt this evening—never mind about the cost—and look up Kronshagen. Brief him on the situation and then try to secure his general approval. You can leave the rest to me. Are we agreed? '

' It would appear so,' Tantau said cautiously.

On the evening of the same day, April 20th, Karl Schulz was

standing in the spare-room of his flat, hitherto rented by Marlene Sonnenberg.

Schulz noted the casual way in which the furniture had been shifted around. Stray articles of clothing hung over the chairs or trailed across the floor. The sight offended his sense of neatness, and his nostrils twitched at the stuffy, sweetish smell that pervaded the room.

Eva, who was standing in the doorway, said: 'You mustn't take it too hard.'

Schulz shrugged. 'It's my own fault. I must have been mad to look at her twice.'

'You were in love with her,' Eva said softly, 'I know you were.'

'Nonsense!' Schulz protested. 'Love's for the young. The war was on when I was the same age as you and Claus. There wasn't any time for that sort of thing. I missed my chance, that's all.'

'What if she wanted to come back?'

'I'd tell her to get lost.'

'I'm not sure you would,' Eva said with a smile. 'But she won't come back.'

Karl Schulz shook his head dismally. 'You never get a second chance. That's why you've got to hang on to the good things in life. Make sure you do that with Claus.'

'I'm going to give him all the freedom he wants,' Eva said firmly. 'That's the best way of hanging on to a man.'

Conrad Gisenius sat behind his desk, brooding.

'You know, Bennicken,' he said, 'it's good to feel there's someone I can rely on.'

'All the way,' Bennicken assured him. 'Anything I can do?'

'You've done more than enough already, but I'm afraid you're an exception to the rule.'

Bennicken was moved. 'Good of you to say so,' he grunted.

'You understand me,' Gisenius continued. 'You have an unspoiled natural intellect, Bennicken, did you know that? You're not like the rest of these emasculated products of an over-refined civilization.'

'If you say so,' Bennicken said heavily.

' I do say so, and I'm right. That's why you're probably the only person who appreciates how worried I am by recent developments. You know my attitude towards Meiners. I deplore the fact that we had to act as we did—it was a tragic choice to have to make—but I'd regard it as even more deplorable if we all ruined our lives for the sake of one man.'

' It'd be a crying shame! ' growled Bennicken.

' Yes indeed,' sighed Gisenius. ' We strain every nerve in the struggle for a place in the sun, we fight our way to the top and carve out a niche for ourselves by perseverance and hard work, and what happens? A ridiculous coincidence threatens to destroy everything we hold most dear. Ought we to take it lying down? '

' Never! '

' But what's the alternative? I tell you in all honesty, Bennicken, I'm beginning to think there's only one course of action possible—but which of us has the moral courage to take it? '

Willy Kerze was sitting beside the fire at home, watching the flames that spurted from the logs in the grate. He glanced across at Marlene Sonnenberg.

Marlene, also gazing into the fire, said: ' It's lovely, being here with you like this, Bill.' No one had ever called him ' Bill ' before, but he liked the cosmopolitan flavour of the nickname.

' You make up for a lot of things,' he said.

' I'm glad you think so, Bill, but some people wouldn't agree with you—your housekeeper, for instance.'

' Don't worry about her.'

' But she hates me.'

' She hates me too—at least, you'd think so sometimes. These pig-headed moods of hers can last for days, but it doesn't stop her running the house properly. She comes to heel in the end. It's just that she takes a bit of time to get used to things.'

' Believe me, Bill,' said Marlene, ' her hatred goes far deeper than you think. I'm not joking! '

Kerze reached for the tongs and put another log on the fire. ' You're imagining it. Anyway, I'm finding life quite difficult enough at the moment without manufacturing more complications.'

'Get rid of her then,' Marlene urged. 'Get rid of her before she does you any harm. I wouldn't put anything past her.'

'Drop the subject!' Kerze shouted in sudden fury. 'All I want is a bit of peace and quiet. I'm not going to have my home life made hideous by a couple of squabbling women, even if I have to get rid of the pair of them!'

Marlene stared at him, dumbfounded. 'Does that include me?'

'It includes anyone who tries to meddle in my private life,' Kerze said viciously. 'I live for my work, and the sooner you realize that the better.'

Tantau found Michael Meiners in his hotel room, working on a daily report for his firm. It was his last report in the current series, and—thanks to various outside distractions—not a particularly satisfactory one.

'Well,' Tantau said, shaking hands, 'was it instructive, meeting all your old friends again?'

'It was pointless.' Meiners's voice was devoid of bitterness.

Tantau nodded. 'There's more than sixteen years between you and them—you're worlds apart.'

Meiners pushed the pile of papers aside. 'Anyway, that's the last they'll see of me. I'm leaving tomorrow. This place revolts me, and so does everyone in it.'

'I sympathize.' Tantau folded his arms and stared into space. 'Thirty or forty years ago I was young and irresponsible enough to try a little experiment. I'd been investigating a case of murder, and it hadn't taken me long to identify the murderer, but for various reasons I concentrated my fire on a completely innocent man. My aim was to work on him, using every method in the book, until he developed a sense of guilt—of actual complicity. In the end, I succeeded.'

'I think I see what you're driving at,' Meiners said with a wry smile. 'You're wondering if there's been any change in my own conception of what happened. Well, there hasn't. My memory's still green enough.'

'I'm glad to hear it,' Tantau replied. 'And yet you were ready to let bygones be bygones. What was your motive?'

'Humanity, if you like. I know it's a much misused word,

but it fits somehow. I wanted to give them a chance to extricate themselves with as much human dignity as possible —but you were right. You can't forgive and forget unless the guilty party acknowledges his guilt first. That was what you said, wasn't it? '

' That's only the first part of my theory of sin and atonement. The second is this: we've established that it's possible to persuade an innocent man of his guilt, but the reverse is equally practicable. Do you follow me? The criminals or accomplices of yesterday have lost all consciousness of their guilt or complicity.'

' You mean they don't want to remember? '

' It's even simpler than that: they've genuinely forgotten. They regard what happened as ancient history. In the interim, the last war has been largely rehabilitated—medals, orders, decorations and all. For years now, people have been attaching far more importance to the meagre virtues war generates than to the crimes it brings in its train—and which occurred on a vast scale. " You only did your duty by the Fatherland and your fellow-men "—that's the implication, and that's what these old soldiers who refuse to fade away are only too willing to believe, deep down inside. After all, how many human beings are courageous enough to make a frank acknowledgement of their past mistakes and weaknesses—let alone their crimes? '

Meiners looked dejected. ' I was beating my head against a brick wall, then.'

' You jolted your self-styled comrades out of a carefully constructed dream-world. You forced them to think and made them feel unsure of themselves. You reminded men who pride themselves on their integrity—most of them, that is —that they were once capable of vileness. You've become a living threat to their way of life, Meiners, which is why you'd be well-advised to leave here at once.'

' What about you, Herr Tantau? '

Tantau stared meditatively out of the window. ' I'm going to give them something else to think about. You never know, one or other of them may discover he's got a conscience after all.'

' There's something you haven't told me.' A look of apprehension came into Meiners's eyes.

'Life follows a pattern, my friend. One thing leads to another and guilt breeds guilt. What does it matter today that an attempt was made on your life sixteen years ago? Who's seriously concerned about the possibility of legal proceedings after all this time? No, something else must have happened, something which might still have serious repercussions, and I'm beginning to realize what it was. Mere conjecture isn't enough, though. I want the whole truth and I'm going to get at it whether you like it or not.'

Going in search of Frammler, Bennicken found him in the embalming-room of his Interment Institute, absorbing kirsch and perusing a morticians' trade magazine entitled *Earth and Fire*.

'Got to talk to you,' Bennicken said, sitting down uninvited on a crate.

Frammler produced another glass from the cupboard. 'You're welcome, especially if it's about helping me to fix up that trolley we discussed.'

'Be glad to.'

'That's fine.' Frammler filled both glasses to the brim. 'I've been meaning to install one for years. Sometimes, when I've finished work on a body late at night, I get an urge to move it into the viewing-room and try out some lighting effects, but I can't haul it in there by myself. With a trolley, it would be dead easy.'

'I'll start on it the day after tomorrow.'

'What'll it cost?'

Bennicken ignored the question. 'Is the Siegert business settled?'

'Ah, that's why you came!' Frammler's eyes twinkled with amusement. 'Don't worry—it couldn't be more settled.'

'Good. I don't want any trouble with the police.'

'Trouble? You're joking! They'll be pinning a medal on you soon for dealing with that chap Lehmgruber so efficiently.'

'Cut it out!' Bennicken said ungraciously.

'Have it your own way.' Frammler took a swig of kirsch. 'Siegert was a push-over, if you want to know. I just went and had a little chat with him.'

'What about?'

'The finer points of my profession,' Frammler replied with a reminiscent chuckle. 'I gave him a lecture on causes of death and explained what a wide range of possibilities there is. I started with head-wounds—a shot in the mouth, for instance, aimed at the upper oral cavity. Then there's the shot in the temple—though you've got to be accurate if you want to do the job properly. Then there's the Cyclops method—you know, a shot between the eyes. That can go wrong too, especially if you're not an expert.'

'Well?' Bennicken demanded, slightly puzzled.

Frammler shook his head with professional distaste. 'As an undertaker, I'm against head-wounds. Let's face it—they're not pretty. You can't do justice to a mutilated lump of meat. It's barbaric. No, I'm all in favour of a clean death.'

'Like what?'

'Like a bullet in the heart. Believe me, Bennicken, the safest and cleanest way of killing yourself or anyone else is to put the heart out of action.'

'Sounds reasonable.'

'That's what I told Siegert, except that I went into a bit more detail,' Frammler said, rubbing his hands gleefully. 'And do you know what he did? He rushed off to the police as fast as his legs would carry him and begged to be allowed to withdraw his statement.'

Bennicken grunted appreciatively. 'You've got your head screwed on the right way.'

Conrad Gisenius was paying a second visit to the young person for whose welfare he had so generously assumed responsibility.

'If only there was some way I could repay you,' sighed Brigitte.

'Being here with you is reward enough in itself,' Gisenius replied, glancing round keenly. Brigitte's bed-sitting-room had undergone a welcome change since his last visit. The couch was covered by a thick blue candlewick bedspread. Various pieces of contemporary furniture—among them an armless canary-yellow chair upholstered in foam rubber and a kidney-shaped coffee table with a plain glass top—were scattered round the room. There was a Mondrianesque rug

335

composed of bold planes of colour on the floor between the window and the room-divider, and a dove-grey record-player stood in one corner.

'You've done so much for me,' Brigitte said humbly.

To her secret delight, Gisenius spurned the foam-rubber chair and seated himself on the bed. 'I wouldn't like you to misconstrue my motives,' he said. 'My life is an unending round of hard work and self-sacrifice. Much of what I do—and I say this in all humility—is done for the benefit of society as a whole. For instance, I help to promote the interests of political parties, organizations, associations and so on. However, these are activities on the grand scale, aimed at the betterment of posterity in general. That's why I sometimes feel impelled to do something more modest for a change, something fundamentally human.'

'It's awfully hot in here,' Brigitte put in. 'You're welcome to take your coat off if you like. I'll slip out of my sweater—if you've no objection, that is.'

'Of course not, my child.'

'I'm not a child—I'm a woman,' Brigitte pouted, throwing out her chest.

'Just in case I haven't made myself clear,' Gisenius said, not without dignity, 'I am the one who is prepared to make sacrifices here. I ask nothing in return.'

'But you can trust me,' Brigitte assured him huskily. 'I know how to keep my mouth shut, never you fear.'

'I'm not interested in your sense of discretion,' Gisenius said firmly. 'In fact, frankness would be more to the point. I came here to pay a social call, nothing more. You must even be able to swear to it if necessary. I arrived just after eight and I shall probably leave again at about eleven. Go on, take a look at the clock. My sole aim is to improve your mind, Brigitte. I mustn't allow myself to be distracted by your physical charms.'

Brigitte sighed. 'What a pity!'

Chief Inspector Sand was seized with a strange feeling of restlessness. After spending the evening at home, he went back to his office, and from there to Rheine-Bergen Central, simply because he felt a need to talk to someone. In this instance, the someone was Sergeant Brahmvogel.

'Not in bed yet, sir?' Brahmvogel asked sympathetically.

'I'm dog-tired, Sergeant, but I can't seem to sleep. I've got to the stage where everything's going round and round in my head.'

'Care for a game of chess?'

At the nod from Sand, Brahmvogel opened his desk and carefully extracted a board with chess-men already set out on it. Taking two pawns, he shuffled them behind his back and held out his hands. Sand chose black.

Minutes passed. Then Sand, wondering whether or not to move his remaining rook, said: 'Tell me, Sergeant, have you ever worked under someone who knew more than you did about absolutely everything?'

'Sounds like a bad dream, sir,' Brahmvogel observed. 'Is there such an animal?'

'There is,' Sand said bitterly. 'Geniuses do exist—even in the police force. You can't put anything over on them, you can't hoodwink them—you can't even keep up with them. All you can do is admire them from afar.'

Brahmvogel shuddered. 'If I were you, sir, I'd go to bed and forget all about it.'

'There are some things you can't forget,' Sand said, aimlessly tapping his queen. 'There are certain combinations of factors which never fail to disturb one. Ordinary mortals like us can guess at their common denominator, but it takes a genius to interpret them.'

Brahmvogel raised his eyebrows. 'Sir?'

'I'm talking about the law of series, Sergeant. There are times when practically nothing happens, and there are other times when people seem to be bitten by a universal bug—God knows why. It may be due to climate, or lunar phases, or sun-spots, or cosmic disturbances or magnetism—the possible explanations are legion, but I don't find any of them convincing.'

'Watch out, sir,' said Brahmvogel. 'There's no need to risk your queen like that.'

'It doesn't matter. Someone's got to win some time—that's another law of nature. What worries me is the unpredictable way in which crime comes in batches. I wonder why?'

' I couldn't say, sir. All I know is, you're checkmate. Would you like another? '

Shortly afterwards, while Sand was still at Rheine-Bergen Central, it was reported that the body of a man had been found near the local refugee camp, between the main road and the gravel-pit. He had been shot through the heart at close range.

The body was identified as that of a man named Michael Meiners.

10. The Disbanding

'Seems a fairly straightforward case,' commented one of Sand's two C.I.D. sergeants, a rat-faced young man named Brasch. 'You can bet your life it comes under one of the seven standard headings—jealousy, probably. I expect he'd been running after one of the girls in the refugee camp.'

'I don't agree,' said Ramsauer, his fellow-sergeant. 'It isn't as simple as that, if you ask me.'

'I didn't ask you,' Sand snapped. 'I've no desire to hear what you think—only what you know. Understand?'

He watched them nod submissively.

'Up to date,' Sand said, 'each of us has been covering a separate field of inquiry. Now let's see whether we can fit the pieces together and make a definite pattern.'

The two sergeants' gaze travelled round the office, a typical public servant's lair sparsely equipped with battered office furniture and enclosed by grey-green walls on which hung street plans, maps and 'wanted' notices, the most recent being:

WANTED FOR ARMED ROBBERY
Anton Lehmgruber
Caution—carries fire-arms
Reward: DM 1000

'Right, let's get down to it,' Sand said, clearing his throat. 'The basic facts, please, Brasch.'

'Last night,' began Brasch, 'the body of a man named Meiners . . .'

'Wrong,' Sand interrupted promptly. 'The phrase "last night" is ambiguous. By tomorrow it will be the night before last. Always give the precise date and time. Also, the body wasn't identified until later on.'

'Yes, sir.' Brasch patiently began all over again.

339

The basic facts were as follows: Date: Thursday, 20 April 1961. Time of discovery: 11.30 p.m. Place: Birkenweg, beside the north-east corner of the slaughterhouse wall. A passer-by returning from the cinema—particulars on record —stumbled over the body of a man. He notified the local police, who notified headquarters.

'Now the medical findings, please.' Sand made a practice of conducting his tuition classes with unnerving attention to detail. 'You, Ramsauer.'

Stripped of medical jargon, Ramsauer's report amounted to the following: the police surgeon had established the cause of death as a bullet through the heart. Death had been instantaneous, and the fatal shot had been fired at short range, probably from about three feet. The estimated time of death was set at 10 p.m.

'The police surgeon completed his examination earlier this morning,' Sand announced. 'He located the bullet. It turned out to be a 7.65 mm. job, so it may have been fired from a Walther automatic. Does that mean anything to you, gentlemen?'

The significance of this appeared to be lost on them. Sand seemed to have anticipated their negative reaction, but he maintained a patient silence.

'The only thing that occurs to me,' Brasch said at length, 'is that an old Walther automatic was found about fifty yards from the scene of the crime. Unless the ballistics boys prove otherwise, it seems reasonable to assume that it was the murder weapon.'

'Quite reasonable,' Sand replied acidly, 'but why didn't the murderer take it with him? Why did he chuck it into a bush only fifty yards from the scene of the crime? What do you think, Ramsauer?'

Ramsauer hesitated. 'Well, sir, it may have been either deliberate or accidental—it's hard to tell what goes on in a murderer's mind.'

Sand permitted himself an indulgent smile. 'It's part of your job to know what goes on in a murderer's mind. All right, let's have the identification report.'

According to an identity card found on the body, the dead man's name was Michael Meiners and he had been born at Immenstadt on 15 March 1924.

' Any further details, Ramsauer? '

Ramsauer reported that Meiners was registered as a guest at the Station Hotel, but had been resident at the *Gasthof zur alten Post* until the day before his death. Examination of his personal effects revealed that he was a representative for a debt-collecting agency. He had only received one or two calls during his stay, each time from the same person.

' Have you found out who his visitor was? '

' No, sir. The receptionist said he was a funny little old man. He didn't sound a very likely suspect to me.'

Sand cast his eyes to heaven. ' You poor innocent! When are you going to learn that you can't take anything for granted in our business? If Meiners only had one caller, I want to know his name. Trace him, damn it! '

Having dealt with Ramsauer, Sand addressed himself to Brasch. ' Have they run a lab check on the Walther yet? '

' Yes, sir,' Brasch said eagerly. ' They got several clear prints.'

' Have you compared them? '

Brasch looked perplexed. ' With what, sir? '

' How dense can you get? I think you said the automatic was a 7.65 calibre Walther. Doesn't that ring a bell? '

' Of course, sir! ' Brasch seemed amazed at his own powers of perception. ' There was that taxi business the other night. The probable weapon was a Walther.'

Sand heaved a sigh. ' It took you long enough to get there, didn't it? All right, Brasch, tell them to run a comparative check straight away. It may be mere coincidence, but it's worth looking into.'

While Brasch was making the requisite telephone call, Sand turned to Ramsauer. ' This is a report compiled by the Federal Bureau in association with Interpol,' he said, tapping a file on his desk. ' It appears that Lehmgruber, alias Schichelberger, is known to Counter-Intelligence. He's been working for the Eastern bloc for years—Poland, Czechoslovakia, the so-called German Democratic Republic and God knows who else besides. He's obviously a scheming agent employed by Communist-controlled regimes hostile to this country.'

Ramsauer emitted a low whistle.

' There's something fishy about this case, and what makes

it even more fishy is that, according to my information, Meiners spent several years in Russia as a prisoner of war and was later employed in the Eastern Zone. He didn't reappear in the Federal Republic until two or three years ago. The connection seems obvious, doesn't it? '

The telephone rang, and Brasch, at a nod from Sand, answered it. He listened in silence for a few moments and then replaced the receiver with an expression of triumph.

'You were right, sir! Lehmgruber's prints are identical with the ones found on the automatic.'

'That's good,' said Sand, '—almost too good to be true.'

Conrad Gisenius looked round sadly. 'I summoned you here today because I have something to tell you. Our old comrade Michael Meiners is no longer with us.'

Hirsch frowned. 'How do you mean? Has he left town? '

'He's dead.' Gisenius bowed his head as he spoke. He might have been overwhelmed with grief.

'How do you know? ' Hirsch demanded.

'I tried to call him at his hotel early this morning, to arrange a private meeting, but it was too late. He was already dead.'

'Meiners was a good lad,' Karl Schulz declared, fumbling awkwardly for a handkerchief and blowing his nose.

'De mortuis,' observed Frammler, leaning back in his chair. 'There's no comrade like a dead comrade.' Turning to Gisenius with a sudden look of interest, he asked: 'Where's the body? '

'Forget about business for a moment, will you, Frammler? ' grumbled Kerze. 'What I want to know is, how did it happen? Was it an accident, or did he just drop dead? '

'According to my information,' Gisenius replied, 'Meiners died at about eleven o'clock last night. He was found shot near the slaughterhouse.'

'How appropriate! ' Hirsch remarked grimly.

'A ghastly business,' said Kerze.

'All the same,' Frammler commented, 'it's an ill wind! '

Karl Schulz slowly raised his head and surveyed his companions with incomprehension. 'Who could have done such a thing? It's our duty to help find out.'

'What's it got to do with us? ' Frammler asked. 'Why should we stick our necks out? '

'I'm with Schulz,' Hirsch said belligerently. 'This concerns us all.'

'You've got a point,' Kerze declared. 'I'm inclined to agree with Schulz and Hirsch.'

'Very magnanimous of you,' Hirsch said sarcastically.

Kerze glared at him. 'That's not fair!'

'Let's keep our heads,' urged Gisenius. 'This is hardly the time for personal squabbles. We must all pull together. On the other hand, what good can it do to meddle in something which is properly the concern of the police?'

'And the undertaker,' Frammler chimed in. 'However, since I'm here in a private capacity, I'll second that.'

'My friends,' Gisenius continued, 'we must try to be objective about this. To recapitulate, all that has happened is this: a former comrade-in-arms, Michael Meiners, re-appeared recently. We were surprised at first because we thought he was dead, and our initial reaction was to doubt whether it really was Meiners. However, we were all delighted when the rumour proved to be correct. Many years had elapsed since our last meeting, but that didn't deter us from welcoming him with open arms.'

'You're right,' said Schulz, 'we gave him a warm welcome.'

'Which touched him tremendously,' Hirsch commented. 'Remember how he burst into tears of gratitude before he clasped us to his breast?'

'No one's pretending it was quite like that,' Gisenius said sharply. 'Meiners had changed, and so had we, but the atmosphere was fundamentally harmonious.'

'Fundamentally—yes,' Kerze agreed.

Gisenius nodded. 'The fact of the matter is this: we saw him once and talked to him for something under an hour. That's all there was to it, and that's the story we must stick to if we're ever questioned.'

'We will be, too, don't you worry,' said Hirsch. 'You were wrong to call Meiners at his hotel, Gisenius. Sooner or later, the C.I.D. will get round to asking whether anyone tried to contact him, and your name will come up. What then?'

Gisenius drew himself up stiffly. 'If anyone asks any questions,' he demanded, 'who better to answer them than me? I know what to say.'

'The main thing is to keep us out of it,' Kerze said.

'I'll try—not that it would be a disaster even if I failed. We'll work out our story in detail for safety's sake, but our best insurance against unpleasant misunderstandings is solidarity.'

'That's it,' growled Bennicken, 'solidarity.'

'Talking about solidarity,' Karl Schulz said, 'I think we ought to turn out for Meiners's funeral.'

'I'd be delighted to arrange the whole thing at cost price,' declared Frammler.

Kerze nodded. 'I'll foot part of the bill, of course.'

'All in good time,' said Gisenius. 'For the moment, we'll adopt a policy of wait and see. Any more questions?'

'Yes,' Hirsch said. 'I've got one. Where were we all between nine and eleven o'clock last night?'

'Hirsch is right,' Gisenius said slowly. 'We ought to be prepared for that question. The police may want to know.'

Hirsch gave a keen glance round the room. 'What would you say if you were asked, Karl?'

'Well,' Schulz replied cautiously, 'I'd tell them I was at home—which I was.'

'Any witnesses?'

'My sister and—and her fiancé.'

'All right,' Hirsch said quickly. 'Kerze?'

'I was at home too. My housekeeper could swear to that, and so could someone else if necessary.'

'Very satisfactory,' remarked Hirsch. 'Where were you, Bennicken?'

'At Frammler's,' Bennicken grunted.

Frammler glanced briefly at Bennicken before speaking. 'That's right, we had a few drinks together—just the two of us. We were discussing a trolley he's going to make for me.'

'Dead right,' said Bennicken.

Hirsch looked across at Gisenius. 'How about you?'

'This is a little embarrassing,' Gisenius replied, after a moment's carefully contrived hesitation, 'but—well, just between friends, I spent the time in question with a young lady.'

'Congratulations!' exclaimed Frammler.

'My compliments,' said Kerze.

344

Karl Schulz looked dumbfounded. 'I'd never have believed it!'

'Never mind,' Hirsch said drily, 'it's a nice watertight alibi.'

Gisenius rounded on him. 'What about you, Hirsch? Where were you at the time?'

'Out walking.'

'Nowhere near the slaughterhouse, I suppose?' Frammler asked gleefully. 'That would make my day!'

'No, nowhere near the slaughterhouse. Near Schulz's flat, if you want to know.'

'Got any witnesses?'

'Don't worry, nobody's going to pin anything on me.'

'Don't be too sure.' Frammler shook with laughter. 'From the look of it, you're the only possible suspect.'

'Don't let's exaggerate,' said Gisenius, his eyes gleaming with satisfaction. 'We can't afford to indulge in mutual suspicion. Let's stick to the facts. Much as we all regret it, Michael Meiners's death does have its brighter side.'

Kerze nodded. 'It's going to save us a lot of trouble.'

'It means,' said Gisenius, 'that the Meiners episode is closed—permanently closed.'

'What about that old sleuth-hound of yours?' Hirsch asked.

'He's probably with Kronshagen at this moment.'

'I'll simply call him off.'

'Aren't you being a little hopeful? Once Tantau's got the bit between his teeth, there's no stopping him.'

'There's nothing more conclusive than death.'

Karl Schulz cleared his throat. 'I think we ought to raise a glass to the poor fellow's memory. I suggest we meet at the *Drei Kronen* this evening, as usual.'

'I second that proposal,' Gisenius said quickly. 'It will also give us a chance to iron out what we're going to say in the event of an official inquiry.' He paused for comment, but no one spoke. 'Till this evening, then. Let us look forward, gentlemen, to burying the past once and for all.'

'I'm acting for Herr Gisenius,' Tantau said amiably.

Kronshagen knit his brow. 'Gisenius? Never heard of him.'

'No? Herr Gisenius is a lawyer. He practises in Rheine-Bergen.'

' I'm not familiar with the name of every provincial lawyer in the register,' Kronshagen said indifferently. ' What does he want from me? '

Tantau had encountered little difficulty in finding Kronshagen, who was a junior public prosecutor whose greatest ambition was to become senior public prosecutor.

' You commanded a company during the closing weeks of the war, did you not? '

' I did.'

' Do you remember someone called Karl Schulz? He was one of your senior N.C.O.s.'

' A good man,' Kronshagen said, adding promptly: '—as far as I could judge at the time, that is. What's his connection with Gisenius? '

' Gisenius was in Schulz's section, though you naturally can't be expected to remember every individual in your company.'

' Naturally not.'

' Do you recall what happened on April 20th 1945? '

The fingers of Kronshagen's right hand started to drum on the desk and a deep furrow marred the smoothness of his lofty brow. Then he said: ' Before I answer that question, Herr Tantau, I should like to know your motive in asking it.'

' I'm merely acting on instructions. My job is to collect information, that's all. On April 20th 1945 Sergeant Schulz's section was detailed to bar the Russian advance from a position on the edge of a wood known as Copse 307.'

Kronshagen gave a nod which might have denoted assent.

' So much for the facts,' Tantau went on. ' The question is: are you, as Schulz's former company commander, prepared to confirm that you gave such an order, and add a rider to the effect that the prevailing situation was chaotic? '

' Why? Is someone thinking of writing a regimental history? '

' Not exactly. My clients would like you to provide them with a sort of testimonial for private use. Would you be prepared to supply such a thing? '

' What do you mean, for private use? '

' Well, let us assume that someone is trying to blackmail the ex-members of Sergeant Schulz's section for reasons arising out of their conduct on the day in question. A testimonial from their former company commander would virtually quash any such imputation.'

'What sort of imputation do you mean?'

'Complicity in the rape and murder of a girl the previous night and responsibility for the alleged death of a fellow-soldier, brought about either by beating a premature retreat, i.e., indirectly, or . . .' Tantau paused a moment before continuing '. . . by more direct means.'

Kronshagen drew himself up to his full height and glared at Tautau with icy disdain. Then the storm broke.

'I've never met such effrontery in my life!' he said scornfully. 'You waltz in here and expect me to fall into a trap set for someone else? Well, you've picked the wrong man!'

Tantau experienced an unashamed sense of pleasure. 'Have I?'

The provocative gleam in Tantau's eye was not lost on Kronshagen, who made an effort to regain his self-control. He folded his hands on the desk in front of him.

'Herr Tantau,' he said in business-like tones, 'I don't know how deeply you're involved in this affair, nor do I care. All I'm certain of is that you weren't a member of my company. I have an excellent memory.'

'I'm happy to hear it.'

'I flatly refuse to associate myself with anything which may prove to have been a criminal act.'

'It's not always too easy to draw the line between a criminal act and a military operation.'

'To send a man into the firing-line and then deliberately leave him in the lurch is a criminal act, though I admit it mightn't be easy to prove it. But you mentioned something else, I think. Rape and murder in a barn . . . well, at least that's something more concrete to go on.'

'Your memory really is excellent,' Tantau commented admiringly. 'I didn't say anything about a barn.'

Kronshagen flushed slightly, either with embarrassment or annoyance. 'I can't recall any details, of course, but I did hear that something of the sort had occurred. However, I never received an official report on the matter, and my unit was disbanded almost immediately afterwards.'

'How convenient.'

347

'Kindly keep your provocative remarks to yourself. I decline to hush up an alleged crime by shielding potential criminals.'

'I quite understand your position,' Tantau said affably. 'If it ever came out it would mean the end of your legal career.'

'Personal consequences are immaterial when justice is at stake.'

'Movingly put,' Tantau ventured. 'Would you still maintain the same edifying attitude if I told you that Herr Gisenius, on whose behalf I came here today, is tipped as a future Secretary of State in the Ministry of Justice of his province?'

'It wouldn't affect my attitude in the least.'

'Then you're the kind of lawyer I take my hat off to,' Tantau said. 'Unless, of course, you happen to vote a different ticket from Gisenius. In that case, I'd have to wait a while before removing my hat.'

'All right, it's true,' Kronshagen admitted. 'I do belong to a different party, but that has nothing to do with my concern for justice.'

'You amaze me more and more,' Tantau said delightedly. 'You not only have an excellent memory but you're obviously clairvoyant into the bargain. A moment ago you said you didn't know who Gisenius was, and now you know the colour of his political opinions. I congratulate you!'

'How dare you speak to me like that!' roared Kronshagen. 'Get out of here at once!'

'With pleasure,' Tantau replied, rising to his feet. 'And tell your cronies I've no intention of sticking my neck out for them. On the contrary, I shall make it my business to see that an immediate inquiry is instituted.'

'There you are at last!' Sand took Tantau by the arm and hustled him along the corridor into his office.

'We've established that you recently paid a number of visits to a man called Michael Meiners. You did, didn't you?'

'I expect Kronshagen 'phoned you, and you put two and two together,' Tantau said. 'He doesn't let the grass grow under his feet, I'll give him that.'

Sand looked bemused. 'I don't follow you.'

'But it's obvious! He's determined not to be dragged into anything which might put him in an embarrassing position, so he acts on the principle that attack is the best method of defence.'

'There's something wrong here,' Sand said, shaking his head.

'What do you mean? I'm in absolutely no doubt as to Kronshagen's motives. He's been handed a hot potato and he's simply handing it back.'

'No, no! It's got nothing to do with that.'

Tantau regarded him alertly. 'We seem to be talking at cross-purposes, Sand. There must be something I don't know about—something which you take it for granted I ought to know already.'

Sand came to an abrupt halt in the middle of the room. 'That's it, of course! You haven't heard about it yet. When did you actually leave for Frankfurt?'

'Last night, just before eleven.'

'Last night, at about 10 p.m., according to the medical evidence, Michael Meiners was murdered near the abattoir. Someone shot him through the heart.'

It was some time before Tantau spoke. 'Do you know who did it?' he asked in a low voice.

'On the basis of our inquiries so far,' Sand said cautiously, 'we have a strong suspect—yes.'

'Do I know his name?'

'I doubt it.'

'Then he's not the right man,' Tantau said promptly. 'But we'll find him, Sand—we'll find him!'

After a strenuous morning divided between his friends and his factory, Willy Kerze was on the point of retiring for a brief siesta when the latest in Frau Brandstädter's long succession of housemaids appeared, clutching a letter in her hand.

Kerze accepted the missive, which bore his name but no address. He recognized the paper as part of a Christmas present which he had given his daughter. 'Where did this come from?' he demanded, turning it over gingerly.

'From Fräulein Kerze,' the maid said meekly. 'Fräulein Kerze gave it to me.'

'When?'

'This morning.'

'Why didn't you deliver it before?'

'Fräulein Kerze told me specially: not before two o'clock.'

'If you want to keep your job, my girl,' Kerze said irascibly, 'get this straight: only one person in this house gives orders, and that's me.'

The maid gave a chastened nod and gazed at her large, impressive employer with awe. She admired everything about him, from his forceful voice to his strong, fleshy hands, which were now tearing open the envelope.

Kerze unfolded the single sheet and began to read:

I've been wondering what to do for ages now. I only know one thing, and that is, I can't go on living the sort of life I'm living now. Somehow, somewhere, I'm going to make a completely fresh start. I've found someone who'll help me—someone I trust more than anyone else I've ever met. Don't worry, though—I don't love him in that way. He's like a father to me, and that's what I've always wanted, so I'm not unhappy—perhaps you'll be glad to hear that. I'll get in touch again some time, but it won't be for quite a while.

Karen

P.S. *Tell Bartosch he can marry anyone he likes, as long as it isn't me.*

Kerze read the letter through twice, the angry flush on his cheeks growing deeper as he did so. Then he ground the sheet of paper into a ball with fierce movements of his large hands.

'Does the Herr Direktor require anything else?' the housemaid asked, her timidity mingled with wonder at such a robust display of male temperament.

'Get out!' roared Kerze, disregarding the stab of pain which shot through him as he gestured violently at the door.

While he was still meditating on the world's ingratitude he received an unexpected visit. Marlene Sonnenberg walked in unannounced.

'Glad to see me?' she demanded vivaciously.

'Of course!' Kerze assured her.

'I don't know what I'd do without you,' Marlene sighed, nuzzling his cheek.

'Has something happened?' he asked, his suspicions aroused by this wealth of flattery and caresses.

350

'Karl Schulz kicked me out!' pouted Marlene. 'He behaved like an absolute boor. I thought he was going to throw my cases downstairs after me.'

'Now, now,' Kerze said soothingly.

'And do you know what he called you?' Marlene regarded Kerze with a look of triumph. 'My sugar-daddy! Go on, move in with your sugar-daddy—that's what he said!'

Kerze frowned. 'What infernal cheek!'

'I wouldn't stand for it if I were you, Bill.'

'Don't worry, I'll have it out with him,' Kerze declared with dignity. 'He can't go round bullying my ...' he hesitated '... my intimate friends.'

'You're a darling.' Marlene nestled against him. 'What ever would I do without you?' she said, feeling his arms go round her. 'I feel so safe here with you.'

'You're more than welcome,' he said, panting slightly.

'You really mean it?' Marlene held him at arm's length and gazed fervently into his eyes. 'In that case, I'll tell the taxi-driver to bring my bags in. He's waiting outside.'

On that note, Marlene Sonnenberg moved into the Villa Kerze—temporarily, as she put it. Although Kerze was hardly enraptured by the invasion, he decided to tolerate it for the sake of the amenities it offered, and while Marlene was installing herself he returned to his favourite arm-chair and resumed his cogitations.

In view of all that had happened, he brooded, he was even more determined to bury himself in his work. No one—and that included Marlene Sonnenberg—was going to stop him. When the time came he would dispose of her like a line of obsolete merchandise.

'I've no idea why you want to see me, Chief Inspector,' Gisenius said urbanely, 'but since you do, here I am.'

'Thank you for coming, sir.' Knowing the sort of person he was dealing with, Sand felt a trifle uneasy. Only a fool would prejudice his career by deliberately antagonizing a man like Gisenius.

'May I ask if you've heard about the sudden death of a man named Michael Meiners?' he asked cautiously.

Gisenius placed his finger-tips together. 'I have.'

'May I inquire the source of your information?'

' I telephoned the Station Hotel and was informed accordingly. But you knew that already, I imagine.'

' I always like to receive corroboration of anything I'm told, sir. It helpes to eliminate mistakes. You knew Meiners, then? '

' Of course,' Gisenius said promptly. ' I and several of my friends knew Meiners extremely well. He served with us in the war. As a matter of fact, we celebrated a little reunion with him only yesterday afternoon.'

' And in order to bring about that reunion you employed a Herr Tantau to trace his whereabouts? '

' Herr Tantau has undertaken sundry commissions for me and my clients. For instance, a few days ago he handled some formalities arising from a road accident. In conjunction with this and other assignments he was asked to find the whereabouts of Michael Meiners.'

' What gave you the idea in the first place? '

' That's quite simple. Some of my friends thought they had seen him in town, though they weren't absolutely positive. Since it was just conceivable that our old comrade-in-arms really had turned up here, we asked Tantau to trace him. We wanted to see him again.'

' What about Meiners? Was he keen to see you? '

Gisenius made a gesture of regret. ' Meiners was an extremely shy, retiring person. Esprit de corps was not his strong point, if you follow me.'

' I think I do,' Sand said quietly.

' On the other hand, he was an old friend, and his death has come as a great shock to us all. In fact, we've already decided to club together and give him a decent funeral.'

' Are you familiar with the name Kronshagen? '

' A Lieutenant Kronshagen was my company commander during the closing weeks of the war.'

Sand nodded. ' That's the man. He's a public prosecutor now, and he's anxious to clarify the events of April 20th 1945.'

Gisenius made no reply for several seconds. His face betrayed not the slightest change of expression. In a toneless voice, he said: ' Quite possibly, but I don't see the connection. Meiners's death is one thing. An incident which may or may not have occurred sixteen years ago is quite another.'

' Herr Kronshagen does not share your opinion.'

352

'Your opinion is the only one that counts, Chief Inspector.'
'In the first instance, yes,' Sand replied, 'but not in the second. The directorate of public prosecutions is pressing for an official inquiry.'
'But that's ludicrous!' Gisenius protested. 'Besides, from the purely legal angle, the case you refer to is covered by the statute of limitations. What's the point of raking it all up again? Meiners is dead.'
'That's just it, sir. He's dead.'
'Chief Inspector,' Gisenius said, with a sudden show of candour, 'am I to gather that you suspect me of complicity in the murder of Michael Meiners?'
'God forbid!' Sand said in a shocked voice. 'There's no question of that.'
'Very well, then. That's all that matters.'
'I'd like a few details, though,' Sand persisted.
'My dear Chief Inspector,' Gisenius said suavely, 'you're well aware what public inquiries mean in practice. They arouse unwarranted suspicion, encourage conjecture and promote gossip. They can even ruin a man's career. Knowing this as you do, are you prepared to expose me to the consequences of such a course of action?'
'Certainly not, sir. I told you—there's no question of your personal involvement.'
'Can you prove any definite connection between Meiners's murder and something which happened sixteen years ago?— Well, can you?'
'No,' Sand said truthfully.
Gisenius permitted himself a smirk of satisfaction. 'That settles it, then. By all means do your best to solve Meiners's death, but as far as Kronshagen's attempts at interference are concerned, you can quite justifiably reject them out of hand. And that, I think, covers all there is to say on the matter.'

Tantau sat down in the most comfortable chair in Hirsch's office and gave the hotelier a mocking grin. 'Do you regard it as a profession, managing a hotel, or just another job?'
Martin Hirsch grinned even more mockingly. 'I might ask you the same sort of question. Is interrogating people an art or just a bad habit?' He paused. 'I hope you're comfortable, by the way?'

'Perfectly, thank you.'

'I think I've got something that'll make you feel even more at home.' Hirsch pressed a bell and Gisela Wandel appeared from next door. She glanced at him inquiringly and then, in response to a nod, stood aside.

The head waiter entered, bearing a tray covered with a napkin. He placed it before Tantau, bowed and made his exit, followed by Gisela.

Tantau's nostrils twitched as Hirsch removed the napkin to reveal what the old detective had half-expected to see: a silver bowl filled to the brim with sweets and chocolates.

'No!' Tantau protested. 'You shouldn't have done that —it's not fair. I come here to tell you a few home truths and you try to bribe me with sweets. It's positively inhuman of you, Hirsch.'

'Don't worry,' Hirsch said. 'They're from Karen, not me.'

'What a strange little thing she is,' mused Tantau. 'The poor girl goes around hawking her heart, but no one ever offers her a fair price for it. She pinned a lot of her hopes on you, Hirsch.'

'Perhaps, but what was I supposed to do?' Hirsch complained. 'I'm too old to marry her and too young to be her father.' He shrugged. 'Never mind, she seems to be on the right track at last. She's packed her bags and left this hell-hole —and I'm pretty certain I know who put her up to it.'

Tantau was already eating. He devoured a candied lemon-slice, a cube of nougat and a marzipan heart in quick succession, blinking like a contented cat.

'How did you manage it?' Hirsch persisted. 'Karen won't listen to reason, especially when there's something serious at stake.'

'You misjudge her. Fundamentally, Karen's no better and no worse than most other girls of her age. I talked to her quite straightforwardly—more or less as I talk to myself when I'm alone. She understood.' He munched in silence for a moment. 'That's how I'd like to talk to you now.'

'Go ahead. What are you trying to prove?'

'For one thing, that esprit de corps isn't necessarily sacrosanct.'

'I get you.' Hirsch grinned. 'Divide and conquer—isn't that your plan? You want to undermine my group solidarity.

Well, fire away. There are innumerable chinks in my armour. You're bound to find a couple if you try hard enough.'

'Stop play-acting,' Tantau said indulgently. 'You're not half as unscrupulous as you try to make out. Your main trouble is an overdose of tolerance. Of course one has to tolerate stupidity—it's unavoidable. One laughs at the pompous nonsense talked about esprit de corps, even though some people enjoy it and others think it serves a useful purpose. But when the expression is used to provide camouflage for a bunch of bibulous morons with a taste for strong-arm tactics or a semi-criminal clique whose members lie for their mutual protection—then, my dear Hirsch, the joke wears thin.'

'You may be right,' said Hirsch, 'but you know what covering fire means, don't you? One bloke charges while the others try to pin the enemy down.'

'Yes, except that some people seem to do all the charging while the others stay under cover. Which category do you belong to?'

'You don't seriously think I'd risk my neck if there was a nice deep hole to crawl into?'

'You mean no one in his right mind would? What about Bennicken, for instance?' Tantau eyed his bowl of sweets with apparent concentration. '—and Frammler. Do you really imagine that he'd have any scruples about adding you to his collection?'

'You're wasting your time if you think you can put the wind up me like that. Brawn without brains doesn't scare me.'

'What about Gisenius and Kerze, then—or ex-Sergeant Schulz?'

'My dear Herr Tantau,' Hirsch said, growing abruptly serious, 'I'm not sure what you're driving at and I don't particularly care, but leave Karl Schulz out of it. In the first place he's a genuinely nice chap, and in the second place place he wasn't responsible.'

'If you're implying that responsibility for everything rests with someone called Kronshagen, allow me to disabuse you. I saw Kronshagen today, and he almost exploded when I even suggested it. What's more, he doesn't vote the same party ticket as Gisenius, so the whole thing dropped into his lap like a ripe plum.'

Hirsch stroked his chin. 'And if I know you, Tantau, you

did your best—very discreetly, of course—to see that Kronshagen seized his opportunity with both hands. Well, let
Gisenius handle him, but keep Schulz out of this. I won't
have him used as a scapegoat.'

'Someone will have to suffer some time,' Tantau said,
'and Schulz is an obvious candidate. The question is, can
you suggest an alternative?'

'You expect me to betray someone I served with?'

'Yes,' Tantau replied with disconcerting candour, 'that's
just what I do expect, though I wouldn't describe it as betrayal.
That sounds a bit too much like something out of a magazine.
Let's call it a just decision, intelligently arrived at.'

'I always knew you were a crafty old man, Tantau.'

'My dear Hirsch, don't try to pretend you're a helpless
victim of circumstance, because you aren't. For instance,
what prompted you to mistake that harmless oaf Siegert for
Meiners?'

'You don't believe it was a genuine mistake?'

'No. You're the last person to have made such a blunder.
It was a deliberate piece of deception. You were trying to
dragoon your old army friends into revealing the truth. You
wanted to confirm something you weren't sure about. You
sensed the existence of a guilty secret, just as I do, and you
wanted to find out for certain.'

Hirsch gave a wry smile. 'You won't catch me out by
theorizing, Tantau, you know that perfectly well. I've a strong
feeling you know something definite. If you want me to do
anything you'll have to let the facts speak for themselves.'

Tantau sat back, pushing the bowl of sweets aside. 'You
know I investigated little Konstantin Kerze's death?' he said
quietly. 'Well, in the course of my inquiries I looked into
Saffranski's activities in the Kerze household, and do you
know what he was up to? He was working his way through
a bunch of papers relating to the *Hotel Drei Kronen* and, in
particular, to the manager of that establishment.'

Hirsch's laughter, a little forced at first, became louder,
heartier and less inhibited. 'So that's it!' he said. 'My
devoted friend Kerze wants to squeeze me out, does he?'
I suppose it's his way of expressing his gratitude and appreciation for services rendered to the female members of his
family!' He put his thumb on a buzzer and kept it there.

'Just before you got here I reached a certain decision. I now see it was the right one.'

The door burst open and Gisela Wandel hurried in, looking apprehensive. 'I thought the office was on fire,' she said resentfully.

'Your great moment has come!' Hirsch announced. 'Herr Kerze is acquiring an interest in this hotel, and his first move will be to demand my resignation. However, I've forestalled him. I resigned five minutes ago.'

Gisela Wandel stood in the doorway, regarding Hirsch with disbelief. She said: 'I trust that isn't your final decision.'

Hirsch got up. 'I'll be only too pleased to recommend you for the vacancy. You know the ropes—you virtually run the place as it is. They couldn't find a better replacement.'

'If you go,' Gisela said, 'I go too.'

'Good girl!' Tantau exclaimed cheerfully.

Hirsch walked across to Gisela and stood staring down at her. 'It's no good,' he said, 'I'm sick and tired of putting things off.'

'So am I,' said Gisela, looking him in the eye.

Hirsch shook his head. 'It'll be to your advantage if I go.'

'Come, come!' Tantau sounded profoundly astonished. 'I don't see any difficulty here. Each of you has the other's good at heart, so what's the logical answer? Martin Hirsch goes and Gisela Wandel goes too. As to where you go—well, I'm sure you'll be able to come to some arrangement.'

'If you only knew what I have to put up with, you'd sympathize,' Kerze said bitterly.

'I'm sure I would, but there isn't time to go into that.' Gisenius, who was dabbing his brow with a handkerchief although the managing director's office at Stabilator Limited was kept at an even temperature, spoke without his customary suavity. 'Every minute counts. It's a matter of life or death.'

Kerze raised his eyebrows. 'I thought Meiners was dead,' he remarked cynically.

'He is, but someone else has come to life with a vengeance —Kronshagen! The man's a public prosecutor, and he's hell-bent on making trouble for us.' Gisenius licked his thin

lips. 'Never mind, there's bound to be some way of stopping him. It's just a question of deciding on the right approach.'
'Have you got any ideas?'
'I'm working on the problem now. That's why I came. You're the one who must act—not directly, but with Bartosch's help. You must make it abundantly clear to him that what is at stake is the honour, reputation and livelihood of a family to which he will shortly belong.'
'It's no use,' Kerze said mournfully, 'Karen won't marry Bartosch. She's gone, and I don't even know when she's coming back—if she ever does.'
'Women!' Gisenius said with scorn. 'They talk big but they always come crawling back in the end. Anyway, even if Karen has gone, need Bartosch know? Maybe she won't marry him, but there's no point in disillusioning him for the moment.'
Kerze's telephone conversation with Councillor Bartosch was extraordinarily successful. He began by conveying his daughter's fond regards and then disclosed the awkward predicament in which he and his friends now found themselves. He solicited the Councillor's aid and understanding, both of which Bartosch enthusiastically guaranteed—not omitting to send cordial greetings to his future bride.

'I don't know what your plans for the future are,' Karl Schulz said, ' but I'll try to help you as much as I can.'
Eva smiled. 'That's very sweet of you, Karl, but I don't know what we're going to do myself. That's for Claus to decide.'
'Of course.'
'He likes you a lot, you know.'
'I like the boy too, but you can't expect me to fling my arms round his neck and thank him for taking my sister away from me.'
Schulz sat down at the kitchen table and watched Eva darning his socks. The sight brought a lump to his throat, but his tender reverie was interrupted by the sound of the door-bell, which gave two short rings followed by a long one.
'That's Claus!' Eva cried. She ran to answer the door. With a rueful shake of his head, Schulz got up and prepared to greet the new arrival.

'I'm glad you're here, Karl,' Claus said. 'I've got a couple of things to discuss with you.'

Schulz took Claus's hand and shook it warmly, mollified by the easy assurance with which the boy had used his Christian name. 'Sit down—unless you want to be alone together.'

Claus gave a mischievous grin. 'We'd go to Eva's room if we did.'

'It's high time you two got married, really it is,' grumbled Schulz.

'Any time you like.'

'But you haven't even got a proper job.'

Claus radiated self-confidence. 'I've got a pair of hands, haven't I? I'm not a fool. I can read and write and I've got a few ideas of my own.'

'Where were you thinking of living?'

'Well, we'll have to draw in our horns to begin with. One room will do us for a start.'

'My room,' Eva put in.

Karl Schulz brightened perceptibly. 'You mean you'd move in here?'

'Why not? Wouldn't that suit you?'

'Would it!' Life began to take on new meaning for Schulz. 'I'd be only too happy to share the flat with you. Besides, there's always the other room—the one we've been letting. You could have that as well.'

'I was coming to that,' Claus said, and a touch of diffidence crept into his smile for the first time. 'I know the room's empty, but I've thought of another use for it—with your permission. You see, if I moved in I wouldn't come alone. I'd have to bring my mother too.'

'Good heavens, boy!' Schulz looked perturbed. 'You can't do that. Your father would go up in smoke.'

'My father doesn't burn easily—he's not the inflammable type.' Claus regarded Schulz steadily for a moment. 'It's no use disguising the fact, Karl—you'll have to make a definite decision: either an old comrade-in-arms or a husband for your sister. Under the circumstances, you can't have both.'

Bennicken cautiously pushed open the door of the embalming-room and peered in. 'Is he here?'

359

Frammler nodded without looking up from his work. He was in the process of applying powder to the dead man's face. 'Where else did you think he'd be?'

Bennicken ambled across the room and stared down at Frammler's handiwork while the master busied himself with a few finishing touches.

'I still can't get it into my head.' Frammler carefully traced the eyebrows with an eyebrow pencil. 'I was dead certain it was him I saw lying there on the edge of the wood.'

Bennicken shrugged. 'To err is human, said the cockerel as he climbed off the duck.' He pulled up a chair and sat down opposite Frammler so that the brightly illuminated corpse lay between them. Peeling off his driving gauntlets, he placed them on the embalming-table beside Meiners's head and lit a cigarette. The smoke drifted towards Frammler across the lifeless face. 'Pity, really. He was a good lad.'

Frammler paused and looked up. 'You'll be telling me you loved him like a brother, next.'

Bennicken snorted contemptuously. 'Not me. I don't love anyone or anything.'

'Not even the Fatherland?' Frammler inquired with a grin.

'Maybe, but that's as far as I'll go.'

'Such is human nature!' sighed Frammler. 'Most people crawl through life on their bellies, squatting in church pews or skulking around in dark corners, but one or two do their duty by themselves and others—like the gentleman who did such a sterling job at ten o'clock last night, for instance.'

'Just about the time I was here with you.'

'Were you?' Frammler surveyed his cosmetic masterpiece with satisfaction. 'I don't remember looking at my watch.'

'What's that!' Bennicken slowly stiffened. 'You don't remember?'

Frammler backed away a little. 'Don't worry, it'll come back to me,' he said hastily. 'Everything's a bit vague, that's all.'

'We sat and talked.'

'That's right, we sat and talked—about bodies, wasn't it?'

'About that trolley of yours,' Bennicken amended.

'That's right. We were here talking from about eight-thirty p.m. onwards. We had a bit to drink, too—a bottle—or was it only half a bottle? Anyway, I had most of it. You only took a couple of nips because you were driving.'

'What do you mean by that?' demanded Bennicken. 'Are you trying to make out you were too drunk to remember?'

Still clutching his implements, Frammler raised both hands in a gesture of surrender. 'You know you can rely on me,' he said. 'We talked and talked, and then you said: what's the time, I must be getting home. Wasn't that it?'

'It was.'

'And then I looked at my watch and saw that the time was . . . what was it, can you remember?'

'It was about eleven—just after eleven.'

A sudden look of inspiration flashed across Frammler's face. 'Wasn't it seven minutes past?'

'Seven minutes past,' Bennicken confirmed.

Frammler picked up a comb, bent over the corpse and adjusted its coiffure with extreme care. 'Nobody realizes how versatile you have to be in this business,' he said. 'The public takes hardly any notice of our work. We're an underrated lot, my friend. This is the age of the specialist, but we have to know a bit about all kinds of things—cabinetmaking, metal-work, etcetera—otherwise we can't produce a decent coffin. Then there's the actual presentation of the body, which demands a knowledge of tailoring as well as beauty culture and hairdressing.'

'You don't say!'

'Take a good look at poor old Meiners,' Frammler entreated, 'and then tell me if he isn't a lovely sight.'

'Like a film star,' Bennicken agreed.

Frammler laughed scornfully. 'You don't find them like this in films—or on television either. They're all the same, but Meiners here—well, he looks a personality, doesn't he?'

Bennicken seemed quite affected. 'A nice lad, Meiners. I liked him.'

'Good shooting, that,' Frammler said professionally. 'Straight through the heart.'

Bennicken stared pensively into space. 'He didn't suffer.'

'The wound doesn't show, either. That's very important. I like my clients to look good.'

' Good old Meiners,' Bennicken muttered, blowing his nose.

'Please don't think we're trying to exert any kind of pressure on you,' said Bartosch.

' On the contrary,' Gisenius amplified, ' we want to help you in every possible way.'

Chief Inspector Sand retained his composure with an effort. ' I'm extremely grateful to you, gentlemen, but I really don't know if I need trouble you in this particular instance.'

' All the better,' Bartosch said briskly.

Sand felt thoroughly uncomfortable. He had an excellent grasp of police procedure, but he was no lawyer or ministry official, and the techniques of wire-pulling and compromise were beyond his ken. Gisenius realized this and had naturally told Bartosch, with the result that the two men started to weave their tangled web as soon as they entered the Chief Inspector's office.

After a mere ten minutes' unremitting attention at the hands of his kindly inquisitors, Sand began to flag. Gisenius alone he might have coped with at a pinch, for Gisenius had no official status, but Councillor Bartosch had come armed with ministerial authority.

' The Minister is a man of wide interests,' observed Bartosch. ' He also has an excellent memory. He at once recalled your name and previous career, Chief Inspector. You're pleased to hear that, I trust.'

' Of course,' Sand said uneasily.

' I'm sure the Chief Inspector appreciates the Minister's interest,' Gisenius interposed.

Bartosch gave a winning smile. ' Yes indeed, Chief Inspector Sand, you may congratulate yourself. The Minister's favourable interest can be extremely advantageous—as advantageous as the reverse can be disastrous. The Minister is only too ready to use his good offices on behalf of public servants within his domain and sphere of influence, but he naturally expects them to reciprocate. An act of solidarity, one might call it. You understand? '

' I understand,' Sand replied, frowning. ' I understand all you say, in theory, but I'm a practical man.'

' That's why we're here,' Bartosch said condescendingly.

' You can leave the finer points to us. In years to come, when you're an assistant commissioner, you can try your hand at them yourself. All right, let's stick to practicalities. Have you clarified the circumstances surrounding Meiners's death? '

' I don't regard my inquiries as closed—not for the time being, anyway.'

' Can you say with any certainty who the murderer was? '

' I have my suspicions.'

' Have you found any evidence which might support the assumption that Meiners's murder was in some way connected with a veterans' club headed by a Herr Schulz—Karl Schulz? '

Sand hesitated. ' No.'

' I should hope not! ' Gisenius exclaimed. ' In that case, the matter is virtually settled.'

' Would you agree with that, Chief Inspector? ' inquired Bartosch.

' Not entirely, sir,' Sand said with as much vigour as he could muster. ' You're forgetting the court of inquiry suggested by the directorate of public prosecutions.'

' In case you hadn't heard,' Bartosch said reprovingly, ' the directorate of public prosecutions has dropped its request. I spoke to Herr Kronshagen—after consultation with the Minister—and we explored the matter thoroughly together. We—or, rather, Herr Kronshagen—came to the conclusion that the proposal to hold an inquiry was based on a number of misconceptions. It has therefore been withdrawn.'

Sand felt as if the ground were crumbling beneath his feet. ' Is that official, sir, or is it merely your personal opinion? '

' It's absolutely official,' Bartosch said firmly, ' and I am empowered to see that it is acted upon.'

' Give me a written directive to that effect, Councillor, and we can regard the matter as closed.' Sand contained his rage with difficulty. ' If you don't mind, though, I'll just have a quick word on the internal 'phone.'

Without waiting for permission, Sand dialled the number of the C.I.D. office and Ramsauer answered. ' Anything new on Assignments One and Two? ' he asked.

Assignment One meant: check all available evidence on the Meiners case for anything pointing in the direction of a member of the Schulz group. The reply: nothing to report. Assignment Two meant: find Tantau, inform him that inquiries into Meiners's murder are about to be wound up, and tell him to contact Sand at once if he has any comment to make. The reply: Tantau simply shrugged his shoulders and said nothing.

Sand hung up feeling more hard done by than ever. Time was against him, circumstances were against him, and even Tantau refused to intervene on his behalf.

'I really don't know what more you want,' Gisenius said, raising his eyebrows. 'You have an excellent reputation, Chief Inspector. Why risk it over a case in which the most plausible solution is literally staring you in the face?'

'What's that?' Councillor Bartosch feigned profound astonishment. 'Do you mean to say you're in possesssion of evidence which could provide a satisfactory explanation?'

'The murder weapon was found near the scene of the crime,' Sand said wearily. 'We were able to identify the finger-prints on it.'

'They belonged to a man named Lehmgruber,' Gisenius put in with a look of cool triumph, '—an East German agent wanted by Counter-Intelligence. Quite apart from his espionage activities, there's a warrant out for his arrest in connection with a series of armed attacks on taxi-drivers. The whole of the Federal police force is looking for him.'

Sand eyed Gisenius thoughtfully. 'You're remarkably well informed, sir,' he murmured, '—as usual.'

Bartosch rounded on him. 'Why didn't you tell me all this before, Chief Inspector? It explains everything.' He wagged his head sternly. 'You ought to be grateful for such a solution. It's neat, logical and convincing.'

'And it has one small defect,' Sand added. 'According to reports from East Germany, Lehmgruber crossed the border two days ago, which rules him out as a potential suspect.'

Gisenius blenched slightly, but Bartosch seemed undeterred. 'Good God, man! Surely you don't take such stories seriously, do you? Any child could see through that sort of ploy. It's just one more systematic attempt to blacken the name of the Federal Republic and make it a bugbear in the eyes of the Western world. In short, it's Communist propaganda—and we're not going to fall for that, are we, Chief Inspector?'

Gisenius, who had regained his composure, said: 'I hope you'll assure the Minister that we—and Chief Inspector Sand in particular—are totally immune to insidious cold-war tactics of that kind.'

'I most certainly shall!' Bartosch exclaimed. 'That settles it, then: the murderer is a corrupt, degenerate, stateless individual named Lehmgruber—unless, of course, you care to hazard an alternative solution, Chief Inspector?'

Sand shook his head in silent shame.

Bartosch smiled smugly at Gisenius. 'I didn't imagine you would.'

No. 2 Section's last and most memorable reunion began punctually at eight o'clock the same evening. The place, now hallowed by tradition, was the *Drei Kronen*, and the hotel's Silver Room or banqueting-hall had been reserved for the occasion.

Hirsch had mobilized the hotel's entire resources. The oak refectory table was swathed in snow-white Lyons damask and laid with Nymphenburg porcelain and Venetian glass. The menu listed French specialities in French, and cold electric light had been banished in favour of clusters of wax candles.

'Just like a funeral,' was Frammler's appreciative comment.

'Nothing but the best for my friends,' Hirsch replied with a grin, '—provided they pay for it.'

Willy Kerze circled the table once, wrinkling his nose in distaste. Then he turned to Hirsch and said sarcastically: 'Very nice, but who's footing the bill?'

'I was hoping you would,' Hirsch retorted, turning on his heel.

Even Gisenius was impressed. His verdict was: 'Most creditable.'

Bennicken, who had crammed his bulk into a tight-fitting blue suit for the occasion, declared that it was all very classy, but he'd rather have a foaming tankard and a steaming plate of sausages any day.

'Does everything have to foam and steam when you're around?' Hirsch inquired.

'I like plain fare, that's all,' growled Bennicken, and went off to join Frammler.

Karl Schulz had also donned festive garb. 'Can we begin now?' he inquired.

'They've laid seven places,' said the ever-observant Gisenius. ' We're only six.'

'The seventh place is meant to be symbolic,' Hirsch explained. 'I thought it would be one way of bringing the section up to full strength.'

Kerze gave an exclamation of approval. 'Why, that's positively Nordic! The dead man's chair, etcetera, etcetera ...'

'I couldn't care less,' declared Frammler. 'I could eat my dinner off a coffin if I had to.'

'I respect the decision of the majority,' Karl Schulz said stoutly, regardless of the fact that no decision had been voiced.

Gisenius adopted a more neutral tone. 'Externals don't matter. We're all here, that's the main thing.'

'Hear, hear!' cried Bennicken. 'I'd be just as happy in a slit-trench.'

'If you're as keen as all that, fetch a shovel from the boiler-room and dig in outside somewhere,' suggested Hirsch. 'We'll bring you your dinner in a pail.'

Karl Schulz took a long and enjoyable pull at his glass. 'I think we might get the official part of the evening over now. Gisenius has the floor.'

'Gentlemen—my dear friends!' Gisenius rose to his feet solemnly, 'some acts bring no material reward, just as some heroic deeds never win official recognition. Greatness and nobility often lie hidden, sustained by modest pride. Thus, there are some among us whose lives attain fulfilment in a quiet and unobtrusive way—a very German way, I venture to suggest. In that sense, gentlemen,' Gisenius continued, 'Michael Meiners, too, was one of us. He has been much in my thoughts recently, and I now incline to the view that he has become a sort of symbolic figure who will live in our memories for ever more.'

'What about drinking a toast now and then?' demanded Frammler. 'I'm absolutely parched.'

'Pipe down!' said Schulz.

'The real tragedy of Michael Meiners's death seems to have eluded one or two of us,' Gisenius went on, 'but I feel that we should all do our best to evolve a common approach to it. During the dark days, when we thought we had lost our friend and fellow-soldier, he was, in fact, a prisoner of war.

After spending years as an innocent inmate of various Russian forced labour camps he was eventually released in the Eastern Zone, where he endured many more years of Communist oppression. Then came the day when he found the road to freedom. He trod it hesitantly, as though dazzled by the prospect that awaited him. It was some time before he sought out his friends, and he had scarcely done so when the Red terror struck again. Michael Meiners was shot down in cold blood by a spy and thief named Lehmgruber. That is now official.'

Martin Hirsch clapped ironically. 'Congratulations! So it's official now. What do you say to that, Bennicken?'

Bennicken shrugged. 'I say cheers!'

They picked up their glasses of white Burgundy and drank. Gisenius sat down, and the floor was taken by Frammler.

'Friends,' he said briskly, 'I'll make it snappy, so you needn't bother to put your glasses down.' He paused for laughter, but no one laughed. 'I just want to tell you briefly what arrangements I've made so far. To start with, there's the coffin. This will be seasoned copper beech inlaid with oak veneer. The contrast in grain looks very effective, especially by candlelight. As far as the fittings are concerned, I was in favour of solid silver at first, but then I thought, for the sake of durability and load capacity . . .'

'Send us a brochure,' suggested Hirsch. 'This isn't the time to advertise your wares.'

'What do you mean!' Frammler protested indignantly. 'I'm only trying to show what a splendid investment you're making.'

'That's all right, Frammler,' Gisenius said in soothing tones. 'We have the fullest confidence in you.'

'As an undertaker,' Hirsch added drily.

The next speaker was Karl Schulz. In response to an encouraging nod from Gisenius, he rose and cleared his throat loudly, as he always did when he felt impelled to take the floor. 'Comrades,' he said resolutely, observing the standard rules of procedure governing veterans' reunions, 'I'd like to welcome you and thank you for turning out in force. We're here to mourn an old friend. The place and time of his funeral hasn't been announced yet, but I expect a full turn-out there too. It's also my duty to express our thanks to Gisenius for dealing with a number of problems on our behalf—and, if I may say so, for dealing with them so efficiently.'

The rules now obliged the recipient of commendation to make some form of modest disclaimer, and Gisenius knew the rules by heart.

' Without you, my friends,' he said promptly, ' I shouldn't be where I am today.'

' Granted,' said Hirsch.

Schulz cleared his throat again. ' Thanks are also due to Comrade Frammler for making such generous and efficient arangements for Meiners's funeral.'

' Efficient, maybe,' Frammler muttered. ' I don't know about generous.'

' Furthermore,' Schulz went on, ' I'd like to thank Hirsch for his magnificent hospitality and Kerze—as usual—for his financial help. That wraps up the official part of the proceedings.'

' What about Bennicken? ' inquired Hirsch. ' Aren't you going to thank him? '

' Of course,' Schulz added hastily. ' Bennicken has sacrificed a lot of time and money by putting his taxi at our disposal.'

' Is that all we've got to thank him for? ' Hirsch persisted.

' Thanks be buggered,' growled Bennicken. ' I did my duty.'

Kerze looked across at Gisenius. ' Bennicken's right. Old soldiers don't make a fuss about what comes naturally—they leave that to the pen-and-ink brigade. I suggest we cut the cackle and get down to some serious drinking.'

' Dinner won't be served for a little while yet,' Hirsch said, glancing at the vacant seventh place. ' However, I've thought of an amusing way of filling in the time. There's someone waiting outside to talk to us. I propose we ask him in.'

' No! ' Gisenius called sharply. ' What's the point? This is a private gathering. We don't want any outsiders.'

' No outsiders! ' echoed Bennicken.

' You obviously know who I'm talking about,' Hirsch said, ' so why be obstructive? I think we've all got a right to know the final outcome of Herr Tantau's inquiries. He promised me he'd come here and submit his report. I'm in favour of asking him in. Anyone object? '

' I do,' Gisenius said firmly, raising his hand.

' Me too,' said Bennicken.

Frammler drained his glass. ' I'm easy.'

' What about you, Kerze? ' Hirsch demanded. ' Have you got anything against Tantau? '

' No,' Kerze replied uneasily, not looking at the others. ' Why should I have? '

' I don't know what it's all about,' said Karl Schulz, ' but if Hirsch says it's a good idea I'll take his word for it.'

Hirsch smiled grimly. ' That makes two votes against, one abstention and three in favour. Herr Tantau will be asked to submit his report.'

' I advise against it! ' said Gisenius, striving to conceal his agitation. ' I advise against it most strongly! '

' Delighted to see you all again,' declared Tantau, ' especially as I fear it may be the last time you have a chance to parade at full strength—comparatively speaking,' he added, indicating the vacant chair. ' Do you mind if I sit here? '

Tantau pulled back the empty chair and sat down.

' Where shall I begin? ' he asked, leaning back in his chair. ' I was given certain clearly defined instructions, and I carried them out.'

' And that completed your assignment,' Gisenius said sharply.

' Not my assignment,' Tantau amended gently, ' only the one you gave me.'

' Let's not quibble about phraseology,' retorted Gisenius. ' You did your job and now you're our guest. We want you to feel at home.'

' Cheers! ' Bennicken said ponderously, but no one else drank. Tantau studied Gisenius as though he were reading a book, and the others were surprised to see that it was Gisenius whose eyes dropped first.

' Everyone has his vices,' Tantau said. ' My main one is curiosity. If I'd gone into the bookbinding business, for instance, I'd probably have wanted to read every book I bound. As it is, my business is people. I have to make inquiries about them, analyse their motives, find out what makes them tick —whatever the current requirement may be. However, I'm so inquisitive by nature that I'm never satisfied with half the picture—I must see all of it—or more than half, anyway. For example, when I'm given the job of tracing a man, I feel an irresistible urge to ask why my client is so anxious to find him.'

'But you don't leave it at that, do you?' Gisenius interposed.

'No, that's only the next stage, not the last.' Tantau shrugged. 'It's a vice, I realize that. One question almost always raises another. To pursue our little analogy still further: when I've established the man's whereabouts, I immediately develop an interest in the man himself.'

Frammler wagged his head. 'You must have plenty of time on your hands.'

'You could put it that way,' Tantau replied without rancour. 'In this case my instructions were to trace Michael Meiners. It was a fairly simple job, finding him—too simple, I venture to say, compared with the evident importance attached to it by my clients. Nevertheless, it remained a purely routine case until I stumbled upon a date. April 20th 1945 sticks in my mind because it happens to be the date on which I was transferred from one prison to another.'

'You—in prison?' Hirsch exclaimed. 'What for?'

Tantau smiled. 'I was put inside because I'd arrested a sex-murderer. That was all right, except that he happened to be the local deputy gauleiter, and a colleague of mine tried to prove I'd framed him for political reasons.'

'And had you?'

Tantau shook his head. 'I'm afraid not. I've never been anything more than a policeman, and in those days it wasn't enough to be a policeman—just as it wouldn't have been enough in this case if I'd acted as a private inquiry agent and left it at that.

'But to return to April 20th 1945. I was transferred to another prison where most of my cell-mates were convicted criminals. Thanks to a calculated indiscretion on the part of a warder, the other prisoners got wind of my identity. They promptly fell on me and started to kick me around like a football. They'd have killed me if one youngster of about nineteen hadn't thrown himself on top of me and shielded me with his body.

'Later that day, the warder told the boy that I was an

enemy of the people, a traitor to Greater Germany and a betrayer of the Führer's ideals—and this on April 20th 1945, mark you! The boy spat in my face and wept with rage and shame at having helped an unpatriotic swine to survive.'

'Absurd,' Gisenius said deprecatingly. 'You're exaggerating an isolated case—an exception.'

'All the same,' Tantau pursued, 'there were plenty of young people who still believed in Hitler, Greater Germany and God knows what else besides, even in the throes of defeat. If they were told to blow up a bridge, they blew it up. If they were ordered to mine a road, they mined it. And if their instructions were to open fire on an overwhelmingly superior force of enemy from the edge of a wood, they duly opened fire. Why? Because they believed—either in the Fatherland or their fellow-soldiers. Michael Meiners was a boy like that.'

'Herr Tantau,' Schulz said, 'you don't know me and I don't know you, but I'd like to make one thing perfectly clear: everyone in my section behaved correctly.'

'Herr Schulz,' Tantau replied, 'it may be a point in your favour that we hardly know each other, but your assertion is quite unfounded. Disregarding the fact that each man is a mystery in himself, how can you know what six other people think, discuss or do when you're out of earshot? You yourself may be a man of honour, by contemporary standards, but the same doesn't necessarily apply to everyone who's been associated with you over a long period.'

Karl Schulz set his jaw. 'I can vouch for my men.'

'Give me another quarter of an hour,' Tantau said coolly, 'and you may change your mind.'

'In any case,' Schulz persisted, 'even if something did happen, the responsibility was mine. I was in command.'

'You may revise your ideas on that too,' Tantau observed with a faint smile. 'But first let me get a few platitudes off my chest—for example: ninety per cent of all the inmates of every prison or penitentiary claim to be innocent. They've all got some explanation for their unfortunate predicament. But, whether what they say is partially true or merely a lame excuse, the interesting feature is that most of them are trying to deceive themselves as well as others. An additional factor comes into play, you see—a peculiar factor known as time.

Given enough of it, persistent auto-suggestion can transform supposition into certainty and fiction into fact. In short, the guilty man goes on persuading himself of his own innocence until he finally believes in it, firmly and implicitly.'

' Very interesting,' Hirsch commented, and this time his voice was devoid of irony. ' I find your platitudes enlightening, Herr Tantau. They help to explain a great deal.'

' Pure conjecture! ' said Gisenius, licking his lips nervously.

Schulz said: ' It's all beyond me.'

' There's nothing to understand,' scoffed Bennicken. ' It's a load of rubbish.'

' Let's get down to cases,' Tantau said. ' Meiners arrived here in Rheine-Bergen and was seen, in the first instance, by Herr Schulz. That's important, because I'm inclined to credit Herr Schulz with what is commonly called a conscience.'

' Stand up and take a bow, Schulz! ' Frammler called.

' Schulz's encounter and his reaction to it affected different people in different ways,' Tantau went on. ' Some began to panic, some were resentful, one refused to believe the story and another found it entertaining.'

' Touché! ' said Hirsch.

' I only realized later why your initial reaction was one of amusement, Herr Hirsch. In the first place, you're blessed with the gift of irony, which makes life a great deal easier for you, but you also saw the events of sixteen years ago in a different light from the others. You were unaware of one or two pertinent facts, just as Schulz was. Frammler's refusal to believe in Meiners's reappearance stemmed from a straightforward blunder on his part.'

' It might have happened to anyone,' grumbled Frammler.

' Quite, but the effect of your blunder was to protract matters. Thanks to you, everyone felt convinced that Meiners had died long ago, and that gave the poison time to work. Schulz was thought to have been mistaken: twenty-four hours wasted. Finally, Hirsch's imaginary encounter resulted in a further loss of time.'

' I vote we terminate this unpleasant conversation,' Gisenius broke in. ' Schulz, you're in the chair.'

' Not so fast,' called Hirsch. ' I'm sure Karl's as anxious as I am to hear who was responsible for Meiners's death.'

' We already know that. It was Lehmgruber.'

' What if Herr Tantau could put forward another name? ' Hirsch insisted.

' It would be dangerous speculation on his part, nothing more,' snapped Gisenius, gripping the arms of his chair tightly. ' I call upon Schulz to bring this farce to an end and request Herr Tantau to leave the room. I'm sure my view is shared by everyone, with the possible exception of Hirsch.' He glanced at Kerze. ' Am I right, Willy? '

Willy Kerze lowered his eyes and fidgeted nervously with his cigar. Then he stole an oblique look at Tantau, who was regarding him with a challenging smile.

' I don't see what harm it can do to hear what Herr Tantau has to say,' he replied in a subdued voice.

The colour drained from Gisenius's cheeks and his mouth dropped open.

' All right, Tantau,' Hirsch urged, ' if you can suggest an alternative to Lehmgruber, let's hear it.'

' By all means,' said Tantau, ' now that we've laid the psychological foundations—in this case, a dormant or atrophied sense of guilt. Meiners arrived in town without the slightest idea that his presence would spark off an explosion—and a guilty conscience coupled with a way of life in jeopardy make an explosive combination, especially in successful men.'

' Go on,' Hirsch said grimly.

' Acting on that basis, I looked around for a plausible motive, and I didn't have far to seek. Almost automatically, I singled out six men who might have had an interest in eliminating Michael Meiners.'

' Now wait a minute! ' Schulz exclaimed angrily. ' You don't mean us, do you? '

' Yes. Six men are five too many for this sort of crime, of course, not that one can rule out the possibility of collusion or complicity. The most reliable way of identifying a murderer is to narrow the field systematically. Instead of asking who did it, one asks who didn't do it. The last man left is the murderer. All right, let's begin by eliminating everyone who can't have done it.'

Frammler grinned. ' There's me for a start. I wouldn't hurt a fly.'

' You may be right,' commented Tantau, ' but I'll have more to say about your delicate sensibilities later. No, the

373

first man I'd eliminate is the one who knows me least, mainly because there's been no reason for us to become closely acquainted. I refer to Herr Schulz, a man who is prepared to sacrifice himself for the sake of others.

'The next to go is Herr Kerze. Herr Kerze is far too bound up with his personal affairs to have taken a direct hand in Meiners's elimination. Apart from that, his factory is his whole life. He'd be prepared to shed millions of marks to safeguard it, but not a drop of blood. As a business man, he knows that blood is the sort of debt which all the money in the world can't wipe out.

'Number three in the elimination stakes is you, Hirsch. I ruled you out from the start, and for various reasons, the main one being that you enjoy life far too much to risk it by murdering someone.'

Hirsch's only reaction was to pick up his glass and stare moodily into it.

'I almost hesitate to utter the name Gisenius,' Tantau went on. 'When I think of Herr Gisenius I involuntarily see a picture of a man in a white robe wearing a halo. No one who creates that sort of impression commits murder. On the other hand, even though his nostrils might twitch with distaste at the very scent of blood, his mind is as sharp as a scalpel. I can't imagine anyone within his sphere of influence taking a major decision without his prior approval.'

'I trust you realize that any statements you choose to make about me are based on speculation?' Gisenius's voice was cold and scathing. 'The whole thing's absurd,' he went on stiffly. 'And even if it weren't, an incident which occurred sixteen years ago is subject to the statute of limitations.'

Tantau nodded. 'Quite so, but there's more to it than that. People were slaughtered in droves during the final stages of the war so why all the fuss, why all the panicky counter-measures? The answer is quite simple; Michael Meiners's elimination was not the product of chance but, from a certain warped point of view, a wholly logical step.'

Gisenius watched Tantau spellbound as the old detective fortified himself from the glass which Hirsch pushed across to him. 'Why do some men die a violent death?' he continued. 'Either because they have too much or know too much. How did Meiners qualify for a one-way ticket to eternity? Because

374

he knew what had happened on the night of April 19th 1945. A girl was found dead, but who was responsible for her death? Meiners was aware of the true facts. He must have known who the murderer was and who was directly or indirectly implicated in the girl's revolting death. That's why he was dangerous, and why the best plan was to eliminate him.'

Karl Schulz glanced round appealingly, but in vain. Gisenius did not move a muscle, Kerze was nervously manipulating his cigar, Bennicken preserved the immobility of a statue, and Frammler shifted uneasily in his chair.

' I found it a little difficult to form a clear picture of Herr Frammler,' Tantau went on.

The undertaker smirked. ' I'm not an average sort of person.'

' Herr Frammler is a man of wide and varied experience,' pursued Tantau, ' a man who is no stranger to death, a man who at first sight might seem capable of anything.'

' Give me that in writing and I'll use it as an advertisement,' Frammler quipped.

' I devoted a considerable amount of study to Herr Frammler,' said Tantau. ' Most of my data came from a man named Siegert. He told me nothing I couldn't have guessed, apart from a few instructive details about Frammler's method of extracting information. I did learn one thing of importance, however, and that was that Herr Frammler lacks certain qualities which are inherent in the violent criminal, namely, physical strength, determination and coldbloodedness—just the qualities, in fact, which Herr Bennicken possesses to such a marked degree.'

' Do I have to listen to this? ' Bennicken demanded harshly.

'Why not hit him on the head? ' Hirsch suggested. ' That'll shut him up.'

' I first became aware of Herr Bennicken's outstanding qualities when we were searching for Konstantin Kerze's body,' Tantau continued, undeterred. ' It was an oppressive feeling—like being trailed by a bloodhound. My talk with Siegert clarified the picture still further. In his opinion, Herr Bennicken is a potential killer.

' Later on, I remembered an old saying in the C.I.D. to the effect that habitual glove-wearers are either burglars,

royalty, surgeons or car-drivers—or, in this case, cab-drivers.
  'Do you know when I recalled that saying? When the
police found the weapon used to kill Meiners. It belonged to
Lehmgruber—his prints were on it—but there was a link
between Lehmgruber and Meiners which could not be overlooked: a man who wore gloves and so would be unlikely to
leave prints behind. That man was you, Bennicken.'

Bennicken swore beneath his breath.

Gisenius rose, motioning curtly to the taxi-driver to follow
suit. 'Don't say anything that might be misunderstood,
Bennicken. I don't blame you for being annoyed, but keep
calm. He can't make an outrageous allegation like that and
get away with it. Look on me as your legal adviser, and
remember one thing: there's absolutely no evidence against
you.'

  'You're pretty near the mark there,' Tantau said. 'There
isn't much in the way of evidence at the moment, but wait
until the C.I.D. get cracking. They won't take long to find
what they need, and they'll soon be on the right track—I give
you my personal guarantee.'

Signalling to Bennicken to follow, Gisenius strode to the
door with stiff, jerky movements and made his exit.

Frammler rose too, managing to look as bland as ever.
He grinned at Tantau and said: 'If I ever see you again
I hope it'll be in my funeral parlour, stretched out on the
embalming-table.'

  'You may not have long to wait,' Tantau replied quietly.

When Frammler had left the room, Tantau turned to
Kerze. 'What about you?' he inquired, not without com-
passion. 'Don't you feel like a breath of fresh air too?'

Kerze's florid cheeks looked strangely grey and sunken.
'I've half a mind to pack my bags and take a world
cruise.'

  'Why not do that?' Tantau suggested. 'You can
afford to.'

Willy Kerze got up and bowed in Tantau's direction.
Then he squared his shoulders and strode out.

  'You've got to give him one thing,' Hirsch observed. 'He
may not have any breeding, but he puts on quite a good
imitation sometimes.'

  'Your friend Schulz seems to have been struck dumb,'

Tantau said. ' I hope that's not his only reaction to what he's heard.'

' I still can't grasp it,' Karl Schulz muttered. ' I'd never have believed it.'

Hirsch regarded him fondly. ' The world isn't just a nice cosy veterans' reunion on a grand scale, Karl. You'll get used to the idea in the end.'

Schulz heaved himself to his feet. ' This is my responsibility,' he said resolutely. ' I'm going to the police. I want to know the whole truth.'

Tantau glanced at Hirsch and shook his head warningly, but he did not speak until Schulz had left the room.

' If I know him, he really will go to the police.'

' Wouldn't it have been kinder to spare him that? ' Hirsch demanded bitterly.

' Oh no, my friend! ' There was a surprising undertone of vehemence in Tantau's voice. ' If I went to the police with what I know it would be a straightforward case of laying information, but if he does so it will be much more than that. It will be an honest and deliberate attempt at atonement.'

' Schulz the mediator! ' murmured Hirsch. ' It's a peculiar thought.'

' Men like Schulz can be made to do almost anything, provided you know the key-word which activates them. It must be a word with a positive ring, like decency, friendship or unselfishness. But there comes a day when even they begin to differentiate between those who genuinely believe in the freedom of man and those who sacrifice men to preserve their own unrestricted freedom of action.'

' Which brings us back to Gisenius.'

' An unscrupulous man in a position of power can only retain the allegiance of people like Schulz by deception, and even then not indefinitely. Creatures like Frammler couldn't care less who wields power as long as it isn't used against them personally. The Bennickens of this world are born henchmen; no strong-man's entourage would be complete without them. Men like Kerze try to cash in on any situation. Hard-headed as they are, it seldom dawns on them that nothing in life is free.'

' And what's your opinion of the Hirsches of this world? '

' You, my dear fellow, cannot conceive of any world which

377

even approaches perfection, so you tend to pour scorn on each and every way of life. On the other hand, you ought to remember sometimes that imperfection is the rule, and that our job is to reduce the extent of that imperfection.'

'If we're really going to do that we'd better fortify ourselves first.'

Tantau smiled. 'I agree.'

'In that case I'll ring for dinner,' Hirsch said, and the eyes he looked into as he spoke were those of a friend. 'Let the wake commence!'

FINAL REPORT

STENOGRAPHIC RECORD OF A POLICE INTERVIEW

WITH MARTIN HIRSCH

conducted by Chief Inspector Sand
on 1 May 1961
in connection with the events of 20 April 1945

After being informed of the subject of the interview and cautioned, Herr Hirsch made the following statement:

My name is Martin Hirsch. I am thirty-eight years old and a hotelier by profession.

For many years I had no precise or detailed picture of what happened. I suspected something, but I couldn't prove it, and I lacked the moral courage to acknowledge the real truth. I didn't dare give free rein to my imagination.

No. 2 Section—the one I belonged to—was a sub-unit like tens of thousands of others. Admittedly, no two groups of men are identical, but I suppose Schulz's section wasn't unlike a lot of others.

In his own way, Karl Schulz was a barrack-room Parsifal. His intentions were invariably of the best, and he was one of those naïve people—and how many there are!—who sincerely believe that everyone else feels, thinks, sees and acts as they do. Schulz's innate faith in human decency led him astray time and time again. Once, Frammler jettisoned a belt of machine-gun ammunition because he was too lazy to carry it—a very serious offence. When Schulz noticed it was missing, Frammler looked dumbfounded and said someone in the next section must have pinched it—and Schulz believed him. If I lifted a crate of schnapps from somewhere I only had to tell Schulz it was part of a special distribution and he'd swallow the story whole. In the end, Gisenius was able to rush up to Schulz with an order he'd concocted himself and tell him it came from the company commander, and he accepted it without a murmur. But I'm being premature.

379

When we marched into Steinwiesen late in the afternoon of April 19th 1945, all we wanted to do was pack up and go home. We'd covered about twenty-five kilometres in full battle order, so we were at the end of our tether from every point of view. This was completely lost on Schulz, who had been plodding along in the lead. He'd happily have marched another twenty-five kilometres if he'd been ordered to. He carried the M.G. that day, I remember. He always did his bit, even though he was a sergeant, and we found that particularly welcome when it came to sharing out loads.

No. 1 on the M.G. was Michael Meiners. We didn't begrudge him the privilege. To be quite honest, we pressed it on him, because it entailed carrying the damned thing when Schulz was otherwise engaged. Meiners was a comparative newcomer to the section. He'd been posted to us as a replacement for a chap who'd trodden on a mine, which made him the general dogsbody of the outfit.

There was something else about Meiners. He was heart and soul behind the war-effort, even though any fool could tell that total collapse was just around the corner. I can still see him now, listening moist-eyed with emotion to Goebbels's speech in honour of the Führer's birthday. He looked as if he was going to burst into tears any minute. To him, the Führer was a figure from the pages of world history, a sort of demi-god who could do no wrong. Meiners wasn't insane. He was just a hypnotic subject who couldn't help believing in the hypnotist.

Such were the two pillars of our military establishment—a stout-hearted sergeant and a credulous youngster, one a staunch obeyer of orders and the other a devout believer in ultimate victory. The rest of us tended to be more realistic. Whenever we wanted to discuss anything important we got out of Schulz's way and sent Meiners off on some errand or other. Our little conferences had become more and more frequent, too. The others were gradually waking up to something which I—and Gisenius too, I'm sure—had realized long ago, and that was that the old firm had finally gone bust.

Anyway, it was Kerze who first mooted the idea of desertion. The suggestion might just as easily have come from Gisenius, except that Gisenius didn't make a habit of stating his views openly in those days. Frammler fell in with the plan at once, and Bennicken took his cue from Gisenius, as he still does.

Gisenius announced that he had come to the conclusion that total annihilation was not in accord with the meaning of history or divine Providence. Gisenius never talked down to his audience, even in those days. Kerze expressed himself more simply, and I felt so relieved that the time had come at last that I made my views pretty plain too. Operation ' So long, Hitler ' was carried unanimously, and the only remaining question was when to put it into effect.

Prospects looked particularly good on April 19th 1945. Our own army was in utter chaos and the Russians were breathing down our necks. The Americans were closing in from the west and the intervening space was filled with a milling mass of homeless civilians. Anyone with half an eye in his head could see that the only sensible course was to call it a day.

Gisenius had no difficulty in persuading Schulz to select a billet which would suit our requirements. That evening we made our final preparations. I laid in a stock of liquid refreshment and some extra food. Frammler was responsible for obtaining civilian clothes, and Gisenius, who escorted Schulz to the company commander's briefing session, took care of documentation. This didn't present any great problems, I may say, since every orderly-room clerk with any claims to intelligence had already pocketed a selection of official rubberstamps for use in an emergency. Bennicken's job was to keep Meiners busy, which he did by getting him to clean every weapon in the section. This effectively distracted the attention of both the outsiders from our preparations for departure.

There were two reasons why we didn't actually say goodbye to the German army that night. In the first place I'd laid on far too much liquor, and in the second place there were two women in our billet. These women, a mother and daughter, destroyed all our good intentions and boosted our consumption of alcohol enormously. The result was total inebriation and unbridled lust.

The section's interest in the two women grew more and more fevered. I made an honest attempt to monopolize them both for their own sakes, but the others weren't having any. They were so drunk that I might have kept them at

381

bay, but what really put paid to my efforts was the behaviour of the women themselves.

To put it in a nutshell, they were willing—and since they didn't seem to know which one of us they wanted, everyone thought he was the lucky man. You mustn't forget the general situation. Death was just round the corner and the future had never looked blacker, so we all felt like making the most of our time.

Don't ask me to go into details. Competition was brisk, and I don't recall that any of us were reluctant to take advantage of what was on offer, with two notable exceptions. One was the worthy Schulz, who was recouping his energies by sleeping the sleep of the just upstairs, and the other was young Meiners. Our behaviour didn't fit in with his ideas of chivalry, so he called down curses on God and mankind in general. In the end he looked the other way and puked his guts up.

If you ask me how the girl met her death, I can only tell you this: I concentrated on the mother. She was an experienced creature and extraordinarily willing, and while I was busy with her the others concentrated on the girl. When she went out to relieve herself they trooped after her and dragged her into the barn.

Then, suddenly, Meiners shouted out: ' You swine! I'll get you court-martialled for this!' Bennicken laughed coarsely and told him to shut his trap. He sounded breathless. Then his fist slammed into Meiners's face with a noise like a pistol-shot—I saw the bruise next morning—and the boy collapsed without a word. Bennicken said something like ' That'll teach you to mind your own business!'

But enough of that. The fact was, we were too busy and far too drunk to say goodbye to the army that night, as we'd planned. We were sober enough next morning when we all woke up with ghastly hangovers and realized how stupid we'd been. Quite apart from the risk of being court-martialled on account of the girl's death, there was the chance of getting ourselves blown to smithereens in a pointless, last-minute, last-ditch stand. One thought was uppermost in all our minds, and that was to run for it.

Schulz, who had no idea of our plans, went on waging war by the book. For the time being, all we could do was join in the game, racking our brains desperately for some way of extricating ourselves from the mess we were in. While Schulz reconnoitred the position and Meiners obediently set up his M.G. on the edge of the wood, Gisenius was thinking for all of us.

His plan was simple, as all the best plans are, and he didn't take long to persuade us of its wisdom. One factor in its favour was that Schulz had divided the section into two parties. Meiners and Bennicken were to man the M.G. on the edge of Copse 307 while Gisenius, Kerze and I were to build a road-block. Frammler had been detailed to cope with Frau Boddanski and was still at the farm, and Schulz, like the good N.C.O. he was, trotted backwards and forwards between the two parties at regular intervals, faithfully ensuring that all was as it should be.

The idea was that, when the Russian tanks got closer, Meiners would be left firing his M.G. at them while Schulz would be lured away by a fake message from company head-quarters. This would leave us free to make a concerted run for it and split up later on.

I remember Gisenius taking Bennicken aside and speaking to him. Bennicken hung that great head of his like a dog expecting a thrashing. Then he squared his shoulders and adjusted the grenades in his belt. I saw him glance in the direction of Meiners, who was lying there by himself, frozen-faced, looking like a child on the verge of tears.

While Schulz was checking the M.G.'s field of fire, Kerze caught sight of the Russians through his binoculars. They were advancing across open country, parallel to the road, and they were heading straight for Copse 307. Seemingly endless columns of dust were visible on the horizon, and Kerze iden-tified at least four tanks.

Just then Schulz reappeared and made another inspection of the road-block. Frammler, who had turned up by this time, doubled over to Bennicken and whispered something to him, and at that moment the balloon went up. The first shells started to burst among the trees.

It was time to act. Gisenius shouted to Schulz: 'A runner's just been here. You're to report to Company H.Q. at once!' Schulz obediently trotted off. I think he suspected later that we'd left Meiners in the lurch, but he probably talked himself out of the idea, just as he dismissed his suspicions about the girl's death. His faith in human nature made him incapable of grasping such things, and, anyway, he didn't know anything for certain. All I knew myself until recently was that we left Meiners lying where he was and ran for it. Gisenius and Kerze raced off, ducking low, with me at their heels. Just behind me came Frammler and Bennicken. At the time, I couldn't fathom why Bennicken bothered to turn and throw a grenade in the direction we had come.

Bennicken threw his grenade in the direction of the enemy —or so I thought at the time. In reality, he must have thrown it at Meiners, and death and destruction erupted round the boy's body.

I realize all this now, thanks to Herr Tantau's reconstruction of the incident. The implications are painfully obvious.

Gisenius must have prompted Bennicken—in the most devious and roundabout way, of course—to eliminate Meiners because he knew what had happened the previous night and seemed to be intent on pursuing the matter further. This would have implicated not only Bennicken, the actual murderer, but Gisenius, Kerze and Frammler as well, all of whom had played a part in raping the girl—and Gisenius wanted to feel absolutely safe.

Bennicken did what was expected of him. He disposed of Meiners for sixteen years and then completed the job a few days ago.

Frammler clearly saw what happened, and Kerze, who was considered to be more reliable than I am, was told about it shortly afterwards.

I, Martin Hirsch, suspected the truth but didn't grasp it fully until now. I did not know the full details before.

I have nothing more to add.